HE HAD

Dominique studied Loire over the rim of his wine glass. She was more desirable than all the treasure galleons of Spain, more priceless than the rarest diamonds of Africa.

"Why were you following me?" Loire demanded. "Do you think me a woman of easy virtue, to pursue me so?"

"No, mademoiselle. There is nothing easy about you, I deem."

"Then why?"

"Why would a man sell all that he has to purchase a pearl of great price? Some things are worth giving up all else, Loire."

His intimate tone made her nerves tingle. "You are required to give up nothing, Monsieur Youx, for nothing is what you would get in return."

"Perhaps." He leaned forward, placing his hand on the table dangerously close to hers, and smiled into her eyes. His look seemed to say that he knew all there was to know.

Also by Venita Helton

SAPPHIRE

Available from HarperPaperbacks

Pirate's Prize

⋈ VENITA HELTON ⋈

HarperPaperbacks
A Division of HarperCollinsPublishers

HarperPaperbacks   *A Division of* HarperCollins*Publishers*
          10 East 53rd Street, New York, N.Y. 10022

Cover illustration by Jean Monti

First printing: August 1994

Printed in the United States of America

HarperPaperbacks, HarperMonogram, and colophon are trademarks of HarperCollins*Publishers*

❖ 10 9 8 7 6 5 4 3 2 1

To Mom and Dad: for pirate tales and butterfly nets; for magic in water puddles; for fomenting just enough danger to make life thrilling . . . and for little brothers.

1

"Miz Loire! You better come down here! They say pirates done stole your pappy's ship!"

Loire Chartier nearly dropped the ceramic pitcher she was placing on the top shelf. Clasping it against her breast, she shifted on the high ladder to look down at her housekeeper standing in the doorway of the mercantile. Raindrops mingled with the tears on Ida's broad, dark face.

After setting the pitcher on the shelf, Loire rapidly descended the ladder and crossed the room, her feet tapping on the wide cypress planks, her high-waisted white gown fluttering gracefully. "Who told you such a thing, Ida?"

"I done saw Cap'n Defromage at the levee. He on his way over."

"This cannot be true!" Pushing back a lock of dark

hair that had come loose from her bandeau, Loire hastened outside to look down the rainy street toward the Basilica of St. Louis.

A crowd was coming around the corner of the cathedral, a man in ragged sailors' togs stumping painfully in the lead. Loire did not recognize him until he stopped in front of her and removed his hat, releasing a mop of black hair.

She put out a trembling hand to draw him closer. "Alain, what's happened to you? Where's the barque?"

Defromage winced and passed a grimy hand over his mustache. "It's gone, my dear one. *Mon Dieu,* the bloody bastards took it. They set me and my men off on some godforsaken strand down in the delta."

"Did you put up a fight?" Loire's amber eyes glowed with dangerous intensity. Her fingers dug into Defromage's arm until he pulled away, shaking his head.

"There was no point in it, mademoiselle. We were outgunned. To fight would have been suicidal."

Loire's expression did not soften, but she nodded in reluctant acceptance. "Come in out of the rain."

She led him away from the crowd into the mercantile and offered him a cane-bottom chair. Ida pressed a glass into his hand and splashed wine into it from a brown jug. He lifted one foot onto the opposite knee and took Loire's hand in his as he drank.

"Who were they, Alain? Jean Laffite's freebooters?"

"No. Their brutish captain wore a mask. He spoke Spanish and flew the flag of Cartagena."

"Every pirate flies that flag!" Loire bit her lip to control her temper. "That does not mean he was Spanish. What about his ship?" She pulled her hand from his grasp.

"I've never seen her before. A black schooner, fore-and-aft rigged, with red sails."

"My poor papa," Loire whispered. She went over to a glass-topped counter, leaned her elbows on it, and stared sightlessly at the objects crowding its interior. "How much of his tobacco crop was aboard?"

"A good half of it. And some wool and silver trinkets he'd traded for."

Loire shut her eyes, imagining the lost fortune. "Anything else? Don't try to spare me, Alain."

When he did not answer, she turned and looked him in the eye. He reddened under the layer of dirt on his face, and plucked at his bristly chin. "Some . . . Jamaicans."

"Jamaicans!" Loire shot a glance at Ida and saw her own horror mirrored in the woman's black eyes. "You were running *slaves?*"

"Er, yes. Your papa could not resist the deal, despite the American embargo."

For a minute Loire stared down at him before sinking slowly onto a chair. "Then it was the judgment of God."

Glad to shift the blame away from himself, Defromage said, "It must have been! I told him not to test the patience of God by doing such a terrible thing, but he would not listen!"

"He would not, eh? And how hard did you try to make him listen, *Captain?* Or were you too greedy for your share of the profits?"

"Before God, I—"

"Don't say another word." Coldly furious, Loire rose from her chair and stalked across the store to the open staircase. Halfway to the second floor, she stopped to regard him. "It is fortunate for you that pirates captured the barque, Captain, and you escaped with your freedom, for had you docked in New

Orleans with your cargo of humans, I would've made Governor Claiborne arrest you and lock you in the meanest hole in the city!"

"But, Loire, what of my love for you?"

"That is your problem, not mine! Now get out of my shop."

Loire went onto the balustrade outside her bedroom and gripped the wrought-iron vines of the railing. The morning's rain had gone, leaving the flat roofs of the houses steaming in the sunshine, the cypress and sweet olives dripping on the cobbled banquettes bordering the street.

"You feeling pretty low, child?"

Loire brushed away her tears before looking around as Ida squeezed out through the tall French window. "I'm all right, considering that we're broke and my father's a lying, underhanded *slave trader.*"

Ida draped her arms around Loire's shoulders. "Now don't you be fretting about *that.* Your pappy ain't got good sense, that's all. He like the color of money, and that's the truth. He ain't such a bad man. He set St. John and me free, didn't he?"

"Only because he was afraid St. John would run off sometime and he'd never find another bookkeeper good enough to replace him."

"Well, never mind about the old man's reasons. And St. John say we ain't broke yet!"

Loire released a ragged sigh. "St. John is a dreamer. Our only hope is for Papa to get the rest of his crop off the island without getting plundered again."

Ida chuckled a little. "He will, and ain't he gonna have a *fit* when he hears you ain't marrying the cap'n?"

"I don't care. I never told him I'd marry Alain. He dreamed it up because he thinks no decent gentleman will marry me."

Ida's chuckle died. "Now, honey, don't you say a thing like that. It ain't true."

"It *is* true. Do you think any gentleman would wed the daughter of a whore?"

"Honey, ain't nobody think of you like that!"

"Ha! You've heard the way they talk about me, about *us*. Monsieur Chartier could not control his wife, they say, and his daughter has the same bad seed!"

"Them old biddies is jealous, that's all, 'cause you're a sight prettier than their ugly old daughters! Don't you pay them no mind!"

Loire pushed her hair off her damp forehead. The heat was appalling, blasting over the balustrade like the kiss of a dragon. "I can't breathe out here. Let's go in."

Ida followed her into the room, where she pushed aside the mosquitaire curtain surrounding the bed, plumped up the pillows, and sat down with a sigh. "Your mama used to light up this room like a candle, honey. You remember how pretty she was, her hair all up in curls? You ain't got quite as much curl to your hair as her, but you just as pretty."

"I'm not interested in being like her, Ida," Loire said, then turned away to hide her tears.

Ida said gently, "Maybe she'll come back before long."

"She ran off to Paris five years ago. She's not coming back."

"You don't know that, child. Folks change."

"Not her. I'll show you." Loire reached on top of a cypress armoire for a tattered sheet of vellum and handed it over. "I received this from her a year ago. See, she brags about living at court with one of Napoleon's officers."

"You know I can't read, Miz Loire, and don't start telling me I ain't too old to learn!" Ida folded the letter into fours and handed it back. "Besides, they say Napoleon done gone into exile—your mama'll be back any day. You go on and tear that damn thing up. You'll just get all bent up inside if you keep on reading it."

"This is all I have of her. I can't destroy it."

Thrusting the letter into her bodice, Loire walked out into the hall and down the narrow flight of stairs to the mercantile.

"You been gone some long time," said a deep Jamaican voice.

She stopped at the end of a counter to look for St. John. Someone had closed the front and rear doors, leaving the long, narrow shop dim. It was a moment before she spied the black man high on the ladder leaning against the shelves.

"You ought to open the doors, St. John. No one can see what they're buying in this gloom."

"Ha! You not to worry, Mems Loire. We haven't gotten too many customer since you been upstairs. The only one we get, he want credit."

"Who was it?" she asked, going to open the back door.

St. John climbed down the ladder, folded his arms across his massive chest, and stared up at the shelf he'd just stocked with butter churns, cow bells, and birchwood fragrance balls. The light revealed tufts of white in his wiry hair and deep lines about his eyes and mouth.

"St. John, he is sorry about the barque, Mems Loire," he said, turning his dark eyes on her.

Loire flinched and raised her hand as if to ward off the memory. "You said we had a customer asking for credit? Who?"

"Just some man. I send him away."

"Empty-handed?"

The Jamaican clicked his tongue against the roof of his mouth and raised his hand to the back of his neck. "Mebbe not quite empty-handed."

"Ah-ha!" Loire said. "And *you* lecture *me* about giving away too much, you soft-hearted old possum."

St. John fixed a reproachful gaze upon her. "The man, he say his fishing boat got wash away in the flood. He say he no can feed his children. He say they are hungry. I give him food and mebbe one, two blankets."

"You did the right thing, of course."

"He pay when he can, he say."

"I know. They always say that." Sighing, she leaned against the doorpost. The courtyard was a brick-walled jungle of banana trees, sweet olives, jacaranda, and jasmine. It was so peaceful, so . . . safe. She had played in it for the first time at age three, when her parents brought their family of five boys and one girl from Paris. The cool fountain had sheltered them when a dreadful fire raged through the Quarter; the venerable arms of the magnolia had cradled her while her brothers suffered with yellow fever.

Until today, with Alain Defromage's calamitous news, she had thought her home could shelter her from anything. Now, nothing was certain.

"Do you think the British will attack New Orleans, St. John?" she asked, not looking at him.

"You cry, Mems Loire," he said. He laid his great palms upon her shoulders and, tilting up her chin with his thumbs, looked into her eyes. "The British, they do not come. Many forts guard the big river."

"I know . . . and many British ships block the channel. It was foolish of Papa to try to send the barque this year."

"Monsieur Chartier, he is a gambler, Mems Loire. He knows the risk. He knows that for you, this little shop is everything. Besides, he cannot let the tobacco rot on the island."

"So now it rots in a pirate's hold . . . along with those poor Jamaicans."

"Mems must understand."

"I cannot understand him. I will never understand him. I'm tired, St. John. I need a smoke."

St. John dropped his hands to his hips and regarded her disapprovingly. "The tobacco, she will kill you."

Dashing away her tears, Loire went past him to root around in one of the cupboards behind the counter. Her voice echoed hollowly as she said, "That isn't what the Kaintocks uptown say."

"Eh? And what do them damned Americans say?"

"I'll tell you." Surfacing with a pound tin of tobacco, she pointed at its blue label. A West Indies native was depicted, smoking a pipe with President Madison. "This will prove how wrong you are. Listen."

She began to read the label. "'Ain't life a smoke? We'll tell you true: Tobacco will your Health renew; So thrust off Death and dark Despair, For we've got best Kentucky here!'"

She ignored St. John's groan. "Of course, Papa's tobacco is better, but, well, we can't be sure of getting any this year. We'll have to sell our stock of Louisville weed."

"And you will smoke her."

"I don't do it very often."

"How often?"

Loire shuffled her feet. "Only once before."

"Once too many time," St. John said. He perused her sorrowfully, from her shining hair to the tips of her black leather pumps. She was so pretty, with the youthful figure of an hourglass and the face of an undisciplined angel.

"If Mems Loire were St. John's child," he said, "she would not be fogging herself up with stinking Kaintock tobacco."

"Well, she's not St. John's child!" At this, she grabbed some sulphur matches and a battered clay pipe shaped like a pop-eyed whale and walked out the door.

Shaking his head, St. John walked over to the ladder and rolled it on its iron wheels toward the front windows. Then he climbed halfway to the ceiling and began to rearrange painted trays, bottled herb vinegar, and black wrought-iron toys on a shelf.

Loire stood just outside the back door, waiting for St. John to say something. When he did not, she walked as nonchalantly as she could into the courtyard, feeling his eyes on her the entire way.

She skirted the fountain and settled onto an iron bench beneath the big magnolia tree. She could sense St. John looking out at her. Grumbling, she gathered up her materials and skulked around the side of the house to the porte cochere, the narrow passage leading to rue St. Ann. There, she leaned against the brick wall near the gate and stared out at the cobbled street. A few mule-drawn carriages jolted by, but nothing else of interest.

It was hot between the high, jasmine-covered brick walls, but at least she had a bit of privacy. With difficulty born of inexperience she worked the lid off the tin and tamped some resiny weed into the pipe, muttering when it sprang out as soon as she removed her thumb. Holding the open tin under one arm, she fumbled the glob back into the pipe and struck a match against the bricks. At the moment she managed to light the tobacco, the heavy tin slipped out of her grasp and crashed upside-down onto the cobbled walk.

"By the holy thunder!" she said in French, then glanced guiltily through the wrought-iron gate to see if anyone had heard her swear. The banquette was empty. She scooped most of the tobacco back into the tin and pushed the lid down tight.

As she straightened, she came face to face with a large green-and-black spider dangling from the jasmine. Again the tobacco tin crashed to the ground, this time bashing her right big toe.

Crying with pain, yet unwilling to relinquish her precious pipeful of smoldering tobacco, she poked the stem into her mouth, grabbed her injured toe with both hands, and hopped around on one foot.

"*Mon Dieu!* The savage Creeks conspire to capture Vieux Carré! Here is one making smoke signals now!"

Caught by surprise, Loire lost her footing and fell against the wall. For a long moment she blinked through a cloud of blue smoke at a tall figure in a charcoal-gray waistcoat and breeches standing just inside the gate, his dark eyes flashing in amusement. An instant later, he shot out his hand to wrest the pipe from her mouth.

"Why, how dare you?" She snatched back the pipe and hid it behind her, then kicked him hard in the shin. Fresh pain shot through her toe. "You are a horrid man!"

"*Merci*," he said, bowing gallantly. "My thanks."

His effrontery inflamed her. She reached up to slap his handsome face.

He smiled in an almost predatory way, caught her hand before she could reach his face, and gently brought it to his lips. Then, still holding her hand, he moved one step closer.

For a moment she was too startled to fight, to move, even to breathe. He had just taken control of her entire world, and she hadn't an inkling of what to do about it. His eyes were as black as Bayou LaForge, with the same mysterious depth. She began to struggle.

Instantly he released her and stepped back. He did not attempt to touch her again. She retreated against the wall and stared at him, uncertain whether to run or to kick him once more.

"You are so pretty," the stranger said in French. "It is a shame that you smell like a forest burning down."

"A forest burning— Oh! Oh!" she screamed, suddenly aware that smoke was coming up from her skirts in wisps. The pipe she'd hidden behind her back had caught her dress on fire!

"*Sacrebleu!*" he cried, snatching her into his arms. He rushed her to the fountain and tossed her in.

Loire hit the water with a great splash. She surfaced almost immediately, spluttering and coughing, her hair streaming into her eyes and her bandeau slipping around her neck.

"Are you all right, mademoiselle? You are not burned?"

She pounded the water with her fists. "No, I'm *drowned!*"

"But you are so lively for a drowned woman, mademoiselle," he said, raising one booted foot to the edge of the fountain. He rested his forearms on his knee and leaned toward her. The ruby dragon set in a heavy gold ring on his right hand flashed in the sunlight.

"You are a blackguard, monsieur," she said, slogging through the water to the opposite side of the fountain. As she began to climb out, he walked around to offer his hand. At first she refused to take it, then she yanked it with a vengeance.

The hard tug would have jerked him headfirst into the pool, but he straightened quickly and released her hand. She stumbled and plunged backward into the water.

When Loire surfaced this time, the man was standing in the fountain at her side, water pouring into the tops of his boots. Wordlessly he helped her out of the pool to the bench beneath the magnolia tree and pounded her helpfully between the shoulder blades.

"St. John!" she shouted as soon as she regained her breath. "Throw this wretch out!"

Her shouts echoed off the walls. He did not appear, though she yelled for him three or four times. "What did you do with my bookkeeper—murder him before you attacked me?" she then asked the stranger.

He did not appear to have heard but strode off a few paces, an elegant figure in gray. His snowy cravat contrasted against his darkly tanned, intensely masculine face. He sat down on the grass, pulled off his boots, and emptied each onto a nearby gardenia. Then he stripped off his black woolen stockings and hung them upon the bush to dry.

Loire saw that the tight knee-length breeches covering his thighs were wet halfway to his hips. Fearing that his breeches would be the next items draped across her gardenia, she jumped off the bench and pointed at the gate. "I haven't given you leave to throw your clothing about my garden! Take your things and get out!"

Adjusting the cuffs of his full-sleeved white shirt, his ring flashing with every movement of his hand, he languorously turned his head to examine her. Loire's petticoat of alençon lace peeped sadly through the charred holes in the bottom of her skirt. Her bodice, missing its ribbon, was stained and soaked, and through the wet fabric her breasts glistened in the afternoon light. Her hair hung in strings halfway to her waist. Her feet were bare, as she had lost her shoes in the fountain.

"I told you to get out!" She pushed her hair out of her eyes, smearing soot across her cheek and forehead. "What are you staring at?"

"A belle without compare," he said, looking forthrightly into her honey-brown eyes.

Loire Chartier raised her head haughtily. "You have two seconds to leave, monsieur, before I summon the sheriff."

With the grace of a leopard he came to his feet. Loire stepped back. The Frenchman was broader in the shoulder and bigger than most Kaintocks.

"It will not be necessary to summon the sheriff," he said, his deep voice sending a shiver down her spine despite her determined effort to still her reaction. "I have no desire to alarm you."

"If you had no desire to alarm me, why did you trespass and lay your foul hands on me?"

"It was but a passing fancy—I had never before seen a woman smoking a pipe. My apologies, mademoiselle. I will, of course, buy you a new gown."

A hot flush colored Loire's cheeks. This was exactly the sort of gift her mother would have accepted from a stranger. "You will do no such thing! What sort of woman do you take me for?"

The light in his eyes matched the dragon's-fire ruby on his finger. "I take you for a lady, a lovely innocent without peer. If I have offended you, it is because I am a bumbling idiot. Is there not a way I can make up for my unjustified assault upon your honor, Mademoiselle Chartier?"

"How did you know my name?"

"Does not the sign above your shop say 'Chartier's Mercantile'?"

"Oh." She twisted her fingers together uncertainly. "I want you to go now."

"I was just on my way." He bowed, collected his boots and stockings, and strode barefoot into the porte cochere. Loire caught her bottom lip between her teeth and tried not to stare too hard at his wide shoulders, his narrow hips and straight, muscular legs. She was still gazing after him when he turned as he opened the gate, flashed her a smile, and disappeared from view.

"Me, I told you the tobacco will kill you, Mems Loire. You some mess!"

St. John was leaning indolently against the doorpost, sniffing a huge pink camellia blossom.

"St. John! Didn't you hear me calling?"

"*Oui.*"

"Then why didn't you come and help me? Didn't you see that . . . that"—she struggled for a suitable word—"*swine* attacking me?"

"I see him. He ver' helpful, that man."

"*Helpful!*" Swishing her wet hair back and forth, she stormed across the courtyard and yelled into his face, "If ever a man is that 'helpful' again, I'll take my Kentucky rifle to him!"

"Mebbe you burn up next time you smoke, then.

Mems, she handle a pipe like a newborn monkey."

"A newborn monkey!"

"*Oui*. The older monkey, he know not to put a smoking pipe under his dress."

"I didn't put it under my dress— Wait! You were spying on me, weren't you?" Her rage grew several degrees hotter.

He smiled, retreated just inside the shop, and returned with a copper watering can. "The camellia by the porte cochere, she thirsty. I give her a drink."

Loire glanced at the ten-foot-high bush. "You were hiding there the entire time, yet you didn't throw that rogue out! I cannot believe it!" She stomped past him into the mercantile.

St. John followed her inside. "M'sieu Dominique, he put out the flames ver' fast. Me, I could not do better."

Loire froze with one hand on the banister and turned to look at him. "Monsieur Dominique? You know this man?"

"*Oui*." He strolled down the aisle to the ladder and began to climb it.

Loire followed him. "Who is he?"

"Who, Mems Loire?" St. John said, fiddling with some glass lampshades high on the shelf.

Loire swiftly climbed the ladder and tugged his waistcoat. "You know very well! Come on, tell!"

"Oh, that man? He is Dominique Youx." He pronounced the name "You." Then he climbed to the next shelf and began to rearrange a set of wedges and other tools, whistling under his breath.

"Dominique Youx? Who in the name of St. Joan of Arc is Dominique Youx?"

"Just a merchant."

"I know every merchant in the Quarter. Why haven't

I seen this one before?"

"He is just here from the great war in France. He got a ship and a warehouse."

"How is it that *you* know him?"

"I see him sometime. Do a little business. People say he fight good for the King Bonaparte."

Loire didn't remember having seen the name on St. John's books. "You sell to him?"

"No. Buy."

"Why haven't you told me about him before?"

"You do not ask. You say, 'Hurry, hurry—I do not like books!' So St. John, he hurry."

"Oh." Her wet skirts clung to her legs as she climbed down the ladder, where she stood thinking for several seconds. "I do not wish you to do business with Monsieur Youx again, St. John."

"You do not wish the tobacco?"

"Tobacco?"

"I buy her from M'sieu Dominique."

Loire clenched her fists and started upstairs. Halfway to the top, she looked across to St. John on the ladder. "Smoking is a very bad habit. I do not wish to promote it. No more tobacco."

"Then life, she ain't a smoke?"

"You are very funny, St. John. Now if you'll excuse me, I'll change out of these clothes your good friend Monsieur Youx destroyed."

The bookkeeper's deep chuckle chased her upstairs. Loire slammed the door to her bedroom loudly enough to startle Ida in the sitting room across the hall. As she stripped off her soggy clothes, a lump of paper fell out of her bodice onto the floor.

"Oh, no!"

Folded into squares, her mother's letter was now a

sodden mess. With shaking hands Loire peeled apart the layers and laid it on the Federal-style mantelpiece.

The meddling Dominique Youx had managed to sever her last connection with her mother, cutting her adrift with nothing but a ghostly echo of laughter long faded into the past . . . and a bitter legacy for the present. Heartsick, she leaned her forehead against the mantel and wept.

"Loire," Ida called through the door, "you all right, honey?"

Loire stumbled behind the Oriental screen in the corner. "I'm h-having a wash."

"You been crying again."

"I haven't. I—fell into the fountain." She gripped the washstand and studied her grimy reflection in the mirror. Dominique Youx had seen her looking exactly this way, yet he had named her a belle beyond compare. What a madman! she thought.

"You want me to fill up the tub?"

"No. I need to be alone for a while."

After pouring water into a blue ceramic basin on the washstand, she scrubbed her face with a bar of lemon soap. In the mirror, her eyes looked red and swollen. *You're getting homelier by the second, Loire Chartier. You've got to stop crying!* she told herself.

She could almost see Dominique Youx's handsome face behind her own in the mirror. He was smiling again—an expression she realized instinctively was habitual for him. Red dragons burned in his dark eyes.

Suddenly very tired, Loire dropped down on the canopied bed. A breeze sighed through the window. The mosquitaire fluttered in a ghostly dance.

2

Loire awakened many times that night. She could not banish the handsome rogue from her dreams. Dawn touched the window before she finally gave up on getting rest and climbed out of bed.

After searching wearily among her clothes in the armoire, she chose an embroidered chemise tied at the shoulders with satin ribbons. She gartered her silk stockings in place above her knees, then stepped into light cotton pantaloons, securing her petticoat with knitted braces.

Her sleeveless percale gown of soft peach had pleated skirts that swung just above her feet, flaring slightly behind. She hooked a tatted collar around her throat, then donned a white, short-waisted linen spencer with stiff lapels and elbow-length sleeves.

From the washstand she selected a bud-shaped vial crowned with leaves of green glass and applied a few drops of attar of rose to her face and throat. After piling her hair onto her head, she secured it with a pair of mussel-shell combs.

Over one eye she angled her favorite plumed hat. Finally she tucked a small pistol and a handful of bank notes into the bottom of her reticule—an elegant bag of white satin trimmed with river pearls.

Downstairs, she searched under the counter for her wicker market basket, then unlocked the back door and went out. The air was cool and sweet this morning, the fragrance of the patchwork flowers almost intoxicating. Honeybees circled a hollow cypress stump before diving into the petals or flying over the brick walls out of sight.

Loire could hear Ida singing in the kitchen of the two-story brick *garçonnière* where she and St. John lived. The bookkeeper was probably hunting alligators or wild hogs in one of the bayous outside the city.

Reluctantly, Loire turned away from her garden and walked down the porte cochere. Almost to the gate, she noticed her shattered clay pipe partially hidden in the jasmine sweeping the brick walk.

Almost afraid to touch it, she bent for a closer look. An unwanted sensation burned in her breast— once more she felt the stranger's fiery kiss on her hand. The man had no right to torment her like this!

She quickly gathered up the fragments, intending to dump them into the river on her way to market . . . and Dominique Youx's image with them.

At rue Decatur she was swept up in the crowds surging toward the French Market. After half a block she reached the other side of the street and climbed the steep, grassy levee.

Steamboats, schooners, and barques rocked at anchor on the shining, almost two-mile-wide river.

Bales of cotton waited on the wharves with no takers—silent witnesses to the British blockade of New Orleans, America's principal port.

And what of the Chartier fortune? The pirated barque was only a surface ripple of the maelstrom beneath. If the British won the war, all that her family had ever worked for would be gone!

She brought out the pieces of pipe and shivered at the memory of Dominique's touch. With a sharp cry she pitched the fragments as far as she could into the river, then walked back down the levee to the marketplace.

People of every description crowded the market: Choctaws, Creoles, both slaves and free men of color, Spanish fishermen, Chinese sailors, tall Kaintocks from upriver, Italian vendors.

Blockade or not, the marketeers had plenty of good things for sale: melons, peppers, tiny oranges and lemons, seafood, alligator sausage. Sweating cooks stirred cauldrons of crawfish, okra gumbo, and fish bouillabaisse.

Loire stopped in front of an old Chitimacha squaw sitting on a braided rug, weaving baskets from cane gathered in the swamps and dyed with black walnut leaves and powac roots. Loire ordered three sent to the mercantile.

Beyond a stall decorated with herbs and braided garlic, Loire discovered a group of Kaintocks and free blacks bawling wagers at each other over two big roosters in a pit. A cockfight was no place for a lady, but Loire was intrigued. She clutched the handle of her market basket in both fists and studied the combatants.

She favored the smaller bird—a rogue in tattered

tails and yellow-feathered pantaloons, with a glint in his beady little eyes. He wove in and out of his enemy's range like a boxer, his head bobbing atop a scrawny neck.

Loire gasped when he stretched his head almost casually toward his opponent's breast, leaving his neck vulnerable. The larger bird struck with lightning speed, but the first one sprang nimbly into the air and spurred him down the back. Feathers flew thick and fast.

"Since you have abandoned making smoke signals for gambling," came a deep, amused voice behind Loire, "might I recommend you lay your money on Dandy Leggins, Mademoiselle Chartier? He's the one in the yellow pantaloons."

Anger charged up Loire's spine and set her scalp tingling. She did not have to turn around to recognize the speaker. As if yesterday's humiliating encounter were not enough, today he'd caught her watching a cockfight! She pushed through the crowd in an attempt to get away.

"I had hoped you might join me for a cup of tea."

"And I had hoped never to see you again, monsieur!" She spun around to face him and immediately wished she hadn't. The sight of him took her breath away.

Dominique Youx was a New Orleans gentleman from the top of his tall silk hat to the heels of his shining half boots. Beneath his close-fitting black coat he wore a pearl-gray spencer and a white shirt with a high, stiff collar. His cravat frothed like a cresting wave at his throat. Diamond studs winked at his cuffs, and a red rose trembled in his buttonhole.

With a grin like a slash of ivory in his tanned face,

he swept off his hat and bowed. Loire focused on his thick dark hair curling over the back of his collar. For a moment he seemed so boyish that she wanted to touch his hair there. She held on to her basket for dear life as he straightened to his full height.

He was even more striking than she'd thought him yesterday. He wasn't young—there was a streak of gray over his left temple that she hadn't noticed before—but neither was he old. His eyes were bright and very deep, like a still bayou on a hot summer's day . . . inviting and dangerous. Loire remembered what St. John had said about him: Dominique Youx fought for Napoleon, and he had a ship. Those far-seeing, penetrating eyes belonged to a warfaring seaman.

The crow's-feet at the corners of his eyes deepened with his smile, a magical phenomenon that made Loire's pulse race. Suddenly conscious that she was staring at him, she said in English, "Good day, sir!"

Whirling on her heel, she again began to push into the mob. Jostled this way and that, forced at times to hold her basket over her head, she didn't stop for several minutes. When she finally looked back over her shoulder, he was gone.

"Good riddance to him, and may the heat give him a rash under his collar!"

But when she struggled around the corner to an Italian fruit peddler's stall, Dominique Youx was standing at a booth a short distance ahead, drinking from a crystal brandy snifter. He raised his glass in a silent toast and let his gaze drift slowly over her.

Loire's heart lurched. How had he gotten ahead of her? He was making it look as though *she* were pursuing *him*. What did the scoundrel want? She marched off in the opposite direction.

"My heavens, Babette," said a French voice that penetrated Loire's consciousness, "do you not think the hour is early for such a woman to be about?"

"I do, Marie. But perhaps business was bad last night and she must begin work early."

Loire looked over at two well-dressed matrons leaving a stall, each nibbling a fried *beignet* smothered with sugar. When she recognized her mother's former friends, her words died in her throat.

Looking at Loire out of frosty green eyes, the elder lady moved her skirts aside as she swept past. The younger one followed suit, then looked back over her shoulder and giggled.

Loire stood still, a small island in a sea of people. Two or three of them glanced at her on their way by but, seeing her flushed face and tear-filled eyes, looked hurriedly away.

Would there never be an end to society's memory of her mother and her indiscretions? Very few days had passed in the last five years that Loire had not been forcefully reminded of them. She could not go to mass without hearing whispers.

Creoles of good family continued to do business at the mercantile—but they did not receive her into their homes. It had been a long time since she'd been asked to a ball or the opera.

On the other hand, men came to the store almost weekly with propositions. Most were well-to-do planters wishing to build a love nest in town without their wives finding out. Others were uptown merchants, riverboat captains, gamblers, or Kaintocks. Occasionally one came along and offered to marry her, desiring to take over her business. Loire rejected them all, helping the more stubborn outside with the

Kentucky long rifle she kept behind the door.

Ignoring the people struggling by, she bowed her head and clasped her basket, as if by squeezing hard enough she could blot out the stain attached to the name Chartier.

"It seems that some of these women of good family learned their manners in the pigsty."

Dominique Youx stood beside her, looking after the matrons, a muscle throbbing in his cheek. When Loire did not reply, he said, "It is hot here. Come, I will buy you a lemonade."

She knew she should run. Everyone would believe the worst. Instead, she let him take her arm and clear a path through the crowd with his wide shoulders. She did not look up until he led her beneath the awning of a sidewalk café and seated her on a lace-patterned iron chair. He settled across the small round table from her.

"I—I cannot stay, monsieur."

"The market is not going anywhere. Rest for a moment." He snapped his fingers.

A waiter made his way through the tables with a tall glass of lemonade and set it at Loire's elbow. At a nod from Youx, he retreated into the kitchen and returned a moment later with a bowl of vichyssoise for Loire and a half bottle of wine for Dominique.

"I'm not hungry," she said, looking at the cold potato soup.

"No? Perhaps a bite or two?"

"No!" She pushed the bowl away. "Who appointed you my guardian, Monsieur Dominique Youx?"

If he was taken aback either by her query or by her knowledge of his name, he gave no sign. He simply poured himself a glass of wine, leaned back in his chair, and studied her over the rim of his glass. The dragon on his finger played scintillating games of chase with the reflections of the red wine. He said nothing.

"Why were you following me?" Loire demanded. "Do you think me a woman of easy virtue, to pursue me so?"

"No, mademoiselle. There is nothing easy about you, I deem."

"Then why?"

"Why would a man sell all that he has to purchase a pearl of great price?"

"I do not understand you."

"Some things are worth giving up all else, Loire."

She flushed angrily at his use of her given name, though his tone set her nerves tingling. "You are required to give up nothing, Monsieur Youx," she said, "for nothing is what you would get in return."

"Perhaps, though, I would gladly sacrifice all to discover the truth." Leaning forward, he placed his fingertips on the table a hairbreadth from her naked forearm and smiled into her eyes. His look seemed to say that he knew all there was to know.

Loire leaped to her feet, knocking over her chair. As Dominique started to rise, she pushed out her palm and backed away. "I know your kind, monsieur, and I never want to see it again. Do you understand? Never!" She turned and rushed into the crowd.

Dominique followed her with his eyes until all he could see was her plumed hat. When it, too, had disappeared, he reached into his breast pocket for a miniature portrait done in oil.

The honey-brown eyes of the girl laughed up at him, tantalized him, mesmerized him even as they had since he'd first seen the portrait. To find their owner had eclipsed all other desires. She was more desirable than all the treasure galleons of Spain, more priceless than the rarest diamonds of Africa. He had to have her. He *would* have her.

After dropping a gold sovereign on the table, he stalked out of the café. This time it was not necessary to part the crowd with his shoulders; the dangerous look in his eyes blazed a wide trail before him.

"Me, I never see a woman drive me harder bargain! How you speck a poor Cajun man to eat, eh?"

Loire folded her arms and smiled at the fat merchant she'd been bargaining with for twenty minutes. "You can stop the theatrics, Monsieur Jules. You bought those necklaces for a tenth of what you're trying to charge me. Did you ask the Houmas how *they* were supposed to eat?"

"Injuns eat jest fine, out in the swamp!"

Loire picked up her basket and turned to walk away.

"Eight dollar! Mam'selle give Jules eight dollar and he give her the lot."

"Even that big one in the center?" She pointed at one made of polished mussel shells studded with black pearls.

"*Oui*, eight dollar."

"I'll give you five."

"Five! No! Impossible! Not even for you, mam'selle!"

"Six, but you must also give me that book you've got hidden under your jacket."

Jules stared down at his jacket, shocked. "How did you— Oh, all right, six dollar and I give you my leetle book of poems. Jest please to get out my stall!"

Loire handed him a bank note. Grumbling, he searched in the pouch hanging around his neck for change. Loire rolled the necklaces into the deerskin and placed them in her basket with several items she'd already purchased.

"The book, too, monsieur. You promised."

"The mam'selle has eagle eyes, she has, to look into a poor man's pockets!"

"A promise is a—"

"Promise. All right, mam'selle. I cannot read the damn English words, no way." He reached into his jacket for a slim book with a faded red cover.

"William Blake, *Songs of Experience,*" Loire read, and tucked it into her basket. "It's probably worth ten dollars, monsieur. My thanks."

"Ten dollar! Mam'selle, you must wait!"

But Loire had already moved off into the crowd with a smile and a wave.

"*Mon Dieu,* you some pirate-woman!" the Cajun called after her admiringly, watching her progress up the street. "Mam'selle come back nex' week, eh?"

The convent bells were tolling two as Loire left the French Market. Mule-drawn carriages congested rue St. Philip, and people filled the banquettes. Past the imposing theater, she cut through an alley dotted with cafés to a crumbling brick building.

A rusty gate opened onto a porte cochere. Mosquitoes swarmed over a stagnant pool in the courtyard. Slapping them away, she darted up a cypress stairway to the second floor, knocked once, and walked in.

In the room were a wobbly table and two cane chairs. The tightly closed shutters and a fire blazing in the grate made it feel as hot as an oven.

"Mazy? You here?" she called in English.

"Where else I be, Miz Loire?"

"Dancing with the governor at the Quadroon Ball, maybe?"

"Go 'long, chile!" The reedy voice quavered with laughter.

After setting her basket on the table, Loire rummaged through it for a loaf of bread, a packet of rice, and several links of smoked alligator sausage. She added a parcel of lemons and another of tea to the pile. "How's your rheumatism, Mazy?"

"Tolerable. Tolerable."

A hunchbacked old woman with skin the color of dried coffee grounds shuffled in through a connecting doorway, wearing a faded indigo dress. She clutched a shabby woolen shawl around her shoulders. A tiny amber-colored glass jar dangled from a rawhide thong against her breast.

"Why don't you sit down, Mazy? I'll fry you some sausage."

"No, ma'am." She smiled, showing her tobacco-stained teeth. "You is mighty good to me, Miz Loire, but it ain't fittin'. It jest ain't for the missus to wait on me."

"I'm not your mistress, for heaven's sake! Papa set you free when Mama left, don't you remember? You're a free woman."

"Yeah. 'Cause I done got too ole to work, dat's all."

"I wish you'd quit talking like that."

"Done got too ole to change, too."

Loire sighed. "Why don't you come on back home? Ida says you can have the room next to St. John's and hers in the *garçonnière.*"

Mazy shook her head. "I done spent seventy years answerin' to folk ever' time I needed to pee. I ain't gonna live with nobody no more. When the Lawd ready to take me, He take me. I ain't worried."

"All right, then. But Ida's coming over tonight to cook for you, you hear me?"

The old woman fumbled in her glass jar for a pinch of snuff and pushed it into her cheek. "You got one yet?"

"Got what?"

"A man."

Loire shouldered her basket, aware that her face had reddened a shade more than she could blame on the heat. "No, ma'am, I haven't gotten one since last Saturday when you asked me that same question."

"Mebbe you get one before next Sat'day."

"Maybe. You'll be the first to know. I've got to go now. Ida will be by later. I'll ask her to whip up some jambalaya with that sausage."

"Dat's all right." With a wave, Mazy shuffled back to the other room. Loire heard her pine-straw mattress crackle as she lay down.

Loire was half a block from home when she spotted a huge crowd in front of the mercantile. It looked like the same crowd of loafers that had accompanied Alain Defromage there yesterday. "Sweet Mary, what's happened now?"

Hitching up her skirts, she ran down the street as fast as her feet could carry her. "Let me through! Please let me through!"

"It's Mademoiselle Chartier! Quickly, let her through!"

Loire darted through the path opening in the crowd. In front of the shop she stopped, dumbfounded.

She had never seen so many red roses in her life. Blankets of them covered the pair of dapple grays standing in the traces of a black ebony carriage, piled high with flowers. Honeybees burrowed into the roses spilling across the banquette into the mercantile.

Before Loire could find her voice, a swarthy fellow strolled out of the store, with St. John behind him. Decked out in an ill-fitting jacket decorated with gold braid insignia of the emperor's defunct navy, he stretched up on tiptoe as he walked, appearing taller than his five-foot height. He grinned at Loire and lifted his tricorn hat off a thatch of greasy black hair.

"Here, it's the little lady, herself, or I'll be mastheaded and flayed to me backbone for lying!" he said, parodying king's English for the merriment of the crowd. "If she ain't the pretty one, just like the master said!"

Loire looked down at him as though he were an unpleasant substance she'd discovered on the bottom of her shoe. "Who is this *creature*, St. John?"

The Jamaican smiled. "He say he Renato Beluche, Mems Loire."

His tone betrayed that he knew a lot more than he was admitting. Aware that the crowd was hanging on her every word, Loire said tightly, "I'd like to see you gentlemen inside. *Now.*"

Once she'd moved past them into the store, she dropped her basket on the counter and turned on the sailor. "Are you responsible for that vulgar display outside, Monsieur Beluche?"

His eyes widened in mock innocence as he rubbed a grimy forefinger rapidly across his mustachios. "Vulgar?" he repeated. "You think blossoms to rival those of a Parisian garden vulgar, mademoiselle? But I am cut to the quick!"

"The flowers are from you, then?" She tore her hat

off her head and hurled it on the counter. She had dealt with insulting propositions before, but this won the prize!

Beluche's flamboyant bow propelled a wave of body odor into all corners of the room. Loire stepped back against the counter. St. John wrinkled his nose, his expression of amusement deepening. "I wish I could say they were from me, mademoiselle, but Captain Dominique Youx would kick my derriere back to France for telling such a story."

"Dominique Youx!" Suddenly everything was clear. She dashed around the counter and, grabbing the Kentucky long rifle, leveled the muzzle at his heart. "You have two seconds to get your sorry hide out of my store, collect your blasted flowers, and drive your carriage off my street!"

Renato Beluche shrugged gently. "He said you would be angry."

"He did, eh?"

"But he could not rest until he'd sent his humble apologies for his behavior. He spent three hours in the flower shops purchasing a suitable apology."

"How clever of him to have selected flowers. They will go so well on your crypt, monsieur."

Beluche backed out the door, still grinning. The crowd screamed with excitement when Loire walked out after him with the rifle stock clamped against her right shoulder.

"Monsieur Dominique, he wishes you to have the horses and carriage, too."

"Git!" Loire cried in a fair imitation of a Kentucky yell.

Beluche climbed onto the high seat of the carriage and all but disappeared among the flowers. He picked up a whip decorated with jasmine and touched it to his tricorn.

"You would make a man one hell of a wife, mademoiselle," he said appreciatively, "but not much of a shootist. I should have told you before—you've forgotten to put a flint in the lock. Your gun will not fire."

With a snap of the whip over the horses' ears, he set off at a brisk trot. A trail of flowers and bees marked his progress down the street. The crowd cheered.

Kicking a stray rose out of her path, Loire went into the mercantile and slammed the door with a violence that rattled the panes of glass on either side.

"What are you looking at?" she yelled at St. John as he began emptying the contents of her basket onto the counter.

"A typhoon, I think."

"I am not a typhoon!" She flung her useless gun into the corner. "Damn, damn!"

"Your papa, he would not want you to cuss like the Kaintocks, Mems Loire."

Loire looked him dead in the eye and repeated the word twice more. "There, put that in Papa's pipe and smoke it!"

"It is better than the tobacco, I think, but the pipe, she is broken yesterday."

"Don't remind me!" The whole mess with Dominique Youx had started over that pipe. Why in the world had she put that thing between her teeth? "I'll never smoke again as long as I live!"

"The tobacco, she will tempt you."

"No, she won't!" She reached into the tobacco cabinet and began hurling tins into the wooden dustbin.

"Your father, he lose more money this way." Having dipped a quill into a pot of ink, he painstakingly scratched through several entries in his accounting book. "He think his girl go crazy—throwing out the good tobacco 'cause she fall in love with that man."

Loire froze with a five-pound tin of tobacco in her hand. With menacing slowness she turned her head to look up at him. "What did you say?"

St. John shrugged, dipped his quill, and marked through another entry. "I forget."

"Good. Because if you remember it long enough to repeat it, you'll find yourself out of a job."

"St. John, he take you fishing when you small."

"That's got nothing to do with it! How dare you accuse me of falling in love with that—that *gambler?*"

"Gambler? He is but merchant."

"Ha! He was gambling on a cockfight! He told me which one to bet on!"

St. John dropped his quill and leaned toward her. "You gamble on the rooster chickens? Your papa, he is mad when he find out this thing!"

"La! I've had enough of this!" She flung the last two tobacco tins into the dustbin. Controlling a wild impulse to tear out her hair, she stomped outside to the wellhouse and vigorously worked the handle of a cast-iron pump until water gushed into a large wooden bucket. She filled a second bucket, attached the handles to a yoke, and, balancing the heavy load on her shoulders, staggered into the store.

"St. John will carry that," he said.

"I'll do it myself. I've done it a thousand times." She plodded up the stairs. Near the top she turned cautiously to look down at him. "Ask Ida to bring me something to eat, and tell her to go see Mazy this evening. Maybe she can talk the old woman into coming back."

"I tell her."

"I am going to take a bath. Then I am going to bed. I don't want to be disturbed for any reason. You can take delivery on the things I ordered at the market today."

"They come already."

"Oh. Well then, good night."

St. John closed his book and replaced it on the shelf, smiling to himself in a way that tested Loire's patience.

"If that smelly sailor comes back with his flowers," she said, "you are to stuff them down his throat with my compliments. Do I make myself clear, St. John?"

"Ver' clear, Mems Loire."

"Fine, then."

"Fine."

"One other thing, St. John."

"*Oui?*"

"If Monsieur Youx comes round, tell him I do not receive river scum."

"*Oui*, mems."

"So tell him to throw himself back in the river where he came from."

"This thing I tell him."

"And—and tell him I hated his cartful of wilted dandelion weeds."

The Jamaican walked to the bottom of the staircase and rested his hands on his hips. "You want St. John to make a list of things to say?"

"No. That will be all."

"Good night, Mems Loire." He grinned as she slammed the door in reply. "Me, I hope you sleep better than last night."

3

Renato Beluche was pursuing her through the marketplace with a red rose as large as a cart horse, demanding that she crawl into it. Knowing that Dominique Youx waited inside, she ran through the streets, searching frantically for her mother.

Bells tolled. Loire surfaced from the nightmare, sat up with a jolt, and looked wildly around the room.

Everything was exactly as it had been last night. Her iron tub sat crouched against the wall, with a soggy towel wadded over the high back and her garments scattered on the floor around it.

The bells tolled again, and she realized they were calling early morning mass. Loire crossed to the French windows and looked down the street to the cathedral. She had not been to mass for a long time.

Wearing an indigo dress several years out of date yet more flattering than her fashionable Empire-waisted frocks, she went downstairs, grabbed a wedge of crab quiche left from supper, and repaired to the courtyard with the book she'd purchased yesterday.

Curled up on the bench under the magnolia, she nibbled the quiche and began to read. William Blake's poetry and stunning watercolor illustrations soon enthralled her. Only the rustling of the pages disturbed the cathedral hush in the garden.

After a while she discovered an illustration of a red rose. Remembering her dream, she read aloud: "'O Rose, thou art sick . . . The invisible worm that flies in the night in the howling storm . . . Has found out thy bed of crimson joy . . . And his dark secret love does thy life destroy.'" Discomfited, she closed the book and stood up.

What was she to make of Dominique Youx? No one had ever sent her a carriage filled with roses before. Only a man immensely sure of his own power would have dared such a romantic, larger-than-life deed. But then why had he sent the ridiculous Renato Beluche as his spokesman?

Loire was still thinking of the mysterious Frenchman an hour later when, her face veiled, she slid into the family pew near the front of the basilica of St. Louis. Mumbling the litany, she listened to the priest with only half an ear.

Father Dubourg intoned in Latin, "Let us pray."

Slipping to her knees, Loire discovered the volume of poetry rather than her prayer book in her hands. As she turned it over, the leaves fell open to the disturbing poem. "His dark secret love does thy life destroy . . ."

Immediately the image of Dominique Youx captured her thoughts. She saw him in the café, heard his deep voice proclaim, "Some things are worth giving up all else."

Almost fearfully she peered at the people around her. No flashing dark eyes looked back. No one whispered sweet nonsense with such terrifying intensity. A man like him in church—ha! She could have laughed out loud.

After the final amen, she uncovered her face and waited for the sanctuary to empty. Clutching her book, she walked down the aisle toward the altar.

"You wish to make a confession?"

"Oh! Father Dubourg, I didn't see you."

"I did not mean to alarm you," he said, stepping out of the shadows by the confessional booths. The apostolic administrator of the Diocese of Louisiane pushed his hands inside the sleeves of his black cassock. "May I help you, child?"

"I need to talk to someone. To God, I think." When the priest gestured toward a confessional, she shook her head. "I don't need to confess."

"We all need to confess. Come, it's been a long time since I've heard yours." He disappeared into the booth.

Hesitantly, she entered the adjoining compartment. "I didn't even bring my rosary." She sighed, then plunged into the confession. "Forgive me, Father, for I have sinned . . . but not in the way people seem to think."

When he did not respond, she said, "I've smoked tobacco a few times and perhaps dealt with smugglers when I knew I shouldn't, but I have *not*"—she drew a deep breath—"given myself to anyone, no matter what you might have heard!"

"What I have heard is immaterial. I am here to listen to your confession."

"But I haven't done anything! I'm being blamed for my mother's sin."

"And does Captain Defromage blame you, too?"

Loire was taken aback. "What do you know about *him?*"

"I know that your father wishes you to marry him, and that you blame him for losing your barque. I know that two days ago you broke off your engagement."

"There was no—" She bit her lip. It would do no good to explain. Regretting that she'd come, she stood up to leave.

"People are saying that you led him on."

"Led him on? The gossips are talking already?"

"Is it true?"

She tried to swallow a lump of anger. "I—I considered marrying him at one time. Briefly considered it."

"You used him to keep your father at bay."

"I don't have to listen to this, Father."

"Have you ever contemplated taking the orders?"

The unexpected question made her head swim. Why couldn't this priest see that she needed comfort, not more pressure?

"It would be to your advantage, child," he said. "No one would dare speak ill of a nun."

For a moment she visualized herself swaddled in safely opaque robes. Then Dominique Youx's handsome face loomed before her. She shut her eyes and pressed her knuckles against her forehead.

"Is your father still on his plantation?"

"The one on Isle Châteauroux," she answered wearily. "He sold the other last year, to pay Claiborne's taxes."

"You should get word to him somehow, that you

are considering the orders. He must not continue to believe you will wed his merchant captain."

Loire tried to thrust Dominique's image aside. Lamely she said, "Papa depends on me to run the business here. I cannot take the orders."

"St. John is capable of running the shop."

She could still feel the imprint of his kiss on her hand. *Dominique Youx, why can't you leave me alone?*

Before she could reply, Father Dubourg went on, "I will take you to see the mother superior this very afternoon, child. Come, together we will help you out of this muddle."

Loire got home in time to see two rust-colored mules dragging a freight wagon away from the door. Stacked on the banquette were twenty hogsheads and half a dozen kegs marked TOBACCO. St. John was on his way inside with a hogshead balanced on his shoulder.

"St. John! Put that down!"

"*Oui,* inside, Mems Loire."

She blocked the doorway. "Did you buy that from Monsieur Youx?"

"I did not buy her from him." He attempted to edge around her, but she gripped the doorposts.

"Then where did you get it?"

"I will drop her if mems does not move from the door."

"Good! Drop her on the street, then."

"Mems is most difficult."

"I can become a lot more difficult if you bring that filthy stuff into my shop!"

Grunting, St. John placed the hogshead on the banquette and planted his fists on his hips. "The barque, she got stole on the high seas. Then you throw the Louisville tobacco away yesterday, make your papa more broke. Times, she is hard. I will show mems the books."

"I don't want to look at the books!"

St. John caught the back of her dress as she spun to go. "Mems don't sell tobacco, she don't eat. The shop, she go *psst!* Like that!"

"Did you buy the tobacco from Dominique Youx?"

"Does mems care more for her papa, or her pride?"

"My papa, of course!"

"Then I tell you something. M'sieu Youx, he give the tobacco to say he is sorry. He say he is wrong to take away mems' pipe, burn up her dress. He say smoke as much as mems like, sell the rest to the damn Kaintocks."

"The nerve of that man! I ought to make a bonfire with it right here on the banquette!"

"All right for St. John to take inside the rest?"

"Mon Dieu! You are as crazy as he is!" She dropped her hands in defeat. "Take it if it pleases you so much. Just promise me one thing, St. John."

"Eh?"

"Don't tell him I know where it came from."

Smiling, the Jamaican hefted the hogshead. "St. John, he will keep the secret in his heart."

"Did he . . . say anything else?"

"Just he ver' sorry."

"Oh. Well, did you tell him I hated the flowers?"

"Oui, I tell him."

"What did he say?"

"He say next time he send bigger roses. Maybe you like them better."

"La! I'm going for a walk. Put that tobacco where I won't have to look at it!"

"This thing I will do, and the matches, too. The tobacco, she is not so good for mems."

For two hours Loire walked the streets of the French Quarter, anger driving her feet. How could Dominique Youx be so bold as to think he could buy forgiveness with presents? She'd like to see him just once more to tell him what she thought of him!

St. John was lighting the lamps in the shop when she got back. She sat down on a cane chair, rested her chin on her hands, and gazed out the back door. Twilight cloaked the courtyard. In the magnolia trees, cicadas tuned up for the night.

A soft rap sounded on the front door. Loire said, "Can't they see we're closed? No, St. John, I'll get it."

She crossed the room, slid the bolt free, and swung open the door. "I'm sorry, we're clo—"

Dominique Youx smiled down at her. "Mademoiselle Chartier, may I come in? I have something to say."

4

Hatless, his hair tousled, Dominique Youx wore a black, full-length carrick with tiered cape collars. His ebony carriage waited behind him—this time empty of roses.

Loire could feel herself trembling. Her mind told her to slam the door in his face, but her body didn't listen.

"Mademoiselle Chartier," he began in a low voice, "I apologize for the lateness of the hour—"

"You had nothing to do with the sun's setting, monsieur," she said, "despite your high opinion of yourself. Now, if you will excuse me, I was just on my way to bed."

Dominique shot out his hand to hold the door open. "You may do so in a moment, mademoiselle, after I've said what I've come to say."

"St. John!" Loire said. The Jamaican was leaning against the counter, smiling. "Throw this oaf out!"

His smile broadened into a yawn; his great muscles corded as he stretched. "Ver' sorry, mems, but the old bones too tired to push oafs tonight."

"St. John!" But he only waved and went out the back door.

Dominique swept off his carrick, dropped it on a chair, and adjusted the diamond cuff links in his black spencer. Loire saw his gaze take in the new display of tobacco, and she inwardly cursed St. John's choice of shelving.

"A good man, St. John," he said. "He has the eye of an artist and the soul of a pirate. I like that in a man."

"That scarcely surprises me, sir," Loire said in English, spurning to use the more intimate French. She had to keep him at arm's length, physically and emotionally.

"You do not like pirates, I take it," he said, switching to English.

"I despise leeches of all sorts, with good reason." She stepped behind the counter. "Now what do you want?"

"I have not come to leech off you."

"If you've come with more gifts, throw them into the dustbin!"

"It is not a gift, Loire," he said, his tone deepening on her name, "but a repayment. I always—how do the Kaintocks say it? Square my debts."

"You don't owe me one."

"You are most generous, but I broke something of yours." He reached into his spencer and drew out a small parcel tied with string. "This is for you."

Loire stared at the package as though he were handing her a spider. Curiosity won out, and she set it on the counter between them. The paper fell away from a delicate ivory pipe carved with mermaids and sea anemones. The mouthpiece was of gold, patinaed with age.

"Where did you get this?" she asked reverently, holding it up to the candlelight.

"A merchant comes across things. It is impossible to remember."

Loire lowered the pipe. "St. John says you have a warehouse. Why haven't I seen it?"

"Perhaps you do not venture so far uptown. It is on Tremé, near the cemetery."

"Oh. Still, I would have noticed *you*."

"You would have, had I been in New Orleans longer. I have been in France serving the emperor."

St. John was right, then. She couldn't restrain a burst of national pride and perhaps a little admiration. Unconsciously she broke into French, stepping out from the counter. "My father is very fond of Napoleon. He grieves for him."

Dominique Youx's eyes darkened with pain. "*Oui,* so do we all." He picked up his carrick, looked at the door, and said quietly, "It has been a long war. Maybe that is why my manners are so poor; I have forgotten how to behave."

Suddenly Loire didn't want him to go. She said quickly, "St. John often chides me on my own lack of manners. Smoking, for instance. And waving guns in people's faces."

He looked her full in the face then, amusement chasing the shadows from his eyes. "Renato Beluche mentioned your long rifle. Perhaps you should get a flint."

For a moment they smiled at each other, companions

in a sort of roguish understanding. Then Dominique's expression changed, became charged with electricity. He took half a step toward her and touched her forearm.

At the hot currents she felt coming from his fingertips, Loire instantly moved back. She brought the pipe up between them like a talisman, warding off danger. "This pipe, this was your reason for coming?"

"*Oui*, and to tender my apologies. I would make restitution for insulting you in your courtyard."

"I was not so insulted," she said in a low voice, looking at the pipe. "You did not have to waste money on flowers . . . and tobacco." She raised her gaze uncertainly.

Dominique was looking out the door at his carriage. He tugged at the lock of gray hair over his temple. "Those roses . . . perhaps I went a bit overboard, mademoiselle. On the battlefield, a man imagines doing such foolish things, never believing he will live long enough to do them."

He regretted giving her gifts, then. Perhaps he believed he could have gained what he wished without them.

Perhaps he thought she was as easy as her mother.

Masking her emotions behind a tight smile, Loire marched to the door. "I will, of course, repay you for the tobacco St. John accepted against my orders to the contrary. Good night, Monsieur Youx."

"Good night?" Dominique narrowed his eyes, giving her an uncomfortably penetrating look. "Have I done something to offend?"

"No, not this time." She held open the door and looked away from him, trying to ignore the sparks between them.

"I did not come here to play children's games, Loire Chartier."

She snapped her gaze up to meet his. "Then just why did you come? It was surely not the pipe!"

"No, it was not the pipe, although I wanted you to have it. It belonged to my great-grandmother."

"It is a family heirloom, then? I cannot accept it!"

"I want you to keep it, Smokeflower."

"I have given up tobacco."

A muscle twitched in his jaw. "You never took it up in the first place. Keep the pipe as a token of my esteem, and a pledge that I will never again do anything to hurt you."

Throwing his carrick over his shoulders, Dominique Youx bowed and strode out the door. He climbed onto the driver's seat, picked up the whip, and gathered the reins into his hands. At a sharp crack of the whip, the horses trotted off down the street.

Loire stood in the doorway looking after him, cradling the ivory pipe in her hands. *Smokeflower.* What a very odd thing to call her.

"Ole Mazy ain't doing too good, Miz Loire," Ida said as she carried Loire's breakfast tray into the courtyard the next morning. When Loire didn't stir, she set the tray on the bench beside her and placed her fists on her broad hips. "Somebody done put a dried lizard under her house and witch her!"

Loire stuffed the ivory pipe into a fold in her skirt and looked at her housekeeper. It took a moment to adjust her thoughts to English. "I'm sorry, Ida, what did you say?"

"Mazy doing poorly." She poured rose-hip tea into

a china cup and handed it over. "Somebody witch her."

"You don't actually believe in voodoo?"

The older woman slathered butter onto a thick lard biscuit. "Don't know what to believe. Times is bad. Mazy getting sicker."

"I know, but she won't come back here." Loire stared into the cup and sighed. "Too many years of being a slave."

"Yeah, and she ain't long for this world." Ida added under her breath, "Dried lizards."

"It's not dried lizards. Did you ask her to come home?"

"Ask till my face turn blue as a drowned man's. She ain't going nowhere. She been pining over that boy of hers, Tim, ever since your pappy sold him to ole man Villeré."

Loire winced. "Papa's got a heart of stone."

Ida moved the tray and sat down beside her. "Me and St. John, we got money saved up. I want to ask you to do something."

"Of course, Ida. Anything."

"Go ask ole Gen'ral Villeré to sell him back. I'll give you the money."

Loire's eyes burned with tears as she laid her hand gently on Ida's knee. "I've already asked his son, Major Gabriel. He said no."

"But if we give you more money—"

"It's not the money. He said Tim is"—she choked on the word— "*prime*. He won't part with him for any price. Says he needs more like him in the cane fields."

"Then it ain't no use." Ida's chins wobbled as she began to cry. She heaved herself off the bench and walked across the grass to the *garçonnière*. As she went inside, she said, "Mazy good as dead! Tim, too!"

Loire drew a deep, shuddering breath. Ida was right. If Tim wasn't returned soon, the old woman would surely die of grief.

There was only one thing to do. She'd have to ride out to the Villeré plantation and try again.

Five and a half hours later, Loire stalked out of Gabriel Villeré's house in a flaming temper. After jumping into her green, high-topped buggy, she cracked the whip over her mare's ears and shot out of the yard, scattering chickens and dogs.

The river road to New Orleans ran along the levee for nine miles. Loire had covered five when she spied a big man on horseback beneath a moss-draped cypress tree ahead. While dragging her mare to a halt, she fumbled in her reticule for her pistol and aimed it at his head.

"If you're thinking of robbing me, you'd best carry your Kaintock hide back where it came from!" she shouted in English.

"And why would I rob you, Mademoiselle Chartier, when I merely wished to inquire after your health?"

Dominique Youx emerged from the shadows on a magnificent black stallion. He was clad this time in a fringed buckskin shirt and cottonade leggings.

"You've been following me again!"

"*Oui*." He was unrepentant.

"How dare you, sir?"

Reining in beside the buggy, he touched the brim of his soft frontier hat. If he minded the gun pointed at his forehead, he gave no sign. "I was out for a ride and happened to run into St. John."

"*Happened* to run into St. John?"

"He told me you'd gone off to Gabriel's alone, and I, being a fretful sort of fellow, decided to make sure you weren't accosted by some rogue."

"And I nearly shot the rogue."

"But how droll that would have been, mademoiselle."

"Yes, wouldn't it?" After replacing the gun in her bag, she picked up the whip and leaned back until the leather sides of the buggy top blocked him from view. "Move back so the wheel won't catch your horse."

He placed his hand on the dashboard and leaned into the buggy, studying her as though he were drinking in a work of art.

She became aware that her breasts were tightening as they were fanned by his breath. Her pulse thrilled in her veins, the heat building until she was sure he could see it radiating through her gown. Disquieted, she shifted her gaze and saw her own rapid pulse mirrored in his throat.

"I must leave town for a few days, Smokeflower."

His voice relaxed the spell only slightly. She clung to the buggy whip as he said, "Perhaps you will accompany me to the concert next Saturday evening."

Loire reddened. "We—we hardly know each other, monsieur. I believe you are in jest."

"I would not jest about a Brandenburg Concerto, nor my desire to take you. I will pick you up at nine o'clock, with your consent."

"I—I can't go."

His dark eyes narrowed, giving him an altogether dangerous look. "You have another engagement?"

"No, I—I mean, yes!"

"A pity. This man, may I ask his name?"

"His name? It is . . . it is none of your concern. Now I must be on my way."

Instead of moving away, Dominique slid off his horse and onto the seat beside her. Ignoring her sputter of outrage, he took the reins and chirruped to the mare. The buggy lurched off down the road with the black stallion trotting after it.

"You take a lot of liberties, Monsieur Youx," Loire said, feeling cut off from the outside world within the screening buggy top.

"It is one of my faults, Loire," he said, his cultured French at odds with his words.

"I suppose you would blame it on Napoleon's war?"

Dominique's white teeth flashed as he chuckled. "I wish I could, Smokeflower, but I would be taking liberties with the truth in saying it."

"Then you have no excuse for your high-handedness."

"Such a sharp complement of claws! But I suppose you are right. I came from a large brood in which high-handedness was a necessary quality in obtaining enough to eat."

She softened a bit. "Your family was poor, then?"

"No. Damnably rich, but we had so many mouths at the table that only the fastest and strongest got a second helping."

"And you were the fastest and strongest," she said disapprovingly, glancing out of the corner of her eye at his long, hard body.

His cottonade leggings little disguised the iron swaths of muscle in his thighs, and even his thick buckskin shirt could not hide his bulging chest and biceps. She suddenly wanted to press her lips against his sinewy throat, to nuzzle the chest hair curling against his collarbone.

"Your eyes are pools of fire, Smokeflower."

Embarrassed, she turned her head and leaned forward to look around the side of the buggy.

Dominique perused the classic line of her throat and jaw to her burning cheeks. Spanish combs had captured her shining mass of hair on top of her head, leaving the nape of her neck enticingly exposed. Her white muslin high-waisted gown—a fashion he usually detested—left a great deal of creamy skin bare to his glance. Eyeing her décolletage, he decided he could learn to like the fashion.

He shifted on the seat, aware of the manly stiffening in his breeches, and looked away from her breasts, only to discover that her firm, warm thigh was close against his. Through the thin fabric of her gown he felt her rubbing against him.

We are bound to start a fire this way, he thought. He couldn't trust himself to speak.

"I really think you should go now," Loire said. They were nearing a plantation house set back from the levee. "Someone might see."

"And if they do?" His voice was a ragged whisper.

"Surely even a man with your crude upbringing can guess what would happen to my reputation!"

"Ah, I see." He brought the horse to a halt and for a long moment looked into her eyes. "I promised never to hurt you again, and I will keep that promise. I will cut through the swamp to town. Adieu until Saturday, Mademoiselle Chartier."

"Saturday?"

"The concert."

He placed the reins in her hands, swung onto his

stallion's back, and lifted his hat off his head. Then, with a rakish grin, he wheeled the horse and galloped across the field into an orange grove bordering the swamp.

"You will hear Bach alone that night, Monsieur Youx!" Loire called after him, wrapping the reins around her trembling hands. Several minutes passed before she could summon the energy to drive back to town.

5

Despite her intentions, Loire was in the courtyard Saturday night. Her hair was swept high with a jeweled comb adorned with white egret feathers, silver earrings dangled to her shoulders, and a bracelet of black Rhodesian diamonds sparkled on her left wrist. Draped Grecian style, her low-cut gown of black silk trimmed with ropes of pearls clung to her figure.

"He won't come," she told herself for the hundredth time. And even if he did, she wouldn't go with him. There was something sinister about him, something mysterious that she couldn't fathom. He seemed to know too much about her, almost as if he'd known her in another life . . . almost as if he'd made a study of her.

She folded her arms across her chest and shivered. Why was she pacing this moonlit garden, waiting for a stranger who seemed privy to her secrets, yet revealed little of himself? For example, where had he been all week?

St. John had said Dominique Youx owned a ship. She'd asked about it at the wharves, but no one had known a thing. Or just hadn't told. Surely he hadn't gone off in a ship with the British patrolling the delta.

She glanced at the *garçonnière.* Ida had promised to chaperone her for the carriage ride tonight. If Dominique Youx showed up. If Loire decided to go. Which she wouldn't.

She gazed into the fountain. He was a man used to making instantaneous decisions. Her dress had been on fire, so he had thrown her into the pool. She doubted that even one of Ida's voodoo soothsayers could have foretold such an outlandish encounter.

It seemed rather silly to get all dressed up and then not go, but she hardly knew him. Moreover, he was domineering and too . . . attractive.

As she bent over the fountain to cool her sudden blush, Dominique Youx's reflection shimmered into life in the silvery water. The moon formed a halo around his head.

She spun around in alarm. "Monsieur Youx, what do you mean by frightening me so? Does our every meeting have to begin with my heart springing into my mouth?"

He doffed his top hat of black silk and bowed. Looking tall and elegant in black evening wear, he could have walked into any court in Europe. "My apologies, mademoiselle. St. John told me where to find you, but though I called your name several times, you did not seem to hear. I almost touched your elbow."

"I would have vaulted straight into the fountain!" She couldn't hold back a giggle.

His eyes crinkling with humor, Dominique Youx said, "It seems I am cursed with a propensity for ruining your gowns. I will buy you a hundred new ones someday."

Loire's smile froze.

"You are ready to go?" He held out his arm.

"I'm not sure about this," she said. "Perhaps another time."

His voice echoed softly from the high brick walls as he said, "Release this fear in your heart, Loire."

Tears sparkled in her eyes. "How can you read me so, Dominique Youx?"

With infinite care he stretched out his finger to wipe a tear from her cheek. Instead of pulling back, she closed her eyes, utterly enthralled by his touch. She longed to immerse herself in his dark mystery.

Slowly he traced the path of a tear down her cheek to her jaw. There he stopped, though his eyes continued downward to the swelling curve of her breasts.

How lovely she was, how like a beautiful smoke-flower furled in her silken sheath. Without forming the thought into words, he knew that soon he would own not only the miniature portrait in his pocket, but the woman herself.

He had to clear his throat to speak. "We must go now if we are to arrive on time."

Her lids flickered open. For a moment she felt very young and vulnerable, a child uncertain of her welcome. With a conscious effort, she pulled herself together enough to take his arm. She was much too shaken to speak.

The moon illuminated the cobbled porte cochere as he led her through it to his ebony carriage. Renato Beluche stood by the horses' heads.

"Good evening, Mademoiselle Chartier," he said with a grin. He swept a bouquet of red roses toward her. "And how is your Kentucky long rifle tonight?"

Loire stiffened, on the verge of marching into the mercantile and shutting Dominique Youx and his driver outside.

"Wait, Miz Loire, I'm coming!"

Ida lumbered out of the shop, waving a fox fur wrap. The stays of her whalebone corset creaked as she wrapped the stole around Loire's bare shoulders, then commandeered the roses from Beluche.

"Child'll catch her death out in the night air if these roses don't give her the phystick first!" she snapped.

"I think I'll stay home," Loire said.

"Fiddlesticks, honey, you goin' to the hoedown. Don't pay her no mind, Mistah Youx."

"I would be foolish to pay her no mind, madame," Dominique said, smiling at Loire disarmingly. He dropped his voice. "But pay Renato Beluche no attention, mademoiselle. He meant no insult. He does not have good sense, that one."

"I am on edge tonight, that's all."

"The music will relax you. Let me assist you into the carriage."

Before she could argue, he had settled her onto the backseat and climbed in beside her. Although the carriage was large, the seat was barely wide enough for them to sit without touching. Heat radiated between them, and he tried to draw Loire closer. But she wove her fingers tightly together and focused on Beluche helping Ida onto the driver's seat next to him. "Ida goes everywhere with me," she said. A white lie, but she needed to justify the woman's presence. She only wished that Ida could come into the Théâtre d'Orleans with her, but blacks were not allowed inside unless they worked there.

Beluche cracked the whip, and the carriage moved off along the cobblestones. Light streamed from lamp-posts, bathing the houses warm yellow and attracting countless moths. Loire brushed one off her cheek as the carriage lurched around the corner onto a crowded street. She could sense Dominique watching her. Again she wondered where he'd been all week.

"Your trip went well, I trust?" she asked.

"Well enough, *merci*. And how is business at the mercantile?"

"It could be better. The blockade . . . la, you know how it is. Times are difficult."

He was curiously immobile, watching her. Loire fixed her gaze straight ahead, trying to force away the shivers curling up and down her spine. The heat coming from Dominique's thigh, so close to hers, intensified.

"How—how long have you been in New Orleans, Monsieur Youx?"

"Not long."

"And if I were brash enough to ask your age," she said, looking at him, "I suppose you would say, 'Not young.'"

"It depends on your vantage point. Do I seem old to you?"

She was surprised to hear herself answer boldly, "I'm reading a book called *Songs of Experience*. The poems are full of irony. I think their writer suffered pain that made him older than his years."

Wariness overtook Dominique's expression. "That happens sometimes."

"Did it happen to you?"

All week long he had considered what to say to her

tonight. He had not expected her to demand explanations of his background. Damn it, he had none to give. "A man plays the cards that life hands him as well as he can, Loire."

They turned onto a congested street. From its setting among live oak and magnolia trees, the Théâtre d'Orleans ascended into the velvety-black sky. A wide staircase framed the foundation, and elaborate columns and arched casements swept up the white, stuccoed walls to a tall spire. Carved lions and gargoyles lined the hip roof.

Beluche pulled in behind a queue of carriages, edging nearer the theater as those ahead discharged their passengers. At last they reached the entrance. A slave in white livery opened the carriage door.

Dominique stepped out and reached for Loire's hand, his ring flashing. With his other hand, he caught her slim waist and set her on the cobblestones. For a moment he held her in a motionless dance, a sudden, hot current melding them together. Then he cleared his throat and dropped his hand from her waist.

"We shall go in, mademoiselle."

"Of course," she said, brushing her lips with her fingertips to stop their trembling. She threw Ida a backward glance as Dominique led her up the steps to the loggia. Ahead, she saw elegantly dressed people standing in groups, sipping wine while they waited to be seated.

As Dominique brought her through the archway, every eye turned their way. Dominique acknowledged the radiant smiles of the women with a brief nod, noting that the smiles changed to grimaces of jealousy after they'd digested Loire for a moment.

"They look like a flock of sparrows next to you," he whispered.

Loire scarcely heard him. She recognized many of the leading citizens of New Orleans, all of whom had refused to receive her once news of her mother's disgraceful conduct had gotten around.

Her face blanched when she noticed Alain Defromage across the hall.

"I shouldn't be here," she said, resisting the efforts of an attendant to take her wrap.

Dominique misunderstood. "He will not lose it, *chérie*." He slipped the stole off her shoulders and handed it to the slave. "He will hang it in the cloakroom."

Defromage disengaged from his party and came across the room toward her. He looked dapper in several waistcoats beneath his spencer and evening coat, his dark mustache neat above lips that smiled. But there was no kindness in his eyes as he looked from Loire to Dominique.

"Loire, how pleasant it is to see you here."

"Thank you, Alain." She could feel Dominique's gaze and tried to control her nervous blush but knew she'd failed. "Alain, this is Monsieur Youx. Monsieur, Captain Alain Defromage. He—he is my father's chief captain."

Both men bowed, eyes locked together in mutual appraisal. Loire took a glass of wine from a waiter and sipped it without tasting anything.

"Monsieur, have we met?" Defromage asked at length.

"Perhaps. The world is not as big as it once was," Dominique replied. He took a glass of wine but did not drink from it.

Defromage looked at Loire. She felt her cheeks brightening and swallowed more wine. "Well, then, perhaps we will meet again sometime. My party waits." He clicked his heels together and bowed before returning to his companions. From there he stood watching them.

"Perhaps I have spoiled something for you, Mademoiselle Chartier?" Dominique asked, looking back at the merchant captain.

The arrival of an usher saved her from answering. Tugging at his enormous lace cravat and passing his hand over shiny, slicked-back hair, the usher licked his lips and bowed.

"Monsieur Youx! How good of you to come tonight!"

Dominique bowed in cold response. "Monsieur Seville."

Seville paled under his stare. He bowed to Loire and proffered a program with trembling hands. "Monsieur's box is ready, mademoiselle. If you would please to follow me."

After accepting Dominique's arm, Loire allowed him to walk her through the crowd to a broad staircase at one end of the loggia. Halfway up the steps she heard someone say, "Surely he can afford better than a trollop's whelp." Women laughed.

Loire stiffened, and she looked around into mocking eyes. Coming here had been a dreadful mistake; no one would ever let her forget Madame Chartier's legacy. As the laughter rang in her ears, she dropped Dominique's arm and fled up the steps past the usher. She had to find somewhere to hide until she could slip out of the theater.

Dominique caught her at the top of the staircase. Dismissing Seville with a jerk of his thumb, he pulled her into an alcove.

"Let go of me!" Her bracelet of black diamonds

reflected the anger flashing in her eyes as she struggled to break his hold on her wrist.

"Not until you tell me what this is all about, mademoiselle."

"None of your business!"

Dominique's face darkened with anger. Maintaining his grip on her wrist, he hustled her down the loggia and through a mauve curtain to his private box.

Crystal chandeliers and shaded lamps cast a soft glow over the people on the ornate chairs below while leaving the boxes in shadow. The cacophony of tuning violins and flutes resonated through the luxuriant, forest-green curtains enclosing the stage.

But Loire noticed none of this as her escort pressed her onto a plush, high-backed chair and squatted on his heels beside her.

"Now then, mademoiselle," he said in a low voice, "what was that scene about?"

Loire fixed her gaze on the chandelier near their box. Nervously she began to toy with her right earring. "I sometimes become temperamental, I suppose."

Dominique looked at her until she met his eyes. "You are crying."

"It's the light."

"Loire," he said, his voice dropping in pitch, "there are some burdens that are meant to be shared."

"There are some burdens that it does not help to share." How could she tell this man about the terrible lies? How could she expect him to believe she was different from her mother, when no one else did? And yet he had witnessed her shame in the marketplace last week and had come to her rescue then.

"Dominique," she whispered, unaware that she'd

used his first name, "have you ever been accused of doing something you didn't do?"

"Not very often, Loire," he said, lifting a rakish brow. "I am guilty of most crimes laid to my charge."

Loire did not quite smile, but a good deal of woe left her. "I find this hard to believe, unless you consider giving away roses and tobacco by the wagonload heinous deeds."

Taking her hand, he said, "The truth might surprise you, Loire Chartier. But we were talking of your troubles, not mine."

Loire drew a sigh and looked down at his strong brown hand holding hers. How comforting it would be to crawl into it and close his fingers over her head!

"Perhaps a time will come to share confidences, monsieur, but it would not be proper tonight."

Before he could reply, Seville poked through the curtain with a long brass candle snuffer in his hands. Leaning over the balcony, he extinguished the candles. With a great deal of clinking and clanking, attendants extinguished the other lamps and chandeliers around the great hall. Seville ducked out as the room grew dim.

Dominique slid onto the chair beside Loire. His nearness in the dark box made heat rise to her cheeks. She hoped he would not sense her tension.

From the stage came the throb of stringed instruments. As the curtains opened, a widening band of light swept over the first four rows of seats on the floor. A wind-soft murmur rippled through the audience at its first sight of the orchestra and its conductor elevated on a glittering pedestal.

"The first piece is the Brandenburg Concerto Number Two," Dominique whispered.

Like a sculptor molding a piece of clay larger than himself, the conductor began to blend and shape the magnificent voices of the woodwinds and violins.

Warm currents washed up Loire's spine, chasing away her melancholy. She had almost forgotten how it felt to hear the soul-stirring passion of violins against the earthy counterpoint of cellos and woodwinds. As the orchestra began the Allegro Assai she looked at Dominique Youx out of hungry golden eyes.

"Thank you," she whispered huskily.

Fire kindled in his eyes, locking her in a spell. She gripped the rail for fear she would lose control of her emotions.

"It is my pleasure, Smokeflower." The intensity of his gaze matched the growing swell of the music.

Under his ardent stare, Loire felt her heart climb into the heavens along with the clear high trumpet sound. The rich counterpoint churned like fire in her breast; the low, insistent march of the bass carried her into the smoldering eyes of Dominique Youx.

She picked up the program and fanned her face, hoping he could not read her thoughts, could not sense the roiling excitement in her belly.

"Bach was a master," he said as the piece came to an end. His hand resting on the arm of the chair between them almost touched her side. "A genius."

Loire was too shaken to speak above a whisper. "I've never heard anything so beautiful in my life." She pretended to study the program.

"Have you heard Madame Henri sing?"

"What? Who?" The egret feathers in Loire's hair bobbed as she lifted her head.

Smiling, he turned the program right-side up and

pointed to a name. "Madame Henri, one of the finest sopranos in Paris."

Trembling at the pressure of his finger through the paper on her knee, Loire could scarcely read the soloist's name. Madame would sing Gluck's "Dance of the Blessed Spirits" from the *Orfeo ed Euridice.* Loire thought she would melt if Dominique did not remove his hand.

"There she is now." He replaced his hand on the arm of his chair. Loire could still feel its hot brand. "The large lady coming on stage."

"She is the *only* lady on stage."

"Quite so," Dominique said.

The silver voice of a flute introduced the aria, and Madame Henri began a song of unworldly beauty. Dominique whispered, "The Spirits dance in the Elysian Fields—heaven, you would call it."

Her consciousness wrapped up in him, Loire did not notice her hands folding the program into an accordion. Dominique smiled. Did she know how desirable her very nervousness made her? Closeted as they were in the dark box, it would be a simple matter to take her in his arms and kiss away her trepidation. His hand left the arm of his chair to slide along the back of her seat.

"Mademoiselle Chartier, Monsieur Youx, may I interest you in a glass of wine?" asked Seville as he came into the box and gave a bow.

Dominique sprang out of his chair with the grace of a leopard. One of the glasses tipped onto the floor as he seized the loaded tray and set it on a small table near the rail. "That will be all."

"I will just f-fetch you another glass."

"I said, that will be all!"

Seville shot out of the box like a startled rabbit, yanking the draperies closed behind him. Over Madame Henri's soaring notes, Loire heard his feet pounding down the loggia.

"Why do you treat him so roughly?" she demanded, her own nervousness drowned in a flood of anger.

Dominique adjusted his cuffs before settling back onto his seat. "Seville is not the harmless idiot he seems."

"Oh? He certainly fooled me."

"He would like to fool a lot of people."

"Meaning what?"

Leaning forward, he poured wine into the remaining glass and handed it to her. "Meaning that he sells secrets to the British. He is a spy."

She nearly dropped the glass. "What makes you so sure?"

"I've seen him at it," he said, his voice as low and threatening as the bayou wind.

"You have not been here long, you said. How can you know so much?"

"I know that he spies on Governor Claiborne and other officials who come here, and sends word through Spanish fishermen to the British admiral, Cochrane. Because of him, the Louisiana Legislature has no secrets. Neither has the militia."

"Then why have you not had him arrested?" She set the glass on the table without drinking. "Doesn't your silence make you as guilty as he, monsieur?"

"As I stated before, I am guilty of most deeds laid to my charge."

His remark jarred her. "So you are a traitor."

"A traitor to whom, mademoiselle? To France? To the emperor?" He picked up Loire's wineglass and took a sip. "No. Neither am I a traitor to this country I have adopted."

"Then you should protect her."

"When the time is ripe, I will. You have my word as a gentleman upon it."

Loire leaned toward him to stare boldly into his eyes. "I would first have to accept your word that you *are* a gentleman, Monsieur Youx. I have already made up my mind about *that*."

"And decided to the contrary." Dominique chuckled softly.

She held his gaze despite the flush rising to her cheeks. "A gentleman doesn't throw a lady into the fountain. He doesn't follow her around town, and confront her on the high road and clamber into her carriage uninvited. And he doesn't ruin a lady's important possessions like—like *letters* . . . ."

Dominique's brows drew together in a puzzled scowl. He took a second sip of wine. "Letters? What is this I have done?"

"You ruined my mother's letter," she said, "when you threw me into the fountain. It was all I had to remember her by. I had hidden it in my—my—dress." She twisted her folded program into a knot.

"*Mon Dieu.* I had no idea, Loire. I would not have done such a thing if your dress had not caught fire."

"My dress would not have caught fire without your interference!" Angry tears brightened her eyes.

Dominique, looking into those flaming orbs from a distance of six inches, with Madame Henri's aria ringing in his ears, suddenly lost his sense of reality. One moment he was in the theater box, the next he was dancing with Loire in the Elysian Fields amid swirling spirits.

She was impossibly beautiful, a fiery comet fallen to earth from heaven. How gracefully she danced—a miniature portrait come to life . . . .

"Dominique, Dominique! Are you all right?"

He shook his head, conscious of a strange buzzing in his ears. He swayed dizzily on his seat, dropping his wineglass on the carpet. Massaging his forehead, he managed to focus on Loire's worried face.

"Dominique, shall I summon the manager?"

"No." He pushed to his feet and staggered dangerously close to the rail.

Loire caught him by the arm and pulled him back. "You must sit down until the dizziness has passed."

"I need some air." He pulled her through the draperies into the loggia. The chandeliers drove a million burning spikes into his brain. He groaned and clutched his temples.

"Dominique, sit down! You are ill!"

"Just get me some coffee, Loire. Please." He sank onto a bench by the wall.

She looked for Seville but didn't see him. "I'll be right back." She dashed to the staircase.

Seville appeared at Dominique Youx's elbow, a decanter of wine in his hand. "Monsieur is ill? Perhaps some wine?"

Dominique glared up at him through gimlet eyes. Taking an involuntary step backward, Seville tried to smile, but his greenish pallor spoiled the effect.

"You don't look well, my friend," Dominique whispered, convinced that his head would explode if he spoke in full voice. "Perhaps you should drink that wine."

Seville shot a frightened look at the decanter. "But this is for you."

"Two sips were enough, I think. It is your turn."

"I make it a policy never to drink when there are guests waiting to be served."

"Mademoiselle Chartier will take care of my needs when she returns."

"But there are other guests." He turned to go.

"What did you use, Seville? Arsenic? Oil of oleander? Or something your British masters provided you?"

Seville wheeled about, looking like a fox at bay. "Wh-what, monsieur?"

"What toxin did you put in the wine?" Dominique said. He gritted his teeth against the agony.

Seville stared theatrically at the decanter. Abruptly he let it slip through his fingers, jumping back as it shattered on the floor. "I—I would never do such a thing, I assure you, Monsieur Youx! If the wine was tainted, someone else must have done it!"

Dominique slowly gained his feet. His vision was fuzzy around the edges, and he felt as though his head were being stepped on by a mule. Thank God Loire had taken none of the wine! "You and I will visit the sheriff tonight."

"No! It was an accident, a silly thing!"

"You erred in two ways, monsieur," Dominique said. "The first was in failing to use a stronger concentration of poison. I am sick, but I will not die, I think."

"One thanks heaven for your iron constitution, but I assure you—"

"Your second, and gravest, mistake was in attempting to kill Mademoiselle Chartier along with me."

"She was never the target!"

Dominique Youx wrenched his mouth into a buccaneer smile.

Looking up into the dragonlike eyes, Seville began

to weep. "Please, it will not happen again, monsieur. Here, I have money."

He dug into his pocket and produced a handful of silver and gold coins. "Take it, monsieur! There will be more, I promise!"

"Keep it, my friend. You may need it for burial expenses."

"Burial expenses? Whose?"

"Mine or yours, depending on how clever—or stupid—you are the next time you attempt to assassinate me. I expect great things of such a cunning traitor."

"My God, monsieur, why do you do this to me?" Tugging his hair, Seville went to stand in the arched window overlooking the driveway. "Why do you not just turn me in to the governor if you know so much? You have made my life a living hell since the day I met you. Your men stop me from leaving the city. Why do you not just turn me in?"

"In the first place, you can do no harm if you cannot get to your friends in the swamp to deliver your information. In the second place, you are an American citizen. I am not. Whom do you think Claiborne would believe?"

Seville glared at him. "Claibo would believe me, of course. In which case, monsieur, I suggest you crawl back into whatever sewer you belong and stay away from me. Perhaps I will have *you* arrested!"

Dominique Youx laughed, a low rumble of sound. Quaking before the menace, Seville turned and ran down the loggia to the staircase.

Balancing a cup of coffee on a thin china saucer, Loire moved aside as he stumbled past her. She did not answer when she called after him. Fearing the worst, she took the remaining steps two at a time.

She arrived to find Dominique slumped over the

bench, his face pale and cold, his breath rasping through bluish lips.

"Dominique!" She shook his shoulder. "Open your eyes! Come on, wake up and drink this!"

When he did not respond, she whirled and dashed into one of the boxes, Catching a man by the shoulder, she said, "Please, monsieur, there is a very sick man outside. I need your help."

"William, who is this?" a woman demanded in a Spanish accent.

Loire recognized Sophronia Bosque Claiborne. Realizing that she'd just grabbed the governor, she stepped back. In English she said, "Sir, forgive me for interrupting you and your wife, but, confound it, I need help!"

The governor left his chair, and Loire ran ahead of him to the bench where Dominique lay. The loggia began to fill with spectators.

With the help of two men, Claiborne got Dominique onto the floor and felt his pulse. "He has had too much to drink," he said in disgust. "Take him home to bed, miss."

"He had only two sips of wine," Loire said, "hardly enough to make him drunk! He must have been poisoned!"

Claiborne tugged his side-whiskers. "You've an overactive imagination, miss."

"And you've an underactive intellect, Governor!" Paying no attention to the gasp of the crowd, she hurried to the window and looked down at the line of carriages in the driveway. She couldn't tell which was Dominique's, so she waved her arms and screamed, "Ida! *Ida!* Help!"

"Hang on, honey, I'm coming!"

Loire followed the voice to a carriage near the middle of the line. She saw Ida and Renato Beluche climbing to the ground. "Hurry, I need you!"

"You tell that damn Mistah Youx that I'll bust his head if he touch you again!"

The governor jerked her away from the window. "God Almighty, woman, what a fuss you're making over a drunken Frenchie!"

"He might be dying!" She dropped to her knees to cradle Dominique's head on her lap. Several women fanned him with their programs while she jerked his cravat free and unbuttoned his shirt.

"Git out my way! I gotta save my baby!"

Her eyes popping with rage, Ida pushed the crowd aside, with Beluche jogging in her wake. "Good! You done decked that mashin' son of a polecat!" she exclaimed. "I knowed I oughtn't let you out with no good-looking gentleman snake in the grass!"

"He hasn't done anything, Ida! I think he's been poisoned! *Poisoned!*"

"Why didn't you say so, Miz Loire? Git out my way, you hussies!"

With Beluche holding him around the knees, Loire his waist, and Ida his shoulders, Dominique was soon trundled to the staircase. Glaring back at the crowd, Ida said, "What you white folks standing around for? Come here before we drops him downstairs!"

Claiborne ordered several men to help her. After a few minutes they managed to load him into the ebony carriage. Beluche whipped up the grays and thundered down the driveway to the street.

Again holding Dominique's head on her lap, Loire mopped sweat from his brow. He stirred a little, groaned, and opened his eyes.

"*Par Dieu,* I'm sick," he muttered as the carriage lurched around the corner to Bourbon Street.

"Sick, but alive, *mon cher,*" Loire said, unaware of the endearment. Tears of relief pricked her eyes. "We're taking you to the doctor."

"No!"

"Yes! Do you think I wish to watch you die?"

"I am in no danger of dying," he whispered, "unless a man can die of love."

Loire's cheeks burned. "You are out of your head, monsieur. Renato! To Doctor Kerr's on Esplanade!"

Dominique stared up at her. Excruciatingly conscious of his head against her belly and thighs, Loire dared not look down at him.

"Doctor Kerr's," Beluche said, dragging the horses to a halt before a tall, hip-roofed house.

"This is hardly necessary," Dominique said, trying to sit up. "Let me go home to bed."

"So you can die there? La!" Loire and her companions helped him to the front door. Ida seized the iron lion's head and knocked vigorously, her breasts bouncing in time to her pumping arm.

The doctor fumbled open the door. He was wearing nightclothes, including a nightcap tipped over his eye. His complaints turned to a startled, "Damn my soul, Miss Chartier! What's happened?"

"Monsieur Youx has been poisoned, perhaps," Loire said, steering him down the hall to the examination room. She pushed him onto a leather couch.

"How long ago?" Kerr whipped off his nightcap and shoved a pair of silver pince-nez onto his nose.

"An hour, perhaps less," Dominique said as he started to get off the couch. "I am better already."

"He fell unconscious, Doctor," Loire said, pushing

him down. He was too weak to stop her. "He was barely breathing. I thought he was dead."

Dominique massaged his temples. He had been wounded in battle on more than one occasion but never had he felt quite this feeble. He detested the sensation.

"Did you empty your stomach?" Kerr asked.

"No."

"You will shortly, then."

"I was afraid you'd say that, my friend."

Dominique wrinkled his nose as the doctor dribbled thick, black liquid out of a bottle onto a spoon.

Loire said, "Ida and I will be most happy to hold him for you, Doctor."

"It will not be necessary," he said. "Monsieur Youx is a big boy. I am certain he will behave."

"By the sacred heart," Dominique cursed softly.

Kerr jerked his thumb at the door. "You three wait in the front room." As he began to close the panel, Loire heard him say, "You might find it amusing to know that this emetic is the same stuff you sold me last month, Dominique."

"I should have sunk that damned Spaniard," Dominique said. Then the door closed with a sharp click and Loire could hear no more.

During the half hour that followed, she prowled the waiting room like a caged lioness, starting at every sound. Beluche curled up on a chair and stared morosely out the window. Ida applied her ear to the door of the examination room.

The door opened. Dominique, pale but standing firmly on his feet, caught Ida as she staggered inside. "*La,* madame," he said with a wry grin, "it seems that you, too, are overcome with dizziness. Perhaps some of Kerr's emetic?"

She pushed him away. "I ain't throwing up *my* dinner!" With the majesty of a sternwheeler, she steamed past the doctor and out the front door, slamming it behind her.

Loire clasped her hands firmly together and tried to look calm as Dominique appeared in the hall. Running his fingers through his tousled hair, he grinned down at her. "It seems I will survive, after all, *ma chère,* despite Doctor Kerr's coal oil."

"Laugh if you wish," the doctor said, "but the next time, that British lover might kill you."

"Perhaps I should offer him a bonus if he kills me before you do with your antidotes."

Kerr sniffed. "You are quite the merry-andrew, Dominique, but one of these days your adventuring will win you a crypt. This city is no place for a man with your, shall we say, objectionable record."

"Objectionable record?" Loire repeated. She had just spent a very tense hour worrying over Dominique, and the doctor's intimation that the man was little more than a swashbuckler brought her to a boil. "You make him sound criminal! Tell him, Renato Beluche, tell him how Monsieur Youx served the emperor—"

"Loire," Dominique said quietly, silencing her, "it is time to leave."

After casting the doctor a disparaging look, Loire marched down the hall and out the front door. Beluche assisted her into the carriage. Ida glowered like a stuffed eagle on the driver's seat.

"It seems that the women in my life are just a bit put out, Kerr," Dominique said. Seized by another wave of dizziness, he leaned against the doorpost and rubbed his eyes. "*Dieu,* what a headache."

"Perhaps you should stay here tonight, Dominique."
Kerr spoke loudly enough for Loire to hear. "You are
obviously not over the effects of the poison."

"I will be all right." Dominique shakily descended
the steps and climbed into the carriage.

"The doctor is right," Loire said. "You don't look
well. Perhaps he should give you more medicine."

A shudder passed through Dominique. "Drive on,
Renato."

"But if there is more poison in you—"

"I prefer Seville's to Kerr's," he said, squeezing her
hand. He forced a reassuring smile. "Thank you for
your concern, Loire."

Feeling too full of emotion to look away, she stared
at him out of huge liquid eyes, wishing she could kiss
the lines of pain from his forehead. Her hand burned
in his grasp, and involuntarily she squeezed his.
"Dominique, it is much more than concern. It . . ."
Unable to go on, she looked away to the dark houses
rolling by.

Much more than concern? Should he ask her how
much more? Might her answer drive him into turning
his nightly dreams into reality?

He took her hand in both of his and closed his eyes,
almost glad of the terrible weakness in his body, the
agony in his brain. Without it, he would surely take
her in his arms and slake his thirst whether she willed
it or not.

Par Dieu, how she intoxicated him, consumed him.
For one kiss he would wrest the very scales from a
dragon's back.

"Come home with me tonight, Dominique Youx."

He was dreaming. It was the poison.

"Please, I want to care for you."

Loire was looking at him, her face porcelain white. Fire raged in his breast, igniting his deep eyes with a passion that sucked her breath from her lungs. He could see weakness coming over her and knew he should release her. He did not.

"Renato, to Mademoiselle Chartier's," he said. "Find somewhere to secret the carriage."

Ida twisted around on the seat, her mouth gaping, but Dominique glared at her until she closed her mouth and turned to stare over the horses' heads. Loire folded her hands on her lap.

What would happen when they entered the privacy of her room and turned back the covers on the canopied bed? She could only tremble at the possibilities . . . and wonder what demon possessed her to take such a gamble.

6

Like a woman in a dream, Loire Chartier slid her long skeleton key into the lock and stepped aside. Dominique gazed down at her for a long moment, his face shadowed in the entryway. Then he turned the key, pushed the door open, and led her across the threshold by the hand.

"I'll light a candle," she said.

Dominique said nothing as he closed the door behind him and locked it. A thin shaft of lamplight shone through one of the narrow front windows, illuminating Loire standing between the shelves.

"Where is the candle, Loire?"

His warm breath fell across her naked shoulders and stirred the hairs on her neck, reminding her that she'd left her fox fur at the theater. Her mind seized on the distraction of the fur, turning it over from all angles. It was best not to think about the situation at hand: to do so would make her all the more culpable.

"But I haven't done anything."

"No, you have not, mademoiselle."

Loire started, unaware that she'd spoken the thought aloud. "I'll find the candle."

Lighting it was difficult. The match trembled in her hands, and her breathing bounced the flame away from the wick. She held her breath. The candle sprang into life.

Dominique Youx stood just outside the glowing circle, his gaze impenetrable. Looking at him, Loire felt that she would melt like the slender red candle in her hand. She placed one palm on the counter to steady herself.

"You are frightened, Loire."

"No, I'm not." She wished he would go, yet she feared he would. The candle shook violently.

Dominique stepped forward, took the candle, and set it on the counter. "You've burned yourself," he said, wiping wax from the back of her hand with his fingers.

Loire hadn't noticed the pain. "There's . . . there's water around here someplace." She couldn't remember where.

Dominique did not relinquish his hold. Staring deeply into her eyes, he lifted her hand to his mouth. "I will kiss the pain away, *ma chére.*"

Loire gasped as his tongue flicked over her hand and inner wrist. She tried to pull away, but with gentle pressure he held her fast, his eyes never leaving hers.

"Dominique, you make me feel very . . . strange."

"There is a better way to define your feelings, Smokeflower." He pulled her firmly against him. Softly at first, then with increasing ardor, he kissed her temples, her forehead, her nose and cheeks.

Moaning softly, Loire sought his lips with hers, but he slid his tongue down over her throat to her collarbone. She arched her neck and closed her eyes, her heart pounding harder with every stroke of his tongue.

"By thunder, you are beautiful!" he said.

He claimed her mouth in a hungry kiss that stole her breath and made her knees weaken. She would collapse if he let her go . . . she would *die* if he let her go.

No, she mustn't let this happen, mustn't let herself be devoured like a candle in the hot kiss of a flame. She tried to let him go but found she could not. His muscles were hard as iron beneath the rich fabric of his coat, inviting her deepening caresses.

She could feel his hands sliding down her back. Without a corset, she could hide nothing from his touch. She trembled when his warm fingers glided down to the garters holding her stockings around her thighs.

"I am mad for you, Loire."

"Perhaps you should not kiss me again."

"Ha! I gladly bid adieu to sanity." Locking his arms around her waist, he again engulfed her in a searing kiss, reached up with one hand, and plucked the jeweled egret feather comb from her hair. The heavy mass fell around her shoulders.

Dominique broke off the kiss. Pain etched his face as he stepped back, hands to his temples.

Frightened, Loire pressed him onto a chair and, for the second time that night, pulled off his coat and unbuttoned his shirt. "I'll find Renato. We must get you back to the doctor!"

"No! This thing will pass." He opened his eyes fractionally. "Renato has hidden the carriage. To rush him here will call me to your neighbors' attention."

"I don't care!"

Dominique caught her wrist as she went toward the door. "I forbid it. I will leave here quietly when I am well enough to do so."

"You might die, Dominique—"

"Because of a traitor's tiny drop of poison?" He forced a chuckle, then winced at the pain it caused behind his eyes. "Not so. I have drunk absinthe many times," he said, referring to the bitter drink made of wormwood, "and if that could not kill me, nothing can."

"Blast it!" she swore, sounding like a Kentuckian. "You are not immortal!"

Dominique sat back in his chair. "No? But this is the first I've heard of it."

Loire's breasts rose and fell with anger. "I can see there is no point arguing with such a cocky Frenchman. Upstairs with you, and into bed."

"I will not be much use to you there in my present condition, mademoiselle." The words hung in the air between them.

The sudden flush rising to Loire's cheeks belied the frostiness in her tone as she said, "I have no intention of using you, monsieur. I intend to make you well. If you refuse Doctor Kerr's treatments, why, you will simply have to abide mine."

He stood up, steadying himself with a counter. "Perhaps I should summon Renato Beluche after all."

"Men! Any one of you would prefer a sword wound to a spoonful of medicine."

"The former is a more manly way to die," he said lightly. Then he broke into a cold sweat as the pain concentrated in a white-hot pinpoint of light behind his left eye.

"Dead is dead," she said, leading him slowly up the

staircase. She showed him a chair in the sitting room. "Wait here while I light a lamp."

Dominique sat down. Moonlight played through the mosquitaire-draped windows, tinting Loire's face a ghostly gray green. She raised the glass globe off a lamp, struck a match, and applied it to the wick. Then she settled the globe onto its base and stepped back, her skin tones changing to creamy pink.

She rummaged in a desk, found a small bottle, and pulled out the cork with her teeth. "Charcoal suspension. Drink it, please. All of it."

Casting her a boyish look of disgust, he drained it quickly. "Acch!"

"It wasn't so bad." She handed him a cup of water and a towel. "Rinse your mouth, and then you must lie down."

She crossed the hall to the bedroom, pushed back the draperies around the bed, and folded down the white linen sheets.

Dominique stopped just inside the doorway to slowly peruse her private sanctuary, his gaze touching the bed before coming to rest on the woman beside it.

"Perhaps you wish to change your mind, Loire."

"Nonsense. You need to rest. I promised to . . . nurse you tonight." She blushed, remembering the wild embraces in the store below. She lit a lamp on the mantelpiece but forgot to turn down the wick. The three-inch tongue of fire licked the glass globe.

Dominique joined her at the fireplace. As he reached up to lower the wick, his eye fell upon a letter on the mantel. The paper was crisp and wavy, the ink blurred. He picked it up.

"Don't touch that!"

He laid it down and looked at her. She was staring at the letter, tears in her eyes.

"The letter I ruined, Loire?"

She nodded, tried to smooth the paper.

"If I could take back that day, *ma chére,* I would."

She sighed, a soft, willowy sound. "I believe you. Now get to bed."

"*Sacrebleu,* Loire, will you not let me touch your heart for even a moment?"

"Have you not touched it already, monsieur?" She stamped her foot and began to cry. "Are you not aware of what you do to me? I have not even looked at a man since my mother brought this family down in shame, and now you come into my life and make love to me, and then speak to me as though I am a cold, heartless whore!"

Before she could run away, he pulled her into his arms. She struggled against him, sobbing, but he held her all the tighter, crooning against her hair and rocking her until her aching shudders died away.

For the first time in his life Dominique Youx experienced a strange mixture of pain and possession, the paternal emotion that cuts and wounds even as it binds and heals. He loved her. Deeply. Without constraint. Without the ability to recant, no matter what she might do. He suddenly realized that he would never, *could* never, stop loving her.

Ignoring his throbbing headache, he lifted her beneath the knees and shoulders and carried her to bed. He swept aside the mosquitaire and laid her on the thick feather mattress, then lowered himself beside her. The mosquitaire drifted back into place, a fluffy cocoon of intimacy. Without speaking, he lay on his side, propped his head upon his hand, and watched her.

She settled her head deeply into her pillow, feeling

too drained to leave his side. Briefly she studied his bronzed chest framed in the open neck of his shirt, then, shuddering, closed her eyes.

This made it worse, for although he did not touch her, she could feel the heat emanating from his body, his breath stirring her damp tendrils of hair about her face. More than that, she sensed his spirit, the tangible aura of power he possessed. Her lashes trembled against her cheeks.

The cathedral bell tolled two. As its tones died on the humid river air, Dominique said, "I am sorry about your mother."

Loire stiffened. She kept her eyes firmly closed as she asked, "What do you know about her?"

"Only what you've said. Sometimes people do things we do not understand."

"Oh, I understand her," Loire said bitterly, opening her eyes. "It does not take a palmist to explain her behavior to me."

"But what would it take to forgive her?"

"*Forgive* her? Why should I forgive her?"

His eyes burned more intensely as he waited for her to answer her own question. "Things happen sometimes, Loire, that cause people to behave in ways that seem erratic."

"Erratic? Do you call becoming the whore of New Orleans *erratic?*"

The hall clock ticked loudly in the silence. Loire stared through the mosquitaire at the dark fireplace. She could see a corner of the ruined letter sticking out over the edge of the mantel. At last she said, "How do you know so much about my mother? Have people been talking?"

"They've answered a few questions, that is all."

"So you've been asking questions about my personal life, have you?"

"*Oui.*"

"You boor!" She tried to rise from the bed but discovered her hair was caught beneath his shoulder. She tugged at it, but he made no move to free her. She finally dropped her head back on the pillow and folded her arms.

"You would carry a grudge, too," she said, "if your mother ran away to Paris to live with some officer, and your father preferred life on a dismal island plantation to living with you. Neither of them care what happens to me."

"How old are you, Loire? Twenty-two, twenty-three?"

"If you know, why ask? Why play childish games with me?"

"I do not play games. You play them with yourself."

Sputtering angrily, Loire resumed the struggle to free her hair.

"Lie still, woman with the mind of a child!" He pushed her back on the pillow.

"How dare you!"

"Don't shout. My head is splitting."

"Maybe I should get out the hatchet and help it along!"

"Loire, there are things I've learned that might prove useful to you."

"If I wanted a sermon I would go to mass."

"You didn't listen to the sermon the other day."

"What! You were in church Sunday? Why didn't I see you?"

"I wasn't there. One of my friends was."

"One of your friends? You've been *spying* on me!"

"Not on you. There are intrigues in New Orleans.

You cannot imagine how close the British are to invading the city. It is left to a few of us to protect her—the damned governor can't seem to do it."

"Having spies in church won't help our cause." Loire glared at the canopy, deeply suspicious. "I don't understand why you care. You belong to Napoleon, don't you?"

Dominique smiled sadly. "He is in exile, and quite powerless . . . . But we were talking about your mother."

"I have no wish to talk about her."

He continued as though she had not spoken. "You should try to understand other people's motives. Your mother had reasons that made sense to her."

"I don't want to talk about her. Let me go!"

Dominique caught her wrists on either side of her head until she stopped struggling. Tears welled up in her eyes as she glared at him, trapped but undaunted.

His handsome features twisted in a look of frustration. "I would not hurt you, Smokeflower."

"Then why don't you stop talking about my mother?"

"Because she has her life, you have yours," he said, releasing her wrists. "You are not joined at the navel anymore."

"Monsieur!"

His words had clearly shocked her. He thought how ironically innocent she was as she lay in bed with him. "Her tragedies had nothing to do with you," he said. "She buried her sons. She did not lose you."

So he knew about her brothers, too. How thorough his spies had been! "You should not remind me of such sorrow, monsieur."

"There is nothing wrong with remembering, Loire,

so long as you do not let your memories of the past destroy the present."

"As you do," she said, challenging him.

A look of pain crossed his face. "It is hard to forget the war . . . and other things."

"So you pretend to be a merry-andrew." Some of the fire had gone out of her tone, but her eyes were hostile as she said, "And you chase about New Orleans, pretending to be a great hero who will save us all from the British, and some of us from the scorn of our own neighbors."

He touched his finger to her cheek and trapped a teardrop. "If I can save you from scorn, I will, Loire," he said.

"What are you, then?" she whispered. She felt herself falling into his fathomless eyes. He was like Bayou LaForge, pulling her down deep before she could strike out for shore. "Who is Dominique Youx?"

In a deep voice that penetrated her to the marrow, he said, "The man who loves you."

"You—you should not toy with me so cruelly."

"I would never toy with you, Smokeflower."

"I've heard enough!"

"All my life I have searched for you," he said, his voice low and insistent.

"That is a timeworn cliché."

"*I* have not worn out the sentiment. I have never said it, never thought it, never felt it before. As I told you in the French Market when I found you crying, there comes a time when a man gives up all he owns to possess the one pearl of great price. That time has come, Loire. *You* have come. I have found you."

"And what will you do with me, now that you have found me, monsieur?"

"I would marry you."

She could not answer him. Once, a few years back, she had been standing on the wharf when the boiler exploded in a steamboat alongside. She'd been knocked off her feet and deafened for weeks. Dominique's proposal made her feel the same way.

"I . . . hadn't thought of that," she said.

"But you should."

"I don't know what to say."

"Then say yes."

"Impossible!"

"Why? I love you. I think you love me."

"I never said that!"

"Your eyes said it. They're saying it now."

Loire looked away.

"You and Dandy Leggins are two of a kind," he said.

"Dandy Leggins? What are you talking about?"

"That little rooster that I recommended you bet on."

"So now I remind you of a rooster, do I? Thank you very much!"

"You are much prettier than he."

"Again, my thanks." A ridiculous image of herself dressed in feathered pantaloons and a red comb came to mind. "I suppose you would keep me in a chicken coop?"

"Certainly not," he said, smiling into her eyes. He softly circled her cheek with his fingertips, making her tremble. "I will build you a castle, fair mademoiselle, of pearl and amethyst, jade and lodestone. I will buy you a golden coach pulled by four silver dragons studded with rubies, and adorn you with Chinese brocades and Ethiopian ostrich plumes."

"You are raving," she said, pushing away his hand.

"I am not raving, my beautiful Smokeflower." His

fingers returned to trace her eyebrows. She was a translucent pearl against the soft mosquitaire-draped bed. "But perhaps I *am* raving, for you, my sublime delusion, are much too beautiful to be real."

"I'm as real as Dandy Leggins," she said. "Would you please get off my hair?"

He raised his shoulder a little to release her.

"Father Dubourg thinks I should enter a convent." She sat up on the side of the bed and propped her elbows on her knees, her chin on her hands. The mosquitaire clung to her face, but she did not seem to notice. The world outside the netting was muffled; there was no reality beyond the borders of the bed. "It's . . . hard to know."

He caressed her back, his fingers describing a feathery fleur-de-lis. "What does your heart say, Loire?"

What indeed? If it was right that she take the orders, would she feel such desire for a man welling up in her? Were these feelings something she had to first experience, then overcome, in order to present herself to the Church?

"Do you like children?" she asked, without looking at him.

There was a brief pause, then, "Very much. I have seven brothers and sisters."

She shifted to look at him. "Living?"

Dominique smiled sadly and reached up to finger a lock of hair tumbling down her back. "No, not all."

"I am sorry."

"And I am sorry for your brothers. Yellow fever?"

"Yes. Papa caught it, too, but he did not die."

"And your mother cared for all of you."

She shut her eyes. "You will not leave it alone, will you?"

"Not so long as it poisons you, Loire. To hate one's parents is a grievous thing."

"I don't hate my parents."

"Then forgive. It is the only way you can ever be free."

She would have argued, but he sounded very tired. Instead she reached back impulsively and stroked his dark hair, gently pushing it back from his forehead. "You are a strange man, Dominique Youx. A puzzle. I don't know what to make of you."

"Marry me, Loire," he said as he dropped off to sleep. "You're all I want."

"Dominique." She shook him gently, but he only sighed and mumbled her name.

She considered sending for the doctor, but his face was relaxed, his breathing deep. Perhaps sleep was all he needed to shake off the lingering effects of the poison. Hesitantly she lowered her head to his wide chest and closed her eyes.

As the bells tolled three, thunder rumbled across the wide Mississippi River. A breeze rushed along the cobbled streets of Vieux Carré and fluttered the flags on the Cabildo. The zephyr sprang through the bedroom window, whipping up the lamp flame until a thousand shadows danced upon the walls.

The faded letter on the mantelpiece stirred, lifted, and swirled into the air. Around and around it whirled before coming to rest among the dust balls beneath the armoire.

7

Rain patter against the slate roof awakened Loire late in the morning. Why was she still wearing her black evening gown? she wondered.

"Oh, no, no!" she cried, remembering the previous night. Dominique would be seen leaving the house!

The bed was empty. On the pillow where his head had lain was a small, folded note. She snatched it up and, parting the mosquitaire for better light, read his strong, flowing script.

Beloved Smokeflower,

I thought it best to leave before daylight. You were beautiful asleep—please forgive the stolen kiss.

I will call for you at eight o'clock tonight. Some business associates are hosting a garden ball. Perhaps we will announce our engagement then?

Undying Love,
Dominique
Postscript: Your charcoal emulsion is a miracle cure. Someone should tell Kerr.

Her heart pounding, Loire reread the note twice before slipping it under her mattress. Behind the Oriental screen she stripped off her clothing and washed.

"Dominique Youx wants to marry me," she whispered to her reflection in the mirror. "He wants to build me a palace and give me dragons for horses. He wants to tell all of New Orleans tonight."

Sinking onto a brocade stool, she closed her eyes and tried to remember every word and gesture that had passed between them: the touch of his hands, the hungry look in his eyes, the firm, hot pressure of his lips. Her veins flooded with fire.

There was bewitchment between them, but it was not enough to make her agree to marriage when she knew so little of him. He'd nimbly thwarted her every attempt to learn who and what he was. She couldn't assemble the few pieces she'd managed to gather into a whole man.

Perhaps she should go to his warehouse on Tremé today. If there was a warehouse. She had her doubts.

She dressed, as her father used to say, with the speed of greased lightning. After girding her high-waisted dress of white linen with a blue sash, she pulled up the skirt and tugged on her stockings, then stepped into her pink slippers.

She raked her hair into a loose chignon and topped it with a wide-brimmed hat, then slipped into a blue redingote with a bright red collar. Finally she pulled on her gloves, took her reticule and parasol, and went downstairs.

St. John, seated on a stool in front of a high, open-fronted desk at the back of the store, looked up from his books and smiled knowingly.

"M'sieu Dominique, he is not such a bad man, *non?*"

Loire flushed scarlet. "I'll thank you to wipe that smile off your face, St. John."

He set his quill pen in the holder by the inkwell and dutifully wiped his smile with his hand. "Mems, she is sassy as a ringtail 'coon. She did not sleep enough last night."

Loire bristled. "You've got it all wrong."

Ida ducked through the front door into the shop, rain streaming off her cape. She plopped a basket of sweet potatoes and corn on the counter and frowned at Loire. "Child, if you ain't in trouble!"

"Me? What did I do?"

Ida waved her arms around. "Bringing that man in here last night! You oughta heard what everybody saying about you in the market this morning! I done pushed two ole heifers that used to be your mama's friends into the gutter!"

Loire's eyes glittered. "What did they say?"

"Worse things than ever, honey. And that ole preacher, Father Dubourg? They say he gonna throw you out your church!"

"He's going to excommunicate me?" Stricken, Loire sank onto a crate. "I'll go to hell, and I didn't even do anything!"

"You come home with Mistah Youx. He done stayed the night in your bed—somebody seen him leaving at daylight. You and him gotta marry quick!"

St. John made a rumbling sound of dissent. He went to stare out at the street, rubbing the back of his neck.

Loire took her hat off and dropped it onto the counter. Her redingote followed. "Monsieur Youx asked for my hand."

"He did?" Ida's face split in a grin. "Then St. John don't have to twist his arm!"

"I didn't give him an answer."

"But . . . ain't you gonna say yes? Think of your pappy."

St. John turned around with a funny look in his eye. "Leave mems be, woman. M'sieu's girl never do nothing she don't want."

"But Mistah Youx done ask her already!"

"He'll change his mind after he hears the gossip," Loire said. "He'll hear that Loire Bretagne Chartier made another conquest, that she only sports with him as she has with so many others."

"M'sieu Dominique, he is ver' big man," St. John said. "He is not fooled by wagging tongues, mems. He knows mems is good."

"The wagging tongues will never still. They'll say we had to marry, and count the months until the first child." She drew a deep, shuddering sigh. "The best thing—for both our sakes—is to stay away from each other."

"So you give up on this man, eh?" St. John said. "Mebbe you are like your mother and run away to Paris."

"I never run. Never!" Loire ran her hands through her hair and pulled down her chignon. "After all that's been said of me before, why should this make any difference? I can't marry him. I don't know him. I don't trust his motives."

Ida unloaded sweet potatoes onto the counter. "Won't surprise me none if them gossips gets a story printed up in the newspaper."

Loire clenched her fists, opened her mouth to speak, then marched outside through the puddles to the fountain. She could still see Dominique standing in the water, helping her up. She could hear his voice last night, helping her to understand her mother, herself.

She could almost hear the gossips in the market, painting such a black picture of her.

It was unfair.

A vivid flash of lightning streaked the courtyard, and thunder cracked deafeningly. Loire's rage burst forth in a shriek. She gritted her teeth and lifted her face to heaven as another fusillade of thunder boomed off the walls and shook the ground beneath her feet.

Then she bolted into the porte cochere and down the street. Rain swept in from the river, soaking her through, as she ran through the Quarter, splashing through the deepest puddles, showering herself with mud. At last she turned down an alley into an overgrown garden, ran up a wobbly flight of stairs, and stumbled into Mazy's apartment.

"Who dat?"

Loire closed the door behind her and sank down before the fire, breathing deep and fast. Mazy hobbled in on her cane.

"I didn't bring anything today, Mazy," she said, resting her cheek on one raised knee. "Sorry."

"You done wet through. You needs coffee, honey,"

Mazy said, reaching for a pot in the fireplace. She poured hot, tar-black liquid into a cracked cup. "Drink up, baby."

"Thank you." Loire sniffed, wiped her nose on her sleeve, and bent her head over the cup. Mazy sat down on a rickety wicker chair nearby. "My boy Tim all right?"

"Yes, ma'am."

Mazy shifted around on her chair and stared into the fire, picking absently at her tattered skirt. "What this all about, then?"

Loire didn't know where to begin, so she began at the beginning and didn't finish until she'd told Mazy everything about her relationship with Dominique. The old woman remained utterly silent during the long recitation. Now her lips began to twitch, her shoulders to shake. Suddenly she slapped her knee.

"The meek gonna inherit the earth, sho, 'cause you white folk gonna let yo' wombs dry up with pride!"

Loire's jaw dropped.

"You ain't the first gal I knowed was too proud for her own good, but you is jest about the foolishest, mm-hmm." She dipped a pinch of snuff from the little jar around her neck, pushed it into her cheek, and began to rock to and fro, humming.

"What on earth are you talking about?"

Mazy seemed almost surprised to find Loire there. She scowled and said, "You got yo'self a handsome man, and a rich one, too, and here you traipse off in a storm whinin' about how mean the world treatin' you. You done it all yo'self. Mazy sick to her stomach at it!"

"You don't understand! I can't see him anymore—Ida says everyone is talking."

"Let 'em talk." She spat into the fire. "Ain't no matter. Them jaybirds ain't got enough to keep 'em busy, that's right."

"I've already had more of it than I can stand. This last bit is too much, and now I might be thrown out of the Church."

"Yo' head preacher ain't gonna do that, so you jest put it out yo' mind. You love dat man?"

"Father Dubourg?"

"You know I ain't talking about no preacher man," Mazy snapped. "Mistah Youx."

Loire clasped her arms tightly around her knees and stared into the red flames. "I haven't known him very long."

"Don't matter."

"I'm not sure how you're supposed to feel when you're in love."

"Yo' gut feel sick all the time?"

"How did you know that?"

"Yo' head hurt when you think about him, and you gets too dizzy to stand up sometime?"

"Well, yes, sometimes."

"You off yo' feed? Yo' food look kinda poorly?"

"Only in the last few days."

"You come over all sweaty and hot when he hold you, and yo' bones go to mush?"

"Yes. Sort of."

"You in love, then."

"You're supposed to feel sick when you're in love?"

"Mm-hmm. If you got a bad case."

Loire mulled that over for a minute or two. "Do you ever get better?"

"Not if you lucky. You stays sick all yo' life if you really in love."

"I thought I had the colic or something."

Mazy cackled and clapped her hands. "You one of the real lucky ones, Miz Loire. You go on with him to that garden party tonight. Have a good time."

"But . . . all the talk. I can't bear to face him."

"Yo' damn pride gonna ruin you quicker'n any ole gossip's tongue!" Mazy's eyes lit up with unholy fire. "Why, if'n you was mine, I'd know what! I'd take this here hickory"—she picked up her cane—"and whup yo' backside till you couldn't do nothin' but crawl to dat man and beg him to marry you quick! I'd roust that devil of pride right out yo' heart, dat's what I'd do all right. Mm-hmm."

"You don't have to whip me, Mazy," she said. "I get your point."

"You gonna go see him, then?"

Loire pushed the toe of her slipper into the ashes. She pictured herself showing up on Dominique's doorstep wet and bedraggled, like a desperate stray kitten. He'd seen her looking like that after he threw her in the fountain. Once was enough. She shook her head. "Uh-uh. I'm a mess."

"Pride! You gonna land yo'self in hell one of these days, chile, and I'll be making faces at you from the bosom of Ab'ham and say, 'Ain't I tell you pride go before the fall?'"

Loire pulled her foot out of the ashes. She didn't intend to accept Dominique's proposal, yet she wanted to see him again and maybe go with him to the party. Maybe.

"You go on now, honey. You tell that man to marry you in the mornin'." Her voice softened to a rusty purr.

"Ain't no shame in being in love, chile, and the Lawd know it."

Loire stood up, gave Mazy an awkward hug, and dropped the shawl around the old woman's shoulders. "Thanks, Mazy. Keep your fingers crossed."

"These ole fingers ain't no good for crossin' no more, but I'll fold my hands together and send up a prayer. Go on now."

"Yes, ma'am." Loire started for the door, then stopped. "Mazy, I'm doing all I can to get Tim away from old man Villeré. You just hold on, all right?"

Mazy ignored her. "When we cross over Jordan we gonna drop dat burden at Jesus' feet," she sang, rocking herself back and forth as Loire left.

Outside, the rain was still falling. Loire was almost to the alley when she stopped, heart in mouth. Two big men in long black carricks and wide-brimmed beaver hats were coming through the battered gate. Something told her to panic, and she turned to run.

"Loire, it's all right."

She stopped in her tracks, suddenly giddy and hot, her bones turning, as Mazy called it, to mush. Her heart galloped madly in her chest.

"By the holy thunder, my sweet, you are a small drowned mouse," Dominique Youx said. He came up the porte cochere ahead of his companion. Loire saw his ebony carriage in the alley, the grays steaming.

"How—how did you find me?"

"St. John came to get me. He figured we'd find you here."

The Jamaican raised the brim of his sodden hat. "Me, I did not think mems would go to a fancy café looking so wet."

She glanced from one man to the other in embarrassment.

Fire ignited in Dominique's loins as he gazed back at her. Her dress was a wet, gossamer web, her nipples visible even to the weakest eye. She was trembling, looking more vulnerable than he'd ever seen her.

He cleared his throat. "You'll catch your death of cold," he said. He whipped off his carrick, wrapped it around her, and settled his hat on her head for good measure.

The hat swallowed her head, and the coat tripped her up as she tried to walk. Tilting her head way back to look at him from under the brim, she said, "I don't think this will work."

"It is easy to mend," Dominique said.

Ignoring her shriek of protest, he swept her off the ground and sloshed to the carriage. After setting her on the driver's seat, he climbed up beside her and took the reins.

"Coming, St. John?"

The Jamaican stuck his hands in his pockets. "No, M'sieu Youx. Mazy, she is needing a visitor, I think."

Loire threw him a pleading look. The confidence Mazy had inspired in her melted like a pail of ice in a blacksmith's forge. "Mazy is taking a nap. Won't you come with us?"

But St. John only chuckled and disappeared up the porte cochere. Loire folded her hands in her lap, looking at Dominique out of the corner of her eye.

He was a breathtaking sight, bareheaded in the rain, his tanned face shining and happy. His sodden white shirt clung to his muscular torso, its sleeves rolled to his elbows. Loire watched the play of muscles as he lifted the whip and chirruped to set the horses in motion. The grays broke into a gallop.

Dominique paid little attention to his driving, letting the horses choose their own way. The carriage wheels seemed to find every pothole and rut in the alley. Loire bounced against him, her hat brim flopping up and down over her eyes.

"You seem to be quite well today," she shouted over the noise, clinging to the seat for dear life.

"*Oui*, thanks to you." His teeth flashed in a smile that lit up his entire face. "Doctor Kerr has lost a patient—not to death, this time, but to another physician."

"What are you going to do about the poisoner?"

Dominique shrugged.

"He might kill you next time."

He snorted.

"Suppose he waits in a window and shoots you as you ride by?"

"He is not that good a shot."

"Maybe one of his friends is."

"Maybe."

"You want to die?"

"When I have all the reason in the world to live? But no, *chérie.*"

"Then why not report him to the governor?"

"There is no proof."

Loire ground her teeth in frustration but said nothing.

"Would you like to see my shop, Loire?"

"People will talk if I go there."

"People will talk no matter what we do," he said, chuckling. "It makes them happy."

"You want them happy at our expense?"

With careless skill he guided the horses onto rue

Burgundy. "Happiness is a commodity I don't mind sharing."

"Their happiness is mean-spirited, Dominique," she said. "The kind that causes people to lose their membership in the Church."

"You think the archbishop will excommunicate you for last night, is that it?"

"So you've heard the stories."

"Of course. And embellished them wherever possible."

"What!"

One side of Dominique's mouth lifted in a smile. "Ssh, Smokeflower, calm yourself. I was teasing."

"I wasn't amused!" Her ridiculous hat slid down over her eyes.

Dominique laughed. "Oh, my pet, will you still be so droll after we've been married thirty years?"

Loire pushed the hat back on her head and studied the bobbing tips of the horses' ears until the carriage jounced through a hole, hurling her against Dominique's hard shoulder.

"I will not live thirty more years if you continue to drive so fast!"

Dominique laughed again. He turned left onto St. Philip and slowed to a sedate pace. "This is more the way to drive my lovely Smokeflower."

"Why do you call me that?"

"To commemorate the first day I laid eyes on you, smoking in the porte cochere."

"Oh." She had secretly hoped for a more romantic reason.

"But there is another reason. Have you ever seen a field of tobacco in full bloom?"

"Yes, on Papa's plantation. It was rather pretty."

"'Rather pretty'? My princess, you have been among

the barbaric Kaintocks too long! Cast your mind back to the flowers covering the field like a flock of butterflies, their wings painted soft pink, yellow, and white, each wearing a golden crown."

Loire remembered. There was no more beautiful sight in the world than the fragile blooms fluttering above the tall, furry green leaves. The sky was always cobalt blue and the ground a rich burnt sienna when the tobacco bloomed.

"Do you see," Dominique said, reading her faraway look, "why I can think of no other endearment that approaches your beauty? No rose is so lovely, no lady so fair as you, my beautiful Smokeflower."

He gathered the reins into one hand and reached down to take her small, cold hand in his other one. Smiling into her eyes, he squeezed gently. His look pierced through to her heart.

"You don't mind what people are saying, then?" she asked.

"Why should I mind the truth? They are saying I slept in your house last night, that you nursed me tenderly."

"I don't believe they are saying I *nursed* you, Dominique."

"Perhaps not, but you and I know the truth. That is enough for me."

"Mazy said you'd feel that way. I didn't believe her."

She broke off as Dominique turned onto Tremé, a street in a filthy, decaying section of town. She finished lamely, "Papa says I am too cynical for my own good."

"One must always be a little cynical to stay alive," Dominique said, watching a group of men in a doorway. He tossed a handful of coins to some urchins playing in the gutter. "Mindless trust is likely to land one in there."

Loire followed his pointing finger to the high stone wall on the opposite side of the street. Beyond it lay St. Louis Cemetery Number One. White burial crypts floated above the rainswept grounds; hosts of carved angels and saints hovered. Loire shuddered.

"I don't think that's quite what Papa had in mind when he said I was cynical. He was just worried I would never find a proper mate."

"And have you found one?" He took her hand again.

The hat slid over her eyes. She extricated her hand from his and pushed the hat back up on her head.

Dominique halted the horses in front of a tall, ramshackle building that looked as though it could use a crutch. There was no sign over the door, and its windows were boarded up. Only the heavy lock and chains holding the porte cochere's rusty gate on its posts looked new.

Sandwiched between two other disreputable-looking buildings, the three-story structure had long since lost most of its white stucco, revealing its inner layer of bricks and cypress posts. An ancient magnolia grew out of the banquette near the double doors, uprooting bricks, insinuating its branches into the very walls.

"This is it," Dominique said proudly, climbing out of the carriage. He reached up for her hand.

She sat unmoving. There had to be some mistake. This was an abandoned building, probably swarming with rats, its flat roof ready to fall in.

Two men in dirty blue jackets embellished with bric-a-brac disengaged themselves from the doorway and slouched forward, nodding at Dominique from beneath their gaudy cocked hats. They stopped ten paces away, raked off their headgear, and bowed. Loire saw that each sported a dragoon pistol, a cutlass, and several knives in his belt.

Dominique Youx broke into a slow smile as he held out his hand. He looked like a prince ready to escort the princess into his castle. Loire placed her hand in his. Within a second she was beside him, water soaking into her shoes.

Dominique adjusted her huge hat until he could see her eyes. "Ready to go in?"

"Perhaps it is not such a good idea. We can come back another day."

"Not to worry, Smokeflower," he said, purposely misunderstanding her. "No gossipy scion of society would be seen dead in this part of town." He glanced across the street at the cemetery and laughed. "Gossips would rather be buried in the nicer one on rue St. Peter."

Loire smiled. The loafers grinned.

"If you're worried about my two friends," Dominique said, "you needn't be." He lifted an imperious brow and the men faded away to take up positions by the cemetery wall. "Better?"

"*Oui.* I did not like their looks."

"Neither do thieves," he said.

He led her across the broken brick sidewalk to the door, pushed a key into a heavy brass lock, and turned the handle, stepping aside with a slight bow. That he was soaked to the skin in no way detracted from his savoir-faire: he was handsome, he was in love, and he cared not a wooden picayune for what anyone thought about him.

Loire, her borrowed carrick trailing behind her and the hat slipping down over her eyes, stepped past him over the threshold into fairyland.

8

Loire stepped into a vast open cavern. The lamps on the worn, gray brick walls illuminated a collection of stained-glass windows suspended from the rafters on tracks and pulleys. One exquisite rose window surrounded by a cypress frame glittered in the midst of saints done in Italian glass. With a feeling of reverence, Loire removed her hat and hung it on a peg.

The hall branched into galleries on either side. A group of men were sorting Oriental rugs in the first gallery, so Loire moved on to the next, where paintings hung. She stopped to look at a portrait of a Viking lifting a white gyrfalcon on his gauntlet, a girl with long red braids beside him.

"Aragon the Dane," Dominique said. "A great warlord."

"A real person?"

"I don't know. The painting is fifteenth century,

but legend says he lived long before that. It's probably another Arthurian tale."

He was so close that she felt, as well as heard, his voice vibrate within her. Last night's passionate embrace suddenly reclaimed her senses, making her feel feverish and weak.

She forced herself to step away. Almost desperately she said, "Tell me about this one."

He looked at the floral watercolor. "Nicolas Robert, a master botanist." His eyes glittered as he shifted his gaze to her. "Were he alive, I would commission him to paint a tobacco flower."

Loire looked down, embarrassed. She trembled as he came closer, knowing instinctively that he wanted to take her in his arms. She could not make herself back away.

But instead of embracing her, he moved past her to a lithograph. A muscle throbbed in his jaw, and his voice was strained as he said, "Pierre-Joseph Redouté. He's contemporary. This one is not," he said, pointing at the one beside it. "*The Annunciation* is over three hundred years old. Roger Van Der Weyden."

"Where did you get such a valuable painting?"

Again he threw her a smoldering glance. "I appreciate beautiful things, Smokeflower."

Within the folds of the long carrick she trembled. She could feel the tension in his body, the vibrant aura of expectancy manifesting his desire.

Drawing a deep breath, she moved along the gallery to a multitude of clocks. Miniature castles and gingerbread cottages housed cuckoo birds; larger clocks girded the foot of the wall.

"From Austria and Switzerland," Dominique said. He found it hard to speak, to pretend interest in time.

When he leaned against the wall by a grandfather

clock, he seemed as tall and straight as the clock case,
and as rigid. Loire could almost feel his pulse beating
slowly with the pendulum.

Aware of him in every fiber of her being, she
moved into a low-ceilinged room crowded with George
Hepplewhite furniture. Serpentine-shaped tables
stood amid gracefully turned chairs, boudoir tables,
bowfront chests and armoires. Brass hardware gleamed
in the lamplight. There was an air of sensuality here
reminiscent of her bedroom.

As Dominique followed her in, the top of his head
brushed the chandelier, and he stopped to caress the
curved arm of a chair. Loire imagined his touch.

"Have you been robbing houses?" she asked. Anything to distract herself.

Holding her in his mesmerizing stare, he reached
out to touch her shoulder. His fingers burned through
the carrick as he followed the curve of her shoulder to
her bare neck.

His touch against her naked skin was like fire.
Currents charged down her spine, setting off flashes
of heat in every nerve. She twisted away, breaking the
connection, and fled into the next room.

Dominique was by her side instantly, although
this time he did not touch her. She forced herself to
breathe deeply, to calm the sweeping waves of panic
and excitement.

She relaxed a bit when he went over to a shelf
stacked with fancy wooden boxes. "Here, you might
like to see this," he said gruffly, flipping open a walnut
box lined with red velvet. He showed her silverware in
a grapevine motif.

"Sterling," he said. He opened another box. "And
this one. Look at this."

"Gold? Real gold?"

"*Oui*. A thirty-two-piece place setting." He grinned dryly. "For someone planning a large dinner party."

"It must be priceless!"

"Very nearly so." He shut the lid and shoved the box carelessly back on the shelf. "China and crystal in the next room. Come."

He led her into a room crammed with barrels, prised the lid off one, and rummaged through the straw. The saucer he found was scalloped around the edges and translucent, and the matching cup was so fragile that it seemed the handle would snap off in his fingers. He replaced them gently in the barrel.

"There are onyx plates in that barrel," he said, "ironstone in that one. Here, look at this." He showed her a wineglass with an impossibly long stem and a lip embossed with gold. "And here, an imperial porcelain." He lifted a cobalt-and-white underglaze vase from a bed of straw.

Loire caught her breath. "Ancient Chinese? Why, you've a king's ransom here!" She had never sold goods approaching even the meanest of what he had. Where had he gotten them? How could he afford them?

Back in the main room, she passed mountains of hogsheads marked TOBACCO. Teepees of rifles and muskets stood alongside boxes of powder. There were handsome painted carriages and goat carts, wheelbarrows and wagons. Finely tooled leather harnesses hung from carved ivory tusks on the wall. Porcelain dolls nodded in glass cases.

Loire paused by a tall cedar framework. A six-foot silver dragon dangled from chains attached to the wooden crosspiece. Breathing a tongue of enamel fire, the winged beast wore a high-backed leather-and-silver saddle.

She shot Dominique a suspicious look. "Only an emperor's son would ride a hobby horse like this."

"Or a Spanish tyrant's," he muttered. He disregarded her surprised expression. "My office is upstairs. Would you like to see it?"

She nodded. Holding her by the arm, he led her to a winding wrought-iron staircase and sent her up ahead of him. Loire felt slightly giddy as the floor dropped away from the rapidly descending rafters. The stained-glass windows swung gently from their tracks, emitting jeweled beams of light.

There were other treasures in the cozy, pecan-paneled anteroom at the top of the building: medieval paintings, Hepplewhite benches, silver lamps under tulip-shaped globes.

Dominique steered her into a long, narrow room. At a row of desks awash with paperwork, several clerks fogged the air with pipe-tobacco smoke.

"Ho, Dominique, you have brought the rose into this den of stinkers?" Renato Beluche climbed off a high stool and made a bow. His cigar stank less than his unwashed jacket.

"Uncle," Dominique said, "you're needed downstairs."

"Meaning you don't want me upstairs," Renato said, smiling good-naturedly. He waved his cigar and strode out the door, his behind protruding beneath his jacket tails.

Loire folded her arms across her breasts. "You called him uncle."

"He is a half uncle only. One cannot help one's genealogy."

"I suppose not. Still, I wonder why you led me to believe he was your driver last night, and the other day with the roses."

"He doesn't let many people know we are related."

"And why is that?"

"Security. He fears for my safety because of his business."

"Does this have something to do with the treasures downstairs?"

Dominique smiled wryly. "You are quick, Smokeflower. Yes, in part, although most is mine. With his little ship, the *Spy*, he has scourged British shipping for two years. Legally," he added.

"Legally?"

"The government employs him as a privateer." He led her away from the clerks. "But Uncle has not always been the honest seaman he is now."

She looked at him warily. "And you, Monsieur Dominique? Are you involved with him?"

His eyes went dark, warning her to tread carefully. "I keep his books for him. He has no head for figures."

She looked back at him for half a minute. Save for that grim undercurrent of warning, his expression gave no hint of what lay beneath.

She turned and walked to a large iron safe, spun the brass combination lock. "Someone poisoned you last night, Dominique, someone who knows about whatever it is you're doing."

"You are making an unfounded guess, Loire. Be very careful."

She spun the dial again. "Maybe the answer lies in this safe." She swung around to look at him challengingly. "And then, maybe Dominique Youx is a puff of smoke, with no substance, and the poisoning was accidental."

Red dragons reared in his eyes, but softly he said, "Maybe."

She stepped toward him, angry that he would not respond more satisfactorily. "You sprang out of nowhere. My father and I haven't amassed a hundredth part of the fortune you claim to own, though we've labored for years. Maybe this warehouse belongs to Renato Beluche, and you've got nothing."

He folded his arms and looked at her unsmilingly, his jaw square and hard. The crow's-feet at the corners of his eyes deepened to emphasize a far-seeing gaze that probed the reaches of her soul. She had never seen him look so stern. Anger smoldered in her breast, fed by a new suspicion.

"You are not the first to think he could take Chartier's Mercantile by marrying me."

He swore, then, a violent burst of sound that scattered the clerks at the desks like a flock of pigeons. They followed Renato Beluche's route downstairs.

Loire stood unmoved before him, tears of wrath in her eyes. "I should have known from the first. How foolish to think you cared, when all you wanted was to compromise my virtue and force this marriage!"

"Stop, damn it, stop!" He moved in and caught her savagely by the arms, jerking her against his chest, pulling her head back to command her gaze. The muscle in his cheek pulsated dangerously, underscoring the raging tempest in his eyes.

"You little hellcat, can you feel my heart? Do you think I pretend this emotion tearing me apart? By the sacred robe, my soul will go down to hell if you speak so again, Loire Chartier. Say it not again! I would rather lay myself across the muzzle of a cannon than hear it!"

His handsome face contorted with anguish, he held her tightly against him, pouring out his desire, his need, his desperation, in a kiss that reached down deep to seize her very soul. His passion terrified her yet opened her mind. She knew without a doubt that he spoke the truth, that no matter what secrets he sought to hide, his love was no deception.

Clinging to him, she sought his deepening kiss, surrendered to his hunger. Tides of emotion buffeted her until she could no longer stand, until he carried her to a bench and laid her down. He knelt beside her, his hands taking the measure of her body, reaching into the carrick to caress her through her wet dress.

"Smokeflower, by the high heavens, I love you," he murmured against her throat.

She entwined her fingers in his hair, crying out softly as he pressed kisses upon her neck. He was as big and powerful as the buccaneer of a maiden's dream, the pirate stealing her away on his velvet ship. She was lost in him . . . lost.

"Dominique . . . this is too soon," she whispered. "Please . . . leave me some dignity."

He went still, his cheek against her breast, his arms tight around her waist. He was breathing raggedly, like a tempest spending itself against the waves.

"Dignity, Loire? I would never—could never—take it from you." Gently he kissed the tears from her cheeks, his reemerging control evidenced in his steadier breath.

At last he stood up and brought her to her feet. The fires in his eyes were banked now, his smile just under the surface. He took her hand and raised it to his lips, but he did not kiss it.

Her lips parted in a silent gasp of expectation, but still his mouth hovered without touching. Slowly he turned her hand to breathe on her palm and inner wrist, wafting sensation along her skin until it gathered in a throbbing ball of fire in her belly. She recognized that he knew exactly what he was doing to her, that she was like clay in his hands. It didn't matter. Sighing his name, she lifted her face to his.

"You make me forget everything but the present, Dominique," she whispered against his mouth. "Nothing seems to matter anymore but you."

"Many things matter, Loire, but none so much as my love for you. Upon that oath I stake my life." His irises lightened to silvery gray, and his voice was the soft grumble of a leopard to his mate. "If there is any doubt remaining in your mind as to my motivation, let me erase it now."

He released her, smiling when she caught the arm of the bench with a shaking hand. "Are you all right, Loire?"

"Just a little weak, that's all."

He went to the safe, twirled the combination lock, and swung open the door. He stepped aside.

Loire was too shocked to utter a sound. Bank notes fluttered to the floor from a mound on the top shelf. Several ledgers and other books filled the second shelf. Stacks of golden Spanish doubloons and smaller coins jostled with a diamond tiara, two emerald bracelets, and a scepter encrusted with rubies.

"H-have you been robbing b-banks, Dominique?"

For answer Dominique reached into the safe and selected a ledger from the row on the second shelf. He

opened it without glancing at the pages and laid it on
a nearby desk for her to examine. Loire could not
resist the urge to read the entries in Dominique's
book. There were a half dozen entries beside the
name "Renato B," but the page was filled with dozens
of lines marked "DY." Loire's eyes widened as she
studied the figures.

"You see, I have no need to take away your business," Dominique said quietly from behind her. She
turned to look at him, suddenly feeling out of place in
his company.

Smiling, he lifted out the tiara and set it on her
head.

She knew she looked ridiculous in her oversize
carrick and wet hair, but she curtsied gravely. And
though his hair and clothing were in no better shape
than hers, he bowed with the same gravity.

She handed the tiara back to him. "I am not quite
dressed for the occasion. Perhaps we can play dress-up
some other time?"

"Whenever you like. The tiara is yours." He smiled
at her wide-eyed stare. "Take it home today, if you
like."

"No, I couldn't."

He shrugged, put it back into the safe, and shut
the door. "Whenever you want it, then, Loire. I meant
what I said. It's yours."

"No."

A touch of sadness shadowed his eyes. "I'll take
you home now. Tonight is the ball."

"Oh. I had forgotten." Had she read the note on the
pillow only this morning? It seemed a lifetime ago.

"You will come with me?"

He looked so handsome and young standing there.

He was richer than most kings, yet he waited for her answer with undisguised worry. Loire was ashamed of herself. "If you still want to take me," she said, "I'll go."

Relief warmed his eyes. He almost kissed her again, but something told him to hold back. The prize was almost, but not quite, within his grasp. He could lose her so easily.

He assisted her down the steep flight of steps to the main storehouse and out to the carriage. The guards still sat on the cemetery wall, but when Dominique and Loire emerged, they ambled across the street and posted themselves in the doorway.

Dominique set the carriage whirring briskly down the street, sending water spraying behind the wheels. This time he avoided potholes. The warm tropical mist smelled like jasmine, the wet streets shone like diamonds, and the tail of a rainbow curved away into the west over the flat roofs of the houses.

"Isn't it lovely?" Loire asked, looking at the old buildings, the brief flashes of gardens.

"Yes, she is," he said. He impulsively kissed the top of her head.

Hesitantly she leaned toward him and rested her head on his shoulder, looking up at his strong, clean line of jaw. "You're the handsomest man I've ever seen," she said quietly. "And I am coming to believe you have the soul to match."

Tears surfaced too quickly in his eyes to blink back. He swallowed hard and placed his hand on her knee. Without looking at her, he said, "You are kinder than I deserve, Loire."

"I'd like to be kinder."

"I couldn't bear it if you were."

She smiled. The horses trotted on, their hooves clattering on the brick cobbles. All too soon Dominique reined in before the mercantile and helped her down. He walked her to the front door and stopped.

"Until tonight? Eight o'clock?"

She nodded, went in, and closed the door.

Loire watched him from the shop window as he set off at a fast trot. In her eyes he seemed a part of the landscape against the pale steel gray horizon at the end of rue St. Ann.

9

"Hello, you in there, honey?"

Loire looked up at her housekeeper, who was peering around the Oriental screen. "Of course."

"Good. I done called your name three times. One more and you'da had smelling salts up your nose."

"I was thinking about something."

"You shouldn't think so much. Mistah Youx'll be here any minute and you'll be saying 'howdy' in your underwear."

"Oh, Ida, the way you talk! Help me button up, would you?"

Ida buttoned her high-waisted dress of emerald-colored silk up the back and tied the gold sash. "I coulda wore this dress twenty years ago. Too many butterbeans since them days."

"St. John likes the way you look."

"St. John a foolish ole goat." She tugged Loire's

square-necked bodice down a little. "Quit pulling it back up!"

"Why don't I just go naked, then?"

"You can go nekkid after you done married. Tonight you just gotta tempt him." Ida pulled it down an inch, then smoothed the folds of the skirt. "You ain't gonna wear no stockings?"

"Horsefeathers, I forgot!"

"You gotta quit that Kentucky talk, honey. It ain't no way for a lady to carry on. You'll be betting on hoss races and cockfights next I knows."

Loire smiled, remembering Dandy Leggins, which led her thoughts back to Dominique. She pulled on her stockings, then looked under the bed for her favorite slippers.

"Has you lost your mind, Miz Loire?"

"What?"

"Purple slippers with a green dress! Next thing I knows, you'll be putting on a yellow hat and parading down Canal Street showing your garters! Mardi Gras ain't till next Feb'rary, Miz Loire Chartier, case you done forgot."

Loire kicked her shoes across the room. "Maybe I'll go in my stocking feet, then."

"Yeah, and poor Mistah Dominique won't never hold up his head in public again!"

"He likes scandal. Stocking feet are nothing to him."

Ida gave her a sideways look. "Then he don't care about them gossips, neither?"

Loire clipped rhinestone buckles onto a pair of black slippers before answering. "So he says."

"Well, you best go on and marry him anyways. Some of us don't like scandal so much around here."

Loire blew out her cheeks in exasperation. "I'm

going out on the balustrade to read until he gets here. St. John can let him in."

She found Blake's poems on the desk in the sitting room. Settling onto a wicker chair on the balustrade, she gazed out across the city, which was fast fading into twilight. The rains had passed into the west, and the warm, misty haze over the roofs dropped slowly to the street. People on the sidewalks appeared and disappeared into the fog.

The cathedral bells tolled half-past seven. Loire closed her eyes, reminded of the clocks in Dominique's warehouse. From there her thoughts clicked to his passionate embraces. She began to feel uncomfortably feverish.

Seeking a distraction, she opened her book. At first she couldn't make sense of the English, then, with a feeling of dread, she saw that the book had fallen open to the poem that had so disturbed her before.

"'The invisible worm that flies in the night in the howling storm,'" she read, "'has found out thy bed of crimson joy . . .'" Her voice trailed off as she closed the book. By memory she finished in a whisper, "'And his dark secret love does thy life destroy.'"

Her lungs burning with sudden, uncontrollable dread, she leaped up and glared at St. Anthony's Square down the street. Roiling fog distorted the trees and made the statues look like ghosts, as in a voodoo tale come to life. Her throat constricted until she could scarcely breathe.

The book trembled in her hand. She drew back her arm and hurled it over the balustrade. It landed in a gutter halfway to the square, sank slowly into the filthy water, and disappeared.

Gripping the railing, she stared at the spot until the

ripples died and the last bubble burst. It took her a moment to unclench her hands, another moment still to calm her labored breathing. She tried to laugh at her fears, but the sound was such a shocking croak that she clamped her hands over her mouth.

Hooves clattered on the cobbles. A carriage turned the corner of St. Anthony's Square, its lanterns glowing. The wheels whipped the fog into fast-dissolving spirals.

As the carriage neared the mercantile, Loire could see Dominique at the reins with Renato Beluche beside him. Dominique's face and hands were dark against his white shirt and cravat. With his tall hat cocked jauntily over one eye, he looked solid and comforting in the lantern light.

He hauled the horses to a stop below the balustrade, tugged off his driving gloves, and looked up at Loire.

She knew he'd been watching her from the moment he'd cleared the fog. Watching her, loving her, wanting to tell her that everything would be all right. With a dry sob, she fled back into the house, downstairs past a surprised St. John, and burst out the front door into Dominique's arms.

"Whoa, I was just coming in to get you, *chérie.* What's happened?" He whipped off his hat and flung it into the carriage.

"Just hold me, Dominique," she said, pressing her cheek against his lapel.

Oblivious of the stares of couples strolling by and the lewd whistle of a carriage driver, he held her tightly. "Are you afraid of the gossips again?"

"No. It was nothing. A passing fancy, that's all."

"*Vive le* passing fancy that rushed you into my arms!"

"But it was awful," she said, stepping out of his embrace. "I imagined something terrible was about to happen."

"The only terrible thing about to happen is Madame Renois's canapés," Dominique said lightly. "She employs a dreadful cook. Let me taste everything first."

She laughed a little. "After last night? I thought you never wanted to drink Doctor Kerr's antidotes again!"

He made a wry face and helped her into the carriage. "Perhaps we'll just have champagne."

Loire laughed again. "You are good for me, I think."

"And you for me," he said, the ardor in his gaze making her feel as if she'd already drunk champagne.

Renato drove carefully along the river road to a plantation on the outskirts of town. A driveway fenced with stately pecan trees led to one of the largest houses Loire had ever seen.

Three-story Ionic columns supported airy galleries along the front of the house. Through the brightly illuminated windows music filtered onto the lawn. A slave in a blue frock coat hitched the grays to the iron fence beside dozens of carriages.

A footman opened the carriage door. Dominique gave him a silver dollar, then turned to assist Loire. He sucked in his breath when her breasts brushed against his hand as she stepped from the carriage. "Ida let you out without your wrap tonight."

She blushed under his stare, resisting the temptation to pull her bodice up higher. "I left it at the theater, I'm afraid."

Dominique's expression hardened. "I'll see that you get it back." He took her arm and escorted her upstairs.

"Ah, Monsieur Youx. How good of you to come to my little soiree." A small, wrinkled woman, wreathed in yards of black taffeta, stood in the doorway, smiling at them. Diamonds glittered on her fingers, and a vast ruby choker winked at her throat.

"Evening, Madame Renois." Dominique made a low bow. He introduced Loire and said, "Madame is my business associate, Loire."

Loire hid her surprise. Madame Renois was one of the wealthiest people in New Orleans; her late husband had amassed a fortune in sugar cane and indigo. Perhaps there was nothing mysterious about Dominique Youx after all. He was a merchant with good connections.

"Let's go into the garden, shall we?" Madame said. "Everyone who *is* someone is here tonight, except for my darling Jean and Pierre."

"Jean and Pierre *Laffite?*" Loire asked.

"None other. Maybe they'll come later—they delight in sneaking past Governor Claiborne's police." Laughing, Madame went into the house.

"She ought not deal with pirates," Loire whispered as Dominique pulled her into the crush of people in the front hall.

"Perhaps not," he agreed, making a detour around the spiral staircase ascending to the fifty-foot ceiling. "What a crowd!"

Loire felt as if the entire roomful of New Orleanians were looking at them. Affixing a smile on her face and holding Dominique's hand tightly, she followed Madame Renois across the chessboard-painted floor.

Dominique stopped several times to introduce her to acquaintances of his. She already knew most of them but accepted the introductions gracefully, hiding her nervousness. All the while, she pretended not to hear the whispers.

At last they reached the courtyard. An arch in the privet hedge opened into the rear gardens, where hundreds of people were mingling. Paper Japanese lanterns glowed on every tree and bush all the way to the fog-shrouded bayou. Tables near a marble fountain groaned under the weight of china and silver.

There were cakes and beignets, smoked-salmon boats, blue cheese canapés, crawfish jambalaya, crystal carafes of wine, lemon whiskey, and a barbecued hog.

In a white gazebo under the crepe myrtles, a string quartet played the lively Cajun reel, "Possum Up de Gum Tree." Wisps of fog swirled among dancing couples.

Madame Renois introduced Dominique to a shipbuilder. Loire listened absently to their conversation until she spotted Major Gabriel Villeré. She had not forgotten her promise to obtain freedom for Mazy's son. Maybe the man would be more receptive tonight.

"Excuse me," she said, "there is someone I must see."

She squeezed through the crowd and touched his sleeve. Gabriel's smile froze when he saw her.

"Ah, Mademoiselle Chartier," he said warily, bowing.

"I wanted to apologize for the other day," she said, giving him her brightest smile.

"There is no need for friends to apologize to one another. I have already forgotten what the tiff was about."

"We were speaking about one of your hands, a man named Tim."

"Ah, yes, the big buck nigger Father bought." He sipped his whiskey.

Loire forced down her anger; temper tantrums would not work with this rich young planter. "I am prepared to offer you seven hundred and fifty American dollars. That is the going rate, I think, for a hand of his caliber." She felt sick, bargaining for a human being.

"The going rate, yes, but we're making a damned good crop of cane this year. You must understand my point of view."

"Which point of view is that, Gabriel?" a familiar voice behind them said.

It was Dominique. Loire looked at him in surprise. "You know each other?"

Gabriel stretched out his hand to shake Dominique's. "Monsieur Youx has been a friend of the family for a long time."

Loire couldn't hide her bewilderment. "But I thought you had not been here long, Dominique."

He smiled enigmatically and ignored the question. "Maybe I have interrupted your business?"

Gabriel laughed. "Mademoiselle Chartier and I were merely discussing one of the bucks on my father's plantation."

"He's not a buck—he's Mazy's son," she said with a burst of fire. "My father stupidly sold him to the Villerés, the wretch."

Gabriel tipped his head in amusement. "Mademoiselle displays a surprising streak of sentimentality."

Dominique smiled. Irritated, Loire turned away, missing the steely look in the eyes studying Gabriel. She went to the buffet table for a glass of wine.

"Mademoiselle Chartier, how nice to find you alone for the moment. Of course, my guests have hardly been falling over themselves to speak to you, have they?"

Madame Renois stood at her elbow, a plate of alligator sausage in her hand. She continued as though not noticing the blush she'd brought to Loire's face. "Since it's against the law for me to hang them for rudeness, suppose we forget about them and have a little chat?"

Loire wasn't sure what to say, so she dipped in a slight curtsy. "I'm at your disposal, of course."

"Most people are, once they've discovered how damned rich I am." Madame Renois gave her a penetrating look. "But you don't care about that, do you?"

"No, madame."

"And you don't care how rich your Monsieur Youx is, either."

Loire answered truthfully. "It's a relief to find him rich—not that I care for his money, but because he's not after mine."

The old woman chuckled. "Your fortune is not so large anymore."

Loire narrowed her eyes. "Only pirates get rich during war, madame. Like those who stole my father's barque."

"I heard about that. A shame." She switched the subject back to Dominique. "I think a great deal of Monsieur Youx."

"You've known him long, madame?"

"Long enough to gain an appreciation for his many talents. And you, mademoiselle?"

"He doesn't talk about himself very much."

"Not surprising. He has had a hard life, a dangerous and unhappy one."

"Yes. He was a soldier."

"Among other things." A teasing light shone in her eyes.

Loire was sorely tempted to ask for details, but she

knew intuitively that Dominique would not like it. Moreover, Madame Renois's air hinted that she wouldn't tell anyway.

"I hope the rest of his life is happier, madame," Loire said.

The old woman's lips drew back, but not quite in a smile. "He has a chance, I think. Try not to take yourself too seriously, mademoiselle. Life is a joke meant to be enjoyed."

"A joke, madame?"

Madame Renois turned and frowned at the Cajun fiddlers. "Peasants," she said. "*That* joke has gone on long enough! I must have real music!"

As Madame Renois walked away, Loire went to find Dominique.

He was standing under the sweeping arms of a live oak, gazing into the bayou. When he saw her he welcomed her with a smile.

"I lost you, Smokeflower."

"I've been talking to Madame Renois. A strange woman."

"And a smart one."

"What sort of business do you conduct with her?"

He hesitated briefly. "We belong to the New Orleans Association."

Her eyes widened. "Gun smugglers!"

"We help the Mexican revolutionaries," he said, shrugging.

"La, but you must hate Spain to engage in such an enterprise."

His dragon ring flashed fire as he ran his hand through his hair. There was a dangerous note in his reply. "I will do all in my power to bring her down, and her British allies with her."

Loire nodded slowly. "My father's barque was stolen by a Spaniard, we think."

He looked at her strangely. "The Spaniards are vultures." Abruptly he cast off his dark mood. "They are playing a waltz. Come, will you dance?"

He gave her no time to reply but swept her into his arms and whirled her in a graceful, solitary dance beneath the live oak. Gradually he led her to the center of the garden, his dark hair glowing in the Japanese lantern light.

Loire knew that the guests were watching, whispering behind their hands. She didn't care. There was no power stronger than Dominique Youx. No one could hurt her anymore.

His face was stern, that of a soldier taking cautious pleasure in a moment of peace. No smile graced his sensuous lips, yet the strong affirmation she sensed projected rivulets of heat down her spine. As the voices of the stringed instruments spiraled in the aria, she felt her heart merging with his.

"You are mine, Loire Chartier." Desire flamed in the touch of his hand on her waist. She turned with him, her emerald skirts brushing against his legs before sliding away.

Did she love this mysterious stranger? Her desire to know heightened as the music crescendoed. Maybe she would find out. Maybe one night they would dance the flaming pas de deux, the consummation of love.

As the final notes drifted away into the bayou, Dominique brought her to quivering rest. He bowed, solemn and princely, and did not release her hand. "Thank you, Loire," he said in a low voice.

She traced his lapel with her fingertip. "I—I don't want to stop, Dominique."

He drew her closer, his look burning where it touched. "You are not speaking of dancing, Loire."

"No," she said softly, dropping her gaze. She could see that he was aroused, his breeches taut over his hips. "No, I don't want to stop. But neither do I want to go too far . . . yet."

"I would not force you," he said, though his breath was coming harder than it should.

They stood motionless, hands entwined, oblivious of the world, each searching the heart of the other. Then another waltz began, and Dominique claimed her again. For long minutes they danced, eyes locked, heat building between them until they lost the rhythm and stumbled to a halt under the live oak.

"Perhaps the performance is at an end, monsieur?"

Loire and Dominique both turned toward the voice. A dark-haired man in gray was moving through the guests toward them, a glass of wine clutched in his hand. Loire drew in a sharp breath as the lantern light played across the face of Captain Alain Defromage.

"Alain, what are you doing here?"

"Maybe I should ask you the same question, mademoiselle."

Dominique took half a step forward, preventing him from approaching Loire. "If there is something you wish, monsieur, you'd best ask for it and be on your way."

Alain's cold gaze flicked over him. "You've got nothing to give, my friend, unless you can return the maiden's virtue."

Loire clutched Dominique's sleeve, not so much for support but to keep him from leaping at Alain. He was as tense as a crouching leopard, his pulse thudding under her fingertips. People began to gather around the trio.

"I will let that remark pass, my friend," Dominique said at last. "Do not be so foolish as to make another."

"Why should my remarks matter, when all New Orleans is talking? It is not I who have brought shame to Mademoiselle Chartier, but you."

"There is no shame attached to her," Dominique said, his voice a deep growl. "The slander you've heard is just that—slander. Lies. An attempt by society to drag innocence into the gutter."

Murmurs rose up in the crowd, but Dominique drew himself up tall, towering over all of them. "Look to your own souls, my friends, and see if any of you has the right to cast a stone at Mademoiselle Chartier."

Loire held his arm tightly, looking from one face to another. She could see Madame Renois in the crowd, her mouth stretched in a thin smile of approval.

Alain appealed to Loire. "Your papa would retire to his sickbed if he knew what you were doing. Has he not had enough sorrow, without your subverting his wishes and chasing after this—this scoundrel?"

"Go home, Alain," she said tightly.

"I am not some boy you can send off, mademoiselle. You are promised to me. I'll not watch you ruin yourself with this man."

He ignored her rising temper and went on, "Can you not sense that something is suspicious about him? I *know* I've seen him before, God help me, and it will not be long before I remember where."

"And then, monsieur?" Dominique asked very softly. "What will you do then?"

The frustration in Alain's face made him look old and at the same time half-wild. "I'll have your head, by God. Your head!"

Dominique's bicep hardened under Loire's fingers,

but his voice was a velvet-smooth purr as he asked, "Do you have the strength to take it, my little captain?"

Defromage's hand swung up. Women screamed, believing he had a pistol, but instead he dashed his glass of wine into his enemy's face. Blood snaked from a wound under Dominique's left eye and stained his shirtfront and cravat.

"I challenge you to a duel, you black-haired whoreson!" Alain's voice rang out over the crowd.

Dominique waited until the horrified gasp of the people died down. A grim smile caught the corners of his lips and pulled them back from his teeth. "I don't duel with cowards."

Alain Defromage's mustache quivered. Pale as death, he flicked back his coat, snatched out a pistol, and aimed it at Dominique's face. "You'll give me satisfaction, or you'll die here and now."

10

Dominique pushed Loire behind him and stood facing down the barrel of the gun, his eyes glittering. He made no move to defend himself. Alain's knuckles whitened on the pistol butt. The crowd fell back silently.

Madame Renois strode forward. "You'll not do any dueling in *my* garden, Alain, Dominique! Carry this affair downtown or I'll summon the sheriff."

A muscle twitched in the captain's jaw. Slowly he lowered the pistol and replaced it in his belt. "Where I spill this scoundrel's blood doesn't matter. Name the place, monsieur."

"St. Anthony's Square in one hour," Dominique said, his voice perilously quiet. "Dragoon pistols."

"Done," Alain said. "I hope you have made out your will."

"It has been gathering dust in my lawyer's safe for years."

*   *   *

Loire stood alone beneath a magnolia, peering through the wispy fog. She wanted no part of the group of excited spectators from the ball.

In the center of the square, a man in a stovepipe hat and frock coat spoke quietly to Dominique and Alain. Renato Beluche and Gabriel Villeré, acting as seconds, stood holding their coats.

"Under the rules of conduct," the judge said, "you are to begin walking at the count of one. At ten you are to turn and fire. Does either of you have any last words?"

Loire waited for Dominique to look her way, to address her just once more. But he did not. Her lips still tingled from his long, passionate kisses on the ride over. Tears hovered behind her eyes, and knots formed in her throat and stomach. Her knees knocked together until she had to lean against the tree trunk for support.

Slowly the duelists turned to stand back to back, raising their long dragoon pistols to the moon. With grave faces, they waited for the count.

"One."

Dominique stepped forward.

"Two. Three."

Dominique would redeem her honor. All New Orleans would know that Loire was a woman worth killing for—or dying for. More important, she would know it.

"Four. Five. Six."

Fog obscured the ground ahead of Dominique. He wondered if he would be able to see his target when he turned to fire. He walked slowly, listening to the count.

"Seven. Eight. Nine."

He heard the crowd draw a collective breath, a piercing sound to a man walking along the edge of a knife. His hand tightened on the smooth wooden pistol grip.

"Ten."

He turned and leveled his pistol at Defromage's head before the man had finished rotating on his heel. Fog drifted between them, and for a moment neither could see the other.

Then the fog cleared. Alain's pistol was aimed at him now. A rictus grin held his lips away from his teeth as his finger tightened on the trigger.

Staring across twenty yards of foggy grass, Dominique slowly folded his arms across his breast, his pistol pointing harmlessly over his left shoulder at the sky.

"*Sapristi!* You idiot Frenchman!" he heard Renato Beluche exclaim. Men cursed and women began to cry. He heard nothing from Loire.

He looked at the pistol, the fist holding it, the arm in its sleeve of expensive gray cloth, the moon-washed features of its owner. He smiled.

The gun wavered slightly, then there was a sudden, loud explosion and a fiery tongue leaped out of the fog. Dominique felt a red-hot demon's kiss along his left cheekbone. At the same moment he saw Alain's look of triumph.

The look faded when Dominique did not fall. The mob screamed with excitement.

"It is your turn, Monsieur Youx," the judge said. He waved the people to silence.

Dominique raised his pistol and sighted along the barrel, his forefinger curling around the trigger.

Alain Defromage stood his ground, his eyes full of despairing rage, the wind corkscrewing his hair around his face.

"Shoot him, Dominique!" Renato Beluche said. "He has made you bleed!"

Dominique's finger tightened another notch. He saw Loire looking at him, her eyes shadowed with fear. He flicked his gaze back to his adversary, steadied his elbow on his left fist, and took aim.

He could see sweat running down Alain's face; he recognized the nerve it took to stand still, waiting for death. Dominique swore softly, raised the pistol ninety degrees, and pulled the trigger. On a leaping tongue of flame the ball charged out of the barrel and disappeared into the night sky.

Alain groaned and staggered weakly against his second. Dominique paced through the fog and stopped half a foot away, transfixing his adversary with a dark look.

"The next time, my friend," he said in a low growl, "I will kill you."

With shoulders slumped in defeat, Alain Defromage turned away. Gabriel Villeré wordlessly handed him his hat and coat, and the crowd fell back to let him pass. He stopped near Loire for a moment, then went on without speaking. Soon his carriage rattled away down the street.

Beluche clapped Dominique on the shoulder and helped him into his coat. The people surged forward to shake his hand, to slap his back, to shout in admiration.

Youx accepted the praise distractedly. Loire had not moved from the tree, nor could he read the look in her eyes. Surely she had not wished him to kill the captain, yet perhaps she did not feel he had sufficiently redeemed her honor. *Mon Dieu*, he thought, was she forever to feel unworthy?

Renato Beluche waved his arms until the noise died down. "My friends, we must all go home. Claibo has outlawed dueling, and it is certain that the sheriff will come. Quickly now, to your carriages!"

With good humor and many a backward wave, the crowd dispersed. Within five minutes the foggy street was empty. Beluche, after tipping his hat to Loire, stumped out of the square and climbed into the ebony carriage.

Dominique moved through the fog toward Loire. He kept his hands at his sides, waiting for a sign that she wanted him to touch her.

"I thought you were dead when you didn't fire," she whispered at last. She fumbled a handkerchief out of her reticule and pressed it against the red slash across his cheekbone. "Oh, Dominique, you mad, impetuous, glorious man, I could kill you myself for scaring me so!"

Dominique pulled her into his arms with desperate strength, staring into her eyes, which were bright with tears. "You are not distressed that I didn't kill him?" he asked.

"Distressed? I have never seen anyone with so much courage, so much honor. Dominique . . . I cannot doubt my feelings anymore. I—I love you."

Fierce joy lit his countenance. "By the apostles, perhaps the captain killed me after all. I must be in heaven!"

"Heaven is where you are," she whispered.

He held her tighter, his emotion stealing his ability to speak for a while. At last he murmured, "I will never let you go, my beautiful pearl. You are beyond price. I will never relinquish you, Loire Bretagne Chartier."

"My heart would break if you did, Dominique Youx."

He laughed for pure joy, then swooped her up and strode into the street, passing Renato without stopping. She was like a tuft of cotton in his arms, a soft, precious burden he loved to bear.

Soon Chartier's Mercantile loomed out of the fog, with a lantern glowing in one of the narrow windows by the door.

Dominique set her down. "Give me the key."

Loire found it in her reticule. Their fingers brushed as he took it from her hand and slid it into the lock. The door clicked open.

She hesitated on the threshold, looking into the dark lochs of his eyes. He could have been killed defending her honor on this warm summer's night. Perhaps the danger was not yet over: Alain Defromage might yet lie in wait for him in a fog-shrouded alley.

"If you go tonight," she said in a low voice, "I may never see you again. Please come inside."

The fires of conflict raged in his face. "I must go away tomorrow on a matter of business. I will be back in a few days."

She grasped his lapels in anguish. "Don't leave me."

He groaned, feeling a stab in his heart like the thrust of a knife. Why should he suffer in his lonely bed tonight, when he'd won her at last? Quickly, lest she vanish into the air, he pulled her into the shop and closed the door.

"You have invited me in," he said. "I will not be cast out."

"I would never try, my love."

"Then come with me upstairs."

Loire was hardly aware of the staircase underfoot, the glimpse of the mercantile sliding away behind her. With her fingers laced tightly through Dominique's, she passed through the door at the top of the steps.

In the bedroom she stopped. Dominique made his way across the dim room to the mantel. His flaring match gave life to the lamp.

Moving to the bed, he swept aside the mosquitaire and pulled down the covers. He turned to look at her.

He had said he would not be cast out, yet Loire knew she had but to say the word and he would leave. But how could she bear to let him go? If something happened to him tonight, she would never feel the passion in her soul ripen to fulfillment. She gave up the last bittersweet shred of resistance.

"Don't go, Dominique," she said, and glided into his embrace.

"This time there will be no turning back, Loire."

"I have made my choice." She raised up on her toes to kiss him.

He returned the kiss with single-minded intensity, feeling her quiver as he freed her hair from its comb. He began to undo the buttons down her back.

"I want to see your beauty," he said, and pulled her gown to her waist. Molding her camisole to her breasts, he breathed upon her until her nipples grew rigid.

"You were born of a dragon," she whispered.

"This dragon burns for you, Loire Chartier."

He pushed the emerald silk down over her hips to the floor. With agonizing slowness he peeled off her petticoat and short undergarment. She stood before him in camisole, garters, and stockings.

"You are more beautiful than a pirate's dream!"

She shivered, uncertain of his plans. His eyes burned where they touched her, turning her belly into a lake of fire. She almost collapsed when he unlaced her camisole and pulled it off.

"You are a statue come to life," he said, tracing her nipples with his thumb. "My own Venus. I must taste you."

His tongue slid into the notch in her collarbone. Slowly he moved down to draw her right nipple into his mouth. After a few moments he released the hot, wet flesh and blew upon it.

"Dominique, I think I'm going to fall."

"I won't let you, Smokeflower."

He pulled her hips hard against his, kissing and caressing until her fevered reactions told him she was ready. He laid her on the bed and knelt between her thighs.

His face hard with passion, he flung his coat on the floor. His waistcoat followed. Finding that his fingers moved too slowly to suit him, he tore at his shirt, buttons popping and flying across the room. The garment fell open, but he did not remove it from his back.

Loire gasped at his mighty expanse of chest, which was tanned a deep mahogany and softened with dark hair. His muscles glistened in the lamplight. There was not a particle of fat on him, nothing but rigid warrior flesh.

"You take my breath away," she whispered. Hesitantly she touched his throat, then slipped her hand down his breastbone to his hard, flat belly. She pulled back when he jolted against her hand.

Dominique lifted her right foot to bend her knee. Slowly, luxuriantly, he caressed her foot, her ankle, her finely muscled calf, smiling when her face grew flushed and her breath rasped between her teeth. His fingers explored her thigh through her silk stocking. He did not touch her above the garter.

His smile, his touch, his breath, taunted her unbearably. She dug her fingers into the mattress and arched against his hard, trouser-covered thighs.

"You are a lioness," he said. Spreading her thighs farther apart, he gazed hungrily at her for a moment, then slipped his fingers over her garters to caress her naked thighs.

"My starving young lioness, let me feed you."

She cried out as his hand moved boldly against her. Racked by delicious torment, she grasped his wrists.

"Touch me, Loire."

She slid her palms up his forearms to the hard mountains of his biceps and shoulders. His strength astonished her. Tracing his collarbone again, she eased her fingertips down over his chest muscles.

In his breathing and the movements of his fingers she could feel how much she excited him. Emboldened, she stroked his abdomen; this time the convulsive jolt of his diaphragm did not alarm her.

"You weave spells about me, Smokeflower."

"And you have bewitched me since the moment you came into my life."

He bent to kiss her, his chest hair brushing her breasts. She caressed his muscular thighs through his trousers, then brought her hands to his belt and slipped them inside. Every muscle in his body contracted at the warm touch of her fingers on his naked hips, and his manhood pressed between her thighs.

"I am playing with fire," she whispered, "and I can't stop."

"Bask in it then, Loire." His tongue thrust between

her teeth as his hand explored her feverishly.

"Love me now, Dominique," she said, breaking off the kiss. "I cannot wait!"

Kneeling, he unbuckled his belt and dropped his trousers. At her look of astonished passion he grew even harder, throbbing with the beat of his heart. He lay down on top of her, rubbing her until she wept and cried his name. Taut with desire, he entered her slowly.

She cried out, her voice as hauntingly beautiful to his ears as wind in the rigging of a ship. He stopped for a long moment, caressing her face, whispering endearments against her mouth until her pain faded and the flames sprang anew.

"By the powers, I love you, Loire."

She could not speak. Gripping his back, she lifted her head to kiss the straining cords of his throat. His body was as hard, as slick, as stone. Burning with need, again and again she met his thrusts.

"You are mine, Loire," he said. "I claim you."

"Claim me, then!" White heat overflowed her belly, scorching her from crown to foot. She was drowning in a lake of lava, its raging fire the most beautiful agony she'd ever known. "Claim me!"

Dominique growled deep in his throat. Holding her in his steely arms, he moved ever faster until at last he erupted in a molten wave of passion, contracting with unimaginable power. Loire clung to him desperately as he continued to move within her, bringing her to a ripening crescendo. She buried her face in his shoulder and screamed.

After a long time he shuddered into stillness. "Oh, my beloved," he said with a low groan. He kissed her damp brow, her flushed cheeks and lips. "Do you know how much I cherish you?"

"I am beginning to realize," she whispered, kissing him back.

A breeze wafted the mosquitaire aside, cooling their damp bodies. Dominique eased off her and pulled her back against his chest so they could look out the window. A star twinkled out of the fog, a small, hopeful beacon in a misty sea.

His quiet voice broke the stillness. "How often over the years I've watched that star from the decks of ships, wishing with all my being to find you."

"But you did not know I existed," she said, touching his cheek.

"I have always known you existed. Always."

"You are an incurable romantic, my darling."

"Perhaps. Yet I remember a night in December when I was only twelve years old, thinking that my wife had just been born."

Loire looked at him in wonder. "I was born in December."

"What day?"

"The sixteenth."

"Mmm, I thought it was the seventeenth. That's what I wrote in my journal: 'December 17, 1791. My future wife has finally arrived. Glory!'"

"You're fooling me, aren't you, Dominique?"

"And why would I, *chérie?*" he asked, kissing her eyebrow.

"Maybe to make me love you even more. You do not have to resort to tricks—I am finding that I love you so much that my heart hurts. You don't have to play games."

"You are very suspicious, for one so young." He touched her forehead, thinking how like a heart her face was.

"I don't mean to be suspicious, but I can't help it. I've seen too many men with ulterior motives—Oh! I did not mean you!"

He ached for her. "If it takes me till the end of my life, Loire, I will finally convince you of your own worth, and of my love for you. You are the everlasting song in my soul, the spirit I knew and cherished before ever we set foot upon this earth."

Tears trembled on her lashes. She tried to speak, but her tongue stuck to the roof of her mouth and she could not utter a sound.

"Loire, will you marry me?"

She had thought she could attain no higher plane of emotion, but his question sent the blood thrilling through her veins. She could refuse him no longer; she didn't *want* to refuse him any longer.

She touched his face, traced the clefts in his cheeks down to his jaw, and grazed his lips. Her voice was a husky whisper as she replied, "You've known from the first that I'd say yes when the time was right."

"And is it right, Smokeflower?"

"It could never be more right, my lovely dragon." She brushed her lips across his. "I ask for only one week to prepare."

A dazzling smile overtook his face. It seemed only natural then to take her in his deepest embrace, to fan the flames of love into a raging storm. For a long time the mosquitaire draperies fluttered and shook around them, as graceful partners in their dance of desire.

At last they lay back on the pillows, spent. Loire rested her head on his chest and closed her eyes, listening to the slow, strong thud of his heart, savoring the feel of his hand on her back.

They had known each other such a brief time, but

somehow it seemed like an eternity. Was there something in what he'd said? Had he known her in some preexistent sphere and come to this earth in order to find her?

He was a strange man, dark and mysterious in many ways. He still had not revealed much of himself, and that disturbed her. Madame Renois had said he'd had a dangerous, sorrowful life. Given time, Loire was sure he would tell her all. Yet despite her reassurances to herself, deep in her soul a little fear lurked that she could not dispel.

Something terrible was going to happen. What it was she could not guess, but once more Blake's awful poem marched through her mind.

Desperately she burrowed into the arms he tightened around her. What was this dark secret with the power to destroy her life? Don't let me find out, she prayed. I don't want to know.

11

Dominique kissed Loire's sleeping face and left her bed before the first brushstrokes of dawn painted the city. Then he went down to the dark shop and let himself out, relocking the door behind him and slipping the key through the crack. This time no one saw him go as he disappeared into the fog.

Later, Loire came downstairs to find St. John dragging marbles out of a huge burlap sack by the front door. One by one he tossed them into wooden bins in the window, sorting them by color and size.

"Marbles? We haven't had any for months!" Loire scrabbled in the sack. The cold, shining glass balls clicked and clattered as she withdrew a big cat's-eye. Holding it to the light, she asked, "Where did they come from?"

"Mems cannot guess?"

"You don't mean Monsieur Youx sent them?"

"*Oui.* M'sieu Beluche just now bring them in the wagon."

She shook her head. "It's hard to believe that little privateer is his uncle."

St. John laughed as he tossed a couple of cranberry-colored marbles into a bin. "We all have our cross, *non?*"

"It is so. He says one cannot help one's genealogy." With an expert flick of her thumb she lobbed the cat's-eye into a bin, then selected a clear green pea from the sack. Rolling it around on her palm, she said, "All the little boys in town will raid us when word of this treasure gets around!"

"*Oui,* and their papas, too, I think. M'sieu Youx, he send also wagon bed rivets, plow screws, and seed. Other things, too."

Loire followed his gesture to the counter. Under a canvas cloth she found Hansel and Gretel's gingerbread house, a shepherd's cottage with a big black wolf at the door, and a tiny castle. A leafy pendulum and three iron weights shaped like pinecones rested beside each clock.

"These were on the wall in his warehouse," she said, gently opening a door under the eaves to expose the cuckoo bird.

"He some crazy for you, that man."

"So he says."

St. John's grin stretched wide. "M'sieu Beluche say mems is getting married Saturday."

She sighed. "He spoiled the surprise—I was going to tell you myself. Did you tell Ida?"

"She already uptown, finding mems a dressmaker. M'sieu Beluche say M'sieu Dominique want to buy mems' trousseau."

Loire blushed. "That wouldn't be proper. I'll buy it myself."

"Mems, she *non* have so much money now. Perhaps is best to let M'sieu Dominique buy the dress. He say he already swore to buy mems a hundred."

Frowning, she opened a big glass jar and drew out a string of rock candy. "He should wait until after the wedding."

"Mems is ver' sick soon, eating candy. A biscuit is better."

She hoisted herself up until she was perched on the counter and began to swing her legs, licking the candy. "I don't want a biscuit. I want to go see Dominique before he leaves town."

St. John eyed her. "You see him all last night already."

She stopped swinging her legs. "I saw him at the party, of course."

He grinned. "There, and the square, and—" He broke off and cast his eyes to the ceiling.

"Spy!"

"Your papa, he say keep mems safe."

"Does anyone else know?"

"I tell nobody."

"Good. I don't need your meddling—I can take care of myself." Suddenly noticing that she wore mismatched shoes, she pulled the hem of her dress down over them.

Hiding a smile, St. John resumed sorting marbles. "M'sieu Beluche say Father Dubourg is glad mems will marry."

Loire put down her candy. "How did he find out so soon?"

"M'sieu Dominique see him this morning already, give him money for the building fund."

"Money?"

"*Oui*. Enough to put on spires on the cathedral."

"Why, it must have been a monstrous sum! Why did he do that?"

"He love you, that man."

Loire frowned. "I suppose he did it to keep me from being excommunicated."

"Mems is ver' distrustful."

"I can't help it."

"Why don't mems try to believe in something?"

"I do. I believe in Dominique . . . I just wish he'd told me where he's going this week."

"If you ain't pretty!" Ida said, standing back to gaze at Loire. They were closeted in the *presbytère,* next door to the cathedral. "Your Mistah Youx gonna think he done died and waked up in heaven with a angel."

Loire's dress was all pure silk and lace with a ten-foot train. The low, alençon lace bodice tapered to a point several inches below her waist. Lacy pendant cuffs fell from the underside of her elbow-length sleeves halfway to the floor, fluttering gracefully when she moved her arms.

"Mistah Youx gonna faint when you step down the aisle."

"I just hope he's there when I walk down the aisle," Loire said. "Suppose he hasn't returned!"

"You know he has. You done got his message this morning, and St. John say his carriage is across the street in the park. You just quit worrying."

"I can't help it," Loire said. She poured herself a cup of water from a pitcher and gazed into it. "Do you not think it strange that he's asked Jean Laffite to be his best man?"

"Nope. He done said in his letter that Madame Renois asked him to, as a favor to her."

The cathedral bells began to toll half-past six. Loire raised her voice. "Renato Beluche has asked to give me away. I should have sent for Papa. He will be hurt that I did not even take time to send him a message."

"And who coulda carried it to him, with them British ships thick as water moccasins out there? Ain't nobody but pirates getting in and out of the river." Ida gave a snort that indicated what she thought about pirates. "Ain't likely one of them would help you, no way."

"Maybe I should wait . . . ."

"Wait, my eye! You're a grown woman, gal. You done waited long enough for the right man to come by. Your pappy's gonna be mighty proud, next time he see you. Mebbe you'll have him a grandbaby by then, make him *really* happy."

"Still, I have a strange feeling about this whole thing."

"You just simmer down, Miz Loire." Ida took her by the shoulders. "You all green around your gills. Mistah Youx in the church waiting for a pretty gal, not something an old alley cat'd turn up his nose at!"

"Do I look that bad?"

"A sight worse."

"I love you, too, Ida."

"Now don't go getting mushy. I just wants you happy, that's all."

"I am happy, just nervous."

A knock sounded on the door. Ida yanked it open to find Renato Beluche standing on the mat. He wore a new blue jacket with gold braids, white breeches, and shiny black boots. His hair was slicked carefully back from his forehead, and his mustachios fanned his cheeks. He held a bouquet in his hand and a blue velvet box under one arm.

"Mademoiselle Chartier," he said, bowing. "M'sieu Dominique Youx sends his compliments."

Loire curtsied and took the bouquet. Among the scarlet roses were delicate white-and-pink tobacco flowers.

"He does not wish you to go unadorned, mademoiselle," the little privateer continued. "And so!"

He opened the box and brought out the diamond tiara from Dominique's safe. Lightning seemed to burst from the stones as he turned it. He smiled at the women's gasp of surprise.

"Does mademoiselle have a veil?"

"She got one." Ida settled it over Loire's head, and then Renato stood on tiptoe to place the tiara.

"It seems everyone in town will see the wedding," Renato went on. "There are at least a thousand people in the cathedral. Even Governor and Madame Claiborne are there."

"Oh, my Lord," Loire said.

"Now you gone and done it, Mistah Beluche!" Ida said. "Look at this child! I ain't seen a greener face since she ate two dozen little green apples one time. She as nervous as a cat."

"La, I am sorry, mademoiselle. I did not mean to worry you, but after all, you are getting married, not crossing the Rubicon."

"I know. I'm not planning to turn back, monsieur."

Beluche laughed. "It is that foolish Jean who should turn back. He risks jail, showing himself to Claiborne.

The governor has offered five hundred dollars for his arrest."

"And Laffite has offered a thousand for Claiborne's," Loire said. She smiled at the foolishness of it all. "I suppose neither would spoil the wedding with such unpleasantness."

"But no. And Jean, why, he has volunteered his daughters for this happy occasion." He stepped outside and returned with dark-eyed little twin girls. "Claudia-Marie, Michelle, this is Mademoiselle Chartier. You will carry her train. And this is— *Merde!* Where is Jeanine?"

He went out again, returning after a moment with a very small girl in a pink gown. Her pale hair fell to her shoulders, she had huge blue eyes, and her chubby hands were curled around a basket of petals. "Say hello to the mademoiselle, girls."

"A pleasure, Aunt Loire!" the twins chorused. Jeanine stuck two fingers in her mouth.

"Thank you," Loire replied. *Aunt Loire?*

"Mass has begun," Renato said quickly, shooting the twins a warning look. "Shall we?"

He held out his left arm. Loire accepted it, her heart pounding.

"I'll be in the balcony with St. John and the other coloreds," Ida said. "You speak up loud when the preacher ask does you want to marry that man."

The bells began to toll as the wedding party walked out of the *presbytère* and up the cathedral steps. Gray clouds hung low in the sky, and thunder rumbled in the west.

They went into the shadowy vestibule and looked into the sanctuary. Beeswax candles wearing caps of brass glowed in elaborate sconces along the walls and supporting pillars. A white runner stretched down the aisle to the altar steps. Every pew was full.

"You were wrong, Monsieur Beluche," Loire whispered. "There must be *ten* thousand people here."

He chuckled softly. "All of them will fall instantly in love when they set eyes on you. Do not be afraid, little one."

"Where is Dominique?"

"He will come out soon. Be tranquil."

The organ notes faded as Father Dubourg, flanked by two other priests, entered the sanctuary through a side door. His red-and-white robes swung as he genuflected, then stepped to the first tier before the altar.

The door opened again, and Dominique Youx and Jean Laffite came in, genuflected, and turned to face the congregation.

Clad in a white shirt, black tails, waistcoat, and trousers, his dark hair swept back from his brow, Dominique looked like a prince straight out of a medieval tale. Loire could scarcely hear the organ music over her own throbbing pulse.

"All right, my precious," Renato said, giving little Jeanine Laffite a pat. "Scatter your pretty flowers. Be sure to give one to Governor Claiborne's wife in the first row, and tell her it is from your papa."

The child trotted into the sanctuary and stopped. She jammed her fingers into her mouth and stared at the huge congregation. Then, seeing her father, she pulled a petal out of her basket and dropped it on the white runner. Dropping one petal after another, she wandered up the aisle. She turned aside to give Sophronia Claiborne a flower, then rushed into Jean's arms.

"It is time to meet your groom," Renato said as the

music swelled. The congregation stood and looked back at the vestibule.

For a moment Loire could not make her legs move. Then, through her veil, she saw Dominique smile. Suddenly all was well. She walked out of the shadows into the light, instinctively adopting the stately but hesitant gait of the bride.

"She is like a beautiful princess!" people whispered as she walked by, her long train sweeping back to where the little girls held it in their hands. Loire didn't even hear the murmurs of the crowd.

"You are far lovelier than the morning glory flower," Renato Beluche whispered out of the corner of his mouth. "My nephew thinks so, too. See the way he looks at you!"

Loire trembled when Renato placed her hand in Dominique's and then faded back into the crowd.

"My beautiful Loire."

Tears welled in her eyes. "Somehow I didn't think this would really happen," she whispered. "I worried all week."

"I never doubted it for an instant," he whispered back, and squeezed her hand. "I missed you sorely. May God make each day with you last a hundred years."

Father Dubourg waved the people to their knees. Dominique and Loire knelt on the first step as the prayers and sermons began.

The cathedral dimmed with the fall of night, and still the priest droned on. Loire and Dominique knelt and stood a dozen times or more, the congregation with them, coming step by step toward the sacrament of marriage.

Rain pattered against the windows, and a vivid flash of lightning electrified the great cathedral. The congregation sprang up in alarm as the vestibule doors blew open. Wind swirled down the aisle to claw Loire's train and whip her veil around.

Dominique pulled her against his side and held her until someone managed to shut the doors. Again lightning flashed, turning the congregation a ghastly blue.

Father Dubourg struggled to be heard above the howling storm. "If any man here can show just cause why these two should not be joined in the bonds of holy matrimony, let him speak now or forever hold his peace."

"By the shadow of Death, I'll not hold my peace!"

This time lightning flashed in Dominique's eyes as he turned and located the speaker.

Captain Alain Defromage materialized out of the vestibule, rainwater streaming off his clothes. His boots left a muddy trail down the white runner as he marched toward the altar, pointing at Dominique.

"Alain! What are you doing?" Loire demanded.

Stopping a yard away, Alain said, "There stands the man who stole your father's barque, who plunged you into poverty! Were it not for his plundering, you would not be forced to wed him!"

The congregation waited in silence for Dominique's reply. Loire felt a scream rising to her throat as she looked from one man to the other. "Say it isn't true, Dominique! Tell me he's lying!"

"I do not lie, mademoiselle! This is the Red Dragon himself, the man who stole the barque! He wore a mask and spoke Spanish, but at last I've learned his identity. He works with that bastard, Laffite."

Governor Claiborne leaped to his feet and pointed at Dominique. "Sheriff, arrest this man, and Jean Laffite with him!"

The sheriff of Orleans parish and his constables

pushed through the people surging into the aisle. Laffite somehow escaped in the confusion.

Renato Beluche reached for his pistol before remembering that he'd neglected to bring it. "Damn it to damn, Dominique! You had better run!"

Dominique did not move, merely stared down into Loire's stricken face. "I am sorry, my love. I never meant to hurt you."

"But he did, mademoiselle!" Alain Defromage said.

The sheriff and his deputies shouldered the merchant captain aside. Two caught Dominique by the arms as the others tore open his coat and began to search him.

Buffeted this way and that, Dominique did not try to fight. He did not even appear to notice his captors. "I love you, Loire."

"Don't listen to him! We raided his warehouse and discovered your father's goods." Alain reached into Youx's shirt and pulled out a miniature portrait. "Do you recognize this? Your picture! Your father gave it to me last year. This bastard stole it from me when he took the barque."

"No!" Loire cried, pressing her hands over her ears.

Alain thrust her hands aside. "He's known who you are from the first! He came to Vieux Carré planning to rob you of the rest of your possessions!"

Loire stepped close to Dominique and stared in agony into his eyes. She saw the truth of Alain's words reflected there. "You lying pirate," she said very quietly. "I'll hate you for the rest of my life."

Abruptly she flung off her veil and diamond tiara, then fled past Father Dubourg to disappear through the small door near the altar.

12

Hands clasped behind his back, Dominique Youx paced to the barred window of his cell for the fiftieth time since his incarceration the night before. Beyond the gate, he could see carriages splash through puddles in the street.

He had planned to tell Loire the truth once they reached his grand cottage on Lake Pontchartrain. There he could have asked her forgiveness.

He rested his forehead against the cold, damp bars. What would happen to her now? He had wanted to help her believe in herself, to erase the memory of her mother's shame. Now, instead, she believed him another opportunist. A pirate, at that.

"Merde!" He crashed his fist against the rough palisade wall. He had planned to lay his riches at her feet, to pay back at a thousand percent interest every nickel he had so unfortuitously gained in capturing

the barque. He would still repay her, by heaven, whether or not she consented to accept his suit.

Not for an instant did he believe he would be hanged for piracy. Not only did his letters of marque from Cartagena protect him from the charge, but he employed the best attorney in the business, Edward Livingston.

At noon, the sheriff unlocked his cell. "Your lawyer was here, m'sieu. You are free to go."

"How much did it cost me?"

"There were many expenses, of course."

Dominique didn't bother to point out the jail's filthy accommodations, its lack of even the most basic necessities. "How much, Sheriff?"

"Five thousand dollars." He added quickly, "Even at that, I barely managed to persuade Governor Claiborne to release you."

Throwing his coat over his shoulder, Dominique strode outside. Money was power. Money was freedom. Money could buy anything . . . except Loire Chartier's love.

Renato Beluche was waiting with the carriage. "Dominique, my little nephew, your eye is black! I'll go in and kill that motherless dog of a sheriff who did this to you!"

Dominique tossed his rumpled evening coat onto the backseat and climbed up beside him. He stared at the wilted, bedraggled roses in his horses' manes and tails, the rain spatters on the beautiful ebony carriage.

"Forget the sheriff. Take me to the Villeré Plantation, Renato. Quickly."

*   *   *

The country residence of Major General Jacques de Villeré of the Louisiana militia was a low, rectangular whitewashed structure elevated on brick posts. Tall pecan trees shaded three sides of the house; an orange grove meandered from the front lawn to a cane field bordered by the tepid waters of Bayou Mazant.

Propping his feet on the gallery rail, the major general's son, Gabriel, studied the grove through half-closed lids. Occasionally he roused from his lethargy just enough to flick a fly out of the air with a black bull whip coiled loosely in his fist.

"There you are, you young sloth!" someone called.

Gabriel banged the front legs of his chair down and stood up, grinning as Dominique and Renato drove into the yard. "Dominique! You are out of jail, *mon ami!* Célestin," he called through an open window, "come out and see Captain Youx's splendid black eye!"

Dominique sprang out of the carriage and bounded up four steps to the porch as Gabriel's younger brother ambled out of the house.

"Do you not wish for such a shiner yourself, Célestin?" Gabriel asked, laughing. He flicked a fly off his own hat brim with his whip. "And to have, at the same time, a bullet graze along one cheek is a thing a man would kill for! Think of how the women would comfort you!"

"I would gladly bequeath both wounds to you, my friends," Dominique said.

"Me, I cannot blame you," Gabriel said. "But what brings you so far from the city, after that terrible experience last night?"

"One of your field hands. Tim."

Gabriel rolled his eyes. "Again that nigger!"

"*Oui.* Again. Only this time you will sell him."

"Mademoiselle Chartier is a persistent creature, *non?*"

"I'm here to see that she gets what she wants this time."

Gabriel scratched his head. "But I am confused, after what happened last night."

Dominique's face turned cold. "Your state of mind is not important, my friend. Hers is. You will sell me the Negro."

"You and I have been friends a long time, Dominique. Let us not allow a nigger to come between us."

Dragonfire sparked in Dominique's eyes. "You will sell him."

"My father will not allow me to sell a prime hand. Not even to you, Dominique."

"Then I will take him."

The Creole's voice soared to a high note. "Over my dead body!" He let his bull whip uncoil.

"Do not tempt fate, my friend."

Gabriel's hand that held the weapon began to shake. "You are a pirate, Dominique Youx!"

"Aye, with the keys to your father's plantation. One word from me and Bayous Bienvenue and Mazant will be shut down. The major general's cane will rot in his storehouses this fall, for my ships will not run the British blockade. Furthermore, he will not be able to purchase black market goods from Barataria."

"And what of the New Orleans Association? You and my father are partners!"

"I own the controlling stock; I take all the risks running guns. Your father's contribution is small. Refuse to sell me Tim, and his profits will be less than negligible. He will lose the plantation."

Faced with the prospect of financial ruin, Gabriel did not hesitate. "Take the nigger, then, and may the Eternal blast your soul to everlasting hell!"

"If I do not win back the woman, He may do with my soul as He pleases." Dominique drew a wallet from his shirt and tossed it to the young major.

Gabriel snatched the wallet, dropping the heavy whip on the porch. He opened it and stared at the bills.

"Nine hundred American dollars, Gabriel. You bought him for seven. Not a bad profit, *non?*"

Gabriel Villeré smiled, his good humor magically restored. "Célestin, fetch the nigger's papers from Father's strongbox."

The long fingers of evening's shadows were caressing the brick walls of Chartier's Mercantile when Renato pulled the carriage up in front of it. On the seat beside him sat a young black man, his ragged breeches spattered with mud, his naked back scarred.

Dominique climbed out of the carriage and stared up at him. "You've just reached the Promised Land."

"Master?"

"You'll never have to call another man 'master' again, once you walk through these doors." He indicated the shop with a nod. "Mademoiselle Chartier won't stand for it."

Suddenly Tim couldn't get off the seat fast enough. Dominique handed him a paper. "This belongs to you. Show it to Mademoiselle Chartier."

Dominique turned to rap on the door. Fifteen seconds passed without a response. He rapped again, loudly.

"Maybe she's in the courtyard, Captain," Renato said.

Dominique pushed open the door and went in, with Tim close behind him. The courtyard and *garçonnière* were empty.

"Come, Tim, she must be upstairs."

St. John opened the door at the top of the stairs and looked down at them. He seemed too distracted to comment on the presence of Tim. "M'sieu Dominique, it is a long time ago I ask you to come."

"You asked me to come? When?"

"This morning. I go to the jail. They say m'sieu *non* can see visitors, m'sieu's lawyer get him out soon. I say tell him to come here quick as quick."

Dominique's gut twisted in apprehension. He went past St. John into Loire's bedroom, raked aside the mosquitaire, and stared at the empty bed.

"Where is she?"

"She . . . she go off in her small *Hopscotch*."

"Off to *where*?"

"Isle Châteauroux. She take Ida with her before the rooster crow today. She say she never come back." St. John turned his face to the wall, blinking rapidly.

Dominique cursed long and savagely.

"St. John, he is afraid the British will catch her," the Jamaican said.

"I will not give them the chance to sink her. I am leaving now."

"St. John will come, too!"

"No. You must stay here and mind the shop," Dominique said. "I promise to bring your wife home to you."

Tim said, "I'm coming with you, Mistah Dominique."

"But you are not a seaman."

"No, suh, but I can shoot the eye out of a stinkin' redcoat if I got to. And I owes you."

"You owe me nothing."

"You done paid good money for me." He drew himself up proudly. "I aim to pay you back."

Dominique hesitated only a moment more. "Come, then. I can use a good shot."

Dominique started for the door, then stopped, struck by a thought. Slowly he turned to look at St. John. "Who commands the *Hopscotch*, St. John?"

The Jamaican drew a heavy sigh and looked at the ceiling. "I tell that girl not to, but she is too mad to listen."

"*Who?*"

"M'sieu Youx has guessed already, I think. It is the Captain Defromage."

13

Loire Chartier leaned against the forecastle railing of her two-masted *Hopscotch*, shifting her weight as the brigantine wallowed in the swells. Her eyes were as stormy as the thunderheads on the southern horizon. She could hear the clanking of bilge pumps through the deck; the sailors had manned them continually since shipping out of New Orleans three days ago.

She looked down at the ivory pipe clenched in her right hand, remembering the night Dominique had given it to her. She wanted to throw it overboard, to watch it drown like the clay pipe she'd thrown into the Mississippi River. But she didn't have the courage.

Alain Defromage sidled up to her. "I had not realized you smoked, Mademoiselle Chartier."

"I don't." She hid the pipe in an old-fashioned white pocket tied to her waist.

"Ah, well, good." His gaze touched the white, lace-trimmed tippet crossed over her breasts before wandering down her indigo apron-gown. He cleared his throat. "A full load of grain in the hold would have made handling the ship easier."

She didn't reply.

"Loading a hundred tons more wheat would not have taken much longer."

"Even one more hour in the city would have been too much, Captain."

"Why? The brute was locked in jail, and unlikely to get out."

Loire narrowed her eyes. Her hands tightened on the railing. "I do not care to discuss him, Alain."

"You'll have to discuss him with your father. There are matters we must clear up . . . now that you've regained your senses."

She spun toward him then, shaking with rage. "You are my father's employee, Captain. Nothing else. This voyage does not mean I intend to marry you."

"Your father may say otherwise."

Aching to strike him, Loire looked out to sea. Gradually she brought her anger under control. "Has the lookout caught sight of that sail he glimpsed last evening?"

"No. It was probably nothing to worry about, just another merchantman. We are in the sea lanes, you know."

"I know, and I don't approve. You should adopt another course, Captain, one not so obvious to the British."

"It was my understanding that you wished to reach the islands as quickly as possible. Another route would slow us."

"So would cooling our heels in the hold of a limey ship."

"I will look at my charts," he said tightly. "Perhaps you would join me for supper?"

"I'm not hungry."

"You must eat something. Your woman says you've hardly eaten."

"Ida talks too much."

"She worries about you. So do I."

Loire stared at him coldly. "You're paid to sail this vessel, Captain, not be my wet-nurse. Now go away and chart a new course. By nightfall I want us well away from the shipping lanes."

His lips tight with fury, the captain stalked off to the wheelhouse. Loire wished she had not asked him to take her to Isle Châteauroux, yet she doubted she could have found another captain: no one wanted to brave the British in the Gulf of Mexico.

For the first time since setting sail, she wondered at the wisdom of this venture. Was her own injured pride sufficient reason to risk the lives of Ida and the crew? Perhaps she should have stayed in the city and faced down the laughter.

She could have tolerated the jeers, she supposed, but not Dominique. He had cruelly deceived her. She knew she could not have looked at him without being torn apart.

She raised her hands to her cheeks to brush away tears. Despite the peril in the Gulf, she'd had to run away. On Isle Châteauroux she would try to forget, try to rebuild her life. St. John could run the mercantile without her help, and Ida could return to him on the next ship. As for Loire, there was nothing left for her in New Orleans. She would never go back there again.

The deck shuddered as the crew trimmed sail. With sheets and halyards shrilling through the blocks and metal sheaves, the *Hopscotch* came about on a new course.

Defromage had obeyed her orders. Good. Now if she could only forget the moment when he'd barged into the cathedral and brought her world crashing down in ruins . . . . *His dark secret love does thy life destroy.*

Yet she could not hold Alain responsible. It was Dominique Youx who had stolen the miniature from him and then used it to find her in New Orleans. She leaned against the rail, remembering the night he had bedded her. He had claimed to know of her birth, claimed he'd written in his journal that he would someday make her his wife.

What if he'd gotten her in the family way? She clutched the rail, paralyzed with this new fright. Why had she not thought of it before?

"Sail ho! Sail off the windward bow!"

Off the windward *bow?* The sail the lookout had spotted had been astern. Were there two ships, then?

"All hands on deck!" the captain shouted.

Ida burst out of the companionway hatch. "Come on, get below, Miz Loire!"

But Loire ran to the port rail. For several minutes she could make out nothing. Then a smudge appeared on the horizon.

She rushed astern as Alain turned the *Hopscotch* to run with the wind. The speck grew larger and larger until they could discern its triangular foresails.

"'Tis a British sloop!" the lookout cried. "She'll be on us in less than an hour, Captain! We are no match for her!"

"Run out the carronade!" Alain commanded. "Load muskets! Prepare to repel boarders!"

"Get me a gun," Loire demanded of the mate.

"You ain't gonna do no fighting, honey!" Ida said.

"No? You watch me!"

"*You* watch *me!*" She grabbed Loire by the back of the collar and hustled her into the companionway.

"I can handle a gun as well as any man up there!"

"I don't give a dogtail damn what you *think* you can do, you ain't going up there and getting in no fight!"

"I'm not going to cower down here and let the British sack my ship!"

"They ain't one thing you can do to stop them if your cap'n cain't sail this here boat fast enough, and I ain't aiming to let you get shot full of holes trying to prove how tough you is."

"I should have left you in New Orleans!"

"I shouldn'ta let you run off on this fool trip, no way. You shoulda stayed home and married that man!"

"Are you out of your mind?"

"No, but you is. He ain't never meant you no harm. St. John say he didn't know nothing about the barque belonging to your pappy till he already done took it and all. Too late to give it back."

"He's a pirate!"

"He a privateer. They's a difference."

"There's not a bean's worth of difference! He just found a way to circumvent the law!"

"You just mad 'cause you think he trick you."

Loire stamped her foot. "Hush up! I don't want to hear it!"

"You gonna hear it this time. I done tole you all this after you run out the church, but you wouldn't listen. You was all set to outfit this here worm-chewed tub and run off to your pappy, just like a little baby child."

"Hush up!"

"I ain't gonna hush up, and you ain't got too big to spank, Miz Loire."

"Don't you lay one finger on me, Ida!"

"You listen, then, and maybe I won't."

"I won't listen, and you wouldn't, anyway."

Loire spun on her heel and stomped down the narrow companionway to her compartment, slamming the door after her.

She flounced down on her bunk and slipped her hand between the straw mattress and the bulkhead. Her reticule was just where she'd hidden it. She brought out her pistol and a handkerchief containing several lead balls and powder cartridges. After snapping the small ramrod off the barrel, she began to load and prime the weapon.

Suddenly a roiling blast shook the tiny cabin. At first Loire thought she'd accidentally set off her pistol, but half a second later a louder blast rocked the cabin. The *Hopscotch* canted violently, hurling Loire off the bunk. There were several more explosions and a loud crash abovedecks.

Blood roared in her ears as she crawled across the listing deck and wrenched open the cabin door. Cradling her loaded gun to her bosom, she staggered up the companionway.

"Ida! Are you all right?"

She banged open the hatch, falling twice on her way out as the brigantine lurched out of control. Blue smoke smothered the decks, nearly obliterating the foremast, which was lopped off just above its square course. Canvas, sheets, braces, and tackle littered the deck. Alain Defromage shouted frantic instructions at the sailors chopping the shattered rigging.

Loire shoved her pistol into her tippet bodice and slipped across the slanting deck to help clear the canvas. She was struggling to throw it overboard when a gust of wind blew most of the smoke clear.

Against a sky of sunset red, she could see a British sloop bearing down from astern, its bow carving the burning waves, its forward carronades belching hot clouds of smoke.

Loire dropped her burden to leap over a broken spar and rush astern. There she faced Alain Defromage angrily. "Why don't you return fire, Captain?"

"We have only a single carronade!" he yelled. "We must strike the colors!"

"We will not strike, you bleeding coward!" She yanked out her pistol and leveled it at his head. "Tell your crew to return fire, or I swear I'll send you to Glory this instant!"

"We dare not shoot! They will sink us!"

Loire's finger tightened on the trigger. "Tell them to fire!"

Defromage threw up his hands and gave the command. The gunnery mate thrust his burning linstock into the touchhole and stepped back. Two interminable seconds passed before the carronade roared into smoke and flame, recoiling on its carriage.

"Reload!" the gunnery mate shouted.

Apparently surprised to find his prey biting back, the British captain tacked evasively. Loire knew her advantage could last only a minute, two at most.

"Jury-rig a mast!" she ordered. "Lively now!"

"You'll get us killed, Loire!" Defromage shouted.

"Can't you see that they're winding round to cross our T? They'll blast us to Paris!"

Loire stared at the green-coated British marines lining the decks of the sloop. Intellectually she knew that her position was hopeless, yet her heart cried out against surrender. All her life she had despised the British tyrants. What chance would she and her little band of French Creoles have in the hands of so terrible an enemy?

"By the sacred thunder, I will not give in!" she told Alain in a vehement whisper. "Not while a drop of French blood flows in my veins—"

"And a nickel's worth of Kaintock obstinacy stiffens your backbone, you little idiot!" Alain interrupted.

The sloop prepared to cross their bow. Loire raised her pistol in hopeless rage and shouted at her crew, "Prepare to receive the enemy broadside!"

The lookout shrieked, "Sail ho! Sail! It's a big schooner, coming out of the cloud!"

"*Merde!*" Loire squinted in the direction of his outthrust finger. Alain Defromage grabbed the pistol out of her hand. She didn't bother to try to get it back.

"How many British does it take to sink us?" she demanded angrily. But before she could locate the schooner, the British sloop broke off its attack and jibed to beat a course downwind.

"What in the world . . . ? Why did she not finish us?"

"God knows," the captain said. "Maybe she wants to leave us to the big ship."

Loire could see the schooner now. Under scarlet sails rigged fore and aft, the ebony hull cut through the waves like a speeding shark. Pivot guns gaped from her bows; cannons bristled from her beams.

"Lookout, can you see her colors?" Loire shouted.

"She displays nothing but her teeth. I count forty guns. You cannot fight this one, mademoiselle."

"Tell your men to jury-rig that mast," Loire ordered Defromage. There was still a slight chance of escape, if the schooner ran into a pocket of dead air before she came within range. "Rig it, I say!"

"What is the purpose? The schooner is twice the size of that sloop. If we could not fight her, we certainly cannot fight this one. We are done for."

Loire slapped him hard across the cheek. "Do as you're told, you bilious coward, or I'll have you clapped in irons!"

"This is mutiny!"

"I own the ship!"

Alain decided enough was enough. He shoved her at the mate. "Take her below and lock her in her cabin!"

"Stay away from me!" She ran toward the bow.

She was climbing over the mangled foremast when she heard a groan. The rubble stirred. She heard the groan again, louder this time.

"Help me! Oh, sweet Jesus, help me!"

"Ida!" Grabbing a broken spar, Loire shouted at the mate, "My companion is buried under there! Help me get her out!"

Ida emerged from the rubble several minutes later, bruised and half-suffocated. Loire helped her to the capstan and made her sit down.

Ida's dark eyes fixed on a point beyond Loire. "Guess them damn British done catch us after all."

Loire wheeled around to find the sharp ebony prow almost upon them, its guns threatening silently.

A single glance at the *Hopscotch*'s stern told her that the Stars and Stripes no longer fluttered from the gaff. Alain Defromage was nowhere in sight.

"You better get below, child," Ida said. "The longer them British goes without seeing you, the better."

Loire squared her shoulders. "This is my brigantine. If they take it, then they'll take it with my curse upon their heads."

"I ain't worrying about them taking the boat," Ida said. "I'm worrying about them taking *you*."

A black flag slowly ascended the schooner's gaff. After reaching the brass ball at the top, it curled around the gaff twice and then snapped open with a loud report. A red dragon streamed arrogantly on the wind. Loire's legs were suddenly too weak to support her. She sat down hard. "It's him!"

"Who?"

"Dominique. He's come after me."

Ida whooped like a Kentucky flatboatman. "Didn't I tell you that man love you?"

Loire caught sight of a tall, sun-bronzed figure striding up the deck to the forecastle. He looked like a Viking, shirtless and bareheaded, clad in faded cottonade breeches and a brown leather vest. His only weapon was a straight, single-edged hanger in the baldric crossed over his chest.

Across a hundred feet of deep water, Dominique Youx's dark brown–eyed gaze caressed her. Loire trembled, her heart hammering so violently that her chest hurt. She had to force herself to breathe.

His ship wound deliberately about and scraped the brigantine's hull. Grappling hooks snaked out to pinion the smaller vessel. Because the schooner was twice the length of the *Hopscotch*, its bulwarks towered many feet above Loire's head.

"Boarders, away!" Dominique cried.

Instantly a score of half-naked savages swung into the brigantine and forced the crew to their knees. Dominique Youx remained on his ship, his hands braced on the forecastle rail, his eyes boring into Loire's.

His arrogance infuriated her, renewing her strength to resist. She rose to her feet. "So, pirate, you've made another conquest. Will you throw the men overboard and rape the female passengers, or will you merely set us adrift without food and water?"

Mirth crinkled the corners of his eyes. He bowed gallantly and said, "The choice is my lady's, of course. Which would she prefer?"

"I would prefer you to order your sea scum off my vessel, Captain Youx, and disappear into a maelstrom."

"Such a bloodthirsty little ship's mistress you are, Smokeflower! No one would guess that within that winsome breast beats the heart of Blackbeard."

Loire didn't deign to reply. With one hand holding the rail, she stumbled through the wreckage to the stern. Out of the corner of her eye she saw him parallel her course along the deck of his schooner.

Having pushed her way through the pirates, Loire glared down at the mate kneeling with the other crew members. "Where is Captain Defromage?"

"Me, I have not seen him, mademoiselle."

"A fine thing, to lose the captain at such a time as this! Has he jumped overboard, then?"

"He is not the kind to do that."

"No, I suppose he is too cowardly for suicide."

"Cowardly, Mademoiselle Chartier? Hardly!"

Alain Defromage emerged from the companionway hatch with a musket in one hand and the pistol he'd purloined from Loire in the other. Before the pirates could react, he pointed the weapons at Dominique aboard the schooner.

"Unless you want to see your damned captain dead, you'll get off my brigantine, you filthy cutthroats!"

An angry growl arose from the crew. Loire looked from Defromage to Youx, who braced his palms on the rail and smiled crookedly.

"Get off my ship, I say!" Alain gestured with the pistol. "Tell your men to get off my ship this instant, you thieving scoundrel!"

"Aye, lads, get off the ship," Dominique said softly. "Doff the grappling hooks and watch her sink."

"She will not sink!" Alain cocked the pistol.

"She is listing, my friend," the quiet voice continued. "The British gored her below the waterline. Her pumps cannot keep out the sea."

"Get off my ship!"

"*Oui*, let us stand off her bows a mile or two," Dominique told his pirates, "and watch the British double back to finish her off."

"They are gone!"

"They lie in wait for nightfall, like wolves," Dominique said.

"You God-cursed pirate, I'll shoot you where you stand, so help me!"

"You cannot shoot him!" Loire said. "He has only a sword!"

"Shut up, woman! The whoreson stole one ship from me, he shall not steal another!"

"I have no intention of stealing your little brigantine," Youx said.

Loire glared up at Dominique. "What are your intentions, then?"

"My crew will rig new pumps in your bilges, and man

them. I will escort your *Hopscotch* to Isle Châteauroux."

Her heart leapt. This was not the act of a pirate! With an effort she controlled her expression. Dominique Youx had already proven he could not be trusted. "My father will have you hanged for piracy, monsieur, when he learns what you did to his barque."

"It is a chance I am willing to take, mademoiselle, to assure your safety."

"I will not allow it!" Alain cried.

"You have no choice, my friend," Dominique Youx said, his hard gaze alighting on him once more.

Muttering an obscenity, Alain Defromage dropped to one knee, his forefinger tightening on the musket trigger.

Loire smashed her fist down on the barrel just as it went off. The ball slammed harmlessly into the schooner's hull inches below Dominique's feet.

Pushing Loire aside, Alain raised his pistol. Dominique's men drew their weapons to shoot him down. Loire stood directly in their line of fire.

"Don't shoot! You'll kill her!" Dominique quickly grabbed a halyard and swung down into the brigantine between his men and the woman. Defromage fired.

The ball slammed into Dominique's shoulder with the force of a sledgehammer, tearing him off the halyard. He crashed into Alain, hurling him across the deck. Dominique landed on his feet, clutching his shoulder as he leaned against the mainmast for support. His crew rushed at Defromage.

"Do not hurt the captain," Dominique said. "Lock him in a cabin and see that he doesn't get his hands on another gun. Wait, he's got something that belongs to me."

He strode over to Defromage and shoved his hand

into the captain's breast pocket. Soon he discovered the miniature portrait, brought it out, and thrust it into his belt. He shouted at the crew of the *Hopscotch*, "Unless you want to sink, you'll get busy and tend your damned ship."

Dominique waited until his men had dragged Defromage into the hold before turning to Loire. She was as pale as death.

"Are you all right, Loire?"

"You—you must have your shoulder seen to. It is a terrible wound."

"There is no pain." It was true. The pain would come later, he knew. "You are a very brave woman, Smokeflower. There are few people who would have risked their lives for me as you did."

She didn't wish to hear such things or see that peculiar light in his eye—the tender light she had seen during their lovemaking.

"I would never hurt you, *chérie*. Never," he added.

She almost came into his arms then, almost cried against the shelter of his wide chest and whispered that she couldn't bear to lose him.

But she forced herself to stand still. His lies had already hurt her more profoundly than anything she had ever experienced. She could never forget the nightmare scenario of her dream prince changed into a pirate in the very act of kneeling at the altar. How could she forgive him after such a brutal deception? God help her, she had not the strength to forgive.

Slowly, deliberately, she turned her back and said in the coldest voice she could muster, "Ida will tend your injury, Captain, if you haven't a ship's surgeon."

"I do not sail without a surgeon, Loire. It would be foolish for one of my . . . profession."

"*Oui*, that I can believe!" she said. "There is always much work for a surgeon on a pirate's ship!"

"It seems you want to hate me."

"Of course I do! You've done nothing but steal from my family and deceive me."

"*Par Dieu*, it was cruel fate that blew your father's barque into my path. Ever since meeting you I've tried to repair the damage."

"You've only caused more damage, Captain Youx."

"It was not my intent. Can you not see that a man can change, that love can change him?"

"You know nothing of love, and neither, it seems, do I."

He grimaced as pain lanced his shoulder. "Loire Chartier, you shall not forever be so unforgiving."

She tossed her head and glared out to sea.

"Damn it," Dominique said quietly. He turned to the brigantine's mate. "See to the pumps. Let us get under way before night falls and the British sloop reports our position. Bring the lady and her companion aboard the *Dragon*."

"We will not come aboard your ship!" Loire snapped.

"But you will. Your tub is in danger of sinking."

"I would rather sink than be your guest!"

A ghost of a smile touched Dominique's lips. "Either you come aboard of your own free will or I will have you carried aboard."

"Damn you, Dominique!"

"You are not the first to voice such a sentiment. I have many enemies, and few friends."

"Count me among the former!"

Dominique dropped his hand from his bleeding shoulder and caught her wrist before she could spin away. "You are not my enemy, Smokeflower. No matter what you think now, you will never be."

For a long moment she gazed up at him, her treacherous heart wanting to believe him. And why shouldn't she? No matter what he had been in the past, he could change. He'd tried to make amends for his misdeeds . . . should she not try to forgive?

Once a pirate, always a pirate, her father used to say. *Once stealing gets in the blood, there is nothing a man can do to get rid of it. He'll be a liar and a thief till the day he dies, Loire, and no merchant will be safe from him . . . .*

She snatched her arm away and used her skirt to scrub his blood from her wrist. "We will always be enemies, Monsieur Youx. As long as you make your living in the fashion you do, there will be no harmony between us."

"And if I choose another way of making a living?"

"You no longer have a choice."

"There are always choices, Smokeflower. Now, if you will accompany me to the *Dragon?*"

"Do I have a choice?" she asked, mocking him.

"No. Not this time."

14

Dominique's cabin in the stern belowdecks looked like the great room of a mansion. Lanterns rocked from hooks in the beams, and moonlight streamed through the long row of open square windows in the stern bulkhead. The lighting imparted a rich glow to the dark mahogany paneling and brass fixtures.

Dominique rested on a stack of pillows in a wide bed with high, fluted posts. His left shoulder was swathed in white bandages. In a glass tumbler beside the bed, the lead ball the surgeon had removed from his shoulder tinkled with every roll of the ship.

He was lucky. The bone had not been shattered, and there was little damage to the muscle. He supposed that Defromage had used wet powder. As he reached for a bottle of whiskey on the bedside table, a soft rap sounded on the door.

"Come!"

The door opened slowly, and Loire peered around the edge.

"Please come in, mademoiselle. I was hoping for a visit."

She closed the door behind her, crossed the room, and sat on the chair beside the bed.

"I trust the mate has made you comfortable?" he asked.

"He gave Ida and me his cabin," she said.

"I will give you this one tomorrow."

"I don't want your cabin, monsieur."

"What *do* you want, Loire?"

"You know what I want."

"We play at words, I fear."

"Then let me spell them out. I want to go home to my father. I want you to sail away and never bother me again."

Dominique dropped his gaze over her throat and breasts. He saw her tremble, fancied he could feel her temperature rise.

"You want neither of those things," he said. "You want me to take you back to the cathedral and finish what I started."

"You are presumptuous," she said. "Nothing would humiliate me more than marrying a pirate! I thank God that in His good mercy He saved me from such a fate."

Dominique looked directly at her, his dark eyes smoldering. "I read no trace of gratitude in your heart, Loire. There is only grief in your soul."

"You know nothing of what I feel, Dominique Youx, nor do you care!"

"You surely do not believe such a thing."

"I believe it, yes, I believe it! You care nothing for me!"

"You drink the gall of bitterness and wrap yourself tightly in the mantle of offense."

"I do not!"

"Have I betrayed you?"

Loire stood and walked to the wide, transom-shaped porthole, where she glared out at the night. "You made me a fool in the eyes of all New Orleans."

Dominique sat up on the side of the bed. "That was your pride, mademoiselle, nothing else."

"My pride? Ha! I have no pride!"

"You are consumed by it."

"You see the reflection of your own!"

"I see the woman I love."

Loire stiffened. *Dieu,* why had she come here, when she'd known they would only argue? He seemed to think it his mission to force her into flights of introspection.

"Look at me, Loire."

His deep voice sent a shiver up her spine. She closed her eyes and folded her arms tightly under her breasts.

"Look at me."

She did not budge. "You may go to hell at your convenience, monsieur, and let the devil look at you."

He did not reply, but she heard only a slight creak of the ropes under the mattress. An instant later she felt his breath brush her shoulders. She whirled around.

Dominique Youx was naked except for a loincloth, his darkly tanned limbs gleaming in the lantern light. A small circle of blood stained his bandage. Loire stepped back against the porthole, feeling the cool sea breeze on her spine and the man's hot breath on her breasts.

"I meant what I said, Captain!"

"I have been in hell since the day you left me, Loire." He moved so close to her that she had to tilt back her head to see his face. "Every day, every night, the devil has looked at me, and laughed."

"You're being punished for your sins, then!"

"It is no sin to love you, Loire. I will not be punished for that."

Loire could retreat no farther, could do nothing but stare up at him with wild, angry eyes. She flinched when his naked chest grazed her breasts and he raised his right hand to her cheek. His eyes burned into her soul, mesmerizing, probing, fondling her.

"You know that I love you," he said. "There is nothing I would not do to make you feel it in your heart. Perhaps I was wrong to take your father's barque—"

"Of course you were wrong! There is no defense for what you did!"

"He flew the Spanish flag, Loire." He dropped his hand and took half a step back.

"Aye, to keep the British patrols away. They are allies, you know. You would use such a ruse, too, in his place."

Dominique Youx shook his head impatiently. "Privateering is the way I make my living," he said. "I know the risks, and I take them. Your father is a businessman. He knows the risks, and, like me, he takes them."

"You ruined his business!"

"I do not think so. The Americans have a saying: 'Don't put all your eggs in one basket.' Your father, I am sure, was too smart to have done such a thing. I doubt that the little barque I captured contained his entire treasure."

Loire returned to the attack. "I suppose you thought

it was a good joke, bringing his tobacco to the mercantile, pretending to be magnanimous!"

Sighing, he walked to the bed and sat down. "A drink, Loire?" he asked, uncorking the whiskey bottle.

"No, thank you."

He took a swallow and placed the bottle firmly in the small cradle fastened to the table—a necessary precaution in the rolling ship.

"Returning the tobacco was no joke. It belonged to you, so I sent it back. In my storehouse are wools and Peruvian silver that also belong to you."

"I suppose you sold the Jamaican slaves?"

"Would you approve if I said yes, and handed over the money?"

"Do you take me for a slaver?"

"Hardly. I took the slaves to Grand Terre."

"Jean Laffite's stronghold! How could you? I suppose you sold them at one of his auctions!"

"Calm yourself. I sold no one. Most decided to work aboard my fleet—as free men. Others took jobs on my cattle ranch in Acadia. The people who wish to return home may do so when they have earned sufficient money for the passage."

"You've thought of everything, it seems."

Dominique swallowed another mouthful of whiskey and lay back on the pillows. "Not everything, *chérie,*" he said wearily. "It seems I have not yet thought of a way to win back your love."

"You should not try."

"I will eternally try. I . . . ." His voice trailed off, and he closed his eyes.

Loire waited for him to speak again. When he did not, she tiptoed over to the bed and looked down at him. Tension lined his face, and there was a catch in his breathing. She decided he must be in pain.

She touched his brow, found it dry and warm. With infinite care she lifted the bandage away from his shoulder enough to see his wound: there were powder marks on his skin, and serous fluid oozed around two catgut sutures. She hoped it wouldn't turn septic.

He looked so innocent, so vulnerable. Just as he had the night he swallowed poisoned wine and collapsed at the theater. Only now he had a bullet graze along one cheek and a torn shoulder—both the result of defending her. Heaving a sigh that was half exasperation, half anxiety, she turned down the lamps and sat on the chair beside his bed.

Dominique stirred in his sleep and turned his face toward her, a faint smile curving his lips. He breathed deeply now, anesthetized by the whiskey. Loire knew she shouldn't, but she couldn't help laying her hand on his bare forearm. His muscles felt firm, unyielding under her fingertips, and deliciously warm.

"Captain Dominique Youx," she whispered, "how many nights must I sit beside you, hoping you won't die?"

"Promise to sit beside me every night," he said, opening his eyes, "and I'll never die."

She removed her hand. "You were awake the whole time!"

"Only after I felt your touch, Loire."

She stood up. "Good night, Captain Youx."

"It will not be a good night, if you go."

"It will be terrible, if I stay. Good night." She walked across the slanting deck to the door, looked back at him, and left.

Dominique reached for the bottle, then set it back

on the table without drinking. He got out of bed,
pulled on a pair of breeches, and fastened his belt
buckle with one hand. Donning a shirt would hurt
too much, so he left without it. He walked down the
companionway to Loire's door, paused, then walked
on.

On the other side of the door, Loire stood in the
darkness, listening to his footsteps recede. Breathing a
soft, disappointed sigh, she slipped off her dress and
climbed onto the top bunk. She lay awake a long time,
listening to Ida's snores, wishing she had opened the
door.

At daybreak Loire went on deck. Streaks of light
radiated from the rim of the ocean to color the *Dragon*'s
huge triangular sails a deeper shade of scarlet. The
Hopscotch, an indistinct blur bobbing in the
schooner's wake, gradually brightened until she could
distinguish sailors in the rigging. The brigantine's
lines had been cast off last night, after she'd been
made seaworthy.

Dominique's crew were about their morning routine:
swabbing the decks with seawater after burnishing
them with flat holystones, mending sheets and sail,
polishing the capstan and every piece of brass. While
singing the rollicking chantey "Haul the Bowline," a
gang tightened a halyard with short, quick motions.

"Your captain escaped from the *Hopscotch* during
the night, Loire."

She spun around. Dominique, dressed in breeches
and still shirtless, stood near the mainmast. His eyes
were weary and his face rather pale, but he was smiling
with his usual aplomb.

"How could he have escaped?"

"He took the ship's boat. I must admit, I hadn't credited him with that much resourcefulness."

"Why would he have wanted to escape? He knew he would be set free when we reached Isle Châteauroux." Suddenly her face paled. "You didn't—you didn't—"

"Didn't what? Feed him to the sharks? Shoot him? Dangle him from the yardarm?" He could tell by her expression that he'd hit the mark. "No, Loire. I am not so inhuman as all that."

"I didn't say you were inhuman."

"Just brutish, crude, and unacceptable."

"I didn't say that, either!"

He bowed. "Forgive my presumption, mademoiselle."

"Did Alain take food and water with him?" she asked, still concerned.

She misinterpreted his sudden look of jealousy as indifference. Grabbing his wrist, she said, "He'll die out there without water. We should try to find him!"

"He stole enough food and water to last him several days. We don't know which direction he went, anyway."

"Your men must have been asleep at their watches, to allow him to run off."

"Perhaps, although I think it more likely that your crew helped him escape."

Checked, Loire folded her arms and glared astern at the *Hopscotch.* The brigantine was sailing on a fairly even keel, and her broken mast had been jury-rigged with a shorter one. As the vessel rode to the top of a swell she saw a ragged hole low in the hull, patched with tarred leather.

"That patch won't hold if we run into a storm," she said.

Dominique looked at the cloudless sky and said nothing.

"Or if we're pursued by another Britisher," she added.

"You are very optimistic, *non?* Is this your usual manner in the morning?"

Loire showed her teeth in a contemptuous smile. "That's something you won't find out, monsieur."

"That sounded suspiciously like a challenge."

"Ha!"

"Ha yourself, with gravy on it!" he said, imitating a Kentucky drawl.

Loire couldn't suppress a smile. Despite her steadfast attempts to hold a grudge, Dominique still had the power to charm her.

"How is your shoulder?" she asked, feeling safer with a more serious topic.

Dominique moved his arm around, grimacing a little. "Much better, *merci*. The stupid captain should have loaded his pistol with more powder. The ball barely had a running start."

Loire's jaw tensed. "*I* loaded that pistol, monsieur."

Dominique laughed. "You did? I might have known! Renato Beluche said you knew nothing of guns."

"I do know about guns!"

"That is why you keep a Kentucky long rifle behind the shop door, loaded and primed, but without a flint, eh?"

Loire kicked his shin with the point of her shoe. "You odious pirate!"

He laughed again. "Were I as odious as you believe, I would kiss you, and remove all doubt."

"Keep your hands to yourself!"

"As you wish." He leaned against the mast and gazed

skyward. "Recognize that man up there?"

Loire seized a halyard and looked up. "Which one?"

"The one on watch."

"No. Should I?"

"Probably."

"You're the only pirate I recognize, monsieur," she said.

"I must introduce you around, I see."

"This isn't a society ball. Your companions can go forever nameless, for I'll never see them again after this voyage, I sincerely hope."

Dominique changed the subject. "I'd like you to breakfast with me."

"I'll eat in my cabin with Ida."

"Bring her with you."

Loire hesitated, wanting yet not wanting to refuse. Finally she nodded her head. "All right. But I'll not discuss anything personal with you."

Dominique raised his right hand. "We will discuss nothing but this hellish Caribbean climate."

She shot him a suspicious glance but said mildly enough, "Give me ten minutes. I'll have to wake up Ida."

Twenty minutes later, a cabin boy admitted the two women to Dominique's quarters. A humid tropical breeze drifted through the rectangular portholes, ruffling Loire's white linen dress. A meal of fruit, wine, and broiled mackerel had been laid on an ebony table bolted to the deck.

"Now ain't this pretty?" Ida said. She lifted the lid off a tureen and sniffed. "Mmm, smells good!"

Dominique rose from his chair. His clean white shirt was open at the throat, the long sleeves gathered at the cuffs. Over it he wore a black silk vest and a sword, which hung over his right shoulder by the baldric.

"Welcome, ladies," he said, bowing. He touched his wounded shoulder briefly as he straightened. "Please sit down."

Before he could assist her, Loire seated herself at the far end of the table. He moved past her to help Ida with her chair.

"It ain't right, Mistah Youx," Ida said, twisting her hands together. "Coloreds don't sit down with gentle-mens."

"Nonsense. You're my guest. New Orleans conventions mean nothing aboard my ship. Now, please, let's get started before the fish gets cold."

Ida sat down reluctantly. Dominique took a chair opposite Loire.

"Lemme do that, Mistah Youx," Ida said as he began to serve the food.

"No need, madame," he said, shoveling a portion of fish and a large section of omelet onto her plate. He filled Loire's plate, then his own, and settled down to eat.

Smiling, Ida applied herself to breakfast. Her smile changed to a frown when she noticed Loire sulking over her plate.

"Eat them eggs before you turns into a cane pole!"

"I'm not hungry. They're bound to be rotten, any-way."

"The cook keeps laying hens belowdecks, *chérie,*" Dominique said. "But perhaps you would rather start with the mackerel? Tim caught it this morning and sent it with his compliments."

"Tim?"

Dominique raised his brows innocently and took an orange. "*Oui.* I pointed him out to you this morning,

Loire, but you failed to recognize him on the mast-head."

"That was *our* Tim?"

"He is no one's Tim. He is a free man. Ah, here he is now."

The cabin boy opened the door to admit the young black man. Tim, a red bandanna wound around his head, was dressed in a striped shirt and bleached cottonade pantaloons, and he carried a cutlass and pistol in his belt.

"Tim!" Ida overturned her wineglass in her haste to leave the table. She swept him up in a mighty embrace, asking one question after another. Tim assured her that he was free and that Mazy knew about it. Ida walked outside with him.

Loire gazed across the table at Dominique, who smiled and refilled her glass. "You are pleased, Smokeflower?"

"Very." Being alone with him made her uneasy, especially in light of the debt of gratitude she now owed him. She pushed her omelet around on her plate and said petulantly, "I don't know how you got him away from Villeré, unless you stole him."

"I didn't steal him."

"Then how? I asked Gabriel to sell him three times, and he just laughed!" She dropped her fork next to her plate. "I suppose he spurned to do business with a woman, the lout!"

"Perhaps. These Creoles are stubborn rascals, I've learned. They don't believe women have a head for business."

"I know that. It's insulting!"

"Would it lessen your outrage to know I do not share their view?"

"Don't patronize me, monsieur. I'm well aware of what you're trying to do."

"And what is that, exactly?"

Color bloomed in her cheeks. She chopped her omelet to pieces with her fork and said, "You're trying to keep me from telling Papa about the barque."

Dominique's handsome face lit up. He tugged at the streak of gray hair over his temple. "You cannot be serious!"

"Oh, but I am. Now that Alain is gone, you have only me to worry about. You think that by freeing Tim and playing on my sensibilities, you can keep me silent. You are grossly mistaken."

"Merde!" he said, chuckling. "I must now fear the wrath of a soft little merchant!"

"Papa is not a soft little merchant! He owns an entire island."

"Again, I am moved to terror."

Loire pushed away her plate and folded her arms. "The indomitable Red Dragon, is it?"

He shrugged his good shoulder. "Some have called me that."

"Have they called you conceited, too?"

"More often than not. My mother neglected to teach me humility."

"Maybe my father can do what your mother failed to."

"He is welcome to try, Smokeflower."

"Stop calling me that!"

"As you wish, though it will be difficult. The name rolls so smoothly off my tongue."

Loire left the table, intending to go look out the porthole. The ship yawed, forcing her to catch a post as she slid past the bed.

Dominique was beside her instantly, one hand under her elbow. She looked up at him. "I would not have fallen."

"I suppose not. You are very independent."

"Independent enough to make my way around without your help, monsieur."

Still, she did not shrug out of his grasp. Her arm tingled where his fingers touched it. She wanted him to touch her in other places, to kiss her. The bed loomed in the periphery of her vision.

Finally she let go of the post and crossed quickly to the window to stare out at the green swells. Fat white clouds sat on the horizon, promising rain. She wished it would rain, or storm even. Anything to draw Dominique's attention back to the ship, away from her. Anything to distract *her* attention from *him*.

"How did you persuade Gabriel to let Tim go?" she asked, hardly aware that she'd spoken.

"With a huge sum of money."

"I offered him a huge sum, all that Ida, St. John, and I could scrape together!"

"I paid him more."

"Money, again!"

"Money would not have been enough. I had to threaten to cut him off from Barataria."

"So?"

He sat down on the bed, massaging his wounded shoulder. "His father's plantation is drained by a stream leading to Bayou Bienvenue. Clog the bayou, and the Villeré plantation is cut off from the black market, from the blockade runners who channel its goods to Europe and South America."

Loire threw up her hands. "So, yet another upstanding businessman in league with pirates discovers himself their hostage!"

"Tim seemed to think the good outweighed the bad."

"In his case, yes."

"The Villerés would do anything to keep the bayou open. I merely played on their weakness."

"You are a master of that."

Dominique sighed. "Why do you play this game of hating me, Loire?"

"It's not a game, and I don't hate you."

"Ah."

"I detest, loathe, and despise you."

"So you say. Your body says differently."

"You are dreaming, monsieur. I have no reason to like you."

"I do not believe you are as fickle as you claim. You are angry, yes, but anger alone is not sufficient to banish your love. Were it not for Defromage's interference, you would be my wife at this moment."

"I thank heaven for sparing me!"

"Spite does not become you."

"And begging does not become *you*. In another moment I will find you kneeling at my feet, begging me to take you back."

"I would never win you, were I to resort to such a tactic," he said. "You are not a woman who enjoys men who act like jellyfish."

"I don't like barracudas, either, monsieur."

He grinned. "It is a good thing that I am neither."

"Your sharp teeth say otherwise." She turned to look out the porthole. "I should thank you for freeing Tim."

"The pleasure was mine."

"Although it appears he has found slavery of another sort aboard this ship."

"Slavery? He chose to work for me."

"Just as Gabriel chose to sell him to you. Tim had no choice."

Dominique's brows drew together. "Once more you paint the worst possible scenario."

She smiled to herself.

"I am beginning to share the Creoles' sentiment. Women have no head for business, or any understanding of men."

"What?"

"You obviously understand nothing of a man's need to think well of himself. Do you think that because Tim was a slave he has no pride, no desire to work of his own accord, to pay off his debts? Is he not a man in your eyes?"

"Of course he is! How dare you talk to me like that? Of course he is!"

"Then respect his decision. I placed him under no obligation, yet he has chosen to pay me back by working for me."

"It seems I owe you an apology."

"It seems so, but you are under no obligation, either."

"I'll say it anyway. I'm sorry."

"Accepted, forgiven. Do you want your breakfast now?"

Loire blinked. Every time she thought she had the upper hand, he had to say something to throw her off balance. "You are a gentleman pirate, Dominique Youx," she said. "Why?"

A corner of his mouth tightened. "That would take a long time to explain."

She left the porthole and sank down on a chair. "What are you doing for the next couple of hours?"

He stared back at her, obviously suspicious.

"Come, Captain, you've probed into my past often enough. Is it not time to share some of your own?" Her heart thumped, excited by his proximity. He was handsome always, but the solemnness of his expression at this moment made her want to touch him. She could see a pulse throbbing in his throat as his chest rose and fell.

"Would it lessen my stature in your eyes," he asked at length, "if I told you I was a bastard?"

She tried to keep the surprise from her voice. "Did you not tell me that one cannot help one's genealogy?"

He leaned forward and braced his forearms on his thighs. Loire moved back in her chair slightly, keeping her distance.

"Perhaps you will not feel so generously inclined, when I tell you who I am."

Her heart began to beat faster. She wished she weren't sitting quite so near him; he had merely to move his hand to touch her knee.

Dominique remained silent for several moments, watching her with a concentration that discomfited her. His eyes seemed to slowly take fire as he looked into hers. A muscle jumped in his cheek as he clenched his jaw. He appeared to be losing the battle against some inner demon.

"God help me, it's no use," he said in a voice Loire could scarcely recognize.

She leaned closer and touched his wrist. "What is it?" she whispered. "Tell me."

Instead of replying, he grasped her shoulders and pulled her halfway onto his lap. Capturing her jaw in his right hand, he stared down at her with a terrible intensity. In her consternation, she did not try to struggle.

"Dominique, what is this thing that tears at you?"

"Shall I make your hatred for me complete, then?" he asked harshly. "All right, I'll tell you. I am Alexandre Frédéric Laffite. Jean and Pierre Laffite's older brother."

15

She knew she should be angry that he had deceived her yet again. Instead she felt bewildered, even sympathetic. She had rarely seen such pain in the face of another human being.

"You're the brother of those pirates?" she asked softly.

"*Oui.* The elder brother . . . and the bad example. I taught them the art of piracy. *I* set up the Baratarian trade, then turned its administration over to Jean."

"*You* set it up? Then you pretend to be someone else out of fear of the law?"

He drew a deep breath as he sought to regain his composure. "I do not fear the law, and I do not pretend," he said. "Dominique Youx is who I am. I made the name; I made the man. Alexandre Laffite ceased to exist when the person I thought was my father discovered that my mother had cuckolded him."

"And Jean and Pierre?"

"Are his true sons. My *half* brothers."

Some of the fire left his eyes. He released her chin, but instead of letting her go, he tightened his arms around her and dropped his face to her shoulder. He went very still.

The sorrow she sensed in him made her want to give him comfort. She lifted her fingertips to his cheek. He turned his head slightly, and for an instant she felt his lips brush her hand. The sensation sent little currents of heat into her arm.

"Who was your real father, Dominique?"

He was silent for so long that she thought he would not answer, but at last he said, "I never learned his name. He was one of King Louis Seize's personal guards. My mother fell in love with him one summer, at court." He raised his head to look at her. "I was the result."

Despite the gravity of his words, Loire could not stifle a shiver as she met his gaze. His mouth was so very near hers, and the warmth of his arms made her want to close the gap. It took all her willpower to drop her hand from his cheek, to indicate by stiffening her body that she wanted him to release her. With a sigh he opened his arms, allowing her to move off his lap to the chair.

Loire was almost sorry he'd let her go. The urge to return to his arms boiled up inside her, and she had to catch the edge of her seat to remain in place. Her reaction to him worried her.

She made herself ask, "And when Monsieur Laffite found out you weren't his son, he disowned you?"

"*Oui.*"

"How old were you?"

"Sixteen."

"How did he find out?"

"My mother told him."

"But why, after so many years?"

"Guilt, in part."

"And did the admission appease her conscience?"

"You are full of questions," he said testily.

"You can always put me aboard the *Hopscotch* if you dislike answering them," she said with a touch of rancor.

"I do not dislike answering *that* much, Loire." He closed his eyes for a moment, as if looking into the past. "My father was a British soldier—a Scot, actually. He served the king before Britain became our enemy, when it was common for foreign mercenaries to serve our country."

Loire anticipated his next words when she said, "That changed after the Revolution."

"*Oui.* With the Revolution came hatred for everything British. My poor mother was swept up in the nationalistic fever, I suppose. Her Scot was long gone, but she saw her household tainted with foreign blood." He drew another sigh. "Under French law, the eldest son inherits the entire fortune. Her sense of honor couldn't stand that, and she finally admitted the truth to my father."

"What a twisted sort of honor," Loire said.

"You have to think of it in terms of how things were then. She wanted to assure her legitimate sons their rightful inheritance."

"At such terrible cost to you? I cannot understand such coldness in a mother."

"She suffered many sorrows, Loire. War taught her to hate not only the British, but the Spanish. From there it was only a small step to hating anyone who stood in the way of her duty to France."

"But her own son . . . incomprehensible." She wanted to touch him again in order to give comfort but feared both her reaction and his. It would be so easy to lie back on the bed and lose herself in his arms. "I cannot imagine that she experienced a day of peace, after losing you."

His eyes sparked. She winced, realizing that she had just revealed her own feelings for him. Desperately she added, "You said you taught Jean and Pierre the pirate trade, and even turned your business over to them. Why, after what had happened?"

"It is a long tale. For now, it will suffice to say that they wasted their inheritance without providing for the younger children. I did not wish to see my other half brothers and sisters starve."

A pirate with ideals? What a paradox he was.

He smiled bleakly. "Jean, especially, took to piracy as readily as a duck takes to water. Revenge makes a fine teacher."

"This was your revenge? To turn them to crime?"

He shook his head. "No. I speak of Monsieur Laffite's revenge. Our family once had an estate in northern Spain. The government took it, killed Grandfather, and drove us out. Laffite took us to Port-au-Prince, where Jean was born. He made very sure to indoctrinate us against Spain, and against anyone he saw as an enemy. He lived for vengeance. His bitterness ruined my mother."

"How sad."

"*Oui*, and how sad for Spain. My brothers and I have obeyed Laffite's wish." His voice hardened. "Together we have sunk thousands of tons of shipping."

"And have you found satisfaction in piracy, Dominique Youx?" Loire asked. "Have you regained the pride you lost when Laffite cast you out?"

Anger and pain battled for dominance in his eyes. He stood up to go. "Perhaps I will tell you sometime, when you are not so determined to sit in the judgment seat."

Loire was surprised to find herself feeling contrite. She reached out to grasp his wrist. His muscles were tense, angry. "Please, I didn't mean to offend."

"You have not. Some things are difficult to discuss. I must go and see to the schooner now."

He gently pulled away from her and strode out of the cabin, ducking his head under the lintel. Loire sat there for a long time, looking at the door he had closed solidly behind him.

Early that evening, the *Dragon* slid past three brigs anchored in Isle Châteauroux's small harbor and made fast to a weatherbeaten dock. The brigs appeared to have been there for a very long time: their anchor chains were rusty, barnacles had formed black reefs along the beams, and their standing riggings looked like shredded old cobwebs.

The *Hopscotch* limped into port behind the schooner and bumped into the dock, every timber groaning. From belowdecks came the ratchety clank of bilge pumps.

Loire stood beside Dominique at the *Dragon*'s wheel, studying the lemony white shore, the coconut palms rattling in the warm wind. Smoke drifted from holes in the roofs of the shacks huddled near the dock.

About a hundred people were on the beach, talking excitedly and waving at the ships. Most were black slaves and others lighter-skinned mulattos. Several white men watched them from horseback.

"There are tobacco fields just over the rise, behind the shantytown," Loire told Dominique.

"And your father's house?"

"A mile inland, almost in the center of the island. As you can see, Châteauroux isn't very big."

"*Oui*, a narrow spit, only. It must be unpleasant during a storm."

"You won't be here long enough to experience one."

"I suppose not." Dominique left her then, to see to his ship. He was dressed as he had been at breakfast, only he'd added a black tricorn hat to shade his eyes from the sun and a long dragoon pistol at his belt.

He was ordering the *Hopscotch* unloaded when a carriage topped the rise and spun down the sandy road, with a man in a white suit and Panama hat at the reins. Even from a distance, Dominique could see a thick cigar protruding below his enormous black mustache.

After dragging the horse to a halt, the man whipped his hat off his sweaty black hair and leaped off the seat to stride toward the dock. Standing just over five feet tall, he had a round paunch that looked incongruous balanced on his straight, thin legs.

Loire immediately ran down the dock into his arms. Dominique smiled, watching her lift Etienne Chartier an inch or two off the ground. Then he left the ship to meet the master of Isle Châteauroux.

Perched beside his daughter on the driver's seat, Etienne talked almost all the way to his château, bemoaning Napoleon's banishment, swearing to aid the popular movement to return him to power. He barely listened to Loire's account of the British attack on the *Hopscotch*.

Sitting alone in the back of the carriage, Dominique listened to their one-sided conversation. His host's cigar smoke trickled over the seat into his nostrils, and the lowering rays of the sun bathed him with comfortable warmth. The road passed straight and level between verdant green tobacco fields that gave off a sweet, resiny scent. Perspiring slaves bowed as the master drove by.

Etienne Chartier's château was a long white structure on tall stilts skirted by a verandah. Jalousied windows stretched from floor to ceiling. Palms leaned over the roof at crazy angles, and a profusion of wild-flowers grew out of the sandy soil around the porch. Five long-eared beagles lay under the porch, too lazy to offer more than perfunctory woofs when the carriage rolled into the yard.

Etienne flung the reins to a black footman. Without waiting for Dominique or his daughter to climb down, he skipped up the verandah steps into the house.

Dominique took stock of a French flag snapping from a tall pole in the front yard. Around its base, roses overflowed several stone urns bearing the fleur-de-lis. A large brass bust of Napoleon commanded a granite pedestal ten feet from the flagpole.

"You must excuse Papa," Loire said, looking at the shrine. "He is a bit touched on the subject of Napoleon."

"Many of us have a certain favorite subject that dis-arrays our faculties, *chérie.*" His eyes crinkled at the corners as he looked down at her.

She pulled her arm out of his grasp. "Many of us would do better selecting another subject, monsieur, and regaining our sanity."

"It is too late for that, Loire."

She knew what he was implying, and the desire in his expression disturbed her. There was no future for them. Tomorrow, if she had anything to say about it, he would get back on his schooner and sail away.

"I do not believe you feel as coldly toward me as you pretend," he said.

"You are hoping to keep me from telling Papa that you stole his barque."

"You may tell him what you wish."

"Ha! He'll have you thrown into a sand pit."

"Perhaps. Look, there is someone waving at you from the porch. Shall we go in?"

A statuesque woman in a red-and-blue dress was standing on the verandah with the household staff behind her. Loire started up the path.

"Mademoiselle Chartier! How good to see you!" the woman said. She had luxuriant dark hair, brown eyes, and creamy, flawless skin. The demure cut of her gown could not disguise her lush figure. She looked two or three years older than Loire.

"Have we met, madame?" Loire asked, walking up the steps. "Perhaps in New Orleans?"

Etienne came out of the house and passed an arm around her waist, pulling her against him. She was three inches taller than he, though from the look of adoration on her face one might have thought him a knight on horseback. Loire stopped, with one hand on the verandah rail and Dominique behind her.

"Loire, Captain Youx, come into the house," Etienne said, gesturing with his cigar. "My Fabian has cooked the most wonderful supper, haven't you, angel?"

She bent her head to receive his kiss on her cheek, smiling at him. "It is nothing," she said. "Some fish, a few cucumbers. Tomorrow the fare will be better."

"Papa," Loire said, "who is this?"

He looked surprised. "Why, Fabian is my mistress, of course."

The women looked at each other. Unaware of the strain, Etienne led the way into the house, humming a march.

"Calm yourself, Loire," Dominique said quietly. He swept off his tricorn and tossed it to a slave before taking her arm. "Be sure to think before you speak."

"I don't need the advice of a pirate." Nevertheless, she let him escort her into the house.

The château was decorated in grand style. Slender gilt chairs and tables stood on thick Persian carpets; crystal chandeliers sparkled on the ceilings. Oil portraits and silk tapestries hung on walls of pink and mustard stucco. Several slave children stood beside the chairs, stirring the humid air with egrets' and swans' wings.

Before they could be seated for dinner, Etienne bade them turn and look out the window. A group of slaves in ragged French army uniforms marched up the path to the flagpole, in step with the martial anthem played by a drummer and a flutist. As the last rays of the sun touched the slowly descending flag, Etienne placed his hand over his heart and assumed a rapt expression.

"*Vive l'empereur! Vive France!*" he said, then, "Let's eat!"

Loire sat down across from Fabian at a long gilt table. Etienne Chartier took a seat at its head and gestured Dominique to his left.

Loire frowned at the steaming fish in garlic butter on her plate. Slaves served thin, rolled slices of dried ham imported from France, small potatoes topped with Brie cheese, and marinated cucumbers and sea-weed on smaller plates. Etienne poured white wine all around.

Loire couldn't bear to look at Fabian. How could her father flaunt his mistress before her? She wanted to leave the table.

"Captain Youx," Etienne began, his mustache bouncing as he chewed, "Loire says I've you to thank for saving the *Hopscotch* from that damned British sloop."

"Thanks are not necessary, monsieur."

"How was it that you happened upon her?"

Dominique felt Loire tense beside him. "I did not happen upon her, exactly. We were following the sea lanes out of New Orleans. It is good, I think, for merchant vessels to stay within sight of one another."

"Ah, indeed," Chartier said, nodding his head sagely. "I admire your foresight—it saved me a fortune in grain. You received your wound during the battle?"

"The battle was over before my schooner reached the brigantine. The limeys ran like the poltroons they are, once they caught sight of our guns. My wound was a stupid accident."

Etienne laughed. "I, too, have caused myself many a mishap. One time I discharged the Kentucky long rifle Loire keeps in our store. The ball struck a plow blade and ricocheted back at me. Here, let me show you."

"Really, Papa!" Loire said as he stood up and fumbled to get his galluses off his shoulders.

Fabian echoed her feelings with a soft, "No, no, *mon cher,* it is not proper to always show your scar to strangers."

Ignoring her, Etienne turned around and dropped his trousers enough to reveal a crease running down his left hip.

Dominique burst out laughing. "You are fortunate that it was not your scalp, monsieur."

"At least one does not have to sit on one's scalp," he said, pulling up his pants and slipping his galluses back on. "It was a most painful ordeal. I assured myself that I would not have to endure another accident by removing the flint from the rifle."

At this, Dominique looked at Loire but said nothing.

Chartier turned serious as he settled back onto his seat and picked up his wineglass. "So you are from New Orleans, eh? How are things there?"

"Rather dismal, monsieur."

"Those damned Kaintocks must clear a passage for shipping before we are ruined!"

"Commandant Patterson has his hands tied, I fear. The Americans are so concerned with averting war with Spain that they are afraid to go after the British, thinking a stray Spaniard might get in the way. It is amazing how many French and American merchant-men fly the Spanish flag these days."

Chartier flushed. "I must admit that I am one of them. You disapprove of those tactics?"

"I think it is better to be honest . . . and well armed."

Etienne laughed and slapped his knee. "You may be right, though as the damned Kaintocks say, there is more than one way to pluck a buzzard, *non?*"

"So long as one takes care to stay away from its sharp beak."

"And from carrion-eating privateers," Etienne added. He looked at Loire. "You're paler than coconut milk, child. Fabian, take my daughter to her room."

"I don't need to lie down, Papa."

"Of course you do, after your experience with the

damned Britishers. Off with her now, Fabian! Run quickly."

"I have no intention of leaving this table until I've finished eating," Loire said as Fabian stood up.

Sinking slowly back onto her seat, Fabian looked uncertainly from Loire to Etienne, who had reddened with anger.

Dominique stepped into the breach. "Tell me about your plantation, monsieur. Never have I seen such tall, heavily leafed tobacco."

As her father launched into a discourse on tobacco farming, Loire let her mind wander back to the night when she had lain with Dominique. Her hands began to tremble, until she had to set down her wineglass.

"I think I would like to go to my room now," she said faintly.

Dominique rose and pulled back her chair. For a moment their eyes locked in unspoken understanding, and Loire was sure her father and his mistress would know exactly what their relationship had been. Then she disengaged and left the room, with Fabian following.

What was she to do about Dominique Youx? Try as she might, she could not be impervious to his charms. Despite her anger and hurt, she knew in her heart that she loved him. The thought made the pain even worse.

16

Dominique watched Loire go. Slowly he sank back onto his chair as Etienne Chartier began to describe a tobacco beetle he was finding particularly troublesome. Chartier suddenly broke off, clapping a hand to his forehead.

"What an imbecile I am, keeping you at the table with an empty plate! Let us go out on the verandah and have a smoke."

Five minutes later, ensconced on a padded wicker chair with his long legs crossed on the railing in front of him, Dominique held a thick black cigar between his fingers.

Etienne sat on a chair beside him, cigar smoke wreathing his head, his eyes blissfully closed against the falling curtain of night. Crickets chirped in the flowers while the beagles snored under the verandah.

"This is my own piece of heaven," he said, opening his eyes. "It is all mine. Someday it will be Loire's."

Dominique drew on his cigar. He blew a smoke ring and watched it drift out into the night.

"The man who wins my daughter will be rich indeed."

Dominique tapped ash onto the porch. "Lucky soul."

"*Oui*. It is not every day a man wins a ready-made fortune."

"Winning the fair Loire would be fortune enough, I think."

Etienne looked at him. "Ah-ha! I knew there was something between you! Never have I seen my daughter try so hard to pretend a man did not exist!"

"Is that what she was doing, monsieur?"

"You could not tell, *mon ami?* But surely you are not so inexperienced with women as that!"

"Daily I discover how much I do not know."

"Loire is easy to know," he said. "She is like me."

"In what way, monsieur?"

"Looks, charm, a thirst for life! She does not settle for second best, that one, oh no! Loire, she must have it all, or have nothing." His face became woeful. "That is the reason for her father's distress, my friend."

"Surely a father would have no reason for distress with a daughter like her."

"It is exactly because she is such a daughter that I am distressed! If she were an ugly little sparrow, I could be content knowing she could enjoy no higher calling than that of a shopkeeper. But no! She is lovelier by far than Napoleon's Josephine, and capable, I am sure, of bearing me fine grandsons."

"You make her sound like a Kentucky Thoroughbred. There is more to Loire Bretagne than a capacity to breed well."

Etienne gazed at him shrewdly. "You fly readily to her defense. Tell me, Captain, are you married?"

He could not hide a grimace. "Would that I were."

Etienne threw the stub of his cigar over the railing and drew a fresh one from his jacket. Then he bit off the tip and lit it with a candle. Filling his mouth with pungent smoke, he waited for Dominique to go on.

"Monsieur, just how secure are your finances?" Dominique asked.

"I beg your pardon?"

"Many merchants have lost their shirts during the war. I wondered about yours."

"My shirt is firmly upon my back, and my money in the Bank of New Orleans." Etienne drew fiercely on his cigar, scowling at the verandah ceiling.

Dominique massaged his injured shoulder. "Claiborne has been begging Andrew Jackson to come to New Orleans."

"That's just what the city needs," Chartier said with a derisive snort, "another ill-bred Kaintock masquerading as a general."

"*Oui,* so the people say. Still, there is a growing concern that the British will attack the city. If they take it, the United States will fall within two months."

"So there *is* a silver lining behind a cloud of gray!"

"You would rather have British rule?"

"They intend to give New Orleans back to Spain once they've won the war."

"Those are rumors only, designed to enlist the aid of dissidents. Put no faith in them."

Chartier puffed on his cigar. A sliver of moon was rising, illuminating the bare flagpole. "It is hard for a man to maintain faith in anything these days."

Dominique guessed that he was thinking of Napoleon. "It is sad when the old orders pass away."

Chartier pulled a handkerchief out of his breast pocket and blew his nose. "It is sadder still when one has nothing with which to replace them. I have no sons. My wife is gone. My mistress cannot have children. My daughter is determined to remain a spinster. A sad, sad thing for a devout Catholic!"

"Sad indeed . . . but there must be some solace in owning a fortune."

Chartier's shoulders slumped in defeat. "Perhaps it is not as vast as I led you to believe. The war . . ."

"*Oui,* it has drained us all."

"I once had many ships plying the trade routes of the Caribbean to New Orleans and Galveston. Some are bottled up in port, rotting. Others have been sunk. Were it not for you, my little *Hopscotch*—and my daughter—would have shared their fate."

"Were it not for me," Dominique said in a low, resonant voice, "your merchant barque would have turned you a tidy profit in New Orleans by now."

"What? What is this you are saying?"

Dominique stood up and leaned against the rail. "Not long ago I intercepted a barque flying the Spanish flag near the coast of Louisiane. She was carrying silver and wool, tobacco, and a large number of Jamaican slaves."

Etienne Chartier gaped at him, cigar smoke trickling out of his nostrils and mouth.

"I set Captain Alain Defromage and his crew off on a strand and sailed the barque to Grand Terre. The goods I sold on the black market, with the exception of the tobacco, which I sent to Chartier's Mercantile once I'd discovered to whom it belonged."

"And the slaves?" Chartier asked in a cracked whisper. He drew on his cigar to steady himself.

"I freed them, giving them work on my Acadian cattle ranch."

Etienne choked on his cigar smoke and coughed so hard that Dominique had to pound him on the back. When he recovered he gave a great whoop of laughter and slapped his knee.

"That's really very funny! Do you realize you made off with well over a quarter of a million American dollars in goods?"

Dominique had anticipated a number of reactions to his news, but mirth had not been one of them. "It was over half a million dollars, monsieur. Prices have risen enormously with the tightening of the blockade."

Etienne went into a fresh spasm of merriment. He finally wiped his streaming eyes on his handkerchief, shaking his head and chuckling. "You are a brazen rogue, *mon ami,* to stand on my porch and tell me you've robbed me, when I have a score of armed men at my beck and call. You are a man after my own heart. Fabian, my quadroon queen! Come out here and bring us whiskey!"

Dominique flicked the stub of his cigar into the flower bed and blew out one last smoke ring, which slid gracefully into the night. "I did not tell you these things for your diversion."

Etienne crossed his fingers for luck and nodded for him to go on.

"I have deposited the sum of five hundred eighty thousand, two hundred fifty dollars, and seventeen cents to your account in New Orleans."

Etienne choked on his cigar smoke again. He threw the butt on the porch and stood up, coughing. "Five hundred and eighty thou—*Sacrebleu!* Have you lost your mind, my privateering friend? Why did you not keep your mouth shut and retain the money?"

"I have my reasons. Of course, I have not made restitution for the slaves. They would have brought you upward of forty thousand dollars at auction—if you had managed to circumvent the embargo. Bringing slaves to the States is illegal these days, you know."

"*Oui,* I know. I could not resist the temptation." He waved his arms. "The forty thousand does not matter, next to the fortune you have brought me!"

"A favor, then, I would ask."

"Name it! I am your servant!"

"Don't tell Loire."

Chartier put his forefinger to his lips and rolled his eyes at the open window behind him. "I can be the soul of discretion, but why?"

Fabian came out with a bottle of whiskey and two tumblers on a crystal tray. Dominique waited until she had served the drinks and gone back inside before speaking.

"I love her."

Etienne chuckled. "Then all the more reason to inform her of your magnanimity!"

"All the more reason not to. Can you imagine her reaction were she to think I bought her?"

"I see your point. She is very prideful, that one."

Dominique sat down and sipped his whiskey. "I think I shall go mad without her."

"You are already mad, *mon ami,* but in a way that gladdens the heart of a businessman! Tell me, what price to enlist your services in running my wares to New Orleans?"

"You would employ me?"

"But of course! You are eminently resourceful."

"I do not need employment. I am busy enough with my other interests."

"Of these I would like to hear." Etienne refilled their glasses and settled onto his chair.

Dominique told him of his gun-running operation to the Mexican revolutionaries, his fleet of privateering vessels, his warehouses, his cattle ranches in Acadia. He failed to mention the two mansions he owned in New Orleans or his summer cottage on the north shore of Lake Pontchartrain, nor did he allude to his town house in Paris or the one in Venice. Nonetheless, Etienne Chartier was speechless.

Dominique half closed his eyes and listened to the lilting chirr of insects. Isle Châteauroux was a blissful spot, a perfect place to rest and recover for a few days. Of course, on an island this size there were very few places for Loire to hide. They would see a lot of each other.

"I want you to send Monsieur Youx on his way, Papa," Loire said at breakfast the next morning. She and Etienne were seated at a small buffet table on the rear verandah. Wild parakeets flitted among the fronds of the palm trees a few feet away and splashed in the spring-fed pool. Ida was in the kitchen with Fabian, singing.

Etienne chewed several bites of quiche before answering. "Send him away? But that would be ungrateful, after what he did for you."

"I have tendered him my thanks. There is no purpose in his staying on."

Etienne wiped egg and cheese off his mustache with his linen napkin, then lit a cigar. "Perhaps he would take exception to my ordering him off the island. That schooner of his could blast us to oblivion."

"Don't be ridiculous."

"What does my baby have against the man?"

"Nothing."

"You are telling your papa a fib, *non?*"

She went to the railing and stared into the palm grove. Her lacy white skirts wafted gracefully in the tropical breeze, and long tendrils of her hair freed themselves from her French braid to blow about her face and neck.

Should she tell her father about the barque? She had debated the question all night. Her anger at Etienne's taking a mistress complicated her decision. Here on the island with them, she felt cut off from civilization.

Her mother's actions had shamed her. To learn that her father had no scruples, either, felt like betrayal. Yet what scruples had she manifested in going to bed with Dominique Youx? Thank God her monthly cycle had come this morning!

"Monsieur Youx is a cutthroat and a braggart, Papa. He lies and cheats and steals. It is habitual with him."

"He is a Frenchman, then."

"I don't think that's funny. You have no idea what he's like."

"And do you, little girl?"

"I have an idea or two. Alain Defromage could have told you a few things, if Dominique hadn't driven him off."

"*Oui*, some of the crew told me this morning that he slipped off in the ship's boat. An act of courage, to skulk away in the night, *non?*"

Loire said nothing.

"Such a man as he would have a lot to learn from the heroic Captain Dominique Youx," he added.

Loire's eyes narrowed with anger. "You are gullible, Papa, to put your trust in a stranger, no matter how heroic he might seem."

"I have told you before that cynicism does not become a young woman, have I not?"

"You have told me but failed to convince me. I am the way I am. You have your faults, too," she said with a meaningful glance at the jalousied window behind his head. She could see Fabian through the slats, dusting furniture and giggling with Ida.

"You are a judgmental child, in addition to being a cynical one. It is none of your business what faults I have."

Exasperated, Loire walked down the steps to the spring, sat on a wooden bench, and dangled her bare toes in the water. The parakeets hopped aside but did not fly away, turning their pert round heads to her. Loire remembered Dandy Leggins and Dominique's amusement.

"Do you ever hear from Mama?" she asked abruptly.

"*Oui.* She writes me often."

Loire looked up in surprise.

"If you would like, I will show you some of her letters."

"I'll think about it." She stroked the cheek of a bright green bird venturing near her skirt. He screwed his eyes shut and tilted his head.

"Your mama, does she write to you?"

"I've had one letter."

"Did you reply?"

"No."

"I see. It is your attitude at fault again, Loire."

"My attitude? What could I possibly have said, Papa? Her letter detailed . . ." She stopped, not wanting to describe her mother's affair with the army officer.

"I know all about it," Etienne said, tugging at his mustache. "It does not matter. She is a beautiful woman."

"Even beautiful women must shoulder some measure of responsibility."

"Eh? And when will you shoulder yours?"

"Now don't start that again!"

"You are becoming an old woman, *chérie*. Twenty-two, and without a husband! It is unthinkable."

"There are other things in life besides husbands. Important things."

"Shopkeeping, for example."

Loire dropped her hand from the bird and folded her arms. "Someone has to keep the family afloat."

"The family will float nicely on the half a million just deposited in my account. There is no need for you to keep shop."

"Half a million? Half a million dollars? Do you mean to say you've had a fortune in the bank while St. John and I have been worrying ourselves sick over the finances? You perfidious scalawag!"

"I am not!" He drew himself up righteously. "Captain Youx has only just told me of the deposit—*Sacrebleu!*" He clapped his hand over his mouth.

Loire's eyes sparked fire as she bounded to her feet, frightening the parakeets away in every direction. For a moment she could scarcely see her father through the beating wings.

"So he bought me from you, is that it? You're a horrible pair of scoundrels, that's what you are!

Nothing but a couple of Cottonmouth water snakes!"

"You do not understand—"

"I understand everything, you wicked old pirate! No wonder Mama left you, you—you—"

"Come into the house and let Fabian get you a whiskey," he said, descending the steps to take her arm.

"Don't you touch me!" She stomped up the porch steps into the house.

Ida was in the bedroom, putting the clothes in the armoire. With fresh annoyance, Loire remembered that her father had not allowed Ida to ride with them from the harbor the evening before. Instead she had been obliged to ride to the house in the back of a mule-drawn wagon, with the luggage. After arriving late, she'd bedded down on a pallet beside Loire's bed.

"Throw everything back in the trunk, Ida! We're moving out!"

"What the devil?"

"You heard me. We're moving into the cottage at the other end of the island. I'm certain we'll be more comfortable there."

Ida cocked her fists on her hips. "You done lost your sense, hasn't you?"

Loire yanked the gowns off the hooks and threw them into the trunk. She swept perfume bottles off a shelf where Ida had arranged them, hurling them carelessly on top of the clothes.

"What's got into you this time?"

"I don't want to talk about it." She shouted out the door, "Fabian! Tell the footman to get the carriage ready, and send somebody in here to fetch my luggage. Step to it!"

"You been drinking?" Ida demanded.

"No, but I'm thinking about it!"

"Where Mistah Youx at?"

"I don't know, and I'll be fried for a clam before I'll care!"

Ida chuckled. "You having more fits than folk at a tent revival, carried away in the Spirit!"

Loire marched out to the front porch with Ida jogging behind her. Her father was waiting by the carriage. Loire pushed past him and caught Ida's hand to help her inside.

"Go!" she ordered the driver.

"One moment, mademoiselle!" Struggling under the weight of a trunk, the footman came down the steps and heaved it onto the rack behind the seat.

"Never mind the other ones—get in!" Loire said.

He jumped up beside the driver. The carriage rolled out of the yard down the sandy road, leaving Etienne and his mistress standing forlornly on the verandah.

17

In a picturesque grove of cypress ten miles from the main house stood Etienne Chartier's getaway cottage. The nearest habitation was across a wide tobacco field.

Loire went into a shed behind the house and found a fishing net. After stuffing it into a tattered burlap sack, she walked through the woods to the beach.

Having tucked the hem of her skirts into her waistband, she stretched the net into a circle on the sand and gathered its lead sinkers into her hands to form a pouch. Then she walked into the water and cast the net.

After the tenth or eleventh cast she snagged a small barracuda and a grouper. The grouper would be better eating than the barracuda, but in light of her frame of mind, she preferred to let it go and keep the predator.

"Into the sack with you, Captain Dominique," she said. Avoiding the barracuda's razor-sharp teeth, she dropped him into the bag and tied it shut.

Had Dominique found out yet that she'd left her father's house? She wondered where he'd slept last night. Not in the house, certainly, or she would have seen him at breakfast. Perhaps he had gone back to his ship. It was possible that he'd spent the day there and didn't know she was gone.

On the way back to the cottage, she stopped at a wild mango tree and gave it a shake. Several large yellowish green fruits plopped onto the sand. Not wanting to soil them by placing them in the bag with the fish, she thrust them into her bodice and went back to the cottage.

Ida was in the detached kitchen behind the house, lighting a fire in the cast-iron stove in the corner. She gaped at the girl's bulging bodice.

"Good lands, child, you growing titties or what?"

Loire laid the mangoes on a scarred wooden table. "There, better?"

"Mm-hmm. You a natural woman again. Just wish you had the sense to stay out the wilderness."

"I'm where I want to be."

"Sure you is," Ida said skeptically. "What's in the sack?"

"Dinner."

"If that ain't the first sensible words out your mouth today, I don't know what is." Ida started to untie the string.

"Watch out, dinner's got teeth." Loire loosened the string and emptied the fish onto the table, pointing out its vicious underbite.

Ida whistled. "Glad that boy's my dinner and not the other way round. He sure ain't no catfish. What is he?"

"Barracuda. A baby one."

"I'd hate to meet his pappy. Gimme that knife over yonder, lemme clean him. Sure is glad to see this rascal, teeth or no teeth. Looked to me like we wasn't gonna eat nothing but them old dried-up coconuts yonder."

"Ida, you wouldn't have built the fire if you'd doubted my fishing ability."

"Go draw us some water, honey."

Loire took the bucket and went out to the cistern. As she removed the wooden cover, a thick layer of cobwebs came with it. She cautiously looked at the bottom side of the cover. No spiders. Sighing with relief, she filled the bucket and returned to the kitchen.

"I'll be dogged, there ain't a coffee bean one around here!" Ida said, scowling at the dusty shelves. "Might as well throw that water out the door."

"We'll drink it."

"Come on over and lemme learn you how to cook, then."

"I know how."

"Yeah, about like St. John know how. He cook about as good as them preachers in the Ole Testament."

"What, bloody sacrifices and burnt offerings?"

"Mm-hmm."

"I cook better than that. I have my own system."

"You does? Come on fry this bare-cuda fish, then, show me how."

"All right, I will." Loire took a scant spoonful of bacon grease from a metal bucket on the back of the stove and dropped it into the skillet.

"Ain't enough grease. He'll burn up," Ida said.

"No, he won't. Just keep watching. I have a system, remember?"

"Yeah, I hears you. What you doing now?"

"Looking for Creole pepper. Ah, here! Is the skillet smoking hot yet?"

"Hot as a mule shoe."

"Good. Now I'll throw in the spices, like this." She dumped in a thick sheet of seasoning, then laid in the fish. It sizzled and popped. A plume of dark smoke rose to the ceiling.

"Better turn him."

Loire tried to flip the fish over with a wooden spatula but found that it stuck to the skillet. She wrestled with it for a few seconds before the skin sheared off and stayed in the pan, smoking. She raked the fish onto a wooden platter, blackened side up. "Ta-da!"

"You sure he done?"

"Sure I'm sure. Did you cut up the mangoes? Good, let's eat."

They sat down at the table, poured two mugfuls of tepid water, ladled the food onto the plates, and picked up their forks. Ida uttered a brief, fervent blessing.

Not a minute later, Ida dumped the fish back into the pan—this time with a healthy two inches of melted grease. Loire sat at the table, drinking water.

After supper they walked down to the beach. Loire began to build a sand castle, but her heart wasn't in it and she stopped construction before the keep was half-done.

"What's the matter, honey?"

Loire drew a stick man in the sand. "I might as well tell you. Papa sold me to Dominique Youx for half a million dollars."

Ida's brown eyes bugged out, then she laughed and rolled back on the sand. "Half a million for a gal that don't even know how to cook!"

"I know how to do lots of other things."

"Ha ha!"

"What, you don't think I'm worth half a million dollars?"

"President Madison ain't worth that much!"

Loire giggled.

"I wish ole St. John could hear you talk, gal."

"You're laughing enough for both of you." She raised her knees and rested her forearms across them. "Well, maybe he didn't buy me, exactly, but the thought was the same."

"And it ain't good enough for you."

"By my faith, Ida, you make me sound a greedy pig!"

"Folk in Savannah use to say, 'If the shoe fit . . . '"

"Wouldn't it make you mad, in my place, to have men bargaining over you?"

"Use to happen all the time, when I was young."

A blush rose to Loire's cheeks. "Didn't it bother you something fierce?"

"Weren't nothing nobody could do."

"That's awful."

"Mm-hmm. Lots more awful than a good-looking man trying to woo a gal away from her pappy, and making her rich, to boot."

"It's not that simple. There's a matter of pride to consider."

"You got bushels of that."

"Hmmph."

"You ain't got no reason to be all het up like this. Mistah Youx crazy about you. He'd give his right arm—he already done give his shoulder—just to make you happy. And here you is turning up your nose like he a three-day-dead possum. Shame."

"I'm going back to the cottage."

"Go on, then. Run off, just like you always does."

"Hush up!"

"I ain't gonna hush up." Ida was suddenly furious. "You spoilt child, gimme your backside! I'm gonna wear you out!"

Loire ran as Ida clambered to her feet and started after her. She broke out of the woods and was rounding the verandah to the front door when she spotted Dominique coming out of the house, slapping a riding quirt against his thigh. One of her father's stallions was tied to a palm tree.

"What are you doing here?" Loire demanded.

Sweeping off his tricorn hat, he sat down on the top step and smiled at her. "I was in the neighborhood and thought I'd stop by."

"We're ten miles from the main house!"

"And eleven from the harbor. No matter."

"Go away. Shoo!"

"I may, after I've reminded you that there are no locks on your doors."

"Your snooping already reminded me. I'll be sure to nail them shut tonight to keep you out."

"I wasn't thinking of your keeping me out." Noticing Ida hovering near the woods, he raised his voice to include her. "I'm concerned about the other men on the island. You women shouldn't be out here alone."

"We can take care of ourselves."

"No, we cain't," Ida said, marching up to the porch. "Tell this foolish child to go on back home to N'Awleans, Mistah Youx. Lock her in your cabin if you has to."

"Are you *crazy?*" Loire shouted.

"Actually, that was a reasonable suggestion," Dominique said. "A pleasurable prospect indeed."

"One about as pleasurable as a tooth extraction! Out of my way!" Loire stamped up the steps past him into the house.

"That gal moving chairs in front of the door," Ida said. "Come on, Mistah Youx, I'll take you 'round back before she block it, too."

"Thanks, but no. I'll come back tomorrow with more supplies. Chartier said she took off without food, so I brought some things over. You'll find a box in the kitchen."

"Praise the Lawd! She think we gonna live off that mess she pull out the sea."

"I smell smoke. Supper?"

"Mm-hmm. She stubborn about cooking, but I'll learn her."

"She won't need to cook after we're married."

"I'll never marry you, you conceited blowfish, and I'll cook whenever I want to!" Loire cried, looking out at him through a bamboo blind. Before he could speak, she put out her tongue and dropped the sash. He chuckled.

"Don't listen to her sass, Mistah Youx. I'll fix everything up with her."

But Youx only bowed, clapped his hat on his head, and stepped off the porch. As he mounted his horse, he said, "Don't try. I enjoy a challenge."

"You'll find this challenge a brick wall," Loire said.

Dominique swept off his hat. "Would you like to come outside to quarrel where it's cooler, mademoiselle? I'm sure the cottage is growing miserable with all that steam blowing out of your ears."

The blind dropped. Something inside crashed.

"I'll see you tomorrow, mademoiselle," he said, turning the horse to gallop down the road. In response, Loire broke another vase.

Etienne Chartier rode out to the cottage early the next day, leading a white filly. Noticing the closed blinds, he trotted over to Loire's bedroom window and rapped on the wall. "Loire, my pet! Come see what your doting papa has brought you!"

"If it's your charming friend Monsieur Youx, kindly take him around back and drop him in the cistern, headfirst."

"No, no! Look out the window and see! Come now!"

Loire climbed out of bed and raised the blind an inch. Her father was dressed in his white suit and Panama hat, puffing his perpetual cigar. He gestured at the filly.

"You know I can't ride, Papa."

"Nonsense! You used to ride all over the island, just like the wind herself!"

"That was a long time ago. I wouldn't know which end of the horse to face these days."

"You are as stubborn as your mother! Open the door and accept this wonderful present I've brought you!"

"No, thank you." She crawled back into bed, closing the mosquitaire and covering her head with a pillow. She heard her father swear, then his fists banging on the door. She was glad she'd barricaded it last night.

A minute later, the pillow was yanked away. Her father stood over her, glowering into her face. Ida hovered in the doorway behind him.

"Come out here and accept your gift!"

"I'm not one of your field hands to order about! Get out of my boudoir!"

"I will not!"

"You are impossible!" She jumped out of bed, flung a wrap over her nightdress, and stalked out of the room.

"Are you coming outside?"

"Yes, outside to the kitchen for breakfast."

"No, no, *no!* You must come and see the filly!" He attempted to catch her arm to pull her to the front door, but she shook him off and marched to the back of the cottage.

Chartier sighed. Dribbling cigar ash all over his suit, he helped her remove the other barricade. "Loire, I do not understand why you are so angry. What is this terrible demon that drives you to act like your mother?"

"You philanderer, how dare you compare me to *her!*"

"Philanderer?" He shook his finger under her nose. "You dare call your papa names? I will take a cane to you!"

"Miz Loire, Mistah Chartier, maybe you-all needs to get something to eat."

"Silence, woman!" Chartier yelled.

Loire jerked the door open and strode outside, her nightclothes flying in the sea breeze. She went into the kitchen and picked up a knife.

"Now you jest wait one minute, Miz Loire, afore somebody get hurt," Ida said, hurrying after her.

"I have no intention of hurting anyone," she said, laying the knife on a cutting board. She went to a box near the door and pawed through its contents, removing eggs, cheese, fruit, and a tin of chicory coffee.

Too distracted to realize that Dominique had brought the food last night, she set the kettle on the stove to boil, then began chopping bananas into a bowl.

Etienne's head appeared around the door. "Your papa, he believes the fire in the stove needs stirring, *chérie.*"

"Then Papa dear can do it," she said, putting down the knife. She began cracking eggs for an omelet. "Unless he wants cold coffee, of course."

"Lemme do it," Ida said. She opened the door and stirred the coals with a poker.

"Perhaps you will let Ida cook the breakfast, my pet," Etienne said, "while we go look at the filly."

"I already told you how I feel about that." She beat the eggs with a wire whisk.

"Please."

Loire gave an impatient sigh. "All right, show me."

With a spring in his step, Etienne escorted her around the side of the house. "She is yours, my angel."

"Thank you. Why don't you take her back to her stable now, as you leave?"

Etienne flung his hat on the ground. "You are maddening! What is the reason for your infernal stubbornness?"

"A small matter of half a million dollars."

"Why does it anger you that Captain Dominique paid for taking the barque?"

Loire stared at him. "*That's* what the money was for? You knew about the barque?"

"*Oui,* he told me last night."

"And you do not intend to hang him?"

"Hang such a magnificent rogue as he? But no! If I can arrange it, I will give him charge of my merchant fleet!"

"He's Jean Laffite's brother."

It was Etienne's turn to stare. "You knew that, yet you did not tell me?"

She had said too much this time. There was a price on the heads of pirates: perhaps her father would seek to collect it on Dominique's.

Etienne suddenly slapped his knee and guffawed. "So! You've fallen prey to the big buccaneer's charms, have you?"

"No! I just don't want to see him get hurt . . . . Don't forget that he rescued the *Hopscotch*."

"I have not forgotten. He is a most resourceful young man. He would make you a fine husband."

"I am not interested in marrying a pirate."

"So haughty?"

"A woman must draw the line somewhere."

"Do not draw it across young Dominique's neck. He would make strong sons on you. I need heirs."

"If you want sons so badly, Papa, go make them with your mistress."

"Alas, she is barren."

"My condolences. Now good-bye."

She went back to the kitchen and sat down. Ida stood by the stove, tapping her foot.

"Aren't you going to sit down?"

Ida continued to beat time on the floor.

"Why are you looking at me like that?"

"Trying to figger how a gal that look like sugar and spice full up with snips and snails instead."

"Don't forget puppy dogs' tails."

"I ain't forgetting. You full of bulldog tails."

"Thanks so much. Can we eat now?"

Ida yanked a skilletful of scrambled eggs off the stove and planked it in front of her. "Go on and eat, then. I'm going for a walk."

"You're not eating?"

But Ida was already gone. Loire put her left elbow on the table and leaned her cheek on her palm, using a fork with a bent tine to stir the eggs around.

Why was everyone angry with her all of a sudden? Did her father really expect her to forgive Dominique Youx after what he'd done?

She remembered Dominique's mighty thrusts. He had loved her with more than his body that night. Had he not tried to help her understand her mother, and perhaps herself?

She went to the stove for a mug of chicory, which she stirred with a peppermint stick. What would people think if she showed up in New Orleans with Dominique? She had been laughed at so many times because of her mother . . . .

Pride. Pride was all that was stopping her from making up with him. Pride was her greatest weakness. Dominique had cautioned her against it, and so had old Mazy. Loire leaned against the doorpost, sipping her drink. Should she go to Dominique and tell him he still held her heart in his hands?

It was hard. Too hard. How could she tell him a thing like that after what she'd said and done? She wished she hadn't been so quick to flee New Orleans, so ready to release her bridegroom to the sheriff.

She went down the path to the beach, letting the warm water bathe her feet. It would take great courage to go to him now. And what if he laughed?

The idea made her blood run cold. She let her coffee trickle into the sand. What if he rejected her?

She took the thought a step further. What if he had pursued her to Isle Châteauroux just to avenge himself on her for humiliating him at the altar? She had heard such stories before. One did not insult a Frenchman without paying some sort of price.

She remembered Alain Defromage. He had challenged Dominique, and look what it had gotten him!

She walked back to the cottage, put on a turquoise apron-gown and a peach tippet trimmed with alençon lace, and went out to look for Ida.

The sunlight shimmering off the narrow, sandy road winding between the tobacco fields burned her feet through the soles of her shoes. After a mile of steady walking she came upon a group of slaves cutting dark, fuzzy leaves off ten-foot-high tobacco stalks. They tied the leaves into bundles and laid them in wagons to be hauled to drying sheds on the leeward side of the island. Loire walked on.

Another mile brought her to a slave village. The overseer's house stood at the end of a row of shanties. There was a smokehouse, a corral, and a pigpen fenced with stout cane poles. Chickens scratched in vegetable gardens between the houses.

Old women and nursing mothers sat on rush-bottom chairs in an open-sided shed, rolling cigars from last year's tobacco crop. They stood as Loire ducked under the low eaves of the roof.

"Please don't get up," she said. "I was just looking for Ida."

"Over here, Miz Loire."

Ida sat on a chair near the middle of the group, eating red beans and rice. "You over your huff?"

"Yes." Loire sat down to watch a woman lay chopped tobacco in a cured leaf, roll it into a tight brown cigar, and lick the seam to secure it. A little girl took it and placed it in a hogshead.

"You gonna tell your pappy you sorry, Miz Loire?"

"No."

Ida clicked her tongue. "You gonna tell Mistah Youx, then?"

"I don't owe him an apology."

"You owes me one, dragging me out to this hot ole island."

"You wanted to come."

"Ain't no use talking to you. Go on home."

"I'm sorry. I'd rather stay here. It's lonesome at the cottage."

"You making the gals nervous, Miz Loire."

"Why? I'm not doing anything."

"Yeah, you ain't doing nothing but being mastah's daughter, overseeing the hands."

"I didn't come here to boss anyone around."

"Start rolling smokes, then, make everybody feel better."

Loire picked up a leaf and spread it flat on the worktable. It was eight inches wide and almost two feet long, with a resiny texture and a pungent odor. Copying the woman next to her, she folded it in half and laid in chopped black tobacco. After tucking in the ends, she rolled it up as tightly as she could. Then she licked the seam—shuddering at the taste—and held it firmly for a minute.

Gingerly she laid the cigar on the table. The thing was misshapen, one end much fatter than the other, with a squashed middle. As she watched, the seam popped open and the leaf began to unfold.

"I'll let Papa smoke this one," she said, holding up the cigar. Tobacco spilled onto the table.

The slaves laughed. Loire stayed for two hours, talking and learning to roll cigars, while Ida dozed on the chair.

"How do Monsieur Chartier and his overseers treat you?" she asked at last.

The murmur died. Heads bowed, fingers flew. Ida opened one eye and squinted at her. "They ain't gonna talk about that, honey."

"Why not? Maybe I can help."

"Ain't nobody can help. Slaves ain't folk, don't you know that?"

"You don't have to be sarcastic with me, Ida. You know how I feel about slavery."

"Yeah, but you cain't do nothing, honey. Talking to your pappy'd only get you two riled up again."

Loire stood up. "If you-all won't talk to me, I'll just go out in the fields and talk to your men."

"Please, missy!" a Jamaican girl cried. "Your papa, he *non* so bad. He say for overseer to treat slaves good, no whip too much."

"No whip too much? He has no business letting them use the whip at all!"

"Sit down, child," Ida said. "You cain't change that man's nature, he gonna do these folk like he please."

"He's going to answer to me!"

"Yeah. You think. Come on, we going back to the cottage."

"But—"

"Don't 'but' me. You talk to Mistah Chartier tomorrow, after you cooled off some."

"I won't cool off about this."

"Mm-hmm, all right, then. Let's go on back, see what you can catch out the sea this time. Maybe a whale."

Loire knew she was being manipulated, but the main house was eight miles away and she had only her feet for transportation. She wished she'd kept the filly.

Perhaps tomorrow her father would send supplies, and she could ride back with the driver.

They were halfway back to the cottage when Loire heard hoofbeats behind them. She looked over her shoulder. "Oh, no, it's him!"

Dressed in white linen and a cockade hat of black felt, Dominique Youx was galloping toward them on a big black gelding.

"By my eyetooth, if he ain't one good-looking man!"

"Ida! Don't look at him. Just keep walking."

Dominique dragged the horse to a halt and swung down from the saddle, tipping his hat.

"How your shoulder doing, Mistah Youx?"

"Very well, madame, *merci*. Wounds heal quickly in the tropics. See." He moved his arm around. "And you?"

"Cain't complain. Mighty hot, though. Come on to the house and get you something to drink." She moved away from Loire's gouging elbow. "We got coffee and I'll make up some lemonade."

"I would like that very much." He smiled when Loire scowled and turned away to walk rapidly down the road.

"Don't pay her no mind, she just hot and cross."

"So I see. Excuse me, madame, but I must speak to her."

He caught up with Loire, leaving the gelding to trail Ida. Loire lifted her nose into the air and increased her pace. Dominique sped up, his long legs gliding along effortlessly.

"Why are you bothering me, monsieur?" she finally asked after walking half a mile without managing to shake him. She stopped beneath a cypress tree to catch her breath, fanning her face with her hand.

"Can you not understand that I do not wish to see you?"

"Your tongue tells me so, yet in your eyes I read the truth."

Loire looked away. "A gentleman does not speak so."

"A gentleman? Then I am a pirate no longer in your estimation?"

"You are a pirate always. Once a thief, always a thief. You will not change."

"Ah, but you are wrong. I have decided to offer my services to Governor Claiborne."

"In what capacity?"

"As a privateer."

Loire threw up her hands and started walking. "Of course!"

"Privateering is not thievery."

"You play with words."

"No. I will fly under the Stars and Stripes. The tonnage I capture I will turn over to the governor, just as Renato Beluche does."

"And you will gain a huge share of the prize money."

"Such a percentage is necessary to meet expenses and pay the crew."

"And to make yourself richer."

"You, a shopkeeper, do not approve of gaining wealth?"

"Not when the wealth belongs to other people."

"I see. But what if the wealth I gain from the British is used to fill the coffers of the United States government? Would you approve then?"

Loire thought about it. Although she disliked Claiborne, she had no quarrel with President Madison. Unlike many disgruntled New Orleanians, she did not believe Britain would return the city to Spain if the Americans were defeated.

"It is rumored that the American government is bankrupt," she said.

"Yes. General Andrew Jackson has poured out his heart to Congress many times, asking for money to support his army. They have none to give."

"If you are telling the truth about taking British wealth for the Americans, I suppose I cannot fault your privateering," she said reluctantly.

Dominique Youx smiled. He had already anonymously donated many thousands of British pounds and Spanish doubloons to the Americans. With the British knocking at the gates of his adopted country, it was time to put his whole heart into the war effort. If he and his brothers threw their ships against the British, the blockade would be crippled. As soon as he returned to Grand Terre, he would approach Jean with the idea.

"I suppose you are telling me these things as a way to regain my favor," Loire said.

"You are cynical, *chérie.*"

"A fault of mine, monsieur, increased tenfold when my groom was arrested at the altar for piracy."

"The timing was unfortunate."

"That is all you can say? You have a heart of stone!"

Dominique caught a flash of tears in her amber-colored eyes. "Let us go down to the beach and talk of these things, Loire. There is much we haven't said."

"I have said all I am going to say. The matter is closed."

"Your mind is closed. Let me open it."

"No! You've opened quite enough wounds, thank you."

"I have made many mistakes."

"*Oui,* but you will make no more with me. Now go away!" She broke into a run, intending to barricade herself in the house again.

Dominique caught her before she reached the porch steps. He spun her around and pulled her against his chest. She struggled to get free, but he held her in a grip of steel.

"You do not always have to fight," he said. He brought his mouth against hers.

Loire's writhing movements against his hard body only caused him to increase the pressure of his arms around her. She felt the heavy thudding of his heart against her breast, his ragged breath on her face. It was all she could do not to give in to the towering emotion that made her ache to return his kiss.

At last he released his grip and stepped back a pace. She gazed up at him rebelliously, conscious of having won and lost a battle all at the same time.

"If you are quite finished assaulting me," she said, striving to keep her voice steady, "I will go inside and take a nap."

18

Left outside on the porch, Dominique contemplated tearing the door off its hinges and forcibly reclaiming Loire.

"You look like ole Mistah Wolf," Ida said, coming up behind him. She handed him the gelding's reins. "Wouldn't surprise me none to see you go to huffin' and puffin' on the door."

For once Dominique didn't smile. With a dangerous look in his eyes, he lifted down a basket of food tied to the saddle and gave it to Ida, then swung onto the horse. His blood was boiling, and there were plenty of pretty brown girls at the harbor willing to cool it.

The sun was low in the sky by the time he reached the main house, where he was tantalized by the scent of French cooking. He left the horse in the stable and walked over to watch the French flag snap in the breeze. The beagles grumbled softly but didn't trouble to come out from under the verandah.

Fabian straightened from a flower bed near the house and dropped a few blossoms into her cane basket. "Captain Youx, I had hoped you'd join us for dinner!"

He swept off his hat and bowed. "I would not wish to impose, madame."

"Of course you would." She shouldered her basket and smoothed her red skirts over her thighs, smiling at him—a slow, provocative smile that formed a dimple in her chin. "You would not be here if you had not smelled dinner. Admit it!"

"I confess. I could not help myself."

"La! That is good." She linked her arm through his and walked him up the steps. "Etienne is in his study. I must finish the preparations."

Dominique watched her hips as she strolled off on a cloud of expensive perfume. His fists clenched as he pictured Loire's smaller behind, her narrow waist. Damn it, he should have torn that door off.

Etienne was fussing with paperwork at his Hepplewhite desk when Dominique walked into the room. A cigar smoldered in an ivory ashtray by his elbow; a second was clamped between his teeth.

"*Vive l'empereur!*" Chartier said by way of greeting.

"Long life to him, and may he soon return to Paris," Dominique responded automatically.

He looked around at the walls. Heads of virtually every species of cat hung there, along with those of a hippopotamus, rhino, and elephant. A huge white bear stretched across the floor, its mouth frozen in a snarl.

"Do you like them, *mon ami?* I shot every one myself," Etienne said, gesturing with his cigar. "I will tell you about my exploits at dinner tonight."

"I would be most interested," Dominique said. Still tight with anger, he pulled up a chair and lit a cigar, looking through the smoke at a razorback boar.

"How are matters between my daughter and yourself?"

The cigar in Dominique's fingers snapped. Swearing, he laid it in the ivory ashtray. "As well as can be expected, damn it."

"That does not sound so good."

"She was angry about something."

Etienne shifted guiltily on his chair and looked out the window. "My daughter, she is always angry about something these days. She will get over it."

"Perhaps."

Etienne pushed his papers into a pile and stood up. "Come, we'll take dinner in the gazebo."

They followed the torch-lit path past the pool in back of the house. Pointing to the parakeets roosting in the trees, Chartier said, "Loire used to lodge four or five of the little buggers in her room when she came here. Keeping a neat house is not her forté."

Dominique refrained from comment. Loire's room over the mercantile had been very neat and orderly. At least, it had been until their night of wild lovemaking. His loins quickened as he recalled their rumpled clothes strewn on the floor, the sheets torn halfway off the mattress, her flushed face against the pillow . . .

"And here it is, Captain!"

Columns of carved flowers and leaves supported the white gazebo in the clearing. Beeswax candles and flowers adorned the railings, and there was a large spray of palm fronds and pink roses on a table. Fabian's basket of flowers graced one of the steps.

Fabian stood by the table, her hands folded demurely in front of her. Dominique bowed, Etienne rose on tip-toe to kiss her cheek, and they sat down at the table.

Slaves bearing covered silver dishes came down the path through the trees and paraded around the table, lifting the covers to display filet of sole *bonne femme*, shrimp *de jonghe*, scalloped oysters, black bean and rice salad, and half a dozen other dishes.

Dominique paid little attention to the feast. He was still annoyed, yet he wanted to feel Loire's arms around his back, her soft breasts against his chest. He wanted to slide his tongue over her throat and make her sigh.

"You are a thousand miles away, Captain," Fabian said, watching him out of her sloe eyes.

"My apologies, monsieur, madame. I am not doing justice to the meal." He dug into the filet of sole, vaguely aware that the breeze had died. The air felt sticky. He supposed it would rain soon.

"Perhaps if Fabian were to speak to Loire, woman to woman . . ." Etienne began.

"She does not approve of me, Etienne, *mon cher*," his mistress said.

"She will be made to!" He mopped his sweating face with his dinner napkin. "I will make her!"

"She can be made to do absolutely nothing," Dominique said.

"It is the fault of her mother, this irascibility of hers! I should have beaten it out of the girl at a young age."

Fresh anger rumbled in Dominique's breast. "Be thankful she possesses such a temperament, monsieur. She is strong and brave. For such a woman, a man would happily die."

Fabian's eyes found his. "Would you?"

"*Oui.*" His voice dropped to a whisper. "She is a pearl of great price. For her I would give up my life."

Etienne tapped his cheek consideringly. "Those brigs rotting in my harbor are full of last year's tobacco. I have not been able to get it to New Orleans, and already it is harvest again. I'll pay you well to run it in your schooner."

"Payment is immaterial. I will not leave Loire."

Etienne's mouth widened in a smile. "That is the beauty of my plan: run her back to the city with the tobacco."

"You make her sound like a hogshead of black leaf. Would you risk her life, running the blockade?"

"The risk would not be great, with you at the helm."

"You do not know the British," Dominique said darkly.

Fabian looked at him a long moment. Softly she said, "He will do it, Etienne."

Chartier rubbed his hands. "Loire cannot help but fall in love, closeted with so virile a pirate!"

Darkness blanketed the island when Dominique left Chartier's house for the *Dragon*. Spending the night in Loire's vacated room, as the planter had pressed him to do, would only grant Dominique a sleepless night. Breathing in her scent on the pillow would drive him mad.

A stiff wind sprang up as he walked to the harbor. Clouds scudded across the moon. The atmosphere was heavy, oppressive despite the wind, and the smell in the air disquieted him. Ice.

He squinted through the gloom at the *Dragon*

rocking at anchor. She was pointing into the wind, her sleek bulwarks shucking the currents of air.

Again the icy scent. The wind picked up, tearing at his coat. His hat spun away into the darkness. Somewhere in the night he heard howling. Etienne's beagles. The beagles that never got excited about anything.

Cursing, he ran down to the shanties and pounded on the doors. "Typhoon! Get to the leeward side of the island!"

With the wind shoving him along, he ran the mile back to Etienne's house in something less than five minutes. After stopping only to hammer on the door and shout a warning, he vaulted over the verandah rail.

In the stable Etienne's horses danced nervously, feeling the approaching storm. Dominique bridled the black gelding but didn't take the time to saddle him. Mounted bareback, he caught up a coiled rope on his way out. As he galloped away, he glimpsed members of Etienne's household taking shelter in a root cellar under the verandah.

Great raindrops began to fall, and the road was as black as pitch. Sheets of lightning revealed tobacco flattened on the ground. The wind raged in Dominique's ears, a deafening blast of sound unlike anything he'd heard since the battlefield. Palm trees flew through the air like gigantic spears. Dominique knew that the worst of the storm had not yet arrived. Struggling to stay on the road, he prayed he'd reach Loire in time. She was at the low end of the island; water could cover it in minutes.

A violent gust of wind lifted the gelding's forefeet off the road and pushed him into a field. Dominique forced him to go on. After what seemed like hours and days and years, he detected the bulky outline of the cottage. He slid off the horse and struggled toward the verandah. Twice he was blown off his feet and tumbled like a ball of cotton.

"Loire! Loire! Ida! Loire!"

The agony in his vocal cords told him he was shouting their names, but he could hear no sound coming from his mouth. The wind ripped at him, shearing the buttons off his shirt, tearing his trousers.

"Loire! Ida!" Crawling up the steps, he saw that the front door was gone. He fought his way inside.

The back wall of the cottage had been lopped off as if by a monstrous ax. The wind thundered through the gap, shoving furniture against the opposite wall. In another moment the rest of the cottage would collapse.

"Loire!" On hands and knees he struggled outside. The sea broke through the woods in an angry rush, swamping the yard. The current tried to suck him out to sea as he half swam, half crawled to the kitchen building.

"Loire! Ida!"

"Dominique! *Dominique!*"

He could not see her. He kicked forward and caromed into the table, which was upside-down. Loire and Ida were clinging to its legs.

"Hold on, hold on!"

The kitchen couldn't last much longer. Dominique tied the rope he'd brought around Ida's middle, paid out more line, and tied it around Loire's waist. Then he attached himself to the end.

"Come on!" he yelled. "Outside!"

"No! Oh, laws, no!" Ida screamed.

"We've got to—the roof's coming off!" Loire shouted.

Dominique pulled them outside and then saw that the cottage was gone. Both women fell down in the water, but he dragged them on. They hadn't traveled ten feet before the kitchen was torn off its foundation and whirled out to sea.

Fighting the elements with all his might, Dominique reached a stand of cypress fifty yards inland. He tied the rope to a tree and pulled his charges close, trying not to think what would happen if the cypress was wrenched out of the ground.

How long they huddled on the ground while the tempest blasted their world to oblivion they couldn't have guessed, but at last the screams of the wind died and the rain began to fall vertically.

The quiet was almost painful.

"It's over," Dominique said. "But there's going to be a tidal surge. We've got to get off this end of the island."

He untied the rope and led them through the water and black tangle of fallen trees toward what he hoped was the road. Sometimes Loire stumbled against his back. He wished he could transfuse strength into her tired body.

They trudged for more than two hours before daylight streaked the sky. Thunder growled in the distance. In all directions the ripe tobacco lay flat on the ground, much of it underwater. People were poking through the demolished village ahead.

"Let's see what we can do for them," Dominique said.

The white overseer and five of the slaves were dead. Others were missing, probably swept out to sea. Ida went to tend a pair of babies while Loire and Dominique helped their injured mother and several others.

At midmorning Dominique said, "We can't do anything else here until we get supplies. I'll take you to your father's house, Loire."

"It might not even be there. I'll stay here with Ida to do what I can."

He took her by the shoulders. Her hair hung in strings and her face was scarcely recognizable for mud, but the spirit in her eyes stirred him profoundly.

"We must check on your father. We'll come back here with supplies, once we've learned his fate." He dropped his hands from her shoulders and took her by the elbow. Together they walked up the flooded road.

They were three miles from the main house when Dominique pointed out a figure in the distance. "That looks like your father."

"Where?"

"Keep watching—he's gone behind that house. There!"

"Merciful God, so it is!" She would have run to him, but her legs could manage no better than a hobble through the mud. Etienne spurred his horse to meet them.

"My children!" he shouted, swinging down to embrace them both. "How relieved I am to see you have come to no harm! Come, we must go to the house."

"Is it standing?" Loire asked.

"*Oui*. The winds bit more savagely at the southern end of the island, it seems. We were scarcely touched. The crops on the leeward side are not too badly off, either."

"And my ship?" Dominique asked.

"She is safe. I wish I could say the same for mine. The *Hopscotch* and one of the brigs were driven ashore. I have lost much, I fear."

"So have the slaves in the south village," Dominique said. He explained what they had seen.

For the first time Loire saw real pain in her father's

face. "I had hoped not to hear such news. This is a sad day."

"It will be sadder still if we don't get busy," Loire said. She caught the reins of her father's horse and bounded into the saddle. "I'll go to the harbor and round up supplies."

Etienne clapped his hands as he watched her gallop down the road. "I knew she could still ride! I will make her take the white filly!"

"You are strangely buoyant for one who has lost so much," Dominique said.

Etienne's eyes twinkled. "Lost much? I think I have gained a son. Did you see the look in my daughter's eyes? You've won her, I can tell."

"I have learned that nothing is certain when it comes to your daughter," Dominique said, admiration and frustration mingling in his tone. "Come, we'll go back and organize the villagers. It's time to rebuild. And then, my friend, I will explain to you the system of tenant farming I use on my ranches."

"Eh? Why is that?"

"It is the system you will adopt after you've freed your slaves."

"You surely received a blow upon the head during the storm, *mon ami*, to conceive such a scheme!"

"I'm scheming to keep your black little soul out of hell, monsieur, and to help you regain the respect of your daughter. Not only that, but the system will make you rich."

Etienne Chartier's eyes glittered. Taking Dominique's arm, he said, "In that case, Captain Youx, my ears are at your disposal."

19

With the help of Ida and Fabian, Loire converted Chartier's stable into a hospital for the injured. Dominique and his crew dismantled wrecked ships and hauled the lumber to the south village to be used for houses. Everyone worked fifteen hours a day or more.

Gradually life returned to normal. Etienne bemoaned the fate of his crop, uttering dire predictions about bankruptcy next year, when he would have only a third his usual amount of cured tobacco to sell. Privately he urged Loire to marry Dominique.

"How can I marry him, Papa?" she asked in exasperation during dinner one night. "He spends all his time pounding away with a hammer."

"La! And what a sight he is!" Fabian said. She winked across the table at Loire and laid her hand on Etienne's arm. "If only *you* had such rippling muscles, such dark skin! My faith, he makes the women swoon when he takes off his shirt and climbs upon the roof, that man!"

"*I* have made women swoon on more than one

occasion," Etienne said. "It is not important to be a Samson, when one is a Frenchman!"

"Ah, but when one is both!" Fabian fanned herself with a flamingo wing and rolled her eyes.

Loire looked down at her plate. Not a single night had passed without her dreaming of his powerful body, his husky voice. She needed him.

Excusing herself, she went outside to the garden. The parakeets clung to the trees like jeweled ornaments, hiding their heads to shut out the fading light. Loire went down the path as the painted sunset dissolved into the sea and night fell swiftly.

A match flared in the gazebo. Loire stepped back against a tree, recognizing Dominique's profile. He held the match to his cigar, then flicked it into the gloom. The glowing cigar moved from one side of the gazebo to the other.

"Come in and sit with me, Loire."

The deep voice seemed to enter her pores and caress her nerve endings. How had he seen her in the darkness?

"Shall I strike a match to light your way?"

She did not need the match. Drawn to him like a moth, she made her way up the steps, stopping just outside the warm circle of light cast by his cigar.

"I have missed you deeply, Smokeflower."

She held on to the rail and tried to make herself stop shivering. Why did she always have to act like such a schoolgirl in his presence?

"Your father's people have been taken care of. There is no reason to stay here anymore."

She knew that. She'd known it for days. Her life was not here, but in New Orleans . . . with Dominique.

"I promised St. John to bring his Ida home to him," he said.

She realized then that he wanted to leave . . . without her. This was his way of saying good-bye. "He will be glad to see her," she managed to say, trying not to cry.

"He will be glad to see you, too."

"Me?"

"I will not leave you on this windblown strand."

"I thought . . . I had offended you."

He flung his cigar into the darkness. "The Spanish offend me; the British offend me. My Smokeflower does not."

She felt him step closer to her, then his arms came up to pull her against his chest. There was a moment when his breath fanned her face, then his mouth closed over hers in a kiss so full of love and longing that she could barely breathe. She clung to his shoulders, stretched up on tiptoe, and molded her body to his.

"Dominique, *mon cher,* I've missed you so," she said when he released her mouth. She hid her face against his jacket lapel and began to cry.

"Come home, Loire," he whispered against her hair. "Come home and be my bride."

She wanted to say yes unconditionally, but she could not. "I cannot imagine the rest of my life without you, Dominique, but . . . neither can I wait and wonder while you go off on your mysterious trips."

"No more trips."

She leaned her head back to look at him. His gaze was open, direct. No hint of deception.

"No more smuggling . . . no more privateering?"

"I will worry the British from time to time, but only under the American flag like my uncle Renato. Only to help win the war." He smiled mischievously. "No more scourging the waterways to add treasure to my storehouse. I have reformed."

"Then, my dear Captain Youx, I have no qualms about marrying you at last."

Light danced in his eyes. He lowered his head to kiss her hungrily. Humming insects echoed the song of a night bird somewhere in the trees, and in the distance Loire heard the surf drumming upon the beach. Or was it the pounding of her heart?

"Promise you'll never run away from me again, Loire."

"I promise."

"I couldn't bear to lose you again." He stepped back to the table and lit a candle, drawing her into its circle to look at her face. Her eyes were pools of gold, the tears in them shining like diamonds. His heart turned over in his breast. "Earth has never known another so beautiful as you, Loire, my queen."

She wiped away the tears that spilled down her cheeks. He caught her hand and kissed her fingers one by one.

Entwining her free hand in his hair, she sought him with her mouth, but he dropped his head to her throat and arched her against the railing. With agonizing slowness he worked his way down to her breasts. Moaning, she clasped him to her, but when he started to unfasten her buttons, she pulled back. "No, no, Dominique. Someone might come."

"Your father?"

"*Oui.* He often walks in the garden at night."

"Then come with me to my schooner."

"Tomorrow, my love." She feared that if she stayed another moment, she would not be able to resist his charms, so she slipped out of his grasp and fled up the shadowy path to the house. After all that had happened, the joy she felt nearly overwhelmed her. She needed time alone to take it in.

Dominique remained in the gazebo for a long time. He pulled her portrait out of his jacket pocket and held it to the candlelight, thinking how the miniature had turned his world upside-down and led him to unimagined happiness. She had agreed—again—to marry him!

This time, nothing would stop him from making her his wife. She would be his for all time, for all eternity. Death would not part them, nor would any living creature. Loire Bretagne belonged to him, and to him alone.

He replaced the portrait in his pocket and left the gazebo. After circling the house, he presented himself at the front door. Etienne answered his knock.

"I wish to marry your daughter," Dominique said without preamble.

Etienne choked on his cigar smoke. "You have my blessing," he said between coughs, wiping his eyes on his sleeve, "but what does my daughter say?"

"She has consented."

Etienne went into such a spasm of coughing that he had to hold on to the doorpost to keep from falling. "This is news to gladden a father's heart," he said, "but there is no priest on the island. You will have to return to New Orleans."

"We will do so tomorrow, after we've loaded your tobacco aboard."

Loire sat near the wheelhouse to watch Dominique guide the *Dragon* out of the harbor late the next day. After setting half a dozen lookouts to watch for British, he brought the schooner about on a northerly course. He didn't have time to speak much to Loire, but the fiery glances he threw her told her all she needed to know.

When they had gotten out of sight of the island,

Loire went below. Ida was sitting on the bunk in the cabin they shared, fanning herself with a goose wing.

"Hotter than ole Scratch's kitchen down here," Ida said. "I ain't never going with you on a boat again, Miz Loire."

"No? But Dominique wants us to go with him when he attacks the British fleet."

"I ain't chasing after no damn Englishmans— Oh, you just funning. It ain't so funny."

Loire poured herself a glass of water and changed the subject. "I'm dining with Dominique tonight."

"Not alone you ain't."

"I'm not a twelve-year-old."

"Mistah Chartier done tell me to keep a eye on you."

"Maybe he should've come along." She raised her hand when Ida started to argue. "I know, he couldn't leave the island in such a mess. It's all right. He's promised to visit in the spring."

"Yeah, well, I still got to keep a eye on you. He don't want no mischief before the wedding."

"He's a fine one to talk."

"Now don't you go starting on Miz Fabian again."

"I won't. I like her."

"Boil me for a crawdad!"

"It's true. I decided not to hold Papa against her."

"You ain't mad no more on account of your mama?"

"She can handle her own affairs. Just like I can handle mine."

"I ain't letting you go off to that man's cabin by yourself!"

"You did before."

"He done been shot before. He be sassy as a new-hatched tadpole now, and that look on your face tell me I got plenty to worry about."

* * *

Dressed in one of the white, high-waisted gowns Fabian had given her to replace what she'd lost in the storm, Loire knocked on Dominique's door shortly after eight o'clock. A ship's boy let her in, then left the cabin.

Dominique stood by the windows in the stern, a glass of red wine in his hand, his hair glinting in the lamplight. He was garbed in white linen breeches and a long blue jacket.

"You've come, Smokeflower."

"You thought I wouldn't?" She twisted her sash. She went to look at the table, which was set with bone china and sterling and sported a centerpiece of tropical fruit from Isle Châteauroux. Perhaps she should have brought Ida after all. She couldn't understand her own sudden nervousness.

Dominique strode across the canting deck and took her in his arms. "By my faith, if you continue to grow much lovelier, I shall surely die of a broken heart!"

"You may be half Highlander," she said softly, "but you have the Frenchman's gift of exaggeration, Alexandre Laffite."

"Don't call me that," he said sharply, releasing her.

"I did not mean to offend you."

"The name conjures memories I would prefer to forget. Forgive me for snapping."

"Only if you will pardon me as well."

"Done."

But the dark look in his eyes told her he had not altogether recovered. She hoped he would not always react so vehemently to allusions to his past. He had helped her overcome her own demons; maybe, given time, she could help him rout his.

He seated her opposite his chair, lifted the cover from a tureen, and ladled vichyssoise into her bowl. "There is bread, if you care for some, Loire."

"No, *merci.*"

"As you wish," he said.

She picked up her spoon, wondering how to break down the barrier he'd erected so suddenly. "Do you remember one Saturday morning about a hundred years ago when we sat in the café in the French Market?" she asked.

A ghost of a smile touched his lips. "I remember very well chasing you all over the marketplace and trying to feed you vichyssoise. You wouldn't eat it."

"No. So it should come as no surprise to you when I don't eat it tonight."

"Eh? But you are not so nervous now as you were then."

"My state of mind has nothing to do with it. I detest cold potato soup."

He laughed. "That explains why I was unable to woo you that morning!"

"So true. It had nothing to do with the fact that you'd tossed me into the fountain only the day before."

"I saved you from a very bad habit, you must admit."

"You should think about that yourself, the next time you smoke one of Papa's beastly cigars. As St. John points out, 'The tobacco, she will kill you.'"

"And so will vichyssoise." He went to one of the transom-shaped portholes and threw their bowls into the sea, then picked up the tureen and tossed it out, too.

"You impress me, Dominique," she said when he returned to the table. "Never have I met a man of such decisiveness, of such cold objectivity."

"Or of such appetite. Perhaps we will be luckier with the next course." He snatched the lid off a dish and looked at the contents. Puzzled, he whisked off several more lids. "But what is this?"

"Fried chicken, gravy, mashed potatoes, black-eyed peas, and cornbread," Loire said, chuckling. She served a great helping onto his plate. "Try it, my haughty gourmet, it's wonderful!"

"I do not recognize Jean-Claude's cooking."

"Because he didn't cook it." She poured gravy over the potatoes and loaded a fork. "Taste it."

Dominique had to either open his mouth or get mashed potatoes up his nose. He chose the former punishment.

"*Sacrebleu!* Never have I tasted anything so delicious!"

"You've never tasted Ida's cooking, then."

"She did this? I hope Jean-Claude paid close attention!" He picked up his fork and ate like a starving man. "Had I known what Kaintock food was like, I would have sailed straight past New Orleans and gone there at once."

"To the Kentucky backwoods? Why, you're eating good old Georgia cooking, *mon cher.* You won't get anything like it anywhere else, except, of course, wherever Ida greases a skillet. She must have cooked this to please you."

"I must thank Madame St. John. I am a lucky man, to marry a girl trained by such a chef."

Loire smiled ruefully, remembering the barracuda she'd burned. "Yes, well, Ida does most of the cooking."

"I look forward to many more meals, then."

Loire suddenly grew sad. "Dominique, how will we find New Orleans when we return there?"

The laughter deserted his eyes. "You fear the city may have fallen to the British in our absence?"

"I am very much afraid so."

He sat back on his chair. "Just before I left New Orleans, Renato Beluche told me that General Jackson had arrived at Fort Bowyer."

"In Mobile? Then he isn't too far from New Orleans."

"No, but I don't believe Jackson intends to come. Many times he petitioned Claibo to send the Louisiana militia, but the Creoles refused to help."

"So he won't help New Orleans if she's threatened?"

"I didn't say that. He'll try to stop the British at Mobile. He knows the U.S. will fall if the redcoats gain control of the big river."

"And where are the British now?"

He shrugged. "Renato said the Spanish let an English flotilla anchor in Pensacola. Perhaps they're still there."

"That's only a few hours' sail from Mobile!"

"And from there only a short march overland to New Orleans. That is why Jackson must hold Fort Bowyer, to prevent them from landing troops."

"You do not think they would try to reach the city through the delta?"

"There are too many forts on the big river, too many American gunboats. But if they attack overland, they can take the city and go downriver to surround the forts."

"We must convince Claiborne to send troops to Jackson."

"That nervous little clerk of a governor won't be able to rally them. There is another way."

"Which is?"

"To convince my brothers to set aside their pilfering

and aid the Americans. Jean and Pierre's fleet can hardly be numbered. I alone have more than eight hundred men loyal to me, and many fast sloops."

"You're willing to risk them?"

"I told you that I would place myself at the disposal of the government, thus becoming the honest man you would have me be."

"I could kiss you!"

"I would not put up a fight, my love."

She went around the table and dotted his face with kisses. "You are quite the unscrupulous dragon, Dominique Youx, and I would not like to be the British fleet commander when your sail heaves in sight. Still, I am afraid for you."

He stood up, led her to the windows, and looked out at the dark ocean. "There is a star guiding this ship, Loire, the same one I pondered the night you were born. You are my star now, guiding me through perilous straits. Dearly, timelessly, I love you. Remember that, even if darkness closes around us."

Tears started in her eyes. She could find no words, so she laid her head on his shoulder and offered up a silent prayer. *Please God, keep him safe. Don't let his ship sink. Don't let the darkness close . . . .*

Her heart began to pound. Fighting the Royal Navy was a foolhardy venture, one that could get him killed. How could he expect a ragtag band of privateers to stave off the finest navy in the world?

They could sail away. They *should* sail away. Dominique had money; they had the schooner. Nothing was forcing them back to a city that even now might be under siege.

Nothing but Dominique's honor.

She couldn't ask him not to fight. Once, she had

flung the charge of piracy in his face, and she couldn't ask him to go back to his old ways now.

Shivering, she lifted her mouth to his, feeling his love, his desire, his determination, in the kiss he gave her. She clung to him when he carried her to bed.

"You have nothing to fear, Loire," he said. He lay down next to her and stroked her cheeks, his eyes dark and liquid. "You were mine before the world was. You were born the day before I met you, the creation of my thought. Death will not separate us."

"Let us not speak of death!"

"We will speak of nothing but our love."

"I cannot even shape the words to convey the depth of that."

"Then show me, adored one."

She needed him to confirm their very existence, to ward off her fear of darkness. Seeking his deep kiss, she slid her hands inside his clothing and caressed his hot, velvety skin, the dragonfire in his loins.

"Dominique Youx," she said huskily. "Never has there been a man like you. Never!"

He got off the bed and hurled aside his clothing. The bullet wound in his shoulder had left a small red scar. His chest was even darker than before, tanned from his labors on the island. Below his waist, his skin was white. Loire stared at his arousal, her breath coming fast.

"You are so beautiful, Dominique." She raised herself on one elbow. "No, my love, do not move yet. Stay there, like so."

Her hair brushed his belly as she kissed the dragon ring on his hand. At last he pushed her gently against the pillow and lay down beside her, slipping her gown off her shoulders, untying the sash.

"I want you naked, Loire."

"There are buttons down the back, Dominique—
Dominique!" Her dress split down the front with a
loud ripping sound. Her chemise followed.

"Do not look so shocked, Loire," he said, kissing
her breasts. "For each gown that I tear from your body
I will buy a dozen more!"

"Who is thinking about clothes, my love? I will not
have much use for them, I think!"

Her laughter changed to a gasp as he spread her
thighs and slowly entered her. With skillful gyrations
of his hips he guided her in the love dance. He murmured in her ear, imparting his feelings in French, in
English, in Spanish, and in languages she'd never
heard before.

"I covet you, Loire. I cherish you. I love you with
every drop of blood in my veins, with every ounce of
my strength, with every thought in my brain. Always,
always have I loved you. Be mine, my heart, be mine
forever."

His words, his touch, enveloped her in a warm
cloud of ecstasy. She did not recognize her own voice,
crying his name.

"Hold me, Dominique! Hold me!"

"I will never let you go, my darling, my precious
love."

She was safe, oh, so safe. Warm, protected, float-
ing on the cloud. He smiled at her, the perpetual fire
flickering in his eyes. "Where did you go, beloved?"

"You know. You took me there."

He brushed away damp hair from her forehead.
"Are you still afraid, Smokeflower?"

"Yes, a little. We must tell Father Dubourg to leave
out the 'till death do us part' clause."

"He will refuse," he said, stroking her face. "It is a ceremony cast in stone through long tradition."

"Then I shall cross my fingers behind my back when I say it."

"And I will cross mine. The angels pay no heed to that portion, anyway."

The embers of passion flared into life as he stroked her, and again they made love. When it ended, Loire said, "Are you ready to go to sleep?"

"No."

"Good. Neither am I. Shall we . . . talk?"

Sunlight streamed across the bed. Dominique was gone, but his ring rested on the pillow beside her head. She tried it on her fingers one by one. It fit her left thumb, and she held her hand up to the light and watched the glittering red rays pierce the bulk-head.

There was a knock on the door. Before she could answer, Ida came in with a bucket of water in each hand. "You sleep good last night, child?"

Loire pulled the covers up to her chin and tried not to blush. "Tolerably. You?"

"Nary a wink. Stare at the ceiling all night." She staggered across the deck and dumped the water into a small wooden tub in the corner. "Better come on before the water get cold."

"Aren't you going to leave?"

Ida planted her hands on her hips and scowled. "I been seeing your backside since you was a year old. It ain't changed much just 'cause you been to bed with that man."

"Ida!"

"Cain't wait two days to get hitched up at the church."

Clutching the sheet, Loire went over to the tub. She sat down, her feet and legs dangling out on either side. "Some folks ought to try minding their own business once in a while."

"Yeah, ought to." Ida walked over to the table and helped herself to a piece of cold fried chicken. "At least you-all took time to eat first."

"Dominique said it was the best food he'd ever eaten."

"I ain't surprised." She began to tidy the cabin, bending over to pick up Loire's gown.

"Don't bother with that!"

But Ida had already noticed the tear. She clicked her tongue. "You-all just *barely* took time to eat, it look like. Too damn impatient."

"You're embarrassing me."

"Least you got the sense to be shamed of yourself."

"Ida—"

"I gotta get you another dress. Somebody need to explain about buttons to that man. You ain't got but two dresses left." She left the cabin.

"By Saint Cecelia's corset!" Loire said under her breath. Ida was busybody enough for two mothers.

An hour later, dressed in an apron-gown and white tippet, she went topside. Spray burst upward from the bow, wetting the sailors holystoning the decks. Tim waved at her from the mizzen rigging.

"Tim is almost as agile as the rest of the hands," said a voice behind her. "His mother would be proud to see him."

Loire turned around. Clad in black breeches and an open vest of black leather, with his baldric crossed over his chest and his hair blowing in the wind, Dominique looked every inch the privateering rogue. He bowed and kissed her hand.

"I didn't hear you coming," she said.

"I was sneaky."

"You should have stolen a kiss, then."

"I make it a point not to kiss women in front of the crew. It makes them jealous."

"And how many women do you privately kiss on these voyages?"

"Are *you* jealous?"

"No . . . yes."

He touched her cheek. "You needn't be. I was teasing."

"I don't believe it."

"What will it take to make you believe?"

An impish smile curved her lips. "A kiss."

"But, *chérie*—"

"A very small one."

"And you would believe anything I told you, then?"

"*Oui*. You could tell me that your youngest female passenger was ninety-six years old, with a hairy upper lip and a bald head, and I would believe you."

He pulled her behind the mast and kissed her once, hard, his hands dropping to her hips. "She was ninety-nine, with a full beard and only one hair on her head, and her wooden teeth slipped every time I kissed her."

"You're a terrible man."

"She said so, too."

Laughing, Loire moved to the starboard rail. He followed and placed his hands on the rail on either side of her.

"By the mark seven, you are glorious to look at, with your hair wild and your skirts billowing away from your ankles, Loire Bretagne Chartier!"

"You are not too hard on the eyes yourself, my

pirate captain, although looking at you gives me the vapors."

"Faint into my arms, then, Smokeflower."

"Oh, no. Your men would become jealous, remember?"

"We are not far from their sweethearts. They can stand the drought until we reach Grand Terre."

"Grand Terre? I thought we were going to New Orleans."

"We cannot sail up the big river until Claiborne accepts my oath of allegiance—Fort St. Philip would blow us out of the water. We must sail the way of the smugglers, through Barataria Bay and the bayou country."

"Oh. I forgot about Claiborne."

"Tch, tch, do not look so sad. In a very short time I will be an honest seaman, with the Stars and Stripes fluttering upon the gaff instead of the Red Dragon. You will not be ashamed to bear my name."

"I would be proud to bear your name no matter what flag you flew."

"And it does not matter to you that I am a bastard, cut off from the lordly name Laffite?"

"Youx is lordly enough; Laffite means nothing to me. I am sorry for what happened to Alexandre Laffite, but it is Dominique Youx I love."

Pulling her into his embrace, he stared down at her with so much emotion that she almost wept. "With you by my side, the phantoms of my past will cease to trouble me."

"As mine have ceased to trouble me since you came into my life. Dominique, my dear Dominique, you make me whole."

"And you make me feel like a man lost at sea, who

suddenly finds himself in a safe harbor. You bring peace to my soul."

"Maybe God will always make it so." She leaned her head against his chest. An image of his ebony schooner sailing into battle filled her mind.

She remembered hearing terrible stories of battles at sea, of the fire and blood and carnage. The Royal Navy had utterly destroyed the French fleet at Trafalgar. Since then no one had challenged its rule of the sea. Once more she wondered how Dominique hoped to succeed, even with his brothers' help.

Again she considered asking him not to fight, and again she bit her tongue. He had said she brought peace to his soul. She was unwilling to disrupt it now by voicing her fears.

She recalled the old Roman dictum her father had so often quoted: "He who desires peace must prepare for war." The thought brought a lump to her throat. Unwilling to let Dominique see how afraid she was, she closed her eyes before he could notice her tears.

How could she prepare for Dominique's own private warfare, when there was every chance he would die? In her heart, she knew that the wife of a warrior had to be as brave as he.

She would have to pretend to be brave, then, and pray that peace would come.

20

Dominique took her into his bed that night and the next, loving her fiercely, bringing her to soaring heights of passion. He did not guess the depth of terror lurking in her heart.

By the light of a single lantern, Loire studied him while he slept. She kissed the hollow of his shoulder and traced the sweat-darkened line of hair to his belly, then raised herself to her knees to caress the long, hard muscles of his thighs and calves.

"And thus I seal you mine, Dominique Youx," she whispered. "If you go away, I will never look upon a sunset again without seeing your face, or view a field of tobacco without hearing your beloved voice calling, 'Smokeflower . . . Smokeflower.'"

She left the bed and walked to the porthole, staring at the wide sweep of stars. She was a small, forlorn figure with no covering but the hair of her head.

She folded her hands. "Don't let the British take

him from me," she prayed. "He believes You joined us together in a time long ago. Do not separate us now, just when our life is beginning."

Why did God hide eternal verities behind a curtain of silence? If only she could know for certain whether or not Dominique would survive! Her faith, never very strong, was wavering.

She went back to bed and looked down at him. Then she clasped her hands together, wishing for the strength to believe in miracles. Behind her, a shooting star arced across the sky and hissed into the sea.

Just before dawn, Dominique awoke and caught the scent of the river. "Louisiane," he said, climbing out of bed. He went to the wheelhouse to take his mate's report.

"All night we watched, Captain," the mate said, "but we saw no Englishmen. It is a funny thing, *non*, so close to the big river."

"The day is not yet over, my friend. We would be foolish to close our eyes before reaching the safety of Grand Terre's brick fort."

"The war, perhaps she is over by now. Perhaps the Americans have lowered their striped and starry flag over the Cabildo."

"It may be as you say. If so, Mobile is in ruins and the man called General Jackson is dead. I do not believe that. They say he is as tough as hickory with a soul consumed by the fires of hate. Such a man is hard to kill."

"*Oui*, even as you are."

Dominique smiled. "We will learn the fate of New Orleans very soon."

"And will you still sail against the British, if she has fallen?"

"There will be even greater reason to do so."

"Your brothers, they will join us?" the mate asked.

Dominique gazed out to sea, which looked like an undulating sheet of silver. "It is hard to say. Jean hates the British, and the Spanish even more. Claiborne most of all, perhaps."

"He loves himself only, that one."

"Yes, but if the British take New Orleans, they will waste no time driving him from Barataria."

"Entrez!" Loire answered a rap at the door.

A young Rhodesian steward entered and laid breakfast on the table. "Miss Ida, she say she will join you, lady. Ah! Here she is now. Captain Youx, he say stay inside the cabin today. Don't go outside."

Two hours and ten games of chess later, Ida and Loire were tired of each other's company. Loire longed to go outside and see Dominique. She would obey his order to stay inside . . . as long as they were not bothered by the British. A rack near the bed held two loaded muskets and a dragoon pistol, and in the pocket tied around her waist were powder, cartridges, and ball.

"Want to play again, Ida?"

"And let you whup me? Ha! Gimme checkers any day."

"We don't have any checkers. If you'd concentrate on guarding your queen and remembering the movements of the pieces, you might whip me."

"Ain't got all day to watch you stare at the board, figgering which way to move them little preachers in the funny hats."

"Bishops move diagonally."

"They can move theirselves right on off the board and out the porthole, for all I care."

"Well, what do you want to do, then?"

"Eat."

"We just had breakfast."

"You call them paper pancakes breakfast?"

"They were crêpes."

"Taste about as good as the *New Orleans Gazette*."

Loire blew out her cheeks in exasperation. Then she went over to a Hepplewhite bookcase fastened to the bulkhead and selected a volume at random. Gazing at the flyleaf, she read, "*The Art of War,* by Sun Tzu, translated by Father J.J.M. Amiot, published in Paris, 1772."

"You'd think a missionary could find better things to interpret than a Chinese war treatise," she said aloud. "What's this world coming to?"

"Judgment Day, honey. If you'd go to church more, you'd know the Lord's on His way back."

"I hope not. I'm not ready yet." She turned the page, stopping at an inscription written in large, flowing letters. "What is this?" She translated from the French: "'Élan and glory; Cheers for the Grumblers, my friend Dominique! Bonaparte.'"

"What's ole King Bonaparte calling your man a grumbler for?"

"It's his endearment for his Old Guard. By my faith, Dominique must have been one of them!"

"That don't mean nothing to me."

"Don't ever let Papa hear you say that. They were the finest soldiers in France, the cream of the Imperial Guard. The world trembles at the very mention of the name."

"I ain't trembling."

"You're not facing them on a battlefield. *Mon Dieu,* Papa says that even the Highlanders couldn't stand before them! They were the deadliest fighters in all of Napoleon's legions." She looked at the armoire in the corner. "I wonder . . ."

"Hey, you cain't be going in gentlemen's closets, child. Shut them doors!"

But Loire was searching through the clothes. "Ah, this proves it. Look here!"

She lifted out a blue jacket with tails piped in gold. The cuffs were yellow, and the gold-fringed epaulet on one shoulder signified captain's rank. On a peg just inside the door hung a red-and-yellow regimental sash. A two-foot-tall bearskin hat decorated with gold cords commanded the top shelf.

"You can bet your last picayune that the straight saber he wears on his back is part of this uniform," she said, putting the jacket back. "His dragoon boots, too." She touched the bearskin. "He must have looked nine feet tall in that hat!"

"He gonna be like a nine-foot-tall *bear* if he catch you in that closet. Get yourself outa there!"

Loire went to sit by the porthole, gazing thoughtfully at the Gulf. "I wonder why he didn't tell Papa about this?"

"Woulda been cheating."

"Cheating?"

"Uh-huh. If your daddy knowed he one of ole Napoleon's guards, he woulda got out the musket and *made* you marry him. That man, he wanted to win you back by his own self, not cause Mistah Chartier think Napoleon the cat's whiskers."

"Maybe you're right."

"'Course I is."

"I'll ask him about it."

"Ask after you done married. It ain't so smart for a gal to let her man know she a snoop."

"I already knew he fought for Napoleon, I just didn't know how good he was. He's bound to tell me all about himself sooner or later."

"You just keep your mouth shut, make him tell you later. Act real surprised."

Loire sighed. "I wish he'd let me up on deck. I've got good eyes."

"Yeah, and you'd be a-fastening them on him instead of the ocean, and he'd be eyeballing you."

"He's still got the crew."

"They'd be staring at you, too. Ain't nobody'd see no Englishmans till we done blown to Beulah Land. We'd all be up in the clouds of Glory, peeping down at a gunship and scratching our heads, wondering how come we didn't see the damn thing in time."

"You've got a frightful imagination, Ida."

"St. John call it horse sense. He always say somebody oughta put me in charge."

"He's right. You've got more sense in your little finger than Claiborne and his whole cabinet have under their stovepipe bonnets."

"Yeah, they make me head woman over there, I'll send them milktoast militia boys to help out ole Mistah Jackson."

Loire looked at her suspiciously. "Were you eavesdropping on Dominique and me the other night?"

"Nope. I don't butt in folks' business."

"Ha!"

"Now what you wanta go 'ha' at me for, Miz Loire? I ain't never listen in on your private time."

"Then how did you know about the militia?"

"Every niggah in the city know about that. Don't take listening to no white folks' bedroom talk to know how the ground lay."

Loire crossed her arms and frowned.

"You worrying over Mistah Youx agin, 'cause he aiming to go after them British."

"You *have* been eavesdropping!"

"I ain't! Tim done told me all about Mistah Youx's plans— all them sailors knows it. They gonna stick by him, help him chase down that fleet."

"Let's not talk about it."

"I ain't said a word." Closing her eyes, she leaned her head against the back of her chair.

Loire went to the armoire. She gazed at Dominique's uniform for a long time, reminding herself that only the most invincible sort of man could earn the right to wear it.

Six miles long and one mile wide, the island of Grand Terre lay just off the coast of Louisiana. At half-past six in the evening, the *Dragon* fired a signal gun in its direction. A puff of smoke from the small brick fort on the headland signaled her to enter port.

Dominique guided his ship through the narrow channel between Grand Terre and Grand Isle into Barataria Bay, where he anchored a hundred yards offshore.

The beach was virtually deserted. No smoke drifted from the squat brick houses just inside the trees, and only one boatload of doxies greeted his crew. The bay, too, was strangely empty; Dominique counted only a score of ships, luggers, and barges.

"We will spend the night at the Red House," he told Loire as he helped Ida and her into the life boat. "Tomorrow we will transfer your father's goods into a barge and make our way to New Orleans."

Once ashore, Dominique led them down a path through a cypress wood. In a clearing not far inland, brick houses surrounded a big red château on stilts. Lamplight blazed from its long, open windows.

Jean Laffite came out of the house. He was tall and very dark and was dressed in a flashy blue uniform. Four thugs wearing tight military jackets fanned out around him. He squinted into the gloom.

"Dominique? Ah, it *is* you! Welcome!" He jogged down the verandah steps, threw his arms around his half brother, and kissed both his cheeks.

"Where is everyone?" Dominique asked.

Before Jean could reply, two doxies in corsets and brief petticoats came out of the house, ran down the steps, and, shouldering Loire aside, showered Dominique with kisses.

Jean laughed as Dominique extricated himself, throwing an embarrassed glance at Loire. "You must go quickly inside, Dominique, before my heated little ones do more than kiss you in front of the lady. Me, I think they have missed you very much."

Uncharacteristically at a loss for words, Dominique reclaimed Loire's arm and rushed her up the steps. Ida sat down on a rocker on the porch.

"It was not as it seemed, *chérie*," Dominique said, pausing at the door. "Perhaps you will put away the flaming daggers in your eyes."

"It's not so easy."

"They are part of a past I've already forgotten. Please, let us go inside. You will see things here to amaze you. Jean built his Red House to showcase his treasures." He led her inside.

But the house was empty except for a few pieces of furniture and half a dozen wooden crates. Loire followed Dominique from room to room, looking at empty glass cases and squares of brighter paint on the walls where paintings had hung.

Jean came into the high-ceilinged drawing room and flopped down on a green velvet settee. The doxies positioned themselves behind the couch, reaching over to play with his hair.

Dominique sat on the raised hearthstone near a guillotine window and pulled Loire down beside him. "All right, Jean, what news? Where is everyone, and where are your treasures?"

"Go away, girls," Jean said, snapping his fingers. He watched them flee into a boudoir and slam the door. "They are too distracting, that pair. In a moment they will begin calling to me like young titmice, and I shall be obliged to make them wait. There are difficult times in a man's life, *non?*"

"Where are the people, Jean?"

"Pierre has taken most to Côte Allemand above New Orleans. Others have camped across the bay."

"Why?"

Jean's left eye twitched shut. "Me, I am expecting visitors, maybe."

"Let me guess—the Royal Navy?"

"Perhaps. As I say, times, they are difficult."

"Let us dispense with the games."

"It is no game I play." Jean drew a cheroot from his vest and lit it with a candle. "A fortnight ago, Captain Lockyer of the brig *Sophie* arrived here with a hellson named McWilliams . . . . I think he said he is a

Royal Colonial Marine. These two, they gave me a
document promising me thirty thousand American
dollars and a captaincy in their navy."

"In return for what?"

"Why, for my consent to work for them, may the
devil pinch their noses with his red-hot tongs!"

"Obviously you refused."

"Perhaps I was not as strong as I should have been,
mon frère. McWilliams demanded that I, Captain Jean
Laffite, return all the goods and ships I've liberated
from England and Spain as a measure of good faith! It
is a painful thing, to give back what I worked so hard
to earn!"

"I fully commiserate," Dominique said. "What else
did he say?"

"That illegitimate son of a mastiff, he said he would
bring a dozen sloops of war and blast Grand Terre to
hell if I refused."

"And so?"

"And so I put them off, of course," he said, chuckling.
"Me, I told them to come back on the eighteenth and I
would place myself at their disposal."

"That is less than four days from now."

"*Oui.* And so you see, I am evacuating those most
likely to be hurt."

"And your treasures as well."

Laffite had the grace to look ashamed but said
nothing.

"Jean, don't run away. I'll send letters to Governor
Claiborne tonight, indicating our intention to fight on
the American side."

"That finicky clerk, he will throw them in the dustbin with the ones I already sent."

"What is this?"

"The lawyer Edward Livingston forwarded the British papers to Claiborne. The British wish to slip into New Orleans using myself as a guide, since no outsider can find his way through the bayous."

"So Lockyer wishes you to unlock the back door for him. What did Claiborne say about that?"

"That son of a cottonmouth moccasin called the letters a forgery! He did not believe my letter swearing loyalty to the United States, either. He is an idiot with bilgewater for intestines!"

"I suppose you wrote in your usual humble style," Loire said, unable to keep silent a moment longer.

"Your woman, she is very scornful, *non?*"

"She has a point. What did your letters say?"

Laffite affected a hurt look. "They said merely that I am a lost sheep wishing to return to the fold. I offered my men in defense of the city. Also, I told him I would leave this place."

"Why?" Loire asked. "You are in a perfect position to hold the bayous."

"Perhaps, but I would not wish him to believe that I, by staying, have cooperated with the enemy." He blew a lopsided smoke ring at the ceiling. "There is a huge fleet in Pensacola. Lockyer struck Mobile, but the Kaintock, Jackson, held him off. They will come here next."

"We must stand to our guns, then," Dominique said.

"*You* stand to our guns, my big brother," Jean said angrily, leaving the settee. "*Oui,* you stay and hold the petite fortress of Grand Terre."

"And so I will. How many men have stayed nearby?"

"Two, maybe three hundred."

"Not enough to attack by sea. We will have to mount the ships' long guns on the fort and place them in batteries along the shoreline, here and on Grand Isle."

"Do as you wish. Me, I have better things to do than fight for a government who insults me so."

"You spoiled imp," Loire burst out, "you should be ashamed!"

"Me? Shame was not something our mother taught us, was it, Dominique? At least, she did not teach her *true* sons the meaning of shame."

Dominique's jaw tightened, but he let the insult pass. "Stay and fight, Jean. Call back your men."

"No. You be the hero this time. Perhaps it will erase the memory of your shameful birth."

"For every hero there are a dozen cowards," Dominique said in a low growl. "Do not make yourself one of them."

For a moment Loire thought Jean would strike his half brother, but he forced himself to relax against the wall. "To lead my little people to safety is no act of cowardice, Dominique. My descendants will call me a great leader."

"They will call you a pirate," Loire said, "interested only in saving his own skin. And his bloodstained treasures, of course."

"If I save my treasures, it is so my descendants will not begin life as penniless outcasts, like this man!"

Loire rose to her feet. "You are a craven blackguard, monsieur. Alexandre Laffite has done very well for an outcast, no? He is a man of honor, which is more than I can say for you!"

Jean strode across the room to the boudoir. "Girls! Get dressed. We are leaving at once."

Dominique rose from the hearth. "On your way, my brave one, tell the men to get back to the island. There is much work to do tonight, and little time."

Jean's countenance softened. Laying a hand on Dominique's shoulder, he said, "Come with me, *mon frère.* The things I said, they were stupid—the manure of anger. Please, do not stay. It is too dangerous."

"Just send men." He looked at Loire. "And take my betrothed to the city."

"No! I won't leave you!"

"You cannot stay, Smokeflower. There will be a terrible fight."

"I'm not going!" She stormed outside, slamming the door behind her.

"Your lady, she likes you very much, big brother."

"Too much. I will send her and her woman away in the morning."

Laffite's doxies came out of the bedroom and fell into his arms. Smiling sadly, he said, "May God watch over you, my brother."

Dominique looked into the empty fireplace and said, "If you will stay here and call back your men, we can send out enough ships to fight before the British reach the island. We will not have to sit here like ducks, waiting for them to come."

The front door slammed as Laffite left, and Dominique knew it was up to him to stop the British rearward assault on New Orleans.

21

Dominique spent that night and all the next day rounding up Baratarians. By evening he was hungry for Loire. She had refused to leave the island, but he had not seen her since Jean's departure. It was time to see her, to hold her . . . to convince her that she must go home.

He found her in the drawing room of the Red House, roasting sweet potatoes on a spit. "Good evening, my lovely Smokeflower."

"Oh! I didn't hear you come in," she said, brushing ashes from her skirts. Her cheeks were flushed with heat, her hair falling in wisps into her eyes.

"You were supposed to go to New Orleans today," he said. The longing in his eyes lightened the severity of his tone.

"I thought you'd need someone to cook for you."

"A lame excuse, Loire."

She shrugged. "All right, then, I thought you'd need someone to kiss you."

"You're volunteering?"

"With open arms."

He smiled and came across the room to embrace her.

Later she asked, "What do you plan to do about the British?"

"Attack them at sea."

"But I thought you hadn't sufficient men. I thought you were staying on the island."

"No. Five hundred Baratarians returned today. I'll leave two hundred here to man the guns; the remainder will sail a little way up the coast with me to intercept Lockyer."

"I could choke that Jean for running away!"

"He is not as bad as he pretends. Calling him a coward was much like putting sand into the shell of a crawfish. He will fret and try to wriggle out of it, but he'll be back, spoiling for action."

"And when do you intend to sail?"

"Jean said Lockyer plans to come back on the eighteenth, so we'll sail the night before. When the sun comes up, he'll find a wolf pack guarding the gates of the sheep pen."

"I see." Striving for composure, Loire went back to the fire and turned the spit. "Will you take me with you, Dominique?"

"You know I cannot. Naval battles are dreadful things."

"So is waiting and worrying. My place is beside you, with a loaded musket."

"Your place is in New Orleans, warning Claiborne of the peril."

"I've already thought of that. This morning Ida went to the city with one of your men, carrying a note to Claibo written in my own hand. Why are you shaking your head?"

"He will say the letter is another of Jean's tricks. Loire, you must go back to the city and personally ask him to send Commandant Patterson. Together we can snare the British."

He didn't tell her that by the time she traveled two days through the swamps, delivered the message, and convinced Claiborne of the danger, the British would have already attacked. At least she'd be out of the way.

"You'd better sit down and eat," she said, trying not to cry. "It will be a while before you have to brave my cooking again."

"Brave it? If it is that bad, perhaps we should load it into our cannon and fire it onto Lockyer's decks."

"It's just a little crispy around the edges," she said, sniffing. She pushed the food onto a pair of gold-embossed china plates Jean had overlooked and patted the hearthstone beside her. "You'll have to eat it with your dagger—I couldn't find any silverware but this butter knife."

"It is beneath the hearthstone," he said, sitting down beside her. "I doubt that Jean remembered to take it."

Loire folded her skirts under her knees and stared at the flat stone. "Should we take it out?"

"No. It will be more fun to let Jean worry about it when he remembers." He pulled out his knife and poked one of the hard black circles on his plate. "What is this?"

"Half a sweet potato. It has a little soot on it."

"That is just the way I like them." He tried to spear

the potato, but it rebounded and landed on the floor behind Loire. She was sawing away with her butter knife and didn't see it.

Feeling his gaze on her, she looked up, then down at his plate and up again. Affecting an expression of pleasure, Dominique pretended to chew.

"You like it, Dominique?"

He swallowed. "*Oui.* I didn't know you could cook like this."

"I can't, really. This is only the second time I've tried it . . . this year, I mean."

When she continued to watch him, he searched for a piece of potato soft enough to eat. His eyes watered as he chewed. "You are not going to eat, Smokeflower?"

"I don't have much appetite," she said, staring at her plate. Suddenly she thrust it aside and began to cry. "Oh, Dominique, I'm a terrible cook! Ida won't even let me in the kitchen! You don't have to eat it . . . I know it's as hard as brick. Everything I make is either burned or raw."

Chuckling, he pulled her close and rocked her. "You don't have to do *everything* perfectly, Loire, my darling. Let Ida be mistress of the kitchen."

"She's gone, and I don't think there's anything left to cook. You need your strength."

"I am strong enough." He guessed that her tears were due more to his upcoming battle than to her clumsiness in the kitchen. "Come with me outside— there are late oranges on the trees. Come."

He led her along the darkening paths to a tall orange tree. "Watch this," he said, swinging athletically up on a branch. With the brashness of a small boy, he ran up and down, pretending that at any moment he might lose his balance and crash to the ground. Loire's shrieks of alarm mingled with giggles as he windmilled his arms, shouting, "Whoa!" like a Kentucky drover.

"Pick some of those little green oranges while you're up there, why don't you?"

"Promise you will not try to make anything with them?"

"I promise."

He tossed down half a dozen and jumped out of the tree, landing lightly on the balls of his feet. Then he bowed flamboyantly. "Ta-da!"

"You are a madman, Dominique, and I love you. Here, have some supper." She handed him a shriveled orange. "I hope you brought your knife."

But Dominique wasn't hungry for oranges. Dropping it on the ground, he scooped her up and carried her under the low branches of the tree. He cleared away some of the hard, crunchy leaves before lowering her to the ground. Murmuring endearments, he began to kiss her mouth, her cheeks, her eyelids.

Loire slid her hands inside his shirt as he undressed her, enjoying the play of his muscles. In a matter of minutes she was naked, lying on her pile of clothes. "Are you not going to undress, Dominique?"

"No," he said with a pirate's smile. "I will let you do it. It is one of the things you do exceptionally well."

"Oh, dear, I'm afraid I've torn your shirt."

He looked down, perplexed. "But it is intact."

"No, it's torn." She seized his collar and ripped his shirt off his back, playfully scratching his chest with her nails.

"Why, you little vixen!" He pinned her arms to the ground and kissed her face over and over again.

"Be careful, Dominique. I see in my crystal ball that your breeches are torn as well!"

"If you and I do not stop tearing the clothes off each other, every tailor in New Orleans will soon be rich enough to buy himself a fine new house."

"Do not begrudge them a living, *mon cher,*" she said with a wicked chuckle, struggling to break free. Her arching movements brought her breasts into contact with his chest.

Thoroughly aroused, Dominique sat up and stripped off his pants. "There, you cannot believe all you see in a crystal ball."

"Oh, no?" She reached out to stroke him, working her way down and back up again. "I believe I've seen this wonderful thing somewhere before."

"It wasn't in a crystal ball," he said. He lay down on his back and rolled her over on top of him, guiding her up and down until she forgot to laugh or talk and it was all she could to breathe.

"I love you, Loire, my heart, my soul. Give me all of you . . . I want it all."

"Oh, Dominique . . ."

He rolled her onto her back, every muscle in his body contracting in great, quivering thrusts that swept her into a maelstrom of desire, obliterating the memory of all other passions, seizing and tossing her until she had no memory of anything at all, no thought for anything but the flaming wave exploding inside her being.

After unmeasured moments she came to her senses. Dominique felt hot, his breath rasping in her ear, the heavy thudding of his heart only a little slower than hers. "By the sacred thunder, my love," he said, "one of these nights you will kill me."

"Never. What hurts you also hurts me."

"And what pleasures you also pleasures me. I've never known such bliss!"

"You wasted your time on the wrong people, then," she said, kissing his jaw. "You must forever after waste it only on me."

"There are no wasted moments with you, Loire Chartier. None."

"Let's go back to the house before the mosquitoes discover us," she said. "Jean took all the beds, but I made a fine pallet of quilts on the floor of the guest room."

Dominique kissed her cheek, surprised to discover it wet with tears. He pretended not to notice. She was a brave soul, and he loved her for it. "Let's put our clothes back on for the trip. There are some places where I would not like to be bitten."

"La! You are a tender baby, to mind a little itching."

"I do not wish to be distracted by it, darling, when I desire to devote my full attention tonight to your enjoyment."

From boyhood, Dominique had made it a habit to rise two hours before dawn. But on the morning of September 16, nestled in the blankets with Loire, he was still asleep when the shout went up: "Sail ho! Sail!"

He bolted off the pallet stark naked and ran to the window, tearing the curtains off the rod as Tim dashed out of the trees, yelling.

"Dominique, what's happening?" Loire began throwing on her clothes.

"The British have come two days early, curse them!" He leaped into his breeches as Tim began pounding on the front door.

Grabbing his shirt and vest on the way, Dominique rushed to the door. Tim burst into the house.

"They're here already, Mistah Youx!"

"How many?"

"Two schooners, three gunboats. Sneaked up in the darkness and fog."

"Get down to the bay and tell the crews to weigh anchor at once." He looked over his shoulder as Loire came into the room, buttoning her dress. "*Merde!* We must get you off the island!"

"No!"

Taking her by the arm, he forced her out of the house and down the path to the bay. A cannon boomed on the gulf side of the island. Breaking out of the trees, he discovered his sailors swarming up the ratlines, hoisting sail, turning the pirate vessels into the wind. He hoped they could get under way in time. With their sails luffing, they would be sitting ducks if the warships entered the bay.

An explosion shook the ground, and from the gulf side a plume of smoke sullied the air. There was another blast, then another and another.

Dominique grabbed a sailor. "LeBeau, find a pirogue and take Mademoiselle Chartier deep into the swamps."

"I won't go!" she shouted. A cannonball crashed through the treetops into the bay near one of the sloops. "I'm staying with you!"

Dominique thrust her at LeBeau. "Tie her up if you need to, but get her out of here. Move!"

Before LeBeau could touch her, a Baratarian dashed out of the woods, shouting, "It is not the British!"

"What! Who, then?"

"Americans! Commandant Patterson's fleet!"

"*Sacrebleu!* This I must see for myself! No one fires until I give the order! LeBeau, get Loire into the swamp."

Dominique sped off into the trees. Evading LeBeau,

Loire darted after him. She reached the brick fort on the gulf and crowded through the sally port. Buffeted by the defenders, she climbed to the parapet.

Patterson's ships were within a mile of the fort. As Loire watched, smoke belched from a gunboat. She heard a high-pitched whine, then an explosion at the base of the wall. Bricks blasted thirty feet in all directions.

"Hold your fire!"

Dominique stood on the southeast corner of the parapet, drawing his hand across his throat, guillotine-like. "Do not fire on the American flag! Evacuate the island!"

"They will blast the island to pieces, Dominique!" Loire yelled. "You cannot give up without a fight!"

"I cannot fire on them, woman!" He caught her under one arm and hauled her down the steps. The brick wall shuddered and crumbled inward as he dragged her out the sally port. "Go with the men! I've got to go back!"

"I'm coming with you!"

"Damn it, woman, I have no time to argue. Run!"

Again the cannons thundered, tearing trees out of the ground, hurling flaming wreckage in all directions. Loire looked for Dominique and saw him running back into the smoking fort. Again she went after him.

He was trying to free someone trapped beneath a timber. Loire grabbed the freebooter under the arms while Dominique renewed his attack on the timber. It would not budge. He growled from deep in his chest and managed to raise the beam an inch. His muscles stood out in thick, shining coils; his face contorted with the terrible strain. The beam creaked and groaned, rising half a foot.

Loire dragged the freebooter clear. Cradling his head in her arms, she shuddered at the sickening thud of the timber dropping back down. Dominique squatted down beside him and took his hand.

"You have served the Laffites well," Dominique said softly. "Your wife and children will never go hungry, I promise."

"Captain," he whispered. His eyes filmed over, and he was gone.

"We must go, Loire," Dominique said, his voice strained. He gently lowered the freebooter to the rubble. "I must get you away before the marines land."

This time she did not argue. They found the path obliterated by fallen trees. A fire was burning fifty yards away.

"They've stopped firing!" Dominique cried.

"What does it mean?"

Shouts echoed from the beach behind them. They struggled along as fast as they could. There was a loud explosion from the bay. Dominique swore. "Stay here and hide. I must see what is happening. Don't stir from here until I come back."

He discovered American schooners in the bay. Several Baratarian vessels were on fire, the *Dragon* among them. Marines were rounding up crews from the ships and freebooters from the vacated shore batteries.

Dominique heard a branch snap behind him. He twisted around just as a pistol butt crashed into his head.

He came to a few minutes later, tied to a tree.

"So, my friend, we meet again. Hoping for just such an encounter kept me alive during the week I spent in your ship's boat, with the sun burning down on my head."

With considerable difficulty Dominique focused on a man standing in the shadows, leveling a pistol at his heart. It was Alain Defromage.

"It is unfortunate for you that the Americans picked me up, Captain Youx."

"Your rescue has nothing to do with me, my cowardly friend."

Alain walked into the sunlight, his face twisted with rage. "It has everything to do with you, pirate! But for me, Governor Claiborne might have believed those letters Jean Laffite sent."

"You should not have convinced him otherwise, Defromage. The British will be here in two days. Who will stop them? You? This pitiful flotilla of Patterson's?"

"This flotilla was enough to stop *you!*"

"Its *flag* was enough to stop me."

"Bah! You are no patriot, but a fraudulent bastard like your brothers. Patterson is disappointed that Jean ran away, but I am content that I've found you here."

"*Oui.* You are a very great hero."

"If I were in your position, I would not spend my breath on sarcasm. It is a shame my bullet did not kill you aboard the *Hopscotch.*"

"These things happen. Your powder was wet."

"It is quite dry today." He pushed the muzzle against Dominique's forehead and cocked the hammer. "I can assure you that this time, I will not fail to send you to hell."

"You are to be commended for your mercy. A coward's bullet between the eyes is quicker than the hangman's noose."

Alain's gun hand trembled. "You are a fool, as well as a pirate, to speak thus to the man who holds your life in his palm!"

"It is a very bad habit of mine."

"A habit you will have no chance to break in the few seconds of life you have left."

The Red Dragon stared into his eyes. "You will not kill me, Alain. You do not have the guts to shoot an unarmed man."

"You are a fool to taunt me so!"

"Perhaps, but if you manage to shoot me dead, you will still be without Loire."

"Loire?"

"She is what this is all about."

"Yes! You stole the woman I love!"

"She is mine, Alain. Mine forever. She will never belong to you."

"You are wrong, but you have reminded me of something. Be very still now, or I will shoot you between the eyes." He squatted down and felt in Dominique's vest pocket. "Ah! I knew you would have it on you, you romantic fool!"

Ignoring the rage burning in Dominique's eyes, Alain thrust Loire's miniature into his own pocket. "There! She is mine again!"

Dominique looked around at the marines. What would happen when they found Loire? He had to give her to Alain; it was his only chance to protect her. "Loire is in the woods. Go find her before one of these Kaintocks does."

The pistol wavered. "She—she is here? On the island?"

"Three hundred yards back, hiding under a live oak."

"You are lying."

"Damn you, go find her. If you discover I've lied, come back and shoot me. Go on!"

Alain slowly uncocked the hammer and shoved the pistol into his belt. "You'll die later, my friend, do not fear."

Then he entered the woods to search for Dominique's betrothed.

22

Rain blew in through the barred window of the cell, misting Dominique Youx's naked chest. For the sum of fifteen thousand Spanish dollars, his lawyer, Edward Livingston, had promised to gain his release, but after three months the cell door remained locked.

It aggravated him to sit in jail, useless, while every able-bodied male in New Orleans blocked the bayous and roads leading into the city. Andrew Jackson had brought two thousand troops from Mobile and imposed martial law, and while Jackson had to force the recalcitrant New Orleanians into the militia, he laughed at Dominique's repeated offers to enlist.

Renato Beluche had reported that the British fleet was in Lake Borgne, only sixty miles east, grounded at Cat Island. Dominique knew that if they somehow managed to get through the shallow lake, they could slip through the bayous to New Orleans' back door.

"Sapristi!" Dominique swore, curling his hands around the bars. If he could only get free, he could bring up some of his fast sloops hidden in the backwaters, block the mouth of the lake, and blast the British where they sat.

The gate creaked. Flanked by two guards, a woman enveloped in an oilskin coat entered the courtyard. Dominique recognized her instantly.

"Loire!"

He watched her honey-brown eyes widen, then she threw off her hood, hitched her coat around her knees, and came splashing across the courtyard.

She was thinner than he remembered, her eyes hollow, her skin very pale, giving her an ephemeral air. Acute frustration mingled with his joy at seeing her after so long. He wanted more than anything to draw her through the iron bars into his arms.

"Loire . . . oh, my lovely lady," he said huskily, stretching his hands through the bars. "I had nearly despaired of seeing you again. *Dieu,* it's been a living death without you."

Her eyes grew even larger, filling with tears. Rain streamed over her face as she stood on tiptoe to take hold of his hands.

"You are freezing, little one," he said, alarmed. "Are you ill? Damn it, why wasn't I told?"

"I've felt like a block of ice since they arrested you," she said, "but not ill. It freezes my heart that you're here!"

Slightly mollified, Dominique said, "You've been as much a prisoner as I have, under house arrest, my poor Smokeflower."

She tried to shrug off her own problems with a care- less, "Pooh, it was nothing to stay in the mercantile all day, watching Jackson's soldiers buy everything in sight. Besides, I'm on probation now. Mr. Livingston says I can go anywhere I want."

He reached out to cup her cheek, brushing tears and raindrops away with his thumb. There was a catch in his voice as he said, "Edward Livingston says they intend to try you for conspiracy against the government, damn them."

"Yes." Fear shadowed her face for an instant before she masked it with a brave smile. "Papa's come for the trial. Livingston thinks they'll drop the charges, though, before it comes up. We'll see."

"They'll drop them," he said, his voice low and dangerous.

A feverish glint came into her eyes. Digging her fingers into his forearms, she pulled him down a little more and whispered, "I've come to talk the sheriff into letting you go, but if he won't, Papa's going to get you a pistol."

Dominique raised his brows. "A jail break? That is droll."

"Droll, la! I'm deadly serious." She threw a glance over her shoulder at the guards, satisfying herself that they stood on the sidewalk. "I'd give you my pistol right now, but Alain lost it after he shot you on the ship, the wretch, and the militia has every gun in the city. But don't worry, we'll get one if we have to steal it!"

Troubled, he stroked her cheek. "Don't do anything foolish, pirate woman. For once in my life, I must abide by the law."

She stamped her foot. "That's the most misguided thing I've ever heard! Don't you realize that Claiborne wants to either hang you or keep you in jail until you're so old you won't know me anymore?"

"You sound as though you still love me."

"You're trying to change the subject, aren't you? But of course I love you—didn't Edward Livingston give you my messages?"

"He did." He smiled crookedly. "But he also said that Alain Defromage has tried to court you ever since the raid."

"I haven't come to talk about Alain."

Jealous anger kindled in his eyes. "So he *has* been courting you."

She stepped away from his hands. "No! I've slammed the door in his face every time. And St. John caught him when he tried climbing over the garden wall."

Dominique's brow furrowed. "What the hell is this?"

Loire sighed. "Don't worry. Do you remember Alain's little black mustache?"

"*Oui.*"

"It is now only *half* a little black mustache. St. John says it's the closest he'll ever come to scalping someone."

His visage cleared. "One might almost feel sorry for the little captain."

"Don't waste your sympathy. He joined Gabriel Villeré's company of militia and thinks himself quite the high hat, striding through the market, ordering little old ladies and slave children about! Why, if Papa gets hold of a gun, I might shoot Alain in the foot before giving it to you."

"Shh, one of the guards is coming. Say no more of guns."

The guard trudged through the puddles and put his hand on Loire's shoulder. He backed away a pace when she flung him off and demanded, "What do you want?"

"Look, ma'am," he drawled, "I waited long as I could, but you got to come inside."

"It's more private here."

"Yeah, and you said you was comin' to see the sheriff. You cain't stand out here, confabbin' with an enemy of the Newnited States."

"You're full of fermented tobacco juice," she said, "if you think Dominique Youx is an enemy."

"Yeah, well, that's what you say. I got my orders. Now come on, be a good girl, get away from that winder."

"Do as he says, *chérie*. You are growing very wet."

The sheriff of Orleans parish stood when she entered his office, his black hair gleaming under the kerosene lamp that hung over his desk.

"When will Monsieur Youx be released?" Loire asked before he could greet her.

"I cannot say, mademoiselle. There are many irregularities which I, alone, cannot straighten out."

"Such as?"

"Acts of sedition, piracy, and conspiring to help the British against the United States of America."

"Balderdash! He intended to give the British captain a drubbing—Why are you curling your lip at me, sir?"

"I have heard these things many times before from Monsieur Youx and his lawyer. It is a very pretty fairy story."

"It is *not* a fairy story! I demand that you release him at once!"

"You, a fellow suspect, are hardly in a position to bargain for his freedom. Besides, the governor has tried for a very long time to gain sufficient evidence on the Laffites to keep them in jail."

"The Laffites have nothing to do with Dominique Youx."

"They have everything to do with him." The sheriff twirled his mustache theatrically before delivering the thrust. "He is their elder brother. Just last week, we found evidence in his warehouse proving he set up their pirating trade years ago, before going back to France to fight for Napoleon."

Loire tried to interrupt, but he spoke over her, his tone full of malicious satisfaction.

"This Alexandre Laffite, alias Youx, owns a controlling interest in the New Orleans Association, which is just a cover for the Baratarian pirate trade."

Loire's voice soared high with desperation. "You don't know what you're talking about! He—he is not even related to the Laffites. You've apprehended the wrong man."

"Your employee, Alain Defromage, learned his true identity last September, while he was prisoner aboard your brigantine."

"Defromage is a liar," she said in a level voice. "He wishes to marry me to get my father's estate. He would say anything to malign Dominique."

"If you wish to discuss this matter further, do so through his attorney. *Adieu.*"

"I'm not leaving until I've spoken to Monsieur Youx."

He shrugged. "It can do no harm, I suppose. Wait here."

A few minutes later, four guards escorted Dominique into the room. His wrists and ankles were shackled; he was wearing only tight knee breeches.

"Take those chains off him at once!" Loire cried.

"You will stop making demands, mademoiselle," the sheriff said, "or I will have him sent back to his cell immediately."

She cocked her hands on her hips but clamped her lips shut.

The sheriff looked Dominique slowly up and down. The privateer stood unmoving, his shackles glinting coldly against his dark skin. Even chained, he looked as dangerous as a leopard.

With his hand hovering over the pistol in his belt, the sheriff swaggered into Dominique's range and locked eyes with him for a long moment.

"Let me warn you, monsieur," he said, "that my men will be just outside. If you try to escape, your lawyer will draw up your burial papers as his final service to you." He left the room.

Dominique's gaze swept over Loire. She bit her lip, seeming hesitant to approach. He imagined how he must look . . . and smell.

"My apologies, Loire. The sheriff does not often allow me razor and soap."

She came to him then and leaned her head against his chest. "I don't care. All that matters is being here with you."

His chains rattled as he lifted his arms and looped them around her waist. Her body was deliciously warm against his naked chest. He could feel himself trembling with the desire to run away with her, to escape the terrible loneliness he'd suffered for so long.

"Each night has lasted a hundred years," he said hoarsely.

"To me, too." Loire fought back tears. "I couldn't get that stubborn sheriff to listen just now, but I'll see Claiborne today, and Andrew Jackson if I have to. I'll get you out!"

"Livingston will manage it, eventually. Don't give up

on me . . . and don't do anything stupid, like smuggling a gun in here."

Her voice broke as she said, "But the sheriff says Claibo knows who you really are."

He stiffened. "The name Laffite haunts me still, then."

"It's worse than that. He says they found evidence in your warehouse about the New Orleans Association. They know everything. I lied for you, but I know he didn't believe me."

He cursed softly.

"Oh, Dominique, what are they going to do to you?" She sagged against him, her shoulders shaking as she wept.

Dominique tightened his arms around her, almost overcome by the exquisite sensation of her nearness. "Don't cry, Loire. I'll get out of this mess, whether I deserve to or not. *Merde*, one time you accused me of using piracy to regain the pride I lost when Laffite disowned me."

"I shouldn't have spoken that way—"

"Shh," he put his finger to her lips. "You were right. But I want you to know that I've changed— you've changed me. From the moment I captured your barque and took your portrait from Defromage, I've been different. I intend to prove it to the world. God help me, I'll buy my way out of here before long."

"How? Livingston said they've confiscated your warehouse. All those treasures—"

"Were only a tithe of what I have. There's more— lots more. And enough supplies to equip Jackson's little army. He and Claiborne don't want to admit it, but they need my provisions . . . and my knowledge of the terrain. I can plan the defense of the city."

Loire shook her head, unconvinced. "They don't

trust you. If only you could have made them prizes of Lockyer's brigs, they might have been persuaded of your loyalty."

"Such is war. It is a pity Claiborne refuses to admit we were right about the British plot. Renato Beluche says Lockyer came back to Grand Terre, found it blown to hell and Jean Laffite in hiding. He went back to Mobile." He laughed bitterly.

Loire let her head fall back, looking into his eyes. She brushed her fingertip across his lips. "I blame Jean for this mess. He set you up!"

"Only because he hoped I could salvage his stronghold. He knew that if the British didn't get him, the Americans would. He is a businessman, my brother, with bank notes for blood. Let us speak no more of him."

Dominique rested his cheek on her head and breathed in her scent, shuddering with longing. Shackled thus, he could not even hold her in the way he wished. He felt like Samson, shorn of strength, aching for what he'd lost. "Ah, Loire."

She moved closer, her tears wetting his chest. "The darkness has closed around us, Dominique, just as you prophesied. Are we never to know happiness?"

"We'll take it where we find it. Now, in the few minutes we have together."

He kissed her then, conveying his yearning with the potency of the storm outside. Rain struck the windows and pattered violently against the walls. Thunder rolled up from the river, giving the jail a shake. Dominique held her tighter, his chains lying cold against her back, his loins hot, throbbing against her.

The sheriff put his head into the room. "Guards, take Monsieur Youx back to his cell. It seems he has finished talking."

*   *   *

When Loire was ushered into Andrew Jackson's headquarters at 106 Royal Street, she found an emaciated shadow of a man with parchment-colored skin lying on the settee, picking at a bowl of hominy grits. Only his eyes seemed alive—alert and hawkish.

"You are wasting your breath to come begging for this hellish bandit, young lady," Jackson said, not waiting for her to speak.

"But he's got cannons and the crews to man them! Patterson didn't succeed in destroying all his vessels."

"I'll note that on the commandant's war record, blast him."

"How can you be so cold?" Loire cried. "They say there are twenty thousand British marines out there, ready to attack the city! You've got less than a third that number. How can you refuse Captain Youx's help?"

Old Hickory waved a skeletal hand. "Go talk to Claiborne if you want him out so badly. Perhaps he can find a job for him."

"The governor won't release him. You're my last hope!"

"Tch, tch. Then I'll tell you what I've already told Youx's lawyer: I'll have nothing to do with any Baratarian renegade."

Having reached the end of her tether, Loire broke into a vehement flood of French.

"Adjutant," Jackson said, setting his grits on the floor and shaking out a map, "if we are to get anything done here, we must clear the room of hysterical females." He fixed his hawkish gaze on Loire. "Good day, mademoiselle."

23

"*Miz Loire, you gonna get* you and your pappy killed, going out to old Villeré's place! That river road too dangerous! You wait till St. John come back."

"St. John's busy guarding the Chef Menteur road," Loire replied. She pulled on her driving gloves, tipped her hat over one eye, and checked her reticule for money. "I don't have time to wait. Papa says Gabriel will sell us a pistol. I'm not going to stay here, sitting on my hands, while Dominique rots in jail!"

She walked out the front door and waited in the rain for Etienne Chartier to bring the carriage around. She could hear the clear notes of a bugle calling reveille from the Place d'Armes beyond the cathedral, where Jackson's troups bivouacked.

"Your papa, he may get himself killed this time, my little girl," Etienne said after they'd gotten under way. He waved his thick black cigar expansively. "But what a way to die, *non?* My life for that of one of Napoleon's

Old Guard, and the lover of my one and only daughter! I will consider it an honor!"

"You are melodramatic, Papa," she said, squeezing his hand. "Nobody's going to die."

"Bah, it is wartime. People die every day. What is the life of one more old man?"

"I've never heard you talk this way before," she said. Apprehension prickled down her spine. "Please stop. We'll get Dominique a gun. You needn't be anywhere nearby if and when he decides to use it."

"He's a warrior," Etienne said with pride. "A warrior like your brothers would have been, had they lived. He'll use the gun."

Loire sat back on the seat, chewing a knuckle. Dominique had told her not to do anything stupid. Perhaps she would only succeed in getting him killed during the jail break.

"Maybe we should petition President Madison for his release," she said, "and forget the gun."

"Bah, that stupid American would listen no better than his governor. We'll get the magnificent Captain Youx a pistol, and watch him break himself free!"

She narrowed her eyes in thought. "Then see if Gabriel will sell us a flint for my Kentucky rifle. Dominique will need help."

"You want your papa to shoot the sheriff?"

"No. If there's any shooting to be done, I'll do it."

"You are a scrappy woman, Loire, just like your mother, but I will not allow it. I myself will shoot the sheriff *and* his deputies. And the governor, if he gets in the way."

They reached the Villeré plantation just before ten. Except for smoke curling out of the chimneys of the château and slaves' quarters, the place looked deserted.

The fields and orchards sulked beneath a heavy blanket of mist rolling out of Bayou Mazant.

Etienne helped Loire out of the carriage. Gabriel met them at the front door and brought them into the living room, hanging Loire's wet redingote over the back of a gilt chair near the fireplace. He poured them each a brandy and gestured them to chairs.

"You've a pistol for us, *mon ami?*" Etienne asked after he'd warmed himself with brandy.

Before Gabriel could answer, Loire's glass tumbled out of her lap as she jumped to her feet, pointing at the window. "God's mercy, look at that!"

A column of green-coated marines and redcoats moved out of the orchard below the house.

"*Sacrebleu*, it is the British!" Etienne shouted. "Where did they come from?"

"Never mind that, we've got to warn Jackson!" Loire said, running out the door.

"Halt! Halt, I say! Stand where you are!" a soldier yelled.

Loire ignored him and started down the steps, with Etienne and Gabriel right behind her. One of the glass windows near them exploded; a musket report echoed down the bayou.

"The next bullet will be aimed at your head, lady! Halt!"

She stopped, raking glass out of her hair, smearing blood from a small cut on her cheek.

The British fanned out to surround the house and outbuildings. A sergeant relieved Gabriel Villeré of his sidearm. A middle-aged officer bowed to the crest-fallen prisoners.

"Colonel Thornton, at your service. Do you surrender?"

"What choice do we have?" Loire asked rhetorically.

"None, madam." He stepped closer, looking at her cut. "Are you all right?"

"I won't bleed to death, sir, if that's what you're hoping."

"I'll have our surgeon attend your wound."

"I'll tend it myself." She started inside.

"Wait!" Thornton caught her elbow. "I trust you are not armed?"

"If I were, you'd be wearing a hole in that red tunic just over your gorget, sir."

"One thanks Providence for your lack of firepower, then." He turned to an aide. "Send Captain Defromage and the guides back for more troops."

"Defromage?" Loire stared hard at the men in the yard.

A man in the ragged garb of a Spanish fisherman lifted his hat brim, triumph glittering in his eyes. He had only half a mustache. "At your service, Mademoiselle Chartier."

Gabriel Villeré stepped forward in anger. "You turncoat!"

"No turncoat—I've been with them from the first, Major. You are foolish to side with losers."

"You joined my militia company!"

Defromage shrugged. "It was essential to gather information, Major Villeré. I am merely doing my part to liberate Louisiana from the hellish Americans." His gaze flicked to Loire. "You've no love for the Kaintocks, my sweet. Perhaps you'd like to change sides while you still can."

"I'll change sides when you crawl back into the alligator hole where you were hatched, you dirty traitor!" She raised her fist and came down the steps after him, but her father rushed to catch her arm.

"No, Loire, leave the yellow-livered bastard alone. He'll die for this, that I can promise."

"I'll die? Ha!" Alain said. "You'll be the one hanging from the tree, carrion for crows, Monsieur Chartier, you stupid, pompous little man! It is a shame that damned pirate stole your barque, for I had intended to make off with the proceeds myself and only *claim* the ship was lost. Another charge to lay on that whoreson's doorstep! I shall enjoy killing him."

Etienne let go of Loire and went after Defromage, but a sergeant jerked him up by the back of the collar and propelled him toward the stairs.

"Perhaps you see how important you are compared to me," Alain Defromage said mockingly. "The British know how to care for their spies."

"They care for you as a she-snake cares for her young!" Etienne yelled over his shoulder. "They'll swallow you up!"

Alain spat. "You know nothing."

"Your masters will leave you flapping in the wind," Loire said, "just as soon as your usefulness is done."

Thornton stepped in. "Enough of this chatter! Lock them in the bedroom and post a guard. I've got work to do, and this cottage will be pleasant after that ghastly swamp."

Loire pulled away from the sergeant. "Jackson has fifteen thousand men guarding the city," she lied. "He knows you're coming this way."

"I think you are telling stories, madam."

"You'll wish I were, when Old Hickory lights into you."

"Inside," Thornton ordered. Two soldiers prodded them into the house.

Loire fired a parting shot over her shoulder. "You're making a very grave mistake, Colonel."

"I'll let history judge that, madam. For the present, I'll take Captain Defromage's word."

"You're quite the foolish lobsterback to accept the word of a man who takes money from both sides!"

"Into the house!" Thornton bellowed.

In the bedroom, Etienne Chartier flopped down on the bed and covered his face with his hands, while Gabriel paced up and down, muttering to himself.

"This is my fault," he said.

"And exactly why is that?" Loire asked.

"I was supposed to block Bayou Bienvenue. They must have come through there to Bayou Mazant."

"You disobeyed Jackson's orders?"

He ran a hand through his hair. "I blocked the neighbors' canals and left mine open."

"Why?"

"Isn't it obvious? What happens to a plantation cut off from its trade routes?"

"You selfish rogue! Because of you, the British are less than nine miles from the city and Jackson doesn't even know it! Do you know what this means?"

"It means I've opened the back door. God, I think I will shoot myself!"

"You can't," Etienne said dully, "you don't have a gun."

Loire raised a corner of the window shade. It was raining hard, obscuring the marines beyond the picket fence.

"We've got to warn Jackson," she said. "Come on, Papa, get off that bed."

"Perhaps we should wait until dark," Gabriel said.

"New Orleans might be in British hands by dark,"

Etienne said. "Loire, you stay here. Gabriel and I will go."

"We'll all go," she said, sliding open the window.

The sash creaked alarmingly, but when no one came to investigate, she eased it fully open, climbed out, and dropped into the shrubbery. The men joined her, and for half a minute they crouched there, dreadfully exposed, straining their eyes against the downpour.

"I'll go first," Gabriel said, "then you, then Etienne. We'll go over the northeast corner of the fence and get into the stable."

"What if the British are in there?" Etienne asked.

"By the sacred blood, I don't know! Just do the best you can." He sprinted out of cover and vaulted over the fence. Hitching up her skirts, Loire bolted after him, and her father pounded along behind her.

"The prisoners are escaping!"

"Halt!"

"Fire!"

The air burst into white-hot jets of flame. Loire threw herself over the fence and landed on a bush. Her father finished on top of her, jumped up, and yanked her to her feet. He lost her hand as they started toward the trees.

Three redcoats rounded the fence. They fired at Etienne as he disappeared into the trees and kept running. Lifting his musket to high port, a soldier started after him.

"Run, Papa!" Loire shouted. She dove at the soldier, grabbed him around the knees, and rolled through the mud with him. The others rushed to grab her, cursing and laughing when she fought them like a wildcat. They finally managed to pinion her arms.

"Get her inside," ordered the soldier she'd tackled,

wiping dirt off his face with the back of his hand. "Give her a dose of brandy to calm her down."

"Where'd the little fat bloke get to, and the young one?"

"Damned if I know, mate. A couple of boys went after them. Keep your fingers crossed they find them in that damned swamp. We'll catch hell if the buggers get off and warn the bleeding Yanks."

Loire sat at the long table in Gabriel's dining room, pointedly ignoring the officers at the other end. Through the windows she could see campfires twinkling on the dark plain. Two thousand troops had arrived shortly after the escape and bivouacked from the Villerés to neighboring Versailles.

Was her father alive? She chewed her knuckle, remembering his fatalistic words on the drive over. He'd wanted to die a hero, blast him. She hoped he hadn't. She preferred him brash, a little too big for his britches, and alive.

Suddenly an explosion lit up the night. Another blast followed, and another. Loire left the table with the men to run to the window.

"Good God, those are naval guns!" Thornton cried. "Commandant Patterson must have gotten his damned *Carolina* downriver!"

The officers rushed outside. Loire tried to follow, but a soldier grabbed her by the arm and pushed her under the table. "There now, lady, you'll stay there till we find out what the bloody devil's going on."

An explosion rocked the house, pelting the soldier with ceiling plaster. He blew out the lamps and squatted down, staring out the window. There were no campfires on the plain now—nothing but darkness punctuated by roaring sheets of flame.

The bombardment ended half an hour later. Within seconds, crackling rifles and the lusty bellowing of infantry penetrated the gloom. From the cypress swamp came bloodcurdling yells and war whoops and the terrified neighing of horses. Field artillery barked.

A faint cry rose over the din. "Save the guns, men! At all costs, save the guns!"

"Jackson, as I live and breathe," Loire said.

At last the guns fell silent, giving place to the shrieks of the wounded.

Were Jackson's men lying on the muddy plain while the British marched on her beloved city? To Loire, locked in darkness, the end seemed very near.

24

Loire tended wounded British men through the rest of the night. At dawn, the naval bombardment began again. A schooner and a sloop of war, the *Carolina* and the *Louisiana*, turned the plain into no-man's-land, halting the work of the burial crews.

She thought Gabriel Villeré must have gotten through to warn Jackson, precipitating last night's assault. She could only hope that her father had made it, too. Nervously she scanned each casualty brought in, but aside from a few Americans, all were British.

Loire didn't know much about military tactics, but over the next two days of captivity she managed to ferret out the names of regimental commanders and the number of troops each one commanded. Twice she tried to escape but was apprehended and sent back to nurse the injured.

On Christmas Day, Major General Sir Edward

Pakenham, the commander of the British forces, arrived at the plantation. Thirty-seven years old, with a mischievous round face and blue eyes, the commander showed his underlings a royal commission naming him governor of Louisiana. Loire overheard him boast that his wife was aboard the flagship at the mouth of the river, waiting for word to sail into New Orleans in triumph.

Loire's spirits rose when she snooped outside the window, listening to his officers brief him. He grew angrier and angrier when he learned of their untenable position, with the river on one side and the cypress swamp on the other. Defromage and other spies reported that Jackson's troops were digging in on the MacCarté plantation two miles upriver, blocking their overland route to New Orleans.

After she learned his plan to fetch naval cannon from the fleet grounded at Cat Island while his engineers widened Bayou Bienvenue for the barges, Loire tried again to slip out of camp. Once more she was captured.

When the American bombardment began the next morning, Pakenham's new battery of cannon answered through an embrasure in the levee, hurtling hot shot through the *Carolina*'s rigging and setting fire to her deck. Taken by surprise and without wind to fill his ship's sails, Commandant Patterson was unable to save her. He ordered his crew to abandon ship, and within minutes the *Carolina* sank.

Aware that the *Louisiana* would suffer the same fate if he didn't begin kedging immediately, her captain ordered the longboat into the river and lines made fast to the sloop. The strongest sailors leaped down into the boat and seized the oars. With hot shot splashing into the river all around them, the rowers endeavored to tow the sloop upriver. After half an hour, the *Louisiana* was safely out of range and the many small fires on her deck put out.

Loire retired to the bedroom that served as her cell late one night, tired to the bone from caring for the wounded. Stopped by Jackson's artillery, the British had been unable to move their line forward. Wounded men arrived by the cartload every day, many of them scalped by Jackson's Choctaw allies deployed in the swamp.

She pulled off her gown and dropped it on the floor. In her petticoat, she went to the washbasin. She heard a noise behind her, a scrape followed by the tinkling of glass.

Whirling around, she saw an arm reaching through the broken pane to flick the latch. A Choctaw in warpaint stuck his head in the window. She immediately snatched up the lamp and drew her arm back to throw it.

"Stop! It's Dominique," he whispered hoarsely.

"*Mon Dieu!*" She hurriedly snuffed the lamp as he climbed through. He pulled her into his arms.

She couldn't see more than his shadow, but his naked chest felt hard and fit. She clung to the leather baldric crossed over his chest, her other hand seeking the back of his neck to pull him down.

The kiss was a hot, intimate melee that made her burn with anticipation. Slipping her hands down his back, she found he was wearing nothing but a fringed buckskin breechcloth.

"You savage," she said, kissing his throat.

"This savage craves you." He kissed her again, his hands ranging forcefully over her body, pulling up her petticoat until his fringe brushed her bare skin. "I could take you here and now!"

"Impetuous *and* savage," she said, and kissed him hard. She pressed herself against him, stroking the muscles of his hips and thighs. "You know we're surrounded."

He groaned. "Yes. We'll have to crawl to the swamp. *Then* I'll take you!"

Without another moment's delay, he threw her redingote over her petticoat, caught her hand, and helped her out the window. In the rain, they were almost invisible as they crawled slowly to the fence. Dominique climbed over it nimbly and reached back for her. At that instant, a sentry bearing a lantern came around the corner of the house. Loire tried to squat down, but Dominique grabbed her wrists and pulled her over the fence.

"Halt, damn you!" the sentry shouted.

Hand in hand, Loire and Dominique ran among the tents. A musket barked behind them as men began emerging from their sleeping quarters.

"Run, Loire! He won't dare shoot now!"

They ran through camp at top speed, stumbling over soldiers who were crawling out of the tents, pulling muskets stacked like teepees into the mud, and scattering campfires. Dominique slammed his fist into the face of an officer rearing up with a cudgel, knocking him down. Loire ran straight over him.

They plunged into the cypress trees as the British unleashed a volley of musket fire. Balls whined off the trees. Loire felt something tug her redingote and realized she'd almost been shot. She stumbled over a root and fell. Dominique picked her up and forged on as fast as he could run.

Twenty yards into the swamp, they stumbled onto a band of Choctaws and Tennessee militia. The American troops let out a yell and dashed to the edge of the swamp, firing at the British to head off pursuit.

They ran for another half hour before stopping to catch their breath. Dominique enfolded her in his arms and held her tightly as she began to shiver.

"Did they hurt you, Loire?"

"No. You?"

"No."

"Where's my father?"

"Back in town, minding the store."

"Is he all right?"

"Perfectly. Spoiling for excitement. Jackson has to let him patrol the marketplace at night to give him something to do."

"Thank God. And Gabriel?"

"In jail. Jackson's mad at him for leaving the bayou open."

"How did you get out of jail?"

He hugged her tighter. "Once Jackson heard that the British were upon us, he gave all the Baratarians amnesty. I'm a free man . . . in exchange for ships, guns, and men. I'm to command a battery of cannon near the levee."

"So he finally saw reason . . . . Why the warpaint?" she asked, touching his garish face.

"To slip through the British lines. It's excellent camouflage, don't you think?"

"I'd rather be able to see who I'm kissing," she said, and sought his mouth.

He obliged her, his breath hot against her face. Tendrils of desire curled up and down her spine, chasing away the chill of the swamp. He felt naked in his Indian garb, his muscles turgid with need, and she caressed him boldly.

"We'd better get behind Jackson's line," he said huskily, "before the British catch us in a very awkward situation."

Two hours later, they walked around the end of the mud rampart stretching into the swamp and arrived in the American encampment. Troops were stretched out on cotton bales, asleep. Dominique led her past hundreds of others sleeping on the muddy ground, to the MacCarté château.

St. John, Jean Laffite, Renato Beluche, and Andrew Jackson glanced up from a map as they walked in, looking muddy and bedraggled. St. John enveloped Loire in a bear hug.

"Ah, there you are, Youx," Jackson said calmly, as if they'd been out for a Sunday stroll. "You took your time getting back, didn't you? The maid's ready to pour your bath anytime you're ready. Oh, Miss Chartier, your housemaid brought you some clean clothes."

Old Hickory returned his gaze to the map.

"Doesn't he want to hear the information I've gathered for him?" Loire asked, bewildered. "Troop strengths, and commanders . . ."

"He's interested," Dominique said as he led her to the staircase, "but you'd have to feed him to an alligator one piece at a time to make him admit it."

"He ver' proud, that man," St. John added, following them. "He pretend like nothing worry him, like he already know all there is to know. Mems go clean up now, come back later. The general, he will listen then."

*   *   *

Loire and Dominique went down the dark verandah steps to a magnolia tree at the corner of the house. It had stopped raining, and stars shone through breaks in the clouds.

Loire was wearing a muslin gown and velvet cloak. Dominique had borrowed a white, open-necked cotton shirt, dark knee breeches, and a French military cape from Jean Laffite. His warpaint was gone, and his hair was combed back from his brow.

Taking Loire's face in his hands, he said, "You are my heroine, Loire Chartier. If all the folk in New Orleans were like you, Pakenham's men would turn and run for their lives."

"I didn't do Jackson much good, Dominique. I couldn't escape to warn him about the cannons on the levee, in time to save the *Carolina.*"

"Yes, but you did tell him about the troop strengths and casualties. It's bound to help in planning our defense. Good girl!"

"Dominique?"

"Yes, Smokeflower?"

"It's been an hour since we kissed."

"I will remedy that right now."

He kissed her for a long time, unable to bear the thought of sending her back to the city in the morning. Perhaps he wouldn't. Laffite thought Jackson would burn New Orleans if he couldn't hold his line against the British, so Loire might be safer with the camp followers.

Suddenly Dominique held her away from him, scowling. "I forgot your birthday. It is the first time I have forgotten in all the years since I recorded your birth in my journal."

She laughed. "You still stick by that ghost story, do you?"

"But of course."

"Are you always so sentimental?"

"I can become even more sentimental, my love, on the cotton bale behind the house."

"Cotton bale?"

"Yes. Jackson used them to heighten the rampart behind the ditch, but some caught fire during an artillery barrage, so he put them in the swamp for the Tennesseans to sleep on. You saw some on the way in. Renato tells me he put one behind the house for my personal use."

She trembled with excitement as he led her around the house to a huge, burlap-covered bale of cotton against the garden wall. There were trees and enough bushes to give them a great deal of privacy.

"Your boudoir, my princess," Dominique said, lifting her up. He sprang up beside her and covered the rough burlap with his cape. Slowly he pulled her cloak away and unfastened her dress, the manly fire emanating from him warming her against the night wind. He pulled her, naked, into his arms and lay back on the bed of cotton.

Loire moaned softly as he sought her pleasure with intimate thrustings. He was her dragon man, her bayou rogue. No matter what he had done before, she loved him now with all her soul.

Together they'd found peace.

She tried not to think about the huge army across the field.

Jackson decided to celebrate the New Year with a military parade and revue, complete with a band and spectators from town. It was foggy, so he went into the MacCarté house to wait for the dampness to lift.

Suddenly a terrific bang rocked the house. Plaster rained down from the ceiling, and bricks exploded from the walls. Again and again cannonballs struck the house, boring monstrous holes in the walls and ceiling.

On the parade ground, Dominique yelled at St. John, "Loire and Ida are in the house! Come on!"

They ran into the ruined garden, ignoring twenty-four-pound balls tunneling into the soft earth and filling the air with debris. St. John ripped the front door off its hinges.

Old Hickory emerged from a pile of rubble, his eyes glaring furiously from a face white with plaster. He staggered outside, yelling, "Snakes and wildcats, the bastards placed cannons on the plain last night!"

Dominique led the way to the staircase. Just then another ball hit the house, blasting through the wall between the two men. St. John reeled, blood flying from his forehead. Cursing, he stumbled on.

The staircase ended five feet below the second floor. Covered with plaster, Ida and Loire stood on the landing above, looking down.

"Jump!" Dominique commanded.

Loire jumped into his arms. He ran back downstairs and deposited her in the demolished foyer.

"Jump, stubborn woman!" St. John yelled at Ida.

With a shriek, she leaped at him. St. John staggered under her weight and would have toppled over the side of the staircase if Dominique hadn't steadied him in time.

Two more balls hit the house as they all stumbled outside.

"Get into the woods!" Dominique yelled at the women, giving them a shove.

Renato Beluche and most of the crew were in battery number three, loading the big guns. Through a spyglass Dominique studied the enemy cannons positioned behind hogsheads of sugar.

"The British don't shoot so straight, Dominique," Renato said, lighting a cigar. "Me, I don't think they've hit the rampart yet. 'Course, these damn American gunners are not too good, either." He turned his cigar upside-down in a derogatory gesture.

Dominique yelled at the cannon crew beside his, "Get the range first—you're wasting shot. Pass on the word!"

After firing several practice shots, Dominique and Renato Beluche adjusted their cannon for maximum effect on the British.

"Let her off," Dominique said coolly. Flame shot out of the twenty-four-pounders. When the smoke cleared, all that remained of a British gun emplacement was a large crater. Dominique methodically began picking off targets. The field was soon littered with British cannons mired in blood and melted sugar.

Down the line in the cypress swamp, the Tennesseans and Choctaws repulsed an infantry assault, while the Kentucky sharpshooters inflicted terrible carnage on the advancing British. At last the British withdrew from the field, carrying away a hundred dead.

Dominique rubbed the back of his neck thoughtfully. "I think General Pakenham has played with us enough. The next time, he will throw his entire force against our puny three thousand. The fate of the United States, my friends, hangs on that conflict."

25

"*I fear your future papa-in-law* got himself in big trouble this time, my little nephew," Renato Beluche said, slipping out of the foggy night into battery number three. In the light of the lantern, Dominique could see that the perpetual cigar in his mouth was unlit, and his face looked strained.

"I thought Etienne was in town, guarding the marketplace," Dominique said sharply. "What happened?"

"He wanted to be a hero, that one. It seems he floated down the big river in a pirogue to join us, confused himself in the dark, and landed near Villeré's plantation. They got him, our spies say. He is tied up in camp."

"Does Loire know?"

"Not yet, but someone will—how do the Kaintocks say?—let the dog out of the bag."

"The cat," Dominique said. Swearing under his breath, he started taking off his clothes.

"Eh? What the devil are you doing? You think to

comfort the mademoiselle with your big sword at a
time like this?"

"No." Naked, Dominique scooped up handfuls of
mud and smeared it all over his body until he was as
dark as night. "Look in my pack for that breechcloth,
Uncle," he said, strapping his dagger to his thigh. He
slung his sword on his back. "I'm going after him."

Renato lit his cigar and dragged smoke into his
mouth in a contented manner before finding the
fringed buckskin. After handing it over, he sat back
on his heels. "You need help?"

"You're offering?"

"No, but maybe somebody else will."

After St. John joined him, Dominique led the way
through the dark cypress swamp, whispering the
password to the Choctaw sentinels. Snakes coiled
half-frozen in the roots of trees. Alligators roared and
splashed not far away. Snarling, a bobcat dropped
lightly off a branch in front of them and bounded away.

British campfires glowed in the fog beyond the
swamp. Moving like ghosts, the men slipped from tree
to tree, closer and closer.

A British sentinel struck a match to his pipe, illuminating himself long enough for Dominique to see his
musket leaning against a tree.

"Foolish," Dominique whispered, moving closer.

"Allow St. John," the Jamaican said, and moved
past him to strike the redcoat on the jaw. They bound
and gagged him, then tied him upright to the tree so
he wouldn't drown in the shallow water.

Bending low, Dominique entered the field with St.
John just behind him. Cane stubble poked their feet as

they slipped from campfire to campfire with the noise-lessness of swamp hunters. But Etienne was not to be found.

Blanketed by thick fog, they worked their way deeper into the enemy camp, sometimes hugging the ground when a soldier appeared. The field was very quiet and the fog depressing. They moved toward the levee.

"How we find him in the dark?" St. John whispered.

"Like this," Dominique said. "Follow my lead."

"Whatever M'sieu Youx say."

"Indians!" Dominique shouted in English. "God help us, there's a hundred of them!"

St. John unleashed a wild yell and threw a stick at the nearest campfire, sending sparks flying. Soldiers leaped up, cursing with fear, kicking dirt over the fires. Several discharged their weapons. Panic spread through the camp.

Unseen in the fog, St. John and Dominique dodged among the horde, occasionally releasing bloodcurdling screams. In the mist, no one knew friend from foe. Some shot their comrades; others were trampled in the confusion.

Near the levee, Dominique heard someone cursing in French. They headed toward the sound.

Etienne Chartier lay near a campfire by the steep levee, trussed hand and foot. His two guards stood just outside the light, staring into the fog and swearing.

"Those Choctaws, they will scalp you and chop you up into itsy-bitsy pieces!" Chartier yelled to them over the noise. "Your friends will have to pack your remains into whiskey barrels and ship you back to London."

"Shut your trap, ye bleedin' frog!"

"You would do well to take your little selves back down the bayou," Etienne said, "and sail away in your ships. These savages, they are very bloodthirsty. I would not like to be in your boots right now."

"Shut up!" One of them turned on Etienne, sword upraised, eyes crazed with terror. "Shut up or I'll send your bloody hide to hell!"

"And I will be a fallen hero," Etienne said calmly, "just like Napoleon's Old Guards. So to hell with your threats, you British swine."

Snarling, the soldier rushed him. Dominique rose out of the gloom, his sword flashing in the firelight, and parried the blow that was descending on Etienne's head. St. John tackled the other guard, locked his great hands around his throat, and choked him into unconsciousness.

Dominique and the redcoat exchanged quick thrusts, then the guard cried out, stricken in the breast, and dropped to his knees. Dominique struck the sword out of his hand, thrust a gag into his mouth, and swiftly bound his wrists behind his back with his jacket.

St. John had Etienne halfway to the top of the levee when Dominique caught up. He grabbed Etienne's other arm, and together they pulled him over the top.

A campfire burned away the fog where several British soldiers stood, guarding a barge. Surprised, they shot at the trio. Dominique threw himself down the steep, muddy bank and fired his pistol. The ball took one between the eyes. Two others, their muskets empty, went after him with swords.

Bellowing a war cry, Etienne lunged out of St. John's grip and tumbled down the bank like a sack of coal, knocking Dominique and the two soldiers into the river. Cursing, St. John slithered down, yanked the redcoats up as they grappled with Dominique, and banged their heads together. Then he tossed their limp bodies onto the bank.

Etienne climbed to his feet, muddy water streaming off his clothes, and chortled with excitement. "Come on, my friends, we'll steal their barge and pole ourselves upriver!"

"Sacred blood," Dominique swore under his breath. "More work."

He grabbed Etienne by the arm and heaved him into the barge, then he and St. John pushed the vessel away from shore and climbed in. Wielding long poles, they stood at either end and began to move the barge against the current.

Etienne caught Dominique by the fringe of his breechcloth and squinted through the fog at him. "Me, I did good, getting those lobsterbacks off you, eh?"

"Great. My thanks."

Etienne sucked a tooth for a minute. "Napoleon's Old Guardsmen could not do much better, do you think?"

"Not much, Etienne," Dominique grunted, straining against the pole. He cast an eye toward the levee, watching for redcoats. He could see nothing in the fog.

"Maybe you will put in a good word for me sometime, get me into the Grumblers? I have the qualifications—indomitable bravery, the strength of a lion. There is nothing else I lack, eh?"

Dominique had to smile despite their peril. "Only one thing, Etienne."

"And what is that?"

"Height. You must be six feet tall."

Etienne sat down in the bottom of the barge and stared into the gloom. Wistfully he said, "But for the lack of twelve inches . . . But I fought good, no?"

"You did. The emperor does not know what he's missing."

* * *

Dominique Youx strained to see into the cloud-covered field. He, along with St. John, Renato Beluche, and ten Baratarians, was crouching beside the cold, gleaming cannons. On this morning, instinct told him, the British would not retreat.

"The pudding-faces, they will want blood today," Renato Beluche whispered. "There is a score to settle."

"Are you afraid?" Dominique asked quietly.

"Fear is for cowards—your uncle has never been afraid in his life! Eh? But what is this?"

"*Merde!*" Dominique said as Loire slipped into the battery. She was dressed in men's breeches and held her Kentucky long rifle. "You will go back behind the reserves!" he ordered her.

"No. I've come to help."

"Go back!"

"Suppose the fog lifts as soon as I stand up?" she asked. "Suppose the British are waiting not ten yards in front of us?"

"Suppose I bend you over my knee and smack the stuffings out of you?"

She raised her chin in defiance and said sweetly, "My brave papa would scalp you."

"Your papa is busy in battery six, manning the water bucket."

"Then I'll man this one. I refuse to be the only member of the family skulking behind the lines." She kissed him on the nose.

Chuckling, Renato Beluche snatched her rifle out of her hands. "We will use real bullets and flint today, mademoiselle, not pretty toys."

She grabbed it back and pointed at the breech.

"See? Flint. I bought it off Jean Laffite. And here"—she fumbled in a leather pouch at her waist—"is powder and ball."

Dominique bent closer to look into the pouch. "That is the most peculiar ball I've ever seen."

She tried to close it, but St. John leaned across Dominique and snapped the cord, claiming the pouch. He put a hand on her shoulder and held her away while he looked inside. His great shoulders began to shake with mirth. The Baratarian gunners crowded around to see.

"What's she got in there, St. John?" Dominique demanded. "Blackened sweet potatoes?"

The Jamaican poured dozens of shimmering, colored balls out of the bag. "Marbles!"

The men broke up laughing. Loire, trying to be stern, began to scrape the marbles back into the pouch.

Dominique found a glassie she'd overlooked. With a deft flick of his thumb he sent it flying into the neckline of her blouse. She retaliated with a shot that caught him on the bridge of the nose, he lobbed it back, and a fierce artillery battle began to rage.

"You are a Frenchwoman after my own heart, mademoiselle!" Renato shouted over the laughter. "I will be glad to call such an indomitable one my niece. This man of yours, he had better watch out lest I put you on the *Spy,* my favorite ship, and sail away with you. I'll make you my chief artillerist!"

"I wouldn't send her off with a dirty-minded old sea-rat like you," Dominique said, catching her hand before she could bean him again, "even to keep her off the battlefield."

Renato laughed and sucked appreciatively on his cigar. "Maybe my nephew will stick his head too high over the rampart when the British strike," he said, wiggling his brows at Loire, "and they will shoot it out of the ring, just like marbles."

"Little-boy humor, Mems Loire," St. John said. "You *non* listen. M'sieu Beluche, he think he ver' funny." He grinned at Renato, who smiled back and then blew a smoke ring in a self-satisfied way.

Loire settled into Dominique's arms. "You won't do that, will you, Dominique? You *will* be careful?"

"More than usual, now that you're here," he said gruffly, caressing her face. "But I can't stop an incoming cannonball with my bare hands, so keep your head down. And Loire . . ."

"Yes?"

"Don't shoot your rifle. The damned marble will blow up in your face. Let Jackson's men do the shooting, and us handle the big guns."

"All right. But if they come over the rampart, I'll hit them with whatever I've got."

"Agreed. And another thing."

She looked at him suspiciously, knowing he still wanted to send her away. "Yes, Dominique?"

"I love you."

She swallowed hard. Laying her fingers on his cheek, she said, "Then come out of this alive . . . please."

"Of course. I need a hundred years of being with you," he said, and kissed her deeply. His gunnery crews looked away, affording the couple what privacy they could.

The fog lifted all at once. A gasp went up from the Americans at their first sight of the British. General Jackson, riding up and down the line, offering encouragement, jerked his black horse to a halt and roared, "Snakes and wildcats, there's six thousand troops if a one! Where in the eternities did they all come from?"

Riding one of Jackson's Tennessee walkers, Jean Laffite reined in beside him, balancing a slate on his knee. Jackson had made him his chief adviser, partly because he knew the terrain like the back of his hand, partly to keep him in sight at all times. After making a quick notation on the slate, Jean leaned over to speak to the general.

Congreve rockets exploded over the plain in front of the rampart, turning the rising fog into shimmering dust. "That's their signal to advance, God love us!" Laffite said. "Dominique, my big brother, it would help very much if you kill a lot of British today, eh?"

St. John crossed his breast. "You ever see such a sight?"

Loire never had. Divided into two long columns, red-coated regulars, green-jacketed rifle brigades, black West Indians, and Highlanders in tartan trews advanced on the rampart. Her hands tightened instinctively on her empty rifle.

"The pudding-faces placed more batteries of cannon last night," Beluche said. "Look between the Highlanders and their left flank. I count seven, no, eight guns."

"Range, approximately seven hundred yards," Dominique told his crews, who made the adjustments. "Let them off, my friends."

The big guns barked, plowing furrows up the soggy plain. The troops gave no sign of fear, continuing to march in orderly precision, seventy-two paces a minute. Obtaining the range, Dominique and the seven other batteries pounded the British gun emplacements.

"Load canister," Dominique ordered as the British poured relentlessly on toward the hellfire flashing from his guns.

Loire leaned her rifle in the crook of her arm, stuffed her fingers into her ears, and stared over the rampart in horror at the British falling like wheat under a sickle. The English Forty-fourth suddenly bolted back through their lines. For a moment Loire thought the entire column would retreat, then the troops returned with fascines and scaling ladders for crossing the ditch in front of the rampart . . . if they ever got there.

At four hundred yards, Jackson ordered the swamp batteries seven and eight to cease firing. He passed the order down the line: "When the cannon smoke clears, wait until you can see the whites of their eyes. Aim just above the gorget and don't miss. We'll send 'em back to the devil's own bosom!"

Seconds elapsed. The smoke drifted away. The British were already within range. The Kentucky riflemen opened fire, withering the enemy under a continuous sheet of red-orange flame. Still they came on.

Dominique stood and showed himself over the rampart, heedless of flying bullets. His hands clenched on the hilt of his sword as he shouted, "There is no honor in dying like sheep. Retreat and go home to England, you fools!"

The tide of men surged forward. The batteries by the levee roared again, causing the troops with the fascines and ladders to panic. Sacrificing their former discipline, they dropped their burdens and fired wildly at the rampart, taking their comrades in the rear.

General Pakenham, the would-be governor of Louisiana, dashed across the field on a magnificent white horse to rally them. A Kentucky rifleman stood up, tracked him like a flying duck, and shot him in the neck. Pakenham dropped stone dead to the ground.

"By thunder," Dominique swore a second later, "the Highlanders are turning to cross the field in the same manner! It is suicide!"

Loire watched the Ninety-third Highlanders pivot toward them across the field. The continuous roar of the cannon broadsides could not wholly drown out the wail of the pipes: brave, rebellious, mournful. She cried for them and even saw a tear streak the soot on Dominique Youx's cheek.

Dominique commanded his crews to reload. Now, as never before in his life, he felt the blood of Scotland flowing in his veins. For all he knew, his guns might claim a half brother on the plain below.

He lifted his hand and held it, his ring flashing in the sunlight. His crews looked at him, awaiting his order to fire. He glanced at Loire, set his jaw, and looked away.

"Let her off," he said almost too quietly to be heard.

The guns roared. Smoke mercifully obliterated the sight before him, but nothing could cover the terrible sound of death.

Two hours after the Battle of New Orleans had begun, Jackson ordered the Americans to cease fire. Two thousand British lay heaped on the field. Jackson's casualties numbered only thirteen.

Dominique, Loire, and many other Americans went onto the field to give aid to the stricken. Dominique, with anguish in his heart, lent his most feverish effort to the fallen Highlanders.

"You did what you had to, Dominique," Loire said.

"*Oui.*" Still, he looked into each face as though searching for his own. It was a relief when darkness fell at last and he could search no more.

No one in the American camp slept that night. Those who were not caring for the wounded watched the west bank of the river, where Colonel Thornton's troops had crossed in barges during the night and won the battle for the British. New Orleans hung by a thread.

But in the morning, they discovered that Thornton had inexplicably rejoined the main body at the Villeré plantation. New Orleans was safe.

26

Loire waited impatiently for Ida to attach the train to her wedding gown. She could hear her father in the sitting room across the hall, swearing under his breath. She guessed he'd stabbed himself on a thorn as he fumbled to place a rose into his buttonhole.

"You just hold your taters a minute, honey," Ida said. "You as jumpy as a boll weevil in a hot frying pan this evening. That man of yours ain't going nowhere. He down in the mercantile with St. John and Mistah Jean and that old cuss, Renato Beluche, sampling my blackberry wine."

"If it makes him drunk and we can't get married tonight, Papa will probably smash your distillery."

"Your pappy can just simmer down. Ain't nothing gonna stop you getting married this time. Laws, Mistah Youx won't even go on over to the church and wait for you! He done laugh ever' time I tole him it's bad luck to see the bride aforehand."

"He's already seen the bride before, if you'll remember. Are we ready? Is my hair all right?"

"It'd look a sight better if you'd lemme coil it up on your head."

"No. Dominique asked me to leave it down."

"He a romantic fool, that man." She settled the veil over Loire's face. "You ready, child?"

"I am indeed. Thanks." She lifted the veil and kissed Ida's cheek. Then she threw her arms around her neck and hugged her close.

"Me and St. John going on over to the church and sit in the balcony. Mazy and Tim gonna be up there, too," Ida said, extricating herself. She dashed a tear off her cheek. "Don't forget to wave."

"I'll remember."

After Ida left, Loire walked into the sitting room and smiled at her father. He left the French windows and came quickly to take her hands, looking her up and down in wonder.

"My baby is not so little anymore," he said. He had to turn away for a moment to blow his nose.

"My papa is not so little anymore, either," she said, and kissed him on the forehead. "And I'm not talking about your height, you know. Dominique says you freed your slaves."

"*Oui.* They are tenants now. Perhaps it is best."

"I'm sure of it, Papa."

He rubbed his mustache with his finger. "I . . . I wish your mother could be here, Loire."

She felt a throb of pain, and then her expression softened. "I wish she could, too, Papa. But I'll write her soon . . . maybe she'll be here when her grandchild is born."

Etienne Chartier's eyes enlarged. "My baby . . . my baby is having a baby?"

Loire smiled. "Your grandbaby."

"Dominique, my son, does he know?"

"I told him last night. He is still in shock, I think, and quite happy."

Etienne gripped her hands more tightly. Tears of joy brimmed over his lids and down his cheeks. For a moment he seemed about to explode. Then he burst into the French national anthem, spun her toward the door, and marched her to the staircase.

Dominique stood at the foot of the steps, smiling up at them. Dressed in a pearl gray coat and trousers, his snowy cravat spilling over a waistcoat of black satin, he was a princely sight as he lifted his hand in welcome, his ring flashing.

"Smokeflower, my bride," he said, his deep, vibrant voice reaching out to caress her. Etienne brought her downstairs and proudly laid her hand in his.

Jean Laffite moved close to Renato Beluche as he opened a blue velvet box and held it out. The diamond tiara glittered.

"You're lucky I got my hands on it the last time you tried to marry, eh?" Renato asked. "I hid it from the sheriff all this time!"

Dominique placed it on Loire's head. "It should always rest there, my princess, though I know you won't allow it. Perhaps once a year I'll take it out of the safe and crown you, renewing the vows of love we make tonight."

Loire's eyes filled with tears. "Let us go and make those vows, then, my pirate."

Etienne Chartier stretched up on his toes, pecked Dominique on both cheeks in the Gallic way, kissed his daughter, and tried to speak. Finding that he couldn't, he clapped Dominique on the back, pumped his hand, and hurried outside. They heard him whistling the anthem as he went up the street to the cathedral.

Renato and Jean Laffite fell into step behind the bride and groom. The setting sun colored the wet banquettes soft pink and peach and the old mercantile behind them a warm shade of gold.

The bells in the cathedral began to toll as they approached rue Chartres. Buggies lined the curbs, though very few people were about.

Suddenly a man with his face shadowed beneath a black top hat stepped out from behind a black carriage and leveled a pistol at Dominique's heart. "Monsieur Youx."

Dominique stopped dead. As he pulled Loire behind him to shield her, he glimpsed her eyes through the veil. They were shocked, angry. His gaze returned to their assailant. "What the devil do you want?"

"Do you not recognize me, monsieur?" Alain Defromage asked as he hurled his hat into the gutter.

Acutely aware that he carried no gun, Dominique asked again, "What do you want?"

"Revenge." His gaze flicked over Loire before returning to Dominique. "You stole my ship, monsieur. You took the woman I loved. Here, you want her so badly? Take her."

Keeping his pistol dead steady, he fumbled in his pocket, then tossed an object at Dominique. The buccaneer reached up reflexively and caught it. It was the miniature portrait of Loire.

"You humiliated me when we dueled in the square." Alain's voice rose high as he recited the list of

Dominique's sins. "And again on the brigantine. Your worst crime, though, was to help the Kaintocks win their little war. Because of you, I am a pauper hunted by the government for treason!"

"You did it yourself, Alain," Loire said, "when you betrayed us to the British!"

He went on as though she hadn't spoken. "Now I will destroy you, Monsieur Dominique Youx. How fitting that you should die on your wedding night." His finger whitened on the trigger.

A loud boom reverberated off the walls. Loire gasped and caught Dominique's arm.

He remained solidly on his feet. She followed his gaze to Defromage, who lay on the sidewalk, blood soiling his shirt front. He was clutching his right shoulder and moaning. His pistol lay in the gutter out of reach.

Jean Laffite stepped up from behind Loire, the pistol in his hand still smoking.

"My brother was unarmed, *mon ami*," he said to the wounded man, "and I do not play games with villains."

Dominique swept Loire into his arms and hurried around the corner to the front steps of the cathedral. He set her on her feet and, raising her veil, kissed her until she ceased to tremble.

"You are mine," he said fiercely. "No one will ever take you away from me, nor me from you."

"I believe you," she said, touching his cheek. "Pirates and presidents fly to your aid."

"I do not know about presidents, Smokeflower, but sometimes pirates are very useful."

"The bells are ringing, Dominique. Shall we go in before something else happens?"

"Without another moment's hesitation." Taking

her hand, he led her quickly up the steps through the open doors.

When they were gone, Renato turned to Jean Laffite. "We live in interesting times, *non?*"

"Uncle, I have a feeling we always will."

Historical Notes

The War of 1812 was not discussed much when I was in school—probably because it was only a piece of the larger war between England and France—but the impact on the American nation at the time was enormous. Bankrupt and torn by factional strife in the government and among its citizens, the young country hovered on the brink of collapse.

Ironically, the Treaty of Ghent, which officially ended the war, was signed on December 24, 1814, *before* the Battle of New Orleans. Word did not reach Washington until a month later. Some military tacticians surmise that had New Orleans fallen and the British advanced up the Mississippi River, the treaty would have been annulled.

Without the valiant efforts of General Andrew Jackson of Tennessee and his culturally diverse army—which included farmers from Kentucky and Tennessee, Choctaws, Cherokees, Creoles, Cajuns, Irishmen, and free Negroes—the British would have taken New

Orleans, the gateway to the continent. And if so, it's quite possible that we would be speaking the king's English today.

The Jamaican bookkeeper St. John is typical of the skilled freemen who managed the nuts and bolts of daily life and commerce in New Orleans. Though not allowed into white social circles, free blacks enjoyed much greater freedom and opportunity in the French society. For instance, it was perfectly legal for a black man to acquire an education under French rule. In fact, some blacks actually operated plantations of their own, where they grew rice or sugar cane, which are principal crops of the region to this day.

While other works of fiction have given Dominique Youx the persona of Jean Laffite's lieutenant, I discovered archives in New Orleans revealing that he was actually Alexandre Laffite. Alexandre set up the Baratarian pirate trade in Louisiana twelve years before his younger brothers came to New Orleans, but it is Jean who has a national park named after him.

Dominique Youx and his Baratarian freebooters were indeed imprisoned after Commandant Patterson's raid on Grand Terre, as described in this story. Andrew Jackson repeatedly spurned Youx's offers of help, releasing him only at the eleventh hour. The Baratarians' performance in battery number three changed the crusty old general's feelings toward them. He commended their deadly accuracy with the big cannons—the consequence of many years of privateering on the high seas—and swore he could not have held Line Jackson without them.

The name Laffite is commonly spelled *Lafitte*, but since Jean usually used the former spelling in his writings, I chose his version.

The home of Major Gabriel Villeré stood until the early 1920s, as shown in an old photograph in my possession. According to accounts, it was Gabriel who escaped to warn Andrew Jackson of the British invasion. How long he sat in jail as punishment for leaving Bayou Bienvenue open is unknown.

The U.S. Department of the Interior has done a remarkable job of preserving Louisiana's heritage. Jean Lafitte National Historical Park and Preserve consists of three units: the French Quarter, Chalmette, and Barataria.

Park rangers conduct tours through the French Quarter, including the house on Royal Street where Andrew Jackson had his headquarters. The tour also covers the French Market, where the fictional Loire Chartier shopped; the St. Louis Cathedral; and the Mississippi River levee.

Chalmette National Historical Park includes the site of the Battle of New Orleans, which is marked by a tall monument. Its cannon emplacements have been restored. The battlefield is located in St. Bernard Parish on the east bank of the Mississippi River.

The Barataria unit preserves many acres of Louisiana's coastal wetlands. Grand Terre, where Jean Laffite's Red House stood, is visible across Barataria Bay.

AVAILABLE NOW

ONE NIGHT by Debbie Macomber

A wild, romantic adventure from bestselling and much-loved author Debbie Macomber. When their boss sends them to a convention in Dallas together, Carrie Jamison, a vibrant and witty radio deejay for KUTE in Kansas City, Kansas, and Kyle Harris, an arrogant, strait-laced KUTE reporter, are in for the ride of their lives, until one night. . . . "Debbie Macomber writes delightful, heartwarming romances that touch the emotions and leave the reader feeling good."—Jayne Ann Krentz

MAIL-ORDER OUTLAW by Millie Criswell

From the award-winning author of *Phantom Lover* and *Diamond in the Rough*, a historical romance filled with passion, fun, and adventure about a beautiful New York socialite who found herself married to a mail-order outlaw. "Excellent! Once you pick it up, you won't put it down."—Dorothy Garlock, bestselling author of *Sins of Summer*

THE SKY LORD by Emma Harrington

When Dallas MacDonald discovered that his ward and betrothed had run off and married his enemy, Ian MacDougall, he was determined to fetch his unfaithful charge even if it meant war. But on entering Inverlocky Castle, Dallas found more pleasure in abducting MacDougall's enchanting sister, Isobel, than in securing his own former betrothed.

WILLOW CREEK by Carolyn Lampman

The final book in the Cheyenne Trilogy. Given her father's ill health during the hot, dry summer of 1886, Nicki Chandler had no choice but to take responsibility for their Wyoming homestead. But when her father hired handsome drifter Levi Cantrell to relieve some of her burdens, the last thing Nicki and Levi ever wanted was to fall in love.

PEGGY SUE GOT MURDERED by Tess Gerritsen

Medical examiner M. J. Novak, M.D., has a problem: Too many bodies are rolling into the local morgue. She teams up with the handsome, aristocratic president of a pharmaceutical company, who has his own agenda. Their search for the truth takes them from glittering ballrooms to perilous back alleys and into a romance that neither ever dreamed would happen.

PIRATE'S PRIZE by Venita Helton

A humorous and heartwarming romance set against the backdrop of the War of 1812. Beautiful Loire Chartier and dashing Dominique Youx were meant for each other. But when Loire learned that Dominique was the half brother of the infamous pirate, Jean Lafitte, and that he once plundered her father's cargo ship, all hell broke loose.

COMING NEXT MONTH

CIRCLE IN THE WATER by Susan Wiggs
When a beautiful gypsy thief crossed the path of King Henry VIII, the king saw a way to exact revenge against his enemy, Stephen de Lacey, by forcing the insolvent nobleman to marry the girl. Stephen wanted nothing to do with his gypsy bride, even when he realized Juliana was a princess from a far-off land. But when Juliana's past returned to threaten her, he realized he would risk everything to protect his wife. "Susan Wiggs creates fresh, unique and exciting tales that will win her a legion of fans."—Jayne Ann Krentz

JUST ONE OF THOSE THINGS by Leigh Riker
Sara Reid, having left her race car driver husband and their glamorous but stormy marriage, returns to Rhode Island in the hope of protecting her five-year-old daughter from further emotional harm. Instead of peace, Sara finds another storm when her husband's cousin Colin McAllister arrives—bringing with him the shameful memory of their one night together six years ago and a life-shattering secret.

DESTINED TO LOVE by Suzanne Elizabeth
In the tradition of her first time travel romance, *When Destiny Calls*, comes another humorous adventure. Josie Reed was a smart, gutsy, twentieth-century doctor, and tired of the futile quest for a husband before she reached thirty. Then she went on the strangest blind date of all—back to the Wild West of 1881 with a fearless, half-Apache, bounty hunter.

A TOUCH OF CAMELOT by Donna Grove
The winner of the 1993 Golden Heart Award for best historical romance. Guinevere Pierce had always dreamed that one day her own Sir Lancelot would rescue her from a life of medicine shows and phony tent revivals. But she never thought he would come in the guise of Cole Shepherd, the Pinkerton detective in charge of watching over Gwin and her younger brother Arthur, the only surviving witnesses to a murder.

SUNFLOWER SKY by Samantha Harte
A poignant historical romance between an innocent small town girl and a wounded man bent on vengeance. Sunny Summerlin had no idea what she was getting into when she rented a room to an ill stranger named Bar Landry. But as she nursed him back to health, she discovered that he was a bounty hunter with an unquenchable thirst for justice, and also the man with whom she was falling in love.

TOO MANY COOKS by Joanne Pence
Somebody is spoiling the broth in this second delightful adventure featuring the spicy romantic duo from *Something's Cooking*. Homicide detective Paavo Smith must find who is killing the owners of popular San Francisco restaurants and, at the same time, come to terms with his feelings for Angelina Amalfi, the gorgeous but infuriating woman who loves to dabble in sleuthing.